Praise for the novels of

Lexi Blake

"I love Lexi Blake. Read *Ruthless* and see why."
—*New York Times* bestselling author Lee Child

"Smart, savvy, clever, and always entertaining. That's true of Riley Lawless, the hero in *Ruthless*, and likewise for his creator, Lexi Blake. Both are way ahead of the pack."
—*New York Times* bestselling author Steve Berry

"A must-read! Lexi Blake is a master!"
—*New York Times* bestselling author Jennifer Probst

"The love story that develops will touch the hearts of fans. . . . A welcome and satisfying entry into the Lawless world."
—RT Book Reviews

Titles by Lexi Blake

ᦕ

THE BUTTERFLY BAYOU NOVELS
Butterfly Bayou

THE COURTING JUSTICE NOVELS
Order of Protection
Evidence of Desire

THE LAWLESS NOVELS
Ruthless
Satisfaction
Revenge

THE PERFECT GENTLEMEN NOVELS
(with Shayla Black)
Scandal Never Sleeps
Seduction in Session
Big Easy Temptation

Butterfly Bayou

Lexi Blake

JOVE
New York

A JOVE BOOK
Published by Berkley
An imprint of Penguin Random House LLC
penguinrandomhouse.com

Copyright © 2020 by DLZ Entertainment, LLC
Penguin Random House supports copyright. Copyright fuels creativity, encourages
diverse voices, promotes free speech, and creates a vibrant culture. Thank you for buying
an authorized edition of this book and for complying with copyright laws by not
reproducing, scanning, or distributing any part of it in any form without permission.
You are supporting writers and allowing Penguin Random House to continue to
publish books for every reader.

A JOVE BOOK, BERKLEY, and the BERKLEY & B colophon are registered
trademarks of Penguin Random House LLC.

ISBN: 9781984806567

First Edition: May 2020

Printed in the United States of America
1   3   5   7   9   10   8   6   4   2

Cover photos: Golden Retriever © asaStock / Shutterstock;
Lake scenery with old wooden boat © FotograFFF / Shutterstock
Cover design by Vikki Chu
Book design by Alison Cnockaert

For Kim, who knows what it means to be on the bayou . . .

prologue

Lila Daley forced her hands to stop shaking. She wasn't this person. She wasn't the person whose hands shook. Who stammered or couldn't speak in the face of tragedy. She stared straight ahead and her logical mind understood where she was. She was in the waiting room of the ER she'd worked at for years. But when she blinked, the scene changed and all she could see was blood and bodies and the careful walls she'd built shuddering and crashing around her.

"Lila?"

She looked up and her brother was standing there. Her brother. For much of her life Will had been the person she looked up to. Their childhood had been all about staying together, keeping their family intact in the wake of their mother's chaos. Will and Laurel and Lisa. They'd been her whole world for the longest time.

"Yes?"

Will dropped to one knee, his face creased with concern. "The police are asking about taking a statement. I think you need some rest. You can do this tomorrow. I'm going to send them away."

And then she would have to deal with the problem in the morning. Then she would have to know it was still waiting for her, still sitting there and wanting attention. She managed to shake her head, forcing a calm she didn't feel. "Don't. I would rather get this over with. I have to be at work in eight hours."

It was the weekend. She couldn't miss work. The crazies came out on the weekend. And the team was down one because . . .

The team was down one because Maryanne was dead. The team was down one because someone had walked into the ER and shot her friend. Lila was used to having blood on her. Trauma nurses weren't squeamish about blood.

But this was Maryanne's blood.

Trauma nurses weren't squeamish about death.

But she'd watched as the light had faded from Maryanne's eyes.

It had been easier to watch her friend die than it had been to look at the man who'd held a gun on her, told her if she touched Maryanne, if she helped, he would shoot her.

God, it was easier than thinking about the fact that if she'd been the tiniest bit braver, Maryanne wouldn't be dead.

"Lila, you are not going to work," Will said gently. "I think we should get you cleaned up and take you home. You can come with me or you can go to Laurel's if you like. She and Mitch are on their way up here right now. I've already talked to Lisa. She's getting in a car as soon as she can. She'll be here by morning."

Her youngest sister lived in Louisiana. She'd gotten married a couple of months before in a ceremony Lila hadn't truly understood. There had been raucous dancing and an outdoor service where the groom had written poetry for his bride and her sister had looked radiant. Will and his wife and Laurel and her husband had been there. They'd brought their kids.

Her siblings had kids. They were all married and she was alone. She'd sat at her table as they'd all danced and known that she wouldn't have that. She wouldn't glow the way her sisters and Will's wife did. She wouldn't dance the way they did. She would be alone, always holding herself apart from the rest of them because she had work to do, because she couldn't let herself open up.

A brief vision of a muscular man in a tux floated over her brain. Dark hair and striking blue eyes, broad shoulders that seemed to go on for days. He'd smiled at her, a warm, sensual thing that she hadn't returned. When he'd started her way, she'd known he was going to ask her to dance and she'd excused herself quickly so she wouldn't have to say no. She'd been a coward.

Like she'd been tonight when she'd had to make the choice between saving Maryanne's life and saving her own.

"Why would Lisa drive up here? I'm fine." She said the words and was pleased with how perfectly normal they came out. The world around her had turned chaotic again, and it was her job to make sense of it, to force it to be normal through sheer willpower.

"Lila, you were held captive for over an hour," he said gently. "You watched two people die and you couldn't help them. You could have died yourself. I know you're a strong woman, one of the strongest I know, but you're not okay."

Before she could reply that she was fine, that she'd survived and was relieved to have done so, Laurel was rushing in. Her sister's brown and gold hair was up in a messy bun and it looked like she'd done nothing more than throw on a coat before rushing out in the middle of the night.

"Lila, god, I didn't know. I didn't have the TV on." Tears streamed down her sister's face.

They were obviously going to be very dramatic. She forced herself to stand. Will was right. She needed to get cleaned up. She'd stayed in her scrubs because she hadn't been sure if the police would need them as evidence, but that was a ridiculous thought. After all, it wasn't like there was someone to arrest. The man who'd held her hostage was dead, too.

She hadn't saved anyone today. Anyone except herself, and she wasn't sure that was a good thing.

"I'm going to take a shower and change. Tell the police

I'll give them a statement when I'm done." She tried to give her younger sister a reassuring smile. It couldn't have been easy for her to hear about what had happened. Laurel and Lisa had always looked up to her. Where Will had been responsible for having a job and protecting them, she had been the mom of the group. Even when their mother had been out of prison, it had been Lila's job to ensure they had something of a normal upbringing. "I'm fine, Laurel. It was a rough night, but I'm all right."

Laurel looked to Will as though she was confused.

Will simply shrugged. "I think it's shock."

Shock. Her mind focused on the word. It was a word she understood. There were five major types of shock. Anaphylactic, cardiogenic, hypovolemic, neurogenic, and septic.

Hypovolemic shock. It was what happened to a body when more than twenty percent of the blood volume was lost. When blood rushed from a wound. When the wound couldn't be closed because someone held a gun to the head of the only person in the room who could do it, who could save her.

"I'm not in shock. You should know the signs." After all, her brother was a neurologist. "I wasn't physically injured."

But only because at the last moment Maryanne's ex-husband had turned the gun on himself. Had he meant to kill her? She couldn't be sure. She only knew that when the time had come to be brave, she'd looked at that gun and done nothing.

Her brother put his hands on her shoulders and it took everything she had not to step away from him. "I wasn't talking about physical shock. You were held captive. You were forced to watch your friend die. He could have killed you. You are in shock."

"I'm not the one who died." Maryanne was. Maryanne, who'd almost gotten away. Maryanne, who'd chosen to leave her abuser. She'd been brave and it had cost her everything.

Lila had nothing. That was what she'd realized in those moments when she'd knelt on the floor and waited for the bullet that would end her life. She had nothing. Her siblings were starting their lives. They were all married and having kids and building something. She went to work and came home and thought that looking strong meant she was strong.

It should have been me.

It should have been me.

It should have been me.

The world went watery and she felt arms go around her. Someone was crying—screaming, really.

It was her.

Despite the fact that her family surrounded her, Lila Daley had never felt more alone.

chapter one

"I don't understand why you can't stay with us. We've got plenty of room." Lisa Daley's voice came over the car speakers loud and clear, as though reminding Lila that her sister wasn't far away anymore.

Not far at all now. The sign that let her know she was entering Papillon Parish rushed by, or rather she rushed by it. Papillon Parish was on the sign, but her sister often referred to the place as Butterfly Bayou. A quaint name for a quaint place. It had been a long drive from Dallas, and everything she owned was in the back of her crossover. She did not need this argument with her sister. She needed to get to the new house, find the bottle of wine she'd packed, and settle in for the night. Unpacking could wait. "You're still newlyweds, Lis. I'm not going to be the third wheel."

"You wouldn't be," Lisa replied. "You would be like the eighth wheel or something. Remy's family is always around. Well, when Zep's not in jail, that is." There was a soft gasp over the line. "That came out wrong. Zep's not on drugs or anything. He's just really obnoxious, and the police around here know how to deal with his smart mouth."

Lisa wasn't a Daley anymore. It was odd to think of her little sister as a Guidry. Most of her life had been spent trying desperately to keep the four of them together, and now they were all off on their own.

"It sounds like you've got enough family around you." She loved her sister, but she couldn't handle her rowdy in-laws right now.

Was she making a mistake? She'd left a perfectly good fast-track job in a cosmopolitan city in exchange for a tiny clinic in the sticks.

Of course, she couldn't actually walk into that gleaming, high-tech hospital without seeing her friend on the ground bleeding out.

"I love my in-laws, but I miss my sister," Lisa said.

The road went a little watery in front of her and she had to take a deep breath. Ever since that day she'd broken down, it had been a fight to stay in control, to get back the Lila she'd been before.

The Lila who hadn't been happy? The one who ticked off the days like they were a checklist she needed to get through? The one who'd nearly married a man she didn't love because he "made sense"?

Her inner voice had also gotten obnoxiously loud since that terrible day.

"I need some space. I'm sorry. I'm here. I want to spend time with you and be close to you, but I need my space, too." She'd also gotten way more honest. Maybe it had been the seventy-two-hour psych hold they'd put her on or the months and months of therapy.

There was a pause over the line. "Okay. I'm backing off, but you're coming for Sunday supper. Delphine makes the best gumbo."

She wasn't really into spicy foods. She kind of stuck to salads and the occasional steak, but she was new here and that meant giving the place a chance. Even if she got heartburn.

She slammed on the brakes because there was something in her way. Something big and creepy and alive.

"There's an alligator in the road." A massive reptile blocked the path. She had to stare at it for a moment because it was completely surreal. Were the doors locked? She looked and made sure and then wondered how she thought the alligator would open the door in the first place.

"Is he missing the tip of his tail?" Lisa asked as though they were talking about something perfectly normal. If baby sis was worried that her precious sibling was about to be mauled, it didn't sound like it.

Sure enough, the primeval-looking thing in the middle of the road had a tail that ended in a stump. Not that his tail wasn't still long and terrifying-looking. "Yes."

"That's Otis. He's a sweetheart," Lisa said breezily. "Don't worry about him. He's sunning himself, that's all. Are you on the highway? Because as long as you haven't hit the stretch by the water, you should be able to go around him. Now, if you are real close to town, you have to be careful because that ground around the pavement is tricky and you could get stuck. Normally that's not a problem because it's not like Herve has anything else to do, but this is his monthly hunting trip and his son is in charge of the shop. I saw him with his girlfriend earlier and he's useless while he's under Lorraine's spell. Unless she says it's okay, nothing's getting done in that shop today. It's fine. Just get out and shoo Otis off."

Get out of her safe vehicle and shoo off what had to be a five-hundred-pound reptile who probably ate the last person who did that? She glanced around and thanked god there wasn't a ton of water on either side of the road.

"I can get around him, but I need to concentrate on the road." She was almost there, and then she would see what her savings had bought her. Lisa had described the small house on the outskirts of town as a fixer-upper, but the price had been right, and it wasn't like she was afraid of hard work.

"All right. I'm waiting at your new place and I'm super excited you're here. Love you."

The line went dead before she could reply.

Okay. She could drive around this Otis thing and then she would move on. Nothing to worry about. She was from

Dallas. She'd dealt with many, many way scarier things than an animal with a pea-sized brain.

Still, when she'd managed to maneuver around the gator, she hit the gas hard as though the damn thing was going to follow her. She was doing at least seventy-five by the time she blew past the billboard advertising that a shopper could get both bait and Bibles at Fuzzy's Faithful Bait Depot.

That was when she heard the sirens, saw the red and blue lights come on behind her. For the briefest of moments, she went cold, her whole soul going back to that night.

But she wasn't in Texas. She was in Louisiana and it was daytime, and she was safe because she'd gotten away from the alligator. That brief moment of fear was replaced with annoyance because that was a cop behind her and he wasn't going around her in an attempt to go and save someone who needed saving. Nope. He pulled in right behind her and flashed his lights.

What was the speed limit? It had been seventy earlier. He was pulling her over for going five miles over the limit?

With a long sigh, she maneuvered to the side of the road and put the car in park. Surely she could talk her way out of this. Small-town cops liked to ticket out-of-towners, and her car still had Texas plates. She would explain that she was a new resident and he could go back to his donut eating and preying on tourists.

She glanced in her side mirror. He was taking his time. Probably thought he could intimidate her. Well, he was in for a surprise. She'd worked with cops all her life. She could absolutely handle some paunchy small-town deputy who likely had taken the job because there wasn't anything better to do.

The door to his SUV opened and then she was staring for a different reason.

A large man with intensely broad shoulders stepped out of the vehicle. He reached back in and brought out a hat that he settled on ridiculously dark hair that had more curl to it than she'd ever seen on a cop. DPD tended to keep it high and tight, but this man might be able to pull his back in a ponytail. No. That wasn't the word. A queue. Despite the long hair, there was absolutely nothing feminine about the man walking her way. Swaggering.

He was probably six foot four, and if there was an ounce of paunch on that man, she couldn't see it.

He was the man from Lisa's wedding, the one who had slid her that sensual smile.

She shook her head and forced herself to focus. He wasn't her type. She liked academic types. Nice men who were nonthreatening.

Boring. That's the word you're looking for. Boring and easily controlled so you can pretend that they can't hurt you. How'd that work out for us?

A hard tap on her driver's-side window brought her out of her inner monologue and she lowered the window. He wore mirrored aviators that covered his eyes. His jawline was sharp as a razor and there was a hint of sexy scruff coming in across his face.

Lord, the man was hot.

"License and registration, please." His tone, however, was cold as ice.

It was the chill in his voice that allowed her to find her footing again. The man in front of her probably had twenty women dangling on his string, and a wife and kids at home, too. No man that hot didn't. She could handle him. "Would you like to explain why you've pulled me over, Officer?"

He stepped back and for a moment she could have sworn he was surprised, but then she was sure almost no one would question this man's authority. He recovered quickly, his hands going to those lean hips of his. "You were speeding. The speed limit on this part of the highway is forty-five. I clocked you going thirty miles over the speed limit. License and registration."

"The speed limit went from seventy to forty-five? Are you kidding me?"

His lips curled up in a slightly crooked, wholly devastating smile. "That's what speed limits do, ma'am. They go up. They go down. You look familiar. Have you been through town before?"

She wasn't falling for his charm. Maybe invoking her brother-in-law's name would work some magic on him. "I'm Lila Daley. Remy Guidry is my brother-in-law."

That smile went flat, his whole body going back into cop mode. "The last time someone came into town looking for Remy, I got shot. You planning on shooting up the town?"

She winced inwardly. She remembered Lisa saying something about an incident that had led to a police officer being shot in the line of duty. "Sorry about that. No. I'm taking over the clinic in town. I'm your friendly neighborhood nurse practitioner. Next time you get shot, I will totally sew you up."

He stared at her and she wished she could see his eyes. "You're taking over for Doc Hamet?"

How to explain? "Sort of. I'm going to run the clinic, but he kind of supervises." A handful of states let nurse practitioners handle their own practices, but Louisiana wasn't one of them. Neither was Texas. She would have an enormous amount of freedom, but it would be in conjunction with the doctor who had served the parish for over forty years.

She intended to learn a lot from him.

"So you're his new nurse," the cop said. "I didn't know he'd fired the old one."

"No. I'm a nurse practitioner. I'm like a general practitioner, but I can't prescribe certain controlled substances. I can perform some surgeries. I spent over a decade working as a trauma RN before I finished getting my NP. I assure you I can handle the parish's medical needs."

"I don't think you understand the parish, but I'm willing to help out. You have to be better than the doc we have now. You have to catch the man early or not at all, if you know what I mean."

She gave him what she hoped was a friendly smile. "All right, then. Sorry about the misunderstanding. I'll be on my way. I was hoping to get everything in the new house before it gets dark."

"License and registration."

She gritted her teeth and reached for her purse. "The only reason I sped up was to get away from that freaking alligator." A thought occurred to her as she opened the Chanel wallet her brother had given her for Christmas. "Did you put that alligator out there as part of your speed trap?"

The sunglasses came off and she was staring into the bluest eyes she'd ever seen. Well, she'd seen them before, but not up close. They were even more devastating up close. "Did you accuse me of colluding with a reptile?"

"Yes."

His laughter seemed to fill her whole world. When that man lit up so did the sky around him. He doubled over, his laughter infectious. When he finally took a breath there was a chuckle in his words. "Oh, that is absolutely the best joke I've heard all day. Your sister never mentioned your sense of humor."

Probably because Lisa didn't think she had one. "Well, I'm known for my quick wit."

He stared at her for a moment and she could feel the connection. It was like an invisible tether drawing her to him. She'd been right to run the first time she'd seen him. Something deep inside had told her she wasn't capable of handling this man.

Didn't want to handle a man like him, she mentally corrected.

Oh, you had it right the first time. That man wouldn't let you be in charge all the time. He would challenge you.

Bully her was more like it. A man that gorgeous was used to getting his way.

But if it meant she would get out of this ticket, she could flirt a little.

He shook his head and sighed. "Unfortunately, you're also known for your lead foot. License and registration."

She bit back a growl because her first day in the new

town wasn't going the way she'd hoped, and the officer, while gorgeous, was an ass.

Same shit. Different town.

"There are no warrants. No BOLOs," the voice over the radio said. "You know you have a computer in the vehicle. It's connected to everything I have here at the station."

His admin was one hundred percent right. He had a very high-tech system that he didn't completely understand, and it was way easier to get Noelle on the radio and have her run it. Besides, he'd wanted a couple of minutes to consider the problem currently sitting in the tiny Audi crossover that was absolutely going to get stuck in the mud this spring.

Lila Daley. Damn, he'd forgotten how pretty she was. He glanced down at her driver's license. It showed a serious woman. Lovely, but serious. In the photo he couldn't see how long her hair was. It was pulled back and she looked a bit stark.

In real life her eyes were luminous, her lips a little too big for her face and all the sexier for it. Her hair was brown, but that was a stingy word to describe it. There was gold and hints of red threaded through all that warm silk. He wasn't sure why—he'd dated women who were technically more beautiful—but that woman did something for him. Not that he'd managed to talk to her before today. He'd tried to ask the woman to dance at Remy and Lisa's wedding, but she'd proven elusive. She was stuck in his head even all these months later.

"Did you know Doc Ham is replacing himself with a nurse?" He started the paperwork on the ticket. The micro-wave in the break room back at the station was on the fritz, hence today's speed trap. The damn thing either didn't work at all or heated anything put into it to volcanic-lava levels of heat. As he was forced to eat most of his meals in the break room, that microwave was critical, and it wasn't like the damn government was going to gift them with a new one.

He needed to get to Guidry's more often. Guidry's Bar and Grill was the gossip hub of the parish. He might have been ready for Nurse Practitioner Lila Daley if he'd been up on the gossip. There wasn't much to his department. It was him and his two deputies, Roxie and Major, and one junior officer, a young man named Vince. There were two other officers-in-training who would come on in a few weeks. For now, they took turns working night shifts, and he'd gotten to where he spent all his time either at the station house or holed up at home with his daughter. How long had it been since he went out and had some fun? Once a month playing poker at his friend Rene's was about all he'd kept up with after the accident, and only because for the first few months, his friends had shown up on his doorstep and insisted on coming in.

He was ready to start living again.

Maybe he should make it special. He'd been thinking about that woman for months, and now she was here like he'd managed to call her forth through pure willpower.

He probably shouldn't give her a ticket.

"A nurse practitioner," Noelle replied over the line. "I'm a little worried about how that's going to go. She's from Dallas. She's Lisa Guidry's sister, but I've met her and she's not like Lisa. She's very city. You know how people feel about that around here."

He'd spent years in New Orleans as a police officer before he'd come home and run for office. There was something special about Papillon. It could soften up the hardest soul. And if she needed someone to translate Cajun crazy to English, he was her guy. "What's the difference between a nurse and what Lila is? Is there a reason Mabel isn't taking over if we're going to lose the doc totally?"

He'd been the sheriff for years now, and the only medical professional in the parish was a three-hundred-year-old doctor with a Scotch problem and his slightly younger but way more feisty nurse.

Noelle sighed and he could practically see her eyes rolling. Sometimes he had to remind himself that he was barely forty and not the ravaged-by-time old man she seemed to think he was. "It means she's every bit as good as a doctor, but she didn't go to medical school. It means she's very likely practiced for at least a decade, and she was a nurse. She knows more about dealing with the people than the doctor does. Definitely more than any male doc."

Noelle had a problem with the patriarchy. "So she's smart."

"Yes, but none of that will matter around here," Noelle replied. "Is there a particular reason you're asking?" She sighed over the line again, a long-suffering sound. "Tell me you didn't pull her over. Do you understand that if you run her off, we won't have anyone? I'll have to go all the way into New Orleans to get a damn pap smear."

He would do almost anything to not have to hear about Noelle's pap smear. She wielded her feminine physical issues like a mighty sword. "She was going thirty miles over the speed limit."

"Nice. I've been eyeing a new coffeemaker after we replace the microwave." There was enthusiasm in her voice now. "Forget what I said. My pap is only once a year, but I need coffee every day. Go get her."

He glanced up and he could see that Lila's car was packed to the brim. Still, it wasn't much for a woman who was moving in. Did she have a truck coming? Was Remy planning on helping her move in? "Do you know anything else about her?"

A pause came over the line. "Seriously? You go two years without a single date and you're attracted to the city girl? I like it. This is going to be a ton of fun."

She was being crazily optimistic. "So you're saying you don't hate the idea of me asking someone out?"

"You do not have to ask me," she said softly.

But he did. "I don't want to complicate your life."

"Dad, getting you out of the house every now and then would make my life easier, and if you could find someone who could take this crappy part-time job, I would be even happier. I could be a freeloader. How awesome would that be?"

His daughter was a pistol. She was also a teenage girl who had lost her mother and been forced to change her whole lifestyle in the course of one terrible afternoon. "You're not freeloading, child. LaVignes work."

She made a gagging sound. "Yeah, that's what I hear. I guess I'm not getting that coffeemaker, huh?"

The ticket printed out and he glanced down to double check the information. "Why not?"

"Because you're not going to give her the ticket, right?"

He kind of had to now. There wasn't a way to take that back now that it had printed out. "I'll see you in a couple of hours, sweetheart. You start looking for that coffeemaker."

The microwave could wait. He had a very hard time denying his daughter anything. He knew he should limit her caffeine, but every time he tried to be the blustery, hard-nosed father he should be, he remembered she was in a wheelchair and caved in immediately.

He gripped the ticket and flipped off the radio even as Noelle was saying something about needing a female under the age of eighty to talk about her cramps and bloating with. Yep. He didn't need to know that.

This was the right path. She was the only woman in two years who'd sparked his interest, and she couldn't possibly be that bad. After all, she was Lisa Guidry's sister, and that woman was a sweetheart.

Not that he didn't like some sass. A lot of sass. All right, he kind of liked them bitchy, and he definitely liked them funny and smart, and the woman who'd accused him of using Otis to aid in his speed trap was definitely amusing.

It wasn't his fault Otis tended to freak out the tourists and they tried to speed away and didn't notice that the speed limit had gone down. Way down.

It wasn't really his fault Otis liked that stretch of highway and that it had been a perfect place to change the speed limit.

"You took your time," Lila said, those bee-stung lips frowning his way. "Did you find out about my criminal past?"

He gave her his best smile, the one he used at election time. He'd been told his vote-for-me smile worked on young and old, people of all political inclinations. "You're perfectly clean, Miss Daley. Can I call you Lila?"

A single brow rose over her pretty eyes. "Why would you do that, Officer?"

Damn, he hadn't even introduced himself. He was out of practice. "It's Sheriff. I'm the sheriff of Papillon Parish. Name's Armand LaVigne, but my friends all call me Armie."

"Can I have my ticket, Sheriff?"

Yeah, they should get through the bad part first. He tipped his hat her way and handed her the ticket. "Here you go. I'm sure you won't have any more trouble now that you know about the safety zone. Got to watch out for the kiddos."

"Safety zone? Seriously?" She huffed and tossed the ticket in her passenger seat.

"So you have a truck coming?" Small talk was good. At least he thought it was.

"Why would I have a truck coming? Are you going to try to ticket that, too?"

His small-talk game needed some work. "Because you're moving. Given that you're taking a job here, I would assume you're moving."

"Your powers of observation are incredible, Sheriff. And no. There's no truck coming. You're going to have to find someone else to upgrade your break room."

"You don't have furniture coming?"

"I bought a place and it came furnished," Lila explained in her matter-of-fact way. "I didn't really have a lot back in Dallas. I don't need a ton of stuff. I mostly work. All my home needs is a bed and a kitchen and a shower."

"You bought a place?" He sought his memory for any idea about a home that had been for sale. He prayed it wasn't the one he was thinking of. "Tell me you didn't buy that piece of crap Bill Roberts's kids have been trying to foist off on the unknowing public for the last six months."

She frowned again, but it was a curious sort of expression. "I bought a three bedroom on Hall Street just outside of town. I didn't have time to come down and look at it, but Remy told me the foundation was solid."

The foundation might be solid, but there were other issues. "Remy let you buy that place?"

Her shoulders straightened and he had the idea that if she hadn't been sitting in her car, she might have gotten in his space, squaring off with him like a prizefighter.

Yeah, that did something for him, too.

"Remy doesn't make decisions for me. He's my brother-in-law, not my keeper. That house was the only one on the market. It will be fine. The price was right so I'm setting down roots. If there's something wrong with the place, I assure you I can handle it. I learned how to fix things at a very young age."

He hoped she was familiar with plumbing. And electrical systems. And how to deal with hoarding. But that was a problem for another day. "That's good to know, but if you have any trouble, you can call me. In fact, I was thinking since you're new in town, you might need someone to show you around."

That brow was back up. "I have a sister."

"Yeah, but sometimes it's nice to see the town from the view of someone who's lived here all his life." Most of his life, but he wasn't going to point that out. "I know all the nice places." All two of them. "I was thinking after a long day of travel, you might want to get a bite to eat."

"You're asking me on a date?"

He couldn't be screwing it up too much. "We can definitely call it that."

"After giving me a ticket."

She would have to concentrate on that. "I wanted you to understand that there's no pressure on you. So, pick you up at seven? We can go to Guidry's." Maybe she wouldn't want to hang out at her sister's family bar. "Or Lucille's. They're open for dinner tonight. Best shrimp and grits you've ever had. I promise."

"You should back up now."

He took a step back and she gunned the engine, taking off down the highway.

"That's a no, then?" Armie shouted after the car.

She was probably speeding again, but he wasn't going to press his luck.

chapter two

Lila stood in front of the dilapidated ranch house that seemed to back up to some form of water. That must be the bayou portion of Butterfly Bayou, though she didn't see any butterflies. She did see the massive potential for mosquitoes. There was a dock she probably would never in a million years risk walking on, and a boat she was shocked was still floating tied to it.

What the hell am I doing?

She'd left her perfectly good apartment for this? Sure, it had been bland and she'd never bothered to decorate, but at least it didn't look like it was about to fall apart.

"It's not as bad as it looks," Lisa said, stepping in beside her. Her sister had been waiting for her when she'd driven up the gravel drive. "Maybe. I went inside and it's pretty bad in there. I can't believe Bill's kids didn't clean it out."

She felt her eyes widen because she wasn't good with dirt. Blood, she could handle. She fully understood the role of germs in the natural world, but in her own home she preferred the suckers nonexistent. "They didn't clean?"

Lisa turned to her. "Oh, not that. I didn't mean that. I had a maid service clean it top to bottom. I'm talking about all the things."

"They said it came furnished." It was the reason she'd

chosen the place. Well, that and the fact that it was cheap, and she needed cheap. Most of her savings was in her practice now. She couldn't afford a new house. Or apparently one that would be standing in a couple of years.

"Yep, with everything. You bought a ninety-eight-year-old man's entire life."

She wasn't sure that's what she'd planned on. "I thought it was furniture and dishes and stuff like that."

She'd left behind almost all of her own stuff when she'd broken things off with her fiancé. She'd walked away from him and gotten her own bland apartment that served as nothing more than a place to eat and sleep. It hadn't been hard to leave it when she'd decided to move out of Dallas.

"And dentures. He had a surprising collection of those," Lisa pointed out. "Don't worry. I think I got them all. I organized the bathrooms and there are fresh sheets on the bed. And the kitchen. It's spotless, though not decluttered. I wasn't able to get to the rest of the place. It's been crazy at work lately. I'll be here every minute I can to help you. I actually think it's going to be pretty once we fix it up."

It had to be because she was going to live here. She was going to make a home here in this tiny backwater place, where she could maybe hide from the big bad world.

"Lila, are you okay?"

She shook it off. She'd made her decision and she was sticking to it, peeling paint and all. "I'm good. It was a long drive. Thanks for bringing the keys out. And you don't have to help me. I'm sure it will be a good way to pass the time. I certainly won't explore this town by driving around. The sheriff is quick with a ticket."

And he was gorgeous and his smile lit up the world, and he had the most spectacular butt. She'd seen it in her rearview mirror as he'd swaggered away to write her up.

Apparently he wasn't married since he'd asked her out. Well, he'd suggested that they grab dinner together. That was kind of like asking her on a date. She'd been out of the game for a very long time.

Lisa groaned. "Are you serious? I'll talk to him. You

know what? There's a town hall next week. I'll yell at him there. And I'll let him know if he doesn't fix it, he's off the pie list at Guidry's. Don't discount that threat. Armie might look like a man who never eats carbs, but he loves my pecan pie."

She did not want her sister involved. "It's fine. I was speeding, but I swear he's in league with that gator. Are there a lot of them?"

"Gators? Yeah, but they really don't cause trouble," Lisa explained. "You leave them alone and they'll leave you alone. You know you can change your mind. You can still come and stay with me until we get everything up to your standards."

"I have standards?"

Lisa sent her an incredulous look. "Yeah, sis. It's kind of your thing. I remember not being allowed out of the house until I looked picture perfect, and I was all of ten years old."

"You had to look perfect so no one would suspect we were on our own." The first time their mother had gone to jail, their aunt had stayed with them for the whole six months. The second she'd had other things to do. She'd played her part for CPS, but they'd been on their own. It had gone that way for the rest of their childhood. Often Lila had preferred the times when her mother was locked up. It meant one less person to take care of. "We had to be ready in case someone showed up. The place had to be immaculate at all times, and we all had to be perfect in school or questions would be asked."

She'd never gotten out of the habit. It was funny that it hadn't really struck her until that moment. She couldn't tolerate a mess. Not because it bothered her. It made her nervous. It made her worry someone would judge her.

How had she never let that go? How was she still in that place she'd been in when she was a kid?

"You don't have to be perfect here. It's actually way better that you aren't. These people respect authenticity," Lisa assured her. "I'm going to help you fix this place up. It'll be fun. And who knows—maybe there's, like, treasure in there. Probably not. He was on a fixed income. From what I've heard, he didn't get out much after his wife passed. His kids were scattered all over the country. When he got sick, he went into a nursing home up in Thibodaux. The kids didn't want to spend much time here. That's why you got it for such a steal. Remy says the house itself is solid, but it needs some upgrading. He's worried about the water heater. And the air conditioner."

"Yeah, I kind of got that feeling from the sheriff."

"He talked to you about the house? How did he know about the house?" Lisa's eyes had turned shrewd. "Armie's famously tight-lipped when it comes to pulling over drivers. He doesn't listen to anyone. All he'll say is 'License and registration' and then he passes you a ticket. He got chatty with you?"

She could still hear the deep rumble of his voice. "He got weird with me. He gave me a ticket and then offered to show me around town, starting with some place called Lucille's."

Now her sister's eyes went wide. "Lucille's is a date place. No one goes to Lucille's unless they're celebrating something special or trying to get into someone's pants. And it's not here in Papillon. It's thirty minutes away."

"If he wanted to date me, maybe he shouldn't have given me a ticket," she replied, starting toward the front door. Armie LaVigne was big and gorgeous but off-limits because she wasn't going to hop into bed two seconds after she'd gotten into town.

Why?

Because he gave me a freaking ticket.

So? He might also give you an orgasm.

Her inner voice could just shut up because she bet Armie LaVigne hit on every single tourist who came into town. The whole parish had less than two thousand people in it. It wasn't like he had a ton of choices, and she was the new girl. Of course he was going to hit on her. She should probably expect that from most of the single men.

"Don't let the ticket thing throw you off. Armie's pretty hot, and he's a solid guy. And I mean that in several ways. He's responsible and has a good job, and he's been shot a couple of times and always survives it." Lisa went still and her hand went over her mouth. "God, Lila. I'm sorry. I shouldn't have said that."

There it was. That memory of when the gun came up and time had slowed down. It was always there, simmering under the surface of every good moment she had. She blinked and reminded herself Dallas was hundreds of miles away.

"I'm fine." She said those words a lot. She said them to her family and friends. She said them to her therapist. She said them to herself. Of course, if she was fine, why had she felt the desperate need to upend her whole life, move over five hundred miles from the city she'd lived in for years, and spend every penny of her savings on a new start? "I didn't take it that way. I'm glad to know the sheriff of the parish is capable of surviving a couple of bullets. I'm sure no bullet could get through his thick head."

Lisa seemed to want to say something else, but her sister let it go. "You know, you could do worse than Armie."

She wasn't sure how. Getting involved with a gorgeous man who was sure to break her heart when she was trying to build a business and a new life for herself seemed like pretty much the worst thing she could do. "I'm not here to socialize."

She fit the key in the door. It was time to see how much trouble she'd bought for herself.

"Yeah, I wanted to talk to you about that," Lisa was saying as the door opened. "This isn't Dallas."

Precisely why she was here. Papillon was about as far as she could get from Dallas and still be close to her family. When she'd decided on a new start, she hadn't been able to give up being close to at least one of her siblings. She'd thought it through. Laurel had a baby. She'd come through it like a champ, and her brother's wife, Bridget, had given birth twice. They both had access to good healthcare. Lisa was out here alone. If her big Cajun husband wasn't packing some hefty swimmers, she would eat her Louis Vuitton handbag. Lisa would get pregnant at some point, and Lila wasn't leaving her care to anyone but her. "I'm well aware this isn't Dallas."

She got the door open and stepped into the fifties. At least she was pretty sure that was when every piece of furniture had been bought. The newspapers, though, looked like they came from every week of the last fifty years.

"Sorry about the papers." Lisa maneuvered her way around the first of what looked like fifty stacks. "Like I said, the place isn't dirty, per se. Just cluttered. He liked newspapers and magazines. And books. Lots of books. There's also a closet full of buttons. No idea why, but we were told not to open that one. I wasn't talking about physical differences. I was talking about fitting in. I'm not sure if you know it, but sometimes you can be intimidating."

Often in the ER a little intimidation went a long way. "I can't help how other people react to me. I do my job and I do it well."

"See, right there. Intimidating."

She managed to make it to the living room. It was better in here, but the place was covered in tchotchkes. Every available space was littered with snow globes and stuffed animals with the names of various monuments stitched on them. There were commemorative plates and spoons and thimbles.

At least the sofa looked fairly comfy. "Again, I'm not seeing the problem."

"People here aren't used to that," Lisa said, picking up a set of Disneyland salt and pepper shakers and moving them in an attempt to clear off the coffee table. "They're used to a gentler approach. You have to think before you blurt out whatever goes through your head or you'll lose them. The people here aren't used to change. They kind of actively fear it."

"You seem to be getting along well. And this *is* coming

from the girl who got into a fight her first night here and ended up pulling out another chick's weave. So I'm not seeing the Southern manners." Her sister's stories about the town and the people here had been one of the reasons she'd come.

It had seemed like a good place to hide.

Lisa grinned. "They do like drama. And she was coming after my man. They understand that, too. You're amazing at your job. I just want it to be smooth sailing for you."

"It will be." At least her clinic probably wasn't a museum for bad souvenirs. "Why on earth would he keep all these things? The poor man obviously had a mental illness."

"Or he was lonely." Lisa's hands ran over the collection of brightly colored pens. There looked to be tubs of them. "These things probably reminded him of a time when life was good. When he and his family traveled. The only thing the kids asked me for were the pictures. I sent those back. There were lots of pictures of the five of them in a camper traveling across the country."

The Daley family had never done that. Not once. The most they'd traveled as kids was to the prison on visiting days after Will had managed to get his license. They hadn't taken trips, they'd just tried to survive.

Was she still trying to survive? Was she still clawing her way through a day without any understanding as to what it meant? Her family was safe. They were all happy and moving on. They had lives and she was . . . running and managing to stand still all at the same time.

The man who'd lived here, he'd had a life. Maybe it had been a messy one. Maybe he'd been lonely in the end, but he'd lived.

When she'd decided to leave Dallas, she'd packed up her car and had room to spare. She hadn't taken a bunch of things that reminded her of good times.

Because she hadn't really had good times.

Lisa held up a coffee mug. It was emblazoned with the hokiest picture of an elderly couple smiling from inside a big heart. *World's Greatest Husband* was written across the other side of the mug. "I think some of these things were gifts from his wife. Isn't that sweet?"

She'd been engaged at one point in time and she'd handed back the ring without a second thought. She hadn't needed to have a bonfire to burn all her mementos because there hadn't been any. All of his gifts to her had been practical. No flowers for Lila Daley. She needed a pair of gloves. No jewelry. She would rather have orthopedic shoes and new scrubs.

"I used to schedule gifts for myself," she said quietly, studying the books on the shelf. It looked like the man had been heavily invested in old Westerns. Her eyes drifted down to the lower shelf and she found a whole row of what looked like romance novels. "When I was with Brock, I mean. I would schedule gifts because I thought I should. He bought me flowers once and I explained that I would prefer him to spend money on something that wouldn't die on me in a week."

"Okay, that's the single least romantic thing I've ever heard," Lisa said. "I never liked Brock. He seemed cold."

"That was what I liked about him," she admitted.

"Because you didn't have to work too hard?"

"Because I did all the work." She looked to her sister and wished she hadn't given in to the impulse to talk about her private life. But wasn't that what her therapist had told her to do? She held everything in, never admitting her own flaws or weaknesses. It kept her apart from even the people she loved. "I liked doing all the work. And I resented it. I wanted control but when I had it, I hated him for giving it all to me. You think I'm intimidating, but I'm a hot mess when it comes to most things."

A quiet, hot mess. A silent, threatening volcano. A bomb waiting to go off if pressure wasn't released. She usually released that pressure via long runs.

What if she could release it a different way?

"You went through something awful. It's okay to be a

hot mess." Lisa sank down on the couch and patted the place beside her.

It was odd to have their roles reversed. For all her life she'd been the big sister, the one Laurel and Lisa came to, the one with all the answers, and if she didn't have them, she made them up. She was the ultimate fake-it-'til-you-make-it girl. She'd been doing it all her life.

But she had no answers now. Only a million gnawing questions.

"I should be over it." It was what she told her therapist. She'd treated therapy like something she had to get through in order to get on with her life. Like if she sat in the chair and answered the questions, she would be fine.

It hadn't worked that way.

"You're not going to get over it. I think that's a phrase that does not apply to what happened to you. You get through it," Lisa said, reaching a hand out. "This will be with you the rest of your life."

"I couldn't walk into the hospital without being in that moment." It was why she'd quit. She'd gone back to work a month after the incident. She'd forced herself to walk into the building, forced herself to do the job, forced herself to go home, forced herself to take the pills that helped her sleep, and then one night thought about how nice it was to sleep, how if she took enough pills she might be able to stay asleep.

She'd quit the next day, and now she was here and she was going to find a way to want to wake up every morning.

"I wouldn't have wanted to go back there, either," Lisa said. "I think that's normal. I was worried when you went back to work so quickly, but it didn't surprise me."

"I bet me quitting did."

Lisa seemed to consider that for a moment. "Not really. Coming here surprised me. I didn't think you liked it here. You barely talked to anyone at my wedding."

There had been a reason for that. "I know you won't believe this, but I was upset when I broke up with Brock. I knew he wasn't the one, but I think I figured out there might not be a one out there for me. I was jealous of everything my siblings have and I held myself apart. I actually find this place interesting."

She'd definitely found Armie LaVigne interesting. Until he'd given her a damn ticket. Not that she could blame the ticket for her hesitance. He hadn't ticketed her at the wedding and she'd still run as fast as she could.

"Really?" There was a wealth of skepticism in her sister's tone.

She didn't have to lie about this. "Absolutely. From my brief stay here I've figured out that everyone in this town is nuts and they need an adult at the helm."

Lisa pointed her way and Lila had the bad feeling she'd stepped into a trap. "There it is. That's what you can't do here. You can't walk in here and act like you know everything."

"I'm not acting. I do know everything." She couldn't resist poking her sister.

Lisa shook her head. "I know you're smart and good at your job, but you're not in an ER now. You're going to be the main source for healthcare for the whole parish. We're isolated. These people need you, and I'm worried if you put them off, they won't come and see you. I've already heard some rumors that people don't understand what an NP is."

She shrugged. "They'll learn or they'll go without. Like you said, I'm the only game in town. They can't stay away forever. When they get sick they'll come and see me."

It seemed like a pretty simple thing. She would explain her education and training to them and they would understand. If they didn't want to see a female practitioner, there wasn't a lot she could do about that. She'd been assured that Doc Hamet would happily hand over his patients, and part of that had to be getting them ready for the transition. According to her new nurse, she had a full afternoon tomorrow. Three physicals, two follow-ups, a well-baby exam, and there would surely be a couple of walk-ins. All in all it sounded busy for a sleepy little clinic.

Her business was going to be the center of her world. It would be her baby.

"I hope it works like that. Sometimes the people here can be stubborn about change. Be patient with them," Lisa said. "Are you sure you're completely done with Brock?"

Her ex-fiancé was in her rearview mirror. Like the rest of her life in Dallas. "Like I said, I figured out he wasn't the one. I knew I didn't love him. I guess I thought I should get married. It was like checking something off a list. Go to college. Get a job. Get married. I'm sure if I'd done it I would have scheduled sex and built a family plan."

"I know that sounds like the way to do it, but it's not. You have to let some spontaneity in. You can't plan love."

"Well, I don't intend to plan love. It wasn't love with Brock." She'd never been in love, wasn't sure she was capable of the emotion. "I'm not planning on getting involved with anyone."

"That's what I was afraid of. I'm going to ask you for a favor. I've done everything I can to make this transition easy, and you asked me if you could do anything to pay me back."

Lisa had done a lot to make this happen. She'd been the one to deal with the paperwork on the house and the inspectors. Her husband had put in his time, too. "Of course."

She had a little money left over. Not a ton, but she wouldn't be surprised if Lisa needed a loan. The restaurant industry was infamously tough. It wouldn't be a loan, though. She would never ask for it back.

"Keep an open mind."

"What is that supposed to mean?"

"It means you're still checking things off that list," Lisa explained. "It's just that the list has changed. You went through something horrible and you've got a plan for how to get through it. Tell me your therapist didn't mention a change of scenery."

Oh, she had. "I don't think she meant for me to take it this far. She was talking about a vacation or a retreat for a couple of months."

"But you like to do things big," Lisa pointed out. "Lila Daley doesn't do anything halfway. You throw yourself in one hundred percent. You take over and get the job done, but this isn't a job. This is your life, and I think you made the right choice coming here. I think if you'd stayed in Dallas, you would have eventually found another Brock and gotten back on your path. You might have changed hospitals, but you wouldn't have essentially changed your life."

"I assure you my life changed." She could barely sleep through the night without dreaming about it. "I didn't need to do anything to have my entire life turned around but go to work and be in the wrong place at the wrong time. *That* was spontaneous."

"No." Lisa shook her head vigorously. "That was planned. He'd planned to kill her for years, and you know it. That wasn't your fault and I pray you figure that out soon or I worry you'll let your life slip by and you won't ever know the truth."

"What's the truth?"

Lisa leaned toward her, eyes shining. "That you are worthy of love, sister. That you deserve every bit of happiness you can find. That it's time to let go, to find that person who can lift you up the way you always did for me and Laurel and Will. Somewhere along the way you forgot that you need support, too, and I'm going to be here for you."

Emotion welled hard and fast, but she shoved it down. This was too much after an already rough day. "How about you help me find something to eat in this town?"

A smile lit up her sister's face. "That I can do."

Lisa started talking about the new foods to try, and Lila prayed she got through the night. Tomorrow would be better. Tomorrow she could leave all the emotional crap behind and get to work.

Tomorrow her new life began.

Armie stalked into the station house, his stomach grumbling, but he'd promised Noelle he would stop eating greasy burgers and that was about all he could get at this time of the day. It wasn't like he could eat a salad in his car. Not that he wanted to eat a salad.

He bet Lila Daley ate a lot of salads. She had that I-think-about-my-cholesterol glow about her.

Damn but he hadn't been able to get that woman out of his head all afternoon.

He needed intel. That was what had gone wrong today. He'd gone into battle without proper intel. He should have found out that the woman got irrationally angry about perfectly reasonable ticketing practices.

"I can't believe you gave her a ticket for going thirty miles over the speed limit." Noelle looked up from the book she'd been reading. "Do you have any idea how much that is going to cost her? You'll be lucky she doesn't run you over the next time she sees you. You realize that woman is now in charge of your yearly physicals?"

"I have to administer the law equally to everyone. I can't favor the woman who's going to take my blood pressure."

"How about the woman who can order your colonoscopy?"

That made him stop. Another thing he hadn't thought about. "She's obviously a professional." At least he hoped she was. A man's colon was a sacred thing. A doctor knew that. "Our first meeting didn't go as well as I thought it would, but there's always next time. We have to work closely with the clinic. I'm sure I can find a reason to get over there soon."

"There's a next time?" Noelle asked.

He wasn't going to get into this with his teenage daughter. "Don't you have homework to do?"

"I'm three weeks ahead of pacing." She shut the lid to her laptop and wheeled herself from behind the desk.

A junior. His baby girl was a junior in high school. Oh, sure, that high school was online, and she didn't do what other girls her age were doing—like going on dates with boys and giggling with her friends at Friday night football games—but she was a junior.

Had he made the wrong call by not sending her to a

physical school? Had he made the right call letting her hang out at a station house most of the time?

Being a parent sucked.

"She's doing great, Armie," a familiar voice shouted across the floor. "She took her calculus quiz and got a ninety. Smart as a whip, that one."

He sighed and started toward the three cells at the back of the building. It was basically a drunk tank, or a place to hold a prisoner before the marshals came to get him. Or her. Except he rarely had female prisoners. Nope. He did have Zep Guidry. He pretty much always had Zep.

"Do you do this to save on rent?" Not that Zep had rent. He was a twenty-four-year-old who still lived at his momma's. If the kid wasn't so good-looking, he'd be considered pathetic. Somehow those movie-idol looks of his kept the women coming even after they figured out he was the worst bet in the parish.

"I love it here. It's my happy place." Zep sat back on the cot and crossed one long leg over the other. "This particular incarceration isn't my fault. Look at me. I'm perfectly sober and I didn't even get into a fight. What you are looking at is false arrest. I'm going to get an attorney this time."

The only attorney in town was Quaid Havery, and he might bail Zep out, but he was smart enough to know Zep had probably deserved it. There would be no help from that direction. "What did you do?"

"He irritated Roxie." Noelle moved in beside him. "She's out back gassing up her vehicle. I don't think it really needed it. I think she wanted to get away from Zep."

If she wanted to get away from him she shouldn't have arrested him. There was an idea.

Noelle frowned like she knew exactly what had gone through his head. "Dad, you are not going to arrest the new doc so she has to listen to you."

It had been worth a thought. "What's he in for? And can we get rid of him before I have to feed him? He eats a lot, and the mayor told me I can't put prisoners on bread and water."

"We don't have any bread," Noelle said helpfully. "We'll have to order out."

"I'll take the gumbo. Wait, we have to heat that up. Maybe a sandwich. Yeah, I'll have a BLT. Tell my brother to not skimp on the bacon," Zep said, like eating in lockup was an everyday occurrence.

There were times when he wished his deputy hadn't fallen hard for that idiot. Mostly those times were always. He could try to point out that Roxie was showing her affection by arresting him, but that could only make matters worse.

"I'm not calling your brother." He had plans for the night and they did not involve hanging out with a prisoner. Roxie was on nights this week, and he wasn't going to leave those two alone. The world could explode. "What's he really in for?"

"Roxie pulled him over for ignoring a stop sign," Noelle explained.

"I paused," Zep claimed. "Damn, man, there's no one out there for me to hit. I like to think of that particular stop sign as more of a suggestion."

"Then, according to Roxie, he argued with her for twenty minutes, refused to take the ticket, and suggested that she shouldn't be on patrol during her time of the month." Noelle shook her head.

Damn, he'd stepped into it. Still, Zep could cause trouble down the line if he ever did find a lawyer who would do more than try to get him out of his numerous parking tickets. Armie's hands went to his keys and he stopped because he had wanted intel and Zep's brother was married to Lila's sister.

He could use this.

"Noelle, go ahead and put that order in," he said. "I think I should talk to our friend here. Put him on the straight and narrow."

Noelle sighed and turned her chair around. "He's going to grill you about Lila Daley. I'll go see how much money's in the emergency fund because I want some fries. You two should settle in because I'm having Roxie take me out there to pick up the order and we're going to eat there because fries do not travel well."

"I'm actually kind of hungry now," Zep started before he looked to Armie. "Or I can wait. I'm good."

It was nice to know his stare could still make a man think twice. Especially since it didn't do anything to the women in his life.

Zep made himself comfortable as Noelle went off to find Roxie. "So you're interested in Lisa's sister. You've come to the right place, my man. I'm kind of a love doctor."

He was absolutely certain if he wanted to have a skanky one-night stand and end up needing antibiotics or worse, Zep would be his go-to guy. "I only want to know what she's like. I do not need advice. I saw her back at Remy and Lisa's wedding. I was sitting at the table next to hers. I might have listened in. She seems funny and smart."

He wasn't sure why, but she'd sparked his interest in a way no woman had in years.

"Well, if you want my advice," Zep began.

"I just said I didn't."

Zep was not listening. "You should find someone with less baggage. That girl has a ton of it."

"She's a woman."

Zep shook his head. "According to Lisa, she's kind of controlling. She also called me a moron more than once."

That was not a disqualifying characteristic for him. Zep *was* a moron at times. "Why did she decide to leave Dallas? Most people do the opposite." Not a lot of kids stayed here in Papillon.

He was damn lucky Noelle showed no signs of leaving. He wouldn't be able to breathe with her out there. The last time she'd left the comforts of her home, she'd come to his in that wheelchair.

That got Zep sitting up straight. "You didn't hear about that?"

He didn't listen to gossip unless it was about an underground drug-running operation. "No. The only thing I've heard is that she had a high-profile job in Dallas and that she's taking over for Doc. I'm not sure how great that's going to work. I know she's not married and she didn't like Remy at one point in time, but I didn't like him, either. He was an asshole for years."

"Preach, brother," Zep agreed. "Remy treats me like I can't do anything right."

He did not bother to mention the man was in jail. Zep Guidry wasn't the most self-aware individual he knew. "So she decided to come to a tiny parish and take over the practice of a doctor whose patients could likely fill a mental ward?"

Zep turned serious for a change. "Something happened. She had this friend named Maryanne she worked with at the hospital. Maryanne's ex-husband walked in and shot her. He held Lila in a room until he was sure his ex was dead and then he shot himself. I think she's coming here because it's as far away from Dallas as she can handle."

Damn. "So she's not looking for fun, huh?"

Zep's eyes found his, a gravity in them he wasn't used to seeing. "No. She's looking for something, though."

Peace. She would be looking for peace. The last thing she needed was some man trying to climb all over her.

He pulled his keys out and made his decision. "You can go on home, man. Stay out of Roxie's way. She's a good woman."

Zep was on his feet in a heartbeat. "I never said she wasn't."

"Treat her with some respect or you won't be in that cell, you get my meaning?"

"I do."

He let Zep head out and went to find his daughter and his deputy. He would take them all out for supper. They could take a radio and close up the station for an hour or so.

The next time he saw Lila Daley, he would be polite, since he knew what it was like to survive hell.

Now he only hoped she could survive Papillon.

chapter three

 ⟡

"Why would she cancel? It's time for her yearly. It's actually past time. She's three months late." Lila stared at her receptionist. The day was not going the way she'd planned.

After getting next to no sleep, waking up to a ridiculously cold shower and finding the button closet—she should never have opened that door—she'd come to the clinic hoping to lose herself in work.

What she'd found was apparently a full-on revolt.

"Miss Armintage said she'd managed to make it forty-seven years without a woman touching her vagina and she intended to make it forty-seven more. She said it's not natural."

Lila shook her head. "A gynecological exam from a female isn't natural? But a male doctor putting her in stirrups and shoving a speculum up to her cervix is?"

Mabel shrugged. "Her words, not mine."

The door to the clinic opened and a woman walked in, her baby in a sling.

"Hey there, Mabel." She smiled as she reached the front desk and turned to Lila. "I'm here to see Doc. Hi, I'm Hallie Rayburn. We haven't met yet. Are you taking over for Mabel? I hadn't heard Mabel was retiring. Oh, she's the best. You'll have big shoes to fill."

It was becoming brutally obvious that Doc Hamet hadn't mentioned her at all to his patients. Her patients. "I'm sorry. Doc Hamet is moving into more of an advisory role here at the clinic. I'm taking over. Mabel will stay on in her capacity assisting with the running of the clinic and helping me with patients."

Hallie's eyes widened and she shook her head like she couldn't quite believe the words she'd heard. "Seriously? But Doc's been here for years. He delivered me. I thought he would deliver all my kids."

"Contrary to popular belief, the man's not immortal. He's getting on up there. He needed a younger person to take over his practice, so I'll be delivering all the babies. Is this Gracie? I saw from her records that she had a little jaundice when she was born. Let's see how that light therapy worked. Come on in the back." She'd spent the morning going over files and making sure she was ready for her appointments. It was a total about-face from her previous job, where she put out fires all day. Literally, sometimes. Now she was the one who would prevent the fires from happening at all.

Hallie took a step back, holding her baby close as though someone was going to snatch her. "I need to think about this. I don't know anything about you. Is Doc here? Can I talk to him?"

"No. He went fishing." He hadn't mentioned that to her, either. He'd simply handed her the keys, laughed maniacally, to her mind, and driven away. He'd promised to sign every report he needed to with the state—provided she filled them all out for him. She had the number for a GP two parishes over who would oversee her if she needed help.

It didn't look like she was going to need any help at all since she wasn't going to have any patients.

Mabel was on her feet. "She's got a bunch of degrees, Hallie. She knows what she's doing."

"I'll talk to my momma." Hallie practically ran the other way.

Yep, her day was not looking up.

How was she going to live if no one would come to the clinic because she wasn't one of them? They had to give in at some point, right?

"This is insane." She dropped the file on top of the others she hadn't needed. "I can handle a well-baby checkup."

"I told Doc it might not work." Mabel was roughly sixty years old with raven-colored curly hair with wispy hints of silver at the temples and a tiny but mighty body, from what Lila could tell. She was dressed in scrubs and hadn't stopped moving once since they'd opened the clinic at noon. Mabel had answered phones, swept the break room, prepped the two exam rooms, done a thorough inventory of their supplies, and generally made her feel like a slacker. Mabel had done everything except actually help treat a patient.

"Why?" The sheriff had mentioned this could happen. Her sister had mentioned it. She still didn't get how she was throwing the town into a tizzy.

"First off, we've never had a nurse practitioner in here before," Mabel explained. "They don't understand that you're as good as a GP. Now, I think we can fix that, but it's going to take some time and you're going to have to let folks get used to you. I know what Hallie's momma is going to tell her. She's going to tell her to take that baby into New Orleans."

"She would rather drive four hours round trip than let me do my job?"

A triumphant look came over Mabel's face. "And that's where we'll get her. She'll go once or twice. Maybe until the baby is a year old or so, but she'll get tired of it. And when she has another baby, she definitely won't like that drive." Mabel nodded. "And we'll be here. We'll be waiting."

She was missing the salient point. "No, we won't because if no one comes in we won't be able to stay open."

Mabel waved that off. "Oh, this place has never once been financially solvent. Don't worry about it. Once a year

Doc goes fishing with Rene Darois and he funds us for the year. If we need a new piece of equipment, we hold a bake sale. Well, I hold a bake sale. Doc wasn't good at baking. He was good at poker. We got that ultrasound machine from the casino up the road."

Every word out of Mabel's mouth ratcheted up her anxiety. "I'm sorry, what? I looked over the financials for this place. It looked like it supported itself."

"Oh, Doc was never any good with reports and such."

"Someone is." Those accounting records had looked real. They hadn't shown much of a profit, but she hadn't intended to get rich. She had intended to keep the place going without the use of baked goods. "I don't think this is legal."

"Now, see, there you go. You can't keep thinking that way or people are going to see you as uppity."

"I'm uppity because I got ripped off? I sunk a lot of money into this place." Almost everything she had.

"It's about more than money, though, right?" Mabel asked. "It's about helping the public and being part of this beautiful community. Honestly, most of these people can't actually afford our services. I'll talk to Hallie's momma, because they've actually got insurance. Her husband works on the rigs. We really can't afford to lose that group. They're having babies all the time. Men who've been on an oil rig for months think a lot about their wives and getting home to them. Not so much about contraception, if you know what I mean."

She was fairly certain she didn't know a thing.

The door opened again and a woman with long brown hair walked in, cradling her arm.

Mabel sighed and ran around the reception desk. "What happened this time, Carrie? I swear you being out there on your own scares the heck out of me. Come on in."

Carrie gave her a weak smile. "I'm clumsy. I was feeding the chickens and I fell. I thought it was only strained but it was hurting this morning and I could barely make breakfast."

Lila stepped around the desk, too. "Can I take a look at it?"

"Is Doc here?" Carrie asked.

She was going to kill that man and then no one would ask about him again. "He retired. My name is Lila Daley. I'm a nurse practitioner. That means I can do almost everything a doctor can do except I didn't sit through medical school. I learned on the job, not in a classroom. My last job was at a major hospital in the ER and I was excellent at it. I'd like to take a look at your arm and maybe get an X-ray to see if we need to set it."

Carrie's eyes widened slightly and a ghost of a smile flashed on her face. "It sounds like you know what you're doing. It hurts a lot."

Finally, someone who needed her. "Let's take a look."

Mabel was smiling as she led Carrie back.

Forty minutes later, Lila was fairly certain what she was dealing with. She put the X-ray on the lighted display so her patient could see what was happening. Had happened. Likely would happen again. "What you're looking at is a small hairline fracture in your radius, Carrie. It's not serious. I'm not going to need to set it. We'll put it in a sling you'll need to wear for a week or so. It will heal on its own if you let it rest."

A relieved sigh went through her. "That's good news. I'll be way more careful from now on."

Lila wasn't sure carefulness was Carrie's problem. "Was it a bad fall?"

That relief she'd seen briefly fled and Carrie was back to looking worried, though it was obvious she didn't want Lila to know that. "Not bad. I tripped on a rock and hit the ground. Like I said, I didn't think it was bad until this morning."

There were a few things that didn't ring true about her story, but she knew from experience that she had to tread carefully. "It's almost four now. How far out do you live?"

"Pretty far. We have to come by boat. We're on an island out in the bayou. It's my husband's family property."

"I wish you'd come in earlier. I could have saved you some pain. Ice therapy works well if you get it on there fast enough," Lila explained.

The younger woman nodded. "I'll remember that. I waited until Bobby was coming into town. It doesn't make sense to make two trips."

Yes, that's what she'd thought. "Your health is important."

"I'm all right," Carrie insisted.

Lila gestured to the X-ray. "Do you see those wispy lines on the X-ray? Those are healed fractures. I counted five of them."

"I'm real clumsy."

"Is your husband hurting you?"

Carrie slipped off the table, landing on her feet.

She was going to lose her if she pushed too hard. Lila picked up her clipboard. "Sorry, I have to ask. Actually, I have to ask if anyone is hurting you. It's that kind of injury."

She nodded. "Yeah, of course. No. It happened how I said it happened."

Lila gave her what she hoped was a reassuring smile and checked the box on the form. "Of course. I'm also supposed to inform you that if for any reason you're in fear of anyone in your home, you can talk to your healthcare provider about help. Not that you need it. They make us say a lot of things to be in compliance."

"Doc never did any of that." Carrie glanced up at the clock and winced. "Can I get that sling? I have to meet Bobby."

"He's not picking you up?" She would've liked to get a look at the man.

"I'm meeting him by the dock. He's got a delivery he has to wait on. I don't want to cause any trouble." Her eyes came up and for a second, Lila thought she might say something about what had really happened. "How much do I owe?"

Her gut had tightened up and she had to force a smile on her face. "Mabel can get you a bill. I'll go and get your sling."

She stepped away and tried not to think about how her hands were shaking.

Maybe it wasn't the same. Maybe it had happened exactly the way Carrie said it had, but then there was the problem of those wispy lines on the X-ray. There were medical explanations for multiple fractures. She could have a disorder. She could simply be clumsy.

But Lila's gut was saying something very different.

It took every bit of her willpower to not push Carrie. There would be a next time and Lila didn't want to be the reason the young woman didn't seek help. She got her in the sling and gave her information on home therapies and waved as she left.

"That girl," Mabel said with a shake of her head. "She's a little mouse. Always has been. How she manages out there I have no idea. I thought she would leave for New Orleans or Houston like most of her friends. She was a smart one, always with a book in her hand. We were all shocked when she up and married Bobby Petrie. His family has lived on that island for a hundred years."

"Is he a nice man?"

Mabel shrugged. "I suppose. They keep to themselves out there. He and his brother are shrimpers, but Donny's the one who handles the business end."

"She sees the doc a lot?" It would be easy to keep up the abuse if she was isolated.

"Not a ton. She had a miscarriage a couple of years ago. She fell down the stairs. It was tragic."

Yeah, she bet the young woman fell down the stairs a lot. "I'd like to see her records. Could you pull them?"

"Sure. It's not like I have anything better to do," Mabel admitted. "We need to plot and plan because we have two more cancellations for tomorrow. You need to get out and meet the people."

She wasn't sure how meeting people would help. The people here seemed to take one look at her and run.

The door was flung open and an elderly man was being helped in by a younger man who might be his son. A second group followed with another man. He had white hair and wore a pair of Bermuda shorts he'd coupled with dress socks, loafers, and a white tank top. He had a bad gash over his right eye.

"Oh, lord. That's Jimmy Burnes and Abe Rubelle. They live next door to each other and I swear they've regressed back to childhood." Mabel shook her head as the party of injured elderly made their way across the floor. "Tell me they weren't playing chicken with the riding lawn mowers again."

The youngest of the men groaned. "I wish I could. My daddy has lost his mind."

The gentleman he was holding up managed to raise a fist. "I'm living, son. Living. And I won."

"Did not," the other man said. "I was getting back on my mower when you decided to have a heart attack. Game ain't over 'til one of us gives in. Where's Doc?"

Lila sighed and sprang into action. It looked like her day wasn't over yet.

Armie stared across his desk at Gene Boudreaux. Gene owned the local grocery store/tourist information station. He also listened to far too many conspiracy theory podcasts. It hadn't been all that bad when he'd only had network television to draw from. Ah, the good old days. Back then Gene would only come in to talk about potential government takeovers. Armie could usually point out that unless the government wanted shrimp or to take a tour of the bayou, there really wasn't much for them to take over.

But then last Christmas Gene's grandson just had to introduce the man to the wonderful world of podcasts. Now Gene constantly listened to non-experts talk about crimes, and now he saw them going on everywhere. And he constantly proved that he didn't understand what the young people meant by being "woke." It was definitely not being woke to think that every single stranger a person met was likely trying to murder him.

"Do we really know what happened, Sheriff?" Gene looked around like he needed to make sure no one was listening. "It seems odd that Doc would walk away like that."

"He's been talking about retiring for the last twenty years," Armie replied.

Gene's index finger came up like Armie had made his point. "Yes, and he never did it. All these years and he never once retired. Suddenly this woman shows up in town and he's gone?"

"I don't think he's dead. I'm pretty sure he's fishing. Remy said he took the boat out early this morning." Remy Guidry ran Guidry's Bar and Grill and the marina that it was attached to. Many a boat was safely nestled there. Remy hadn't been worried about the doc. The doc went fishing all the time. He'd been a little upset that Doc had left his sister-in-law alone on her first day at the clinic.

The whole Guidry family was worried about how Lila Daley was going to fit in, and from what he'd seen, they were right to be.

"You think? I have a different theory. She could have been on that boat, killed Doc, and taken over his clinic," Gene pointed out.

Sometimes it was best to go with the flow, let Gene get it out of his system. Of course, that didn't mean he wouldn't poke some obvious holes into those theories. "What did she do with the boat? Because it's not here and there isn't another marina for miles."

Gene thought about that for a moment. "Helicopter. She could have had a helicopter pick her up and she left the boat out there. It's perfect. She would have had time to wipe that whole boat down. It'll be like she was never there."

Yes, because she'd been at the clinic. He'd driven by the

damn place three times today and caught glimpses of her through the windows. She'd been behind the desk, staring down at files. She hadn't been in the back dealing with patients.

He was going to have a serious talk with Doc when he got back from his fishing trip. "What exactly makes you think Ms. Daley is a murderer besides the fact that she's from Dallas?"

"They grow them mean in Dallas," Gene said with a nod.

He didn't point out that Gene's third wife had been from Dallas and now Gene thought anyone from Dallas had to be evil. He definitely didn't point out that Charlene hadn't needed to be from Dallas to find Gene annoying. Armie was from right here in Papillon and he wanted to murder Gene on a regular basis.

"She's got that look," Gene insisted. "I went in for my physical. I don't know why I have to do it since I feel perfectly fine, but I can't get my blood pressure medication without Doc signing off on it. He claims there's a reason but we all know that big pharma is in league with the Secret Order of Physicians. Now, that shouldn't be confused with the American Medical Association. That's legit. Mostly, although some people claim it's been infiltrated by Russians."

Armie put up a hand to stop what would likely be a long lecture on the deep state. "She's Remy's wife's sister. She's fully qualified and she's definitely not involved in anything criminal. I looked her up. She speeds from time to time, but otherwise, she's got a perfectly clean record. I'm sorry no one informed you the clinic was changing hands. We should have had a town meeting about it. Doc has been a big part of this community for years."

Gene nodded. "I trust Doc. It's why I don't want that lady doctor to murder him."

There was a light knock on the door and then the potential murderer of Doc Hamet was standing in the doorway. Lila was still wearing the tailored slacks and green shirt she'd been wearing earlier in the day, though before she'd had a white lab coat on. She wore a pair of killer heels. He hadn't been able to see those from his car. They were red and pointy and sexy as hell.

He shook it off, remembering he'd promised himself he would let her settle in before he tried to hit on her again.

"If I promise not to kill anyone, can I have a couple of minutes of your time?" She stepped inside his tiny office. "Sorry, no one was out at the desk so I let myself in. Mr. Boudreaux, that testing is necessary to ensure that the medications you're on aren't damaging your liver or kidneys. It's why I would have done some blood work if you hadn't run out of the clinic. This could all be over by now and you would have your prescription and you wouldn't have to see me again for a year."

Gene got to his feet. "Doc's never done blood work. I don't like needles. You never know where they've been."

"They've been wrapped in sanitary plastic and then they get tossed out as medical waste. If you can't let me do blood work, then I can't give you the prescription," she said flatly.

Gene turned a shade of red Armie was fairly certain no human ever should. "She's trying to steal my DNA. We'll see about that."

Armie sat back with a long sigh as Gene fled the building. "I was going to try to convince him to give you a chance."

"Yeah, that's been a theme today." She didn't look back, merely took the seat Gene had previously occupied.

"Is he going to be okay without his medications?" It was clear he would have to do something about the situation at the clinic, and the easiest place to start was with the woman in front of him.

She shook her head, not an ounce of emotion on her face. "Not at all. He has high blood pressure that requires stabilization. He needs those meds, but I can't prescribe them without ensuring that he's okay."

Maybe she wouldn't be the easiest way to solve the problem. "So you'll let him die because his liver might get damaged."

"I'm not letting him die," she replied. "I'm simply not going to prescribe a medication that might be hurting him without testing. I would be doing him a disservice. I get the feeling Dr. Hamet was very lax in his practice. I don't intend to be."

"A little tolerance might go a long way here." He'd ease her into this because by *little* he meant *a whole lot*. So much tolerance was needed. "I know I'm the sheriff and I understand the need for laws, but I also know there's a time to bend those rules a little for the right reasons."

"Yes, and bending the rules could go a long way to me losing my license. I understand. The doctor was a beloved member of this community and I'm an outsider."

"The doctor is an ass most of the time, but the people around here know him and they trust him."

"I don't know why." Her mouth firmed to a stubborn line. "*I* shouldn't have trusted him at all. He told me the clinic made money."

"I don't know about that, but they do a whole lot of bake sales. What are you going to do about Gene?" He wasn't sure why the woman fascinated him, but it had been so long since he'd wanted anything for himself that he wasn't going to question it. He was going to follow his gut, and his every instinct told him Lila was worth the trouble. "I know he's obnoxious, but he really won't come back into the clinic. And he won't go anywhere else. He'll go without."

She seemed to think about the problem for a moment. "I can give him an extra month. But I can't risk my license and I can't not follow the rules. There are reasons for the rules. I'll write up the prescription and have Mabel take it to him. But you have to work on him. If he doesn't want me to draw the blood, Mabel can."

She was bending and that was all he could ask her to do. "Thank you, Lila."

He wanted to reach out and take her hand in his, but they weren't there yet. The way her eyes held his gave him hope.

She stared at him and the ghost of a smile crossed her lips and then she broke the moment, retreating to her previous businesslike demeanor.

"I'm actually here because of one of those rules we were talking about. I need to inform you that I have reason to suspect a woman named Carrie Petrie is being physically abused by her husband."

Well, he hadn't expected that. "Bobby? He's never been in any trouble before. I won't say the man is a joy to be around, but what makes you think he's hurting Carrie?"

"Her medical records. Did you know she's been in five times in the last four years for broken bones or sprained ankles?"

He didn't like the sound of that, but the Petrie family was a bit of a mystery to him and always had been. "She lives out on the island. They do a lot of manual labor out there. It's not an easy life. How many times has Bobby come in?"

That seemed to make her stop. "I didn't check."

He would bet Bobby had a few broken bones in his file, too. He had to take a cautious approach to any kind of accusation like this one. "What does Carrie say?"

"She says what they all say. She says she fell."

He knew why she was doing this. Her friend had gone through this, had lost her life because of a bad relationship, and now she saw it everywhere. It was a normal reaction to have. "Then maybe she fell. Like I said, it's a hard life out there. They're off the grid. They don't have city services. They're on their own and isolated. They can't even get into town without a boat."

Lila nodded. "Yes, she told me. That was why she slept on a broken arm last night. He wouldn't even bring her into town until this afternoon. He couldn't be bothered."

"You don't know that. There could be a hundred reasons he didn't bring her in." He sat back because it was obvious she was getting irritated with him, but he couldn't open a case without some proof. "What do you want me to do? I can go out and talk to her."

"She'll lie. She's too scared to say anything. Look, I have some experience with this. I can explain to you why I know this is abuse. I can show you the medical records. HIPAA doesn't apply if I believe my patient is in danger."

"Lila, it's your first day here." He needed to be gentle with her. She was doing this for the right reasons. "Shouldn't you settle in and get a lay of the land? I'll tell you what, I will go out there and check things out, but I can't accuse Bobby of anything without proof."

"Medical records are proof," she insisted.

"Not when the alleged victim is telling a different story." It was always the fine line he had to walk. Yes, his job was law enforcement, but he was in a small town, in charge of an entire parish, and that meant he was police officer, mediator, shrink at times. He wasn't merely their authority figure. He had to be an advocate, too, and he couldn't do that if no one trusted him. A situation like the one Lila had brought up was so pitted with land mines, it could be difficult to find his way through.

"She's afraid."

He'd never heard even a hint of gossip about Bobby Petrie being violent. "Like I said, I'll see if I can talk to her."

She sat back. "You won't do anything at all."

He wasn't sure what to tell her and that made his gut churn. He didn't want to be on opposite sides from her. "I'll do all I can do, but you need to understand the way things work around here."

"Apparently things work to protect men. It's a whole lot like the rest of the world." She stood up.

He followed her as she started out of the office. "Hey, I'm not the bad guy here. I'll do what I can, but you know as well as I do that if I can't get her to admit what's happening or actively see it happening, my hands are tied. I know this must have brought back bad memories for you, but we have to deal with what's happening in the here and now."

She kept walking, not turning back his way. "It will continue. She's already had one miscarriage from falling down the stairs."

He hadn't heard anything about her having a miscarriage. "I'll ask her about it."

"And she'll lie. And then one day she won't survive whatever fall she takes. Her clumsiness will lead to something she can't come back from. Who do I need to talk to in order to make a formal notification of my suspicions?" She'd stopped at the reception desk, turning on her heels, her jaw set in a stubborn line.

"I told you, I hear you and I'll look into it." He didn't want to be on the other side, but he also couldn't change the way he did things to please her. And honestly, she wasn't listening to a word he said.

"I want it in writing. I want it on paper that you knew on this date."

It would normally set him on edge, but he'd done an Internet search the night before. What she'd been through would have broken most people. He was willing to give her an enormous amount of leeway. "Lila, this is not what happened to you. I will do everything I can to make you feel safe, but you have to understand that I also have to follow protocol."

Her eyes flared slightly. "What happened to me?"

"I understand the impulse to see your friend in this," he admitted. "You went through something terrible and it hasn't been long." The door swung open and he could see Noelle wheeling in, her backpack in her lap. "Let's go back to my office and talk about this. I'm not discounting your expertise."

She chuckled but there was zero amusement in the sound. "That's exactly what you're doing. Who told you? Does everyone know about the sad-sack victim?"

He wished Noelle hadn't been so quick coming back from the library. He didn't want to have this conversation in front of her. "Zep mentioned something happened to you in Dallas. I looked it up. You're not some sad sack. What the hell were you supposed to do? I wasn't saying something bad about you."

"I don't care what you think of me. I care that you do

your job, but that appears to be writing tickets to innocent tourists."

"He's good at enforcing the dog-doo laws, too." Noelle shoved her glasses up her nose as she looked at the newcomer. "I'm his daughter, Noelle LaVigne. I have an appointment tomorrow."

Oh, he might have found a way out of Lila Daley's trap. If she turned that tart mouth on his daughter, he could ignore his attraction to her for all of time. He kind of wanted it to happen. It was obvious Lila was a difficult woman, to say the least. If she was mean, too, he could shove her out of his brain and go on about his life.

Lila dropped to one knee, obviously not giving a damn about her probably designer clothes. She put that manicured hand on the desk next to Noelle's wheelchair and her whole attitude had softened. "I'm glad to meet you, Noelle. How is that bump healing up? I read in your file that you took a fall a week ago."

"Banged up my knee pretty bad, but then, it wasn't like I could feel it," Noelle said. "It's okay. You can look at it if you like, but I would still prefer to keep my appointment. I have lady things to ask about. If my dad gives you trouble, you should talk about your period. It freaks him out."

"Noelle." He didn't need his own daughter giving him hell in front of the smart, sexy doctor. Almost doctor.

His daughter gave him an impish grin. "You told me I should be nice to the new people in town. After all, we were all new once."

She could be a whole lot of trouble.

Lila wasn't at all cold now. She smiled at Noelle, an expression that transformed her face from pretty but remote to gorgeous. There was a warm, caring woman under her frosty demeanor. "This looks good. I saw the X-rays. Your patella was bruised, but there weren't any fractures. You've taken good care of this wound."

"My dad did it," Noelle admitted. "I forget about my legs since they're useless. I don't think about it. Dad made me change the bandages twice a day. He's obnoxious."

Lila looked back at him and for once she didn't look annoyed. "You did a good job. Often wounds like this can get bad if you don't stay on top of them. This is healing nicely. And I'll look forward to seeing you tomorrow, Noelle. You'll probably be my only patient."

She managed to get to her feet with the grace of a woman who was used to standing in those heels all day. She looked like she had far more to say to him, but she merely nodded Noelle's way and strode out the front doors of the station house.

Noelle whistled. "Damn, Dad. She was pissed and not at me. Did she find out how much that ticket cost?"

"Language." He stared out the glass doors as Lila walked down Main Street. She strode right past Dixie's, not even turning to look inside. It was probably a good thing since everyone in the diner had been looking at her. "She wasn't mad at me about the ticket. She was upset about something else. Hey, have you heard anything about Carrie Petrie?"

Noelle was plugged into the town's gossip center. She ate most of her meals at Dixie's, which ran on grease and gossip. "Besides the fact that Gene is fairly certain they're actually running drugs out of that shack they live in, no. Why?"

He didn't want to spark more gossip. "Just let me know if you hear anything. I need to go talk to some folks."

"You're not going to tell me what she's mad about?"

It appeared that Lila didn't want everyone in Papillon to know about what had happened to her. He was going to have to have a discussion with Zep about talking about Lila's past to anyone who asked. If she didn't want people to know, then that should be her right. "It's between me and her."

"It's going to be the only thing between you and her if you're not careful." Noelle wheeled around to the desk she used.

Wasn't that the truth. Contrary to what Gene thought,

it wasn't the town or Doc in danger from Lila Daley, but he was starting to worry the town might be a danger to her.

She might have some big-city ways, but it was obvious she cared about her patients. If the tender way she'd dealt with Noelle was any indication, she could be good for Papillon.

She could be good for him.

He wanted a shot at figuring out if he might be good for her, too. "So how do we save our nurse from the town?"

Noelle's face lit up. "I was thinking about that very thing."

He leaned against the desk and let Noelle talk.

chapter four

"What's the least spicy thing?" Lila stared down at the laminated menu at Guidry's. The front was a complete listing of everything the restaurant served, but the back contained the story of how the family restaurant had come into being. It talked about the love between Remy's grandparents and their adoration for their town. While waiting for her sister, she'd sat and stared at the two photos, one of a large family standing in front of the restaurant as it had been back in the early eighties. There was a newer photo where Remy had his arm around Lisa. They were surrounded by his family and the men and women who worked at Guidry's. Her sister was a Guidry. Not a Daley. Lisa had a new family and they adored her. Her sister practically glowed in that photo.

Damn but she was jealous of her sister. Not because she wanted Remy. She didn't understand her brother-in-law, but she wanted to feel that way about a man. About anything, really. She wanted to understand why Lisa lit up when Remy walked into a room, why there was a smile on her sister's face, like she had a secret no one else knew.

"Try the jambalaya. I'll make sure they give you the one they make at the tourist heat level. They make two big pots fresh every morning. One is for the locals. You do not want that one. It can clear your sinuses just by walking by that sucker," her sister replied, sitting back in her chair. Lisa's dark hair was up in a bun and she wore her uniform of jeans, sneakers, and a Guidry's T-shirt. "You're looking at me like you do when you don't understand what I'm doing with my life."

She winced. When Lisa had first gotten involved with Remy, she hadn't been so sure it would work out. "I wasn't thinking that. Not exactly." She set the menu down. She'd had a salad for lunch and she'd skipped breakfast. This was her little sister's restaurant. It was time to let her lead the way. "I was thinking about this place and how I never thought you would end up here. I never thought *I* would end up here. But you look happy and I was wondering how you got so happy."

It wasn't a question she would have asked before. Not even to herself.

Lisa leaned forward and reached for her hand. "Oh, sweetie, was it a rough day?"

"It wasn't what I thought it would be. I managed to treat two elderly gentlemen who used the foulest language I've ever heard. Not at me. At each other."

Lisa nodded. "I heard the great lawn mower battle happened this afternoon. Sheriff won't let them drive cars anymore. Jimmy's eyesight is very poor and he's had enough accidents that no insurance will cover him, and Abe has both road rage and a deep need to rage at the machine by not paying his tickets. Now they go all over town on their lawn mowers. They can move surprisingly fast. Don't mistake them for the scooter brigade. They're trying to form their own MC. I don't think they understand what an MC is. Abe and Jimmy gave you trouble?"

She'd seen the outcome of their speed. "They seemed to hate each other, but after I patched them up and was certain no one had a concussion, they were going to get a beer together. I told them they shouldn't have a beer after I gave them anti-inflammatory meds, but they said something in French about *bon temps* and went to a bar anyway."

"*Laissez les bons temps rouler,*" Lisa said with a smile. "Let the good times roll."

"The good times could have drug interactions," Lila pointed out. They hadn't been interested in hearing about how alcohol could intensify the drugs' effects on the central nervous system.

But they'd paid in cash. There was that.

"I don't think Abe and Jimmy care much about that. Are they giving you a hard time? Not Abe and Jimmy. The rest of the town. Remy was surprised when Doc decided to go fishing this morning. He thought Doc was going to stay and oversee the first couple of weeks at least."

"I don't think he's big into the protocols we're supposed to follow." It made her nervous. She followed the rules. Always. She'd played it safe.

Lisa waved the concern off. "I'm not worried about that. We're a tiny town with one healthcare provider. We can skirt the rules a bit. No, I was worried that the townsfolk can be a little nervous around strangers."

"Almost everyone canceled when they figured out Doc Hamet wasn't there." She hated admitting to her sister that she was failing. "I had a couple of minor emergencies, but all of my scheduled appointments canceled. I was supposed to have four appointments tomorrow, but we've got two cancellations, and I'm sure number three will do the same. Although Noelle LaVigne assures me she's coming in."

Her heart had nearly broken at the sight of that young woman in her wheelchair. She'd read the report about how she'd injured her spine. It had been a car accident, one in which she'd lost her mother and her ability to walk.

How hard had it been for the sheriff to make the transition to single dad? How difficult had it been for Noelle to go from normal teen to wheelchair bound in a heartbeat?

I would still prefer to keep my appointment. I have lady things to ask about.

How hard had it been to raise a teenage daughter for the manly sheriff? He was kind of a jerk, but she'd seen how much he loved his daughter.

Lisa smiled at the sound of the girl's name. "Noelle is a sweetheart. I'm glad she's coming in. She's not going to be your problem child. I can think of several others, though."

"Why?" This was what confused her. The sheriff had mentioned it. Lisa had been worried about it. "Why won't they give me a chance? They gave you a chance."

"Who won't give you a chance?" Zep Guidry stood at their table, a notepad in his hand and a roguish look on his ridiculously handsome face. "Because whoever won't is an idiot. I'll give you a chance, *chère*."

Chère, she'd learned, sounded more like *sha*. And she was sure Zep would give her the same chance he seemed to give everyone, according to her sister. Well, everyone with breasts. "I think I'll pass. Why don't you give me the chance to drink? Bring me a New Zealand sauvignon blanc. Nothing too pineappley, though."

Zep stared at her. "I thought wine was made from grapes. I don't think we have any pineapple wine. Is that possible? And our wine comes from New Orleans. We get a shipment every couple of weeks." He gave her his movie-star smile. "It's fresh today."

Lisa groaned. "Tell the bartender to bring my sister a glass of the new Marlborough. I'll take a beer. And stop hitting on my sister."

"Well, she was saying no one is being nice to her. I could be real nice, Lis." Zep winked her way. "Real nice."

He was gorgeous and such a child compared to Armie LaVigne. "When was your last STI test?"

Zep frowned. "Why you gotta go be like that? Fine. I'll go get your drinks. But I still don't understand what pineapples have to do with anything."

Lisa shook her head as her brother-in-law walked off toward the bar. "Sorry about that. He's an idiot, but he's also family. We have a surprisingly large wine selection.

And a delicious muscadine sweet red that is the best. It's like dessert in a glass. Some of the locals make it."

She was not in Dallas anymore. "You used to be a wine snob."

"Not really. I just acted that way when you or Will were paying for dinner," she replied with an impish grin. "Most of what I drank came straight out of a box. Hey, don't look like that. I was a poor college kid. I took what I could get. Let's talk more about how today went. You know it's going to take some time."

"I guess I'm wondering how you made the transition." She'd had a ton of time today to wonder if she'd made the right call. And then Armie had looked at her with that nauseating sympathy in his eyes. He'd known. He'd known what had happened to her in Dallas, and it had obviously made him change his mind. He hadn't asked her out today. He'd treated her with the same kid gloves everyone had for months and months. They still did. Everyone but Lisa, which was likely why she'd come here in the first place.

"I loved Remy," Lisa said simply. "I loved him and I got here and made the decision to love this town. It wasn't hard for me, honestly. This place is weird, and I've always loved weird. Don't get me wrong. I loved the city, too. It's why I'm glad Remy still has jobs that take us to Dallas and New York. I love the theaters and the restaurants, but none of those cities has an Otis."

"That would be a good reason to stay in the city." She'd practically run from the house to her car this morning. She hadn't even let herself look in the backyard. Not that it was a traditional backyard. There was no neat and tidy fence to block out the rest of the world. It was something she intended to work on. A big fence. Like the wall from *Game of Thrones*.

Lisa laughed. "No, you'll get used to him. I promise. There's something magical about this place if you'll open your eyes and let yourself see. You have to slow down here. You have to take things in."

"I can't get much slower." She wasn't used to being bored at work.

"I'm not talking about your work. I'm talking about your life. This is what I was really trying to say yesterday. I want you to slow down and enjoy the world around you. There's a lot to enjoy. There's a lot to learn."

She wasn't sure about that. "I think I learned to not buy a house I haven't seen in person and that small-town doctors like to prey on their big-city counterparts. I'm not going to be able to keep that clinic open if I can't get patients to visit me."

"They'll come around," Lisa promised. "I had Remy beside me. They tend to accept you more if you've got someone vouching for you. It's like a big old family in some ways. If your brother is bringing a woman home, you tend to try to get along with her. That was how it was with me. They knew Remy was serious about me and that's why they gave me a chance."

"It's almost the other way around." Zep put a glass of white wine in front of Lila. "They figured you were interested in Remy, so you wouldn't reject them."

"Reject them?" She was actively trying to recruit these people as patients. She was the one facing rejection. Tons and tons of rejection. "I need them."

Zep set down Lisa's beer. "I don't know if you are aware, but this is small-town Louisiana. We are not known for being the most cosmopolitan of people. Tourists come through to enjoy the food and the bayou, and they often gawk at us like we're some sort of freak show. Not me, of course. The tourists mostly view me as a lovely souvenir experience. The women, that is. But it's not the same for my fellow Papillon residents."

"There are a few stereotypes associated with the bayou and small towns in general," Lisa admitted. "Of course, they have their own stereotypes about people from the big city. Most of which you reinforce."

"What?" She thought about it for a second. She'd been a trailer park kid. She'd had every stereotype possible thrown her way. Maybe in the last few years she had gotten a bit snobby. It wasn't that she'd meant to. She'd been separating herself from that time when she'd felt small. Did she want to make someone else feel small? Not at all. "That might be fair. Is it the shoes? Because I might have overestimated my love for them."

They hurt. She'd thought that since it was her first full day in her own clinic, she should look the part. She owned the place. She was in charge. Those Louboutins showed the world that she was the boss.

They showed the world that she wasn't some trailer park reject with a mom in and out of prison, barely holding on by her fingernails.

But if she'd been back in Dallas in the ER, she wouldn't have thought twice about what to wear. She would have shoved on scrubs and her comfiest sneakers, put her hair in a ponytail, and gone to work. She wouldn't have spent an hour in front of the mirror getting her makeup as close to perfect as she could in case the sheriff showed up. It wasn't that she wanted to look nice for him. She was trying to look nice because they'd started on the wrong foot and he needed to understand that she was a professional. That's what she'd told herself. Then her inner voice had mocked the hell out of her.

"Oh, we have some designer wear around here," Lisa corrected. "The mayor of the town has a serious addiction to Chanel. But she also wears boots when the time is right, and not over-the-knee boots with five-inch heels. I'm talking serious work boots."

"Sylvie makes those look good, if you know what I mean." Zep didn't seem to mind that he had a bunch of tables to work. "You know, if you want someone on your side, you should go to her momma's hair salon. It's where everyone goes to get their hair did."

"And to get love potions," Lisa added with a grin.

"What?"

Her sister shrugged. "Marcelle is also the local hoodoo priestess. It's not as bad as it sounds. Some of the blessings are beautiful. Oh, there's an idea. Miss Marcelle could come bless your house."

"Or you could pretend to date a highly respected member of the community," Zep suggested. "If you were seen out with a man everyone loves, they might calm down and see that you're not snobby. You're one of them."

"Actually, that's not a terrible idea," Lisa mused.

Zep dropped to one knee. "I have some of those every now and then. Where do you want to go first, sweetheart? I think we should let everyone see us at the bar and then we can go back to my place."

Lisa rolled her eyes. "I didn't mean you. All that would prove is that she has terrible taste in men."

Zep put his hand over his heart. "I am wounded by that."

Lisa pointed toward the kitchen. "Go and get my sister the jambalaya. Tourist version. And I'll have the crawfish étouffée. And I swear if we run out of bread pudding, I will murder someone."

Zep got to his feet but he was diligently writing down the order. "You know you get meaner every day, sister. It makes me happy Seraphina never plans on marrying since my siblings bring home partners who can't appreciate my unique talents." He winked Lila's way. "But you still could."

"I could also put you through a lot of invasive medical tests." She knew how to take care of Zep.

Zep frowned and managed to look the tiniest bit prissy. "Meanness must run in the family."

He turned on his heels and walked away.

Lisa's new family was odd.

"I don't know that I want to date a guy so people will like me." Though Zep had a point. She'd been bullied before, known everyone looked down on her. "Maybe I could smile more. Isn't that what they always tell women? Smile more."

She'd heard it a thousand times and it always made her want to smack whoever was saying it, but she was getting desperate.

"Yeah, sometimes you look scary when you smile," Lisa

pointed out. "Not when you mean it, but when you're trying to look happier than you feel, you end up looking like you're about to murder someone."

So she'd been told. "I already got accused of that once today."

Lisa laughed at the thought. "I'm sure it was Gene. He believes the world is way more murdery than it actually is. I think we need to talk about how to introduce you to the town. We made a mistake by not bringing you in earlier and having a nice long transition period. Now, while Zep is not discerning about who he sleeps with at night, he does know the town, and he's right about a few things. I think the two of us having a girls' day at Miss Marcelle's could be helpful."

"I had my hair cut before I came here." She wasn't due for another one for at least six weeks.

"Then we'll get some highlights," Lisa replied. "Or a manicure."

She'd had that done, too. "I don't need . . ."

Her sister interrupted her. "We're going with the flow, Lila. The flow."

Apparently the flow had highlights. She'd never had highlights, wasn't sure she wanted highlights. But she did want patients. "I can try it. But I don't know about the fake-date thing."

"Think about it. Remy's got a couple of friends. They're nice guys. Rene Darois might be right up your alley. Not that you're looking for a boyfriend. I understand that. Rene knows the town and he would totally understand that this plan could work. And who knows, you might like him. You've got a lot in common. He's highly educated."

"You talking about Rene?" Lisa's massive, muscular Cajun husband stood at the table, two big bowls in his hands. He set one down in front of her. "What's going on with him?"

Lisa smiled up at her man as she accepted her dinner. "I'm plotting and Rene might be a piece of the plan. The man meat, as your old boss would say." Lisa leaned over with a conspiratorial wink. "Remy used to be man meat."

The bowl in front of Lila contained rice and sausage and some stuff she wasn't sure about.

But it smelled pretty good. She usually didn't eat rice. Not because she didn't like it. Mostly because she liked it too much.

Why shouldn't you eat it every now and then? Her life had become one long denial. She called it discipline, but it was starting to feel like something else.

Can't you see you're punishing yourself? The problem is there's no need for you to punish yourself. You make everything worse by doing it because the reason you're denying yourself anything that might make you happy is irrational. You should be living a good life to honor your friend. Not this half-life you seem to insist on.

That could have come straight out of her brother's mouth. Maybe she'd left Dallas to get away from Will. He sounded far too much like her therapist.

"You think she should pretend to date Rene? I'm not saying he won't do it," Remy was saying. "He funds that clinic. If she can't win over the town, he'll be the one everyone complains to. But I think she would be far better off with Armie."

Armie. Armand. Sheriff LaVigne, of the broad shoulders and sexy lips.

Lisa wrinkled her nose. "Really? I don't see it, babe. I know my sister. She's more interested in intellectuals. Armie is not her type."

Because intensely gorgeous and manly wasn't her type. Because she wasn't interested in sex. That's basically what her sister was saying. Not that Lila blamed her. She'd scheduled gifts to herself and she'd also scheduled sex. She'd read somewhere that normal couples had sex once a week. Friday had been their sex night.

"I'm not going to fake date anyone." It was a terrible idea. "But I will try to fit in better. I'll go to the hair salon. I'll eat where you tell me to. I'll help out where I can and I'll smile when it's appropriate, and I'll make sure it's not a murder smile."

Remy's face split into the most glorious grin. "Oh, now I'm interested. This is going to be far more fun than I thought it would. I'm going to go save my wife some bread pudding. She gets cranky without her dessert. Can I save you some?"

If she didn't eat rice, she actively ran from desserts. "Sure. I'll give it a try."

Discipline hadn't made her happy. No. That was wrong. Discipline had gotten her the education she'd always wanted. It had gotten her the job she loved. It had lifted her and her siblings out of poverty. Discipline wasn't the problem. Self-denial and guilt were the problems. Insecurity was the problem. Closing herself off from everything and everyone so no one could hurt her was the problem.

Lisa was looking at her like she'd done something brave. "I think you'll like it."

She wouldn't know if she didn't try. "Maybe."

She picked up her fork. Did she eat it with a fork or a spoon? What was proper?

Maybe when one was eating bayou food in a restaurant that sported a big old playpen in the middle of the dining room floor where the patrons let their kids play, it didn't matter.

She took a bite as her sister started talking about plans for the town picnic.

Jambalaya, it turned out, was delicious.

The room was incredibly white. White sheets. White walls. A white light fixture on the ceiling that shone brilliant white light. Oddly, she found it soothing, the same way she found the smell of bleach calming. The hospital was her place, the place where she was in control. She glanced down at her clipboard and ensured that the patient had everything the doctor had ordered. Room 27 was dealing with gastrointestinal issues she was fairly certain would lead to gall bladder surgery later on that night. She understood they needed an ultrasound and possibly a CT scan, but when it looked like a duck and the patient was screaming and holding his upper right quadrant, it was usually gallstones.

She chuckled as she glanced down at her watch. The night shift usually went by at breakneck pace, and tonight was no different. Big-city emergency rooms were pretty crazy any night, but on a Saturday the hits never stopped coming. She'd already missed her break. Damn it. She pushed through the doors and looked around for Maryanne.

Maryanne would cover for her while she choked down a yogurt. She would skip it but light-headedness was not a good thing for an ER nurse.

She stopped because something was wrong. She wasn't supposed to be here. She was supposed to be in Louisiana.

A chill snaked over her skin as she looked across the floor and saw a man entering with a ball cap pulled low on his head.

This was the moment when she would turn and find Maryanne and the man with the ball cap would step inside the room. He would lock the door and then he would pull a gun and fire into her friend's torso, hitting her in the right lung.

Her feet started to move. No. She wasn't going that way. She wasn't going there again.

She screamed but her body kept moving and she knew where this would end.

Lila came awake on a gasp, reaching for the light to prove she was exactly where she was supposed to be. She was in Papillon. She was in her new house, with all the collections of crap she was going to have to go through. It was okay to be here.

It was okay.

Her hands were shaking and she forced herself to take a deep breath.

When would she stop dreaming about it? When would the sight of that man fade from her memory? Sometimes she worried she was doing nothing but marking time to that moment when she could close her eyes and not remember his face.

Three twenty-four a.m. The old-school alarm clock on the bedside table showed the time in red block numbers.

She laid back and wiped away the tears.

Meditation. That's what her therapist had told her to do. Cleanse her mind. Let it go blank. Think of nothing at all.

How the hell was she supposed to think about nothing? Every time she tried to make her mind some kind of blank space, it crept in. When she tried to make her inner vision blank, she could smell the coppery aroma of blood. When she got that scent out of her head, she could hear the way a lung sounded when it had been split by a bullet. When the sound was gone, she could taste bile in the back of her throat.

She sat back up.

She could move five hundred miles away but it meant nothing at all if she'd brought her ghosts with her. She'd dumped most of her life, an enormous amount of the things she'd bought and collected because she'd thought things made up a life. She'd managed to fit everything she now owned in her medium-sized overpriced trendy crossover, but she'd forgotten to dump her memories.

She tried to settle back down in the surprisingly comfy bed and listened to the fan spinning over her head, trying to let the sound lull her back to sleep.

She'd hoped tonight would be different than all the others she'd been through since that terrible moment. She'd hoped she would close her eyes satisfied with the knowledge that she'd begun something.

All she could think about was that young woman with the fractured arm and the big doe eyes. No one would listen to her. No one would believe her until there was a body to deal with, and then they would all shake their heads and talk about how Maryanne should have spoken up sooner, should have done something.

Carrie. Maryanne was dead. Carrie was alive. Carrie

was lying about how she'd gotten hurt and Lila had no idea what to do about it. She knew she'd been a bitch to the sheriff and he was right about his hands being tied, but she hadn't been able to help herself. It was happening again and she felt as helpless as she had in the dream. Things were moving to a terrible place and the world kept spinning like there wasn't anything anyone could do to stop it. Like she would be forced to watch the scenario play out again and again.

Damn it. She wasn't getting back to sleep.

She threw off the covers and rolled out of bed. Along with her guilt and rage at a system that failed women over and over again, she'd brought chamomile tea and her trusty tea kettle. The wine hadn't worked. She was willing to give tea a try.

The floorboards creaked under her feet as she made her way from the bedroom toward the small galley kitchen.

Tomorrow would be better. Tomorrow she had at least one patient, and if no one else came in she would spend her morning poring over all the records the clinic had on Noelle LaVigne. Paraplegics had unique issues and she wanted to be ready to deal with them. The young woman said she wanted to talk about lady stuff? They would spend the afternoon on it. She'd thought she would be incredibly busy, rushing from one patient to another. Well, maybe this would be better. Maybe she would lavish her patients with attention, getting to know each one and being able to be thoughtful about the approach she would use to each problem.

It was exactly what she and Maryanne had always said was wrong with the hospital they'd worked at. Everything moved at breakneck speed and the doctors had to go from one patient to another, often without ever learning their names or histories.

Their practice would be different, they'd promised themselves. Their practice would be about patients.

She shook off the memories. If she didn't have any patients, she couldn't practice at all, so she would follow Lisa's plan.

She would make an appointment with Marcelle Martine, who was apparently also known as Miss Marcelle or Madame Marcelle, depending on whether she was doing nails or working a love spell. Lila would definitely be calling the woman Miss.

Because she didn't need a love spell, though she might be able to use a get-that-man-out-of-her-head spell.

She filled the kettle. All afternoon she'd thought about him. His big manly arms. Those ridiculously blue eyes. That accent. That Cajun accent that rumbled out of his mouth and seemed to come from somewhere deep in his soul.

Why should she want Armie out of her head? It was nice to think about him. The other things in her head were pretty terrible. Armie was merely annoying. And attractive. That wasn't the word. *Attractive* was a word to describe blandly handsome men. Armie was sexy. Armie was disconcerting and distracting.

He wasn't for her.

Except Remy thought he was. Remy and Lisa had argued about her never-going-to-happen fake boyfriend. Lisa believed the well-educated super-rich Rene Darois was the only way to go, but Remy had said it was obvious that Armie was the only man in town who could handle another Daley sister.

She was the only Daley sister left. Laurel was a Bradford now. Lisa was a Guidry. It was funny that she'd once been desperate to not be a Daley because that name meant white trash and prison records. She'd prayed her father would realize she was alive and come get her, give her a name she could be proud of. None of them had the same fathers but they had the same name.

Daley was a good name. She'd made it that way. Or she had until that day. Did Daley now mean coward?

Tears blurred her vision and she tried to shove the thoughts from her head. It was easier during the day. She could busy herself and pretend it wasn't always right there. At night when she was alone, it all crashed in on her.

She needed a hobby. Maybe she could take up electrician training since her damn stove didn't seem to work. She turned the dial to get the burner heating up but got nothing. No heat at all coming from those old-school coils. She held her hand over it. Cold as ice even though the little red light had come on signaling the stove was on.

There was no microwave. Nope. That was apparently far too technologically advanced for this household. If she wanted to boil water, she would have to build a fire.

That was when she heard it. It was a faint sound coming from her left, from the back door, with its pretty window that let the light in and its yellow curtains that framed it. At first she thought it was nothing more than the wind. But there wasn't any wind.

It struck her suddenly that the same window that let in the early morning light was about an arm's length from the lock on the door. If someone wanted to, they could break the glass and get the door open.

She went still. She hadn't heard anything. Not really. She'd had a bad dream and hadn't gotten completely out of that fight-or-flight response fear compelled. It was nothing more than a trick of her mind.

Then the lights went out.

Definitely. She was definitely learning how to fix her electricity. Her heart started to pound, adrenaline, left over from the dream she'd been having, reignited in her system.

It was okay. There was nothing out there. She was alone and despite the ramshackle nature of the house, the doors were secure.

Scratch. Scratch.

She shrank back and stared at the door. It rattled slightly. Definitely not the wind.

Fear shot through her and she scrambled for the phone. There was a landline in the kitchen. She hadn't used a damn landline in years, but Lisa had insisted because cell phone service could be spotty.

Scratch. Scratch.

Who scratched at a door? There weren't any trees close enough to explain that noise. Or the breathing sounds.

Something was at her door. She didn't have a gun. Didn't own a gun.

She should own a gun.

The door rattled again and she bit back a scream. Maybe if she hadn't had the dream again she could have reacted with some kind of calm, but panic was threatening to take over. She could hear that man yelling, see her friend's eyes as the light left them, knowing she was next.

Her cell phone was in the bedroom, but it was likely dead since she hadn't put it on the charger. The landline would have to do. She forced herself to pick up the phone. She would call her sister. Lisa would send Remy out.

She didn't know her sister's number. There wasn't a button for Lisa on this damn last-freaking-century piece of technology. Who used landlines?

She dialed the only number she knew.

"911, what is your emergency?"

She clutched the phone and prayed someone would come soon.

chapter five

Armie slammed the door to the SUV closed and was shocked at how hard his heart was pounding. Every bit of his training told him that this was likely nothing at all. She was new in town and unused to how things sounded in the bayou at night. It could be creepy and weird to outsiders. She was in a new home and she'd been through something terrible. If she didn't have PTSD complete with nightmares, he would eat his hat.

Not that he had his hat. Or his uniform. He was in pajama pants, a T-shirt, and his sneakers. He'd slipped on a jacket emblazoned with the words *Papillon Parish Sheriff* that covered his shoulder holster and the gun he had there, but otherwise he was in civvies.

None of that mattered because from the moment he'd gotten the call that Lila Daley had a possible intruder trying to get into her house, his only thought had been to get to her as fast as he could.

He forced himself to slow down and take stock of his surroundings. If someone was trying to get to her, he couldn't leave her alone to face it because the dumbass sheriff had let himself get shot.

He went still and listened. Nothing. Her house was on a

half an acre and he could see the porch light on at Angie Jones's place down the street, but the rest of her house was dark. Angie had motion-activated lights he'd helped her install. When they came on they stayed on for fifteen minutes at a time. They could have gone off by now.

He approached Lila's house and vowed he would do the same for her. She might not like it coming from him but he would find a way to get more lights on her place. Like Angie, Lila was a single woman living alone, and there wasn't a lot of traffic out this way. She wasn't far from town, but it got dark out here fast. The highway was less than a mile away. It wouldn't take much to find her.

Was she running from more than her past?

He was being paranoid.

He took a deep breath. It was time to let his training take over. The front yard was clear. He was ready to move around to the back, when he saw her in the front window. It looked like she had a flashlight in her hand and she was glancing out into the yard.

When she caught sight of him, she threw open her front door. She rushed out, and he was so damn happy he made a habit of having dispatch inform him of 911 calls. Not that there were ever many. In a couple of weeks, the new deputies would be trained and he wouldn't have had the chance to tell night dispatch to hold off, that he would handle it. Then Lila would have been running toward a man she didn't know and he would be carrying a gun.

As it was, he was disappointed when she stopped herself before she got to him. Her arms had been up briefly as though she was running to him and ready to throw her arms around him.

"Someone's trying to open the back door," she said, and he could see plainly she'd been crying. "Or something. I don't know. It won't stop. I wanted to call my sister. I'm stupid because I don't know her number. She's a button on my phone. There's no damn button on a landline that says 'Lisa.'"

He put a hand on her shoulder and wished he had the

right to hug her. "It's okay. I'm here and I'm going to take care of this, but I need you to go in the house and lock the door."

"You're not coming with me?"

"I'm going around the back of the house. I need to figure out if we're dealing with a person or a critter. If that critter happens to be a gator who isn't as lazy as Otis, I'll be at the front door as fast as my damn legs can run and we'll call animal control." He'd grown up here but he didn't wrestle alligators.

"Okay." She sounded breathless, but it was obvious she was under control again.

"Why are the lights off, sweetheart?" He probably shouldn't call her that, but he liked her and she was afraid.

She sniffled. "I don't know. They went off after I tried to get the stove to come on and that's when I heard it."

He pulled his flashlight. "All right. Get back inside."

She hesitated.

"I'm going to be okay. You get inside and I'll figure this out. When I'm done out here, we'll get your lights back on, too. If anything goes wrong, you call 911 again and lock yourself in the bathroom. You don't come out until you're sure it's my deputy. Her name is Roxanne."

Lila nodded and fled back into the house.

Armie drew his revolver and waited until she was fully inside. He crept around the side of the house. He really would run if it was a damn gator. They were nasty and smelled bad and had a million types of bacteria in those teeth of theirs.

He heard the sound that had terrified Lila. It was a scratching sound and then a low *hurmph*.

Damn it. He knew that sound. He stepped out and pointed his flashlight, shining it on the back of the house, where a big mutt of a dog was trying to get inside.

Armie's gut tightened and he wished like hell he could find Bill's kids and charge them with something. "Hey, Peanut. Where have you been, boy?"

He got to one knee as the dog's head came up and his tail started to wag wildly at the sound of a familiar voice.

"It's a dog." The back door had come open. "I was that scared of a dog?"

She hadn't been scared of a dog at all. She'd been scared of everything that had happened before. Terror like what she'd gone through didn't go away easy. He should know.

Peanut laid a weary head against Armie's leg.

"Yeah." The sight of that dog made him infinitely sad. It reminded him that everyone got lost from time to time. "This is Peanut. He was Bill's dog."

She came down the steps, her feet in slippers. She had a robe around her and a flashlight in her hand. Her hair was up in a ponytail, but it was slightly messy. In the starlight she looked sweetly disheveled. "He wasn't here when I got here. I wasn't told a dog lived here. Where's he been?"

"He was supposed to go with Bill's oldest son." He put a hand on Peanut's neck and sure enough his collar was gone. "They promised me they would either take him home with them or find a place for him. He had a collar. He wouldn't have been able to get it off himself even though he's lost a ton of weight."

She gasped and dropped to her knees beside him. "Are you telling me they dumped this dog?"

"That is the most likely scenario," he concluded. "It happens a lot. They probably took him out a couple of miles, maybe more, and dropped him off. Some folks don't want to be bothered with a shelter. They would rather discard the animal than explain why they're dropping him off. Be careful with him. He's been out in the wild for a while by the looks of him."

People weren't the only creatures who could get PTSD.

"Hey, boy." Lila didn't listen to a word he'd said. She held her hand out, palm down. "How are you? You made it all the way home."

"He's probably covered in fleas and ticks." She would likely be horrified at the condition of the dog.

"Nothing a bath can't fix. Well, I'll have to pull the ticks off. I've got some tweezers." She ran a hand over Peanut's head when he didn't growl her way. "And a set of latex gloves. You stink, boy. We'll have to see if there's some doggy shampoo in that old house."

The dog obviously hadn't lost his sense of direction or his instinct as to who he could manipulate with big doggy eyes. His tail wagged and he moved toward the new girl, dumping Armie in a heartbeat.

"You said you could fix my lights? I know I shouldn't ask, but it's late and I don't want to wake up my sister to get Remy out here to do it. If you could show me, I'll know how to fix it myself next time."

He got to his feet. "Of course. I'll put Peanut out in my car and check the fuse box."

Even in the low light from his flashlight he could see the way she frowned. "He can come inside. According to you this is his home. And he needs food and water. I wondered why there were tins of dog food left in the pantry. I was going to find a shelter and donate them. I'm glad I was lazy about that now." She sighed and scratched behind the dog's ears. "They never planned on taking you with them, did they?" She glanced back up at him. "How long has he been gone?"

"Since the day of Bill's funeral. Almost three months now. I should get him to a vet."

She shook her head. "I think I can handle it. I've taken care of dogs before. Back in the trailer park where I grew up I was the one who took care of all the animals my siblings found. And some whose owners couldn't afford it. Puppies were my first patients. Come on in. I need to see how bad he is."

He followed her up the steps to the little porch Bill had built with his own hands thirty years before. They creaked and groaned under his weight.

He would likely need to look at more than the electricity if Lila was going to stay in this house.

He should talk to Remy about it. Remy was her brother-in-law. Her first thought had been to call her sister. If her phone had been charged, it would be Remy who would be out here right now. Watching her take in a mangy dog. Watching her hips sway as she stepped into her dilapidated house.

"I'll go look at the fuse box. Did it happen in the middle of the night? You tried to turn on the lights and they wouldn't work?" He moved to the utility room, where the ancient washer and dryer sat. There was a fuse box trapped behind a stack of something. "What the hell is in here?"

"Numerous items. If you're wondering what's in that closet, it's comic book boxes, I think. I peeked in there and that's what it looks like. The guy who owned this place before me collected everything. I mean everything."

He could see the outline of her frame in the shadows thrown off by her flashlight. She held it down and away, keeping it from hitting his eyes. It made it easy for him to work. "I haven't been in here in a couple of years. Not since before Glenna passed. I knew he had a record collection and he liked stamps, but I didn't know about the comics."

"Oh, he collected all kinds of stuff." Her voice had regained its composure. She was calm again and he was a bastard because he missed the moment when it sounded like she needed him. "I will say, for a hoarder he was a neat and orderly one. Everything is stacked and organized. I would actually say he probably had a mild case of OCD. He has stamps and coins. I guess they're not worth anything or his kids would have taken them. Though they didn't take the sweetest thing, did they? They didn't take the puppy. Bastards."

The end of her speech was said in that singsong tone women reserved for babies and small creatures. And some not-so-small ones since Peanut had been misnamed. The mutt was part lab, part golden retriever. Armie found the right switch and sure enough it had popped. He flipped it and the lights immediately came back on.

Lila sighed, a sound of pure relief. "Thank you. I didn't know where the box was. That was foolish of me."

"It's a new place and you didn't exactly give yourself a ton of time to settle in before you went to work." He stepped around the stack of boxes and moved back into the kitchen. He'd wondered about why she'd simply moved in one day and gone to work the next. Most people would have unpacked.

Not that she'd brought much with her.

"I didn't see a reason to wait. I don't like to sit around. You know, I'm not normally this woman. I don't flip out. I'm a trauma nurse and I freaked out over a dog." She took a long breath and crossed her arms over her chest. "I'm sorry to have woken you, Sheriff."

"Armie, please."

"I thought you liked 'Sheriff' when you're working."

"I'm off the clock. Hence the lack of a uniform."

She flushed a pretty pink. "That makes it worse. I got you out of bed to deal with my irrational fears."

"They're not irrational. It's a new place and you're from the city. The bayou can be daunting at first."

She sank down to one of the four chairs around the small round kitchen table. "Oh, trust me, the panic I felt was irrational, and worse, it's absolutely not who I want to be. I'm very sorry I got you out of bed. I'll be all right now. The dog can stay here with me until I figure something out."

It did not surprise him at all that she would be hard on herself. He sat down at the small kitchen table. It was covered with a plastic tablecloth that looked like it had been there since the seventies. It was definitely not the kind of décor he saw her using, but then, he was having a hard time seeing her in this house at all. There was an air of neglect that clung to the place, and she wasn't a woman who neglected things. It took her a moment, but she found a small bowl and filled it with water.

"We have a vet but his office is about thirty minutes away. He runs a small shelter." He watched her as she managed to find a can opener. He would offer to do it all for her, but she needed control. It had been stripped from her by fear, and she needed to get it back. He could understand that. "He can help you rehome the boy. You should do that soon or you know what will happen."

She frowned and scooped a couple of spoonfuls of the wet food into a separate bowl. "I can't have a dog. I work long hours."

She got to one knee and Peanut was right there. His tail was wagging like crazy as he wolfed down those bites and looked back up to her for more.

"You also work in a place where no one will question you having a dog at the office." He didn't hate the idea of Peanut staying with her. He might not be much of a guard dog, but he was big enough to scare off people who didn't know how easily he could be manipulated by beef jerky. "I think he's still hungry."

She gave the pup a pat on the head. "He's been starving. I can see his ribs. I've got to go slow or he'll make himself sick. He can have a bit more in an hour or so. The good news is he seems to have managed to not get fleas. I bet his owner kept him up to date on his medications."

"I'm pretty sure the neighbors helped Bill out. Angie or Seraphina would come out here a couple of times a week to see if Bill needed anything. Roxanne had dinner with him at least once a week and I tried to make sure someone could drive him to his appointments."

"So he wasn't all alone?" she asked, her voice turning wistful. "I wondered how hard it was for him to have his kids and his wife gone. I wondered how it felt to be the last one of his family. I know his kids weren't dead, but I don't think they called or spent much time with him."

"I think it was like a lot of families, especially ones from around here. The boys grew up and left town. They married and now they're caught up in their own families. Between the miles and responsibilities, they didn't get down here much. I think Bill spent Christmas with his oldest last year. Don't think too unkindly of them. It can be hard to have so much distance."

"I can think a lot of things about those kids. Men.

They're men now. And fathers," she said with a frustrated sigh. "They should know better. That was one of the hardest parts of my job, having to tell a patient no one is coming for them."

Peanut finally gave up, seeming to understand that pitiful doggy eyes weren't going to move the new girl. He walked through the kitchen, sniffing and reacquainting himself with the home he'd always known. Lila moved to the table and sank down into the chair closest to him.

"You won't have that problem here." There were some good things about living in a small town. "If you have a patient who needs something, all you have to do is call me. I'll make arrangements. Someone will be up there."

"Because you're a family?"

"We misfits have to stick together," he said. "Are you feeling better now? More settled?"

She nodded. "I'm fine. Like I said, this is not who I normally am. Normally I would have gotten a baseball bat and charged in. I'm more used to being angry than afraid, but since . . ."

She trailed off and her whole body tightened up again.

He needed to let her know she wasn't alone in this. "I still have nightmares about the night I got shot. I've been doing this job for a long time. I worked as a police officer in New Orleans for years and managed to not get myself shot, but last year I took a bullet right here in Papillon. It was funny because at the time I powered through. I mean it. I barely felt that sucker. I did my job and took down the criminals and everyone talked about what a badass I am. I don't believe they would think the same about me if they knew how often I wake up in a cold sweat."

Her eyes wouldn't quite meet his. "I do understand that. And you're wrong. They would still think you're a badass."

He let the words sit for a moment. If they were going to have any shot at being even friends, they had to get this out of the way. "You don't like me knowing what happened to you. I'm sorry. I was curious. I didn't mean to invade your privacy."

Her eyes glanced away. "It made you think differently of me."

"Why would you say that?"

She shook her head. "No reason. I'm sorry. I'm tired."

When she started to stand, he reached out and put his hand on hers. "Lila, I ran over here as fast as I could. I damn near broke my legs trying to get to you. Finding out you survived a man killing your friend and himself in front of you didn't make me less interested. It made me think about the fact that maybe you don't need the additional pressure of having a man sniffing around you."

She stood there for a moment, not taking her hand from his but also not twisting it around so she could hold it. "That's not what my sister thinks. She thinks I need a man or I'm going to lose my business."

She sank back down and eased her hand out of his, but her eyes had come back up. It was obvious she wasn't talking about what she needed to talk about. Or maybe she simply didn't want to talk to him about it. The upside? She wasn't kicking him out, and at least she was talking to him about something.

"They'll settle down. I know today was hard, and Doc didn't make it easy. I'm going to talk to him about that. He needs to get out and talk to people, make them comfortable with you." If he could get the man off that boat of his. "They'll get to know you and things will be normal in no time at all."

"Really?"

"Really."

"So we're talking a couple of weeks? Because I'm on the razor's edge financially according to those books."

He waved that off. "I'll talk to Rene for you. He'll write you a check to keep the clinic going."

"Does this Rene guy know the town uses him like a checkbook?" She shook her head. "I don't want to merely keep the place open for emergencies. I want to practice here. I can't do that if I don't have patients. I'm uncertain Doctor Hamet has any intention of helping me past cashing the check I wrote him, so I have to consider my sister's advice."

"What did Lisa tell you to do?" Armie asked.

"She thinks I should do what worked for her. She said I should go to this Rene guy and ask him to fake date me because if people think I'm interested in one of the town's guys, that will somehow prove I'm interested in them. Like spending every dime I have on a clinic that helps them and working my ass off isn't proof. Nope, I need to prove my loyalty by humping one of the guys. It's typical when you think about it."

He didn't see anything at all typical about that, and he was going to have a talk with her sister. "You are not going to prostitute yourself for that clinic."

"I was going to fake prostitute myself," she corrected. "And I wasn't going to fake sleep with anyone. It's going to be a very old-fashioned fake courtship."

"That's the most ridiculous idea I ever heard."

"I said the same thing," she agreed. "So you want to do it?"

"What?"

"Fake date me so people will think I'm one of them. Remy thought it should be you and since you already kind of asked me out, it might not be the worst idea. You said you were willing to show me around. Maybe I should wait and see, but I don't want to waste time. I can't have too many more days like today. I know I'm supposed to be patient, but that's not my strong suit. Maybe it's because it's late, but the whole fake-dating thing is starting to look like a viable option. We could make a schedule for a week or two and then reevaluate as to whether or not the plan is working."

Fake date her? Make a schedule?

Of course, fake dating could lead to real dating. It might be a way to get to know her. Or it might be a complete disaster. It was ridiculous because there was a perfectly fine solution sitting right in front of them.

"Absolutely not. You're not going to pull a fast one on

this town. I know they seem like country bumpkins, but these are smart people. They would figure it out. The reason it worked for Lisa was because it was real. She was madly in love with Remy and everyone knew it."

Her shoulders had straightened and she stood up again. "Understood. Thank you for coming to my rescue, Sheriff. You should get back. I will try to keep my 911 calls to a minimum."

He stayed exactly where he was. "Or you could actually date me. I have zero interest in playing games, Lila. I'm too old for that. I'm going to be open and honest. I'm very attracted to you. I don't normally think about women I haven't talked to, but I've been thinking about you ever since I saw you at Remy and Lisa's wedding. I thought you were beautiful and remote and mysterious. I became a cop because I like a good mystery, and that's what you are to me."

"I'm not a mystery. You know what happened to me."

"There's more to you than one incident."

"I don't know. I think it summed me up nicely." She shook her head. "I don't want to talk about that, Armie. I think you should go."

"And I think I should stay," he replied. "Tell me you won't sleep better if I'm on your couch."

"You don't have to sleep on the couch. I'll be fine."

Ah, but she'd said the magic words. He didn't have to. Not he couldn't. He shrugged out of his jacket. "Go back to bed. I'm going to secure the house and I'll be out here on the couch."

"What about Noelle?" she asked.

Noelle was asleep and wouldn't even know he'd left the house unless she woke up and got his text. "She's fine. She can get around and I've got my radio on me. She keeps hers on at her bedside. We live next to your in-laws. Delphine, Sera, and Zep will all help out if she needs something. Go to bed, Lila."

"Are you sure?"

"I'm sure."

She groaned. "I don't want to be this person."

"The person who needs help every now and then?"

"Yes. That person." She wrinkled her nose his way and sighed. "I'll get you some sheets."

She walked away and Peanut was staring at the empty dish again.

"Yeah, buddy, neither one of us is getting everything he wants tonight." Maybe he should have taken her up on the fake-date thing, but that wasn't what she needed. She needed to really fit in, not make some kooky plan to trick people.

Although kooky plans were pretty much the only plans people made in Papillon.

Peanut wandered into the living room, like he was looking for something. Bill, more than likely.

Armie followed, kicking off his sneakers while Peanut managed to jump up onto the lounger that had been Bill's favorite chair. The dog huffed as he settled in.

"His whole life changed in an instant and he doesn't understand why or how." Lila had a set of sheets in her hands.

That had happened to more than the dog.

"Sometimes all you can do is get through a day." He took the sheet from her and spread it over the couch. "One foot in front of the other."

"Just keep swimming. It's funny. I have a couple of nephews and they like that movie. I was babysitting one night. I liked holding the babies. After what happened, holding John or Brendon was one of the only ways I could calm down. I watched that movie about a hundred times. I was treading water in Dallas. I wasn't swimming. I need to swim, Armie."

He understood what she was saying. He'd been there.

"And you will. You have to be patient." He stood in front of her, letting his hands find her shoulders. She hadn't kicked him out. It was enough for tonight.

She turned those gorgeous eyes up to meet his own. "You won't change your mind? About the pretending-to-date-me thing?"

"I want you to think about actually dating me." He rather thought she was a woman who would appreciate honesty. "I'm not a good bet. I'm forty. I wasn't the best husband the first time. I was a workaholic, and being a cop in the big city sometimes made me difficult to be around. I have a daughter who needs me and might always need me. My current job doesn't pay well, and I'll likely stay in this crazy-ass town for the rest of my life. But I would like to date you. I would like to see if there's anything between us because I felt something the first time I saw you. I felt it again yesterday, and I feel it right now. I'm tired of logic. I'm tired of responsibility. I want one thing for myself."

Her eyes met his and he could see her soften. "You want me for yourself?"

"I want to see if you could be the thing in my life that makes me feel young again. That's how I feel around you. Young. Dumb. Oddly hopeful. Maybe it's a trick of my mind. Maybe it's wishful thinking, but if it's not, I don't want to look back and not have tried."

"You don't know me."

He invaded her space a bit. "But I want to and not because you're worried the town won't like you. They'll turn around. I'll talk to some influential people and fix this problem for you. Whether or not you ever want to date me."

She didn't move away. "Real date you."

Something real. That was absolutely what he wanted, what he was ready for. "Real dates. Real other stuff if the real dates go well."

She bit her bottom lip as though considering the problem. "We could just do the other stuff. You want to lay all the cards on the table? I find you very attractive and I wouldn't mind some stress relief. I haven't had a sexual partner in over a year."

Wouldn't that be easy for her? "Does the incredibly

smart doctor not want to spend too much time with the blue-collar guy?"

She frowned at him. "I'm a nurse practitioner and I don't have problems with blue-collar guys. I grew up poor. I think the incredibly sexy sheriff will figure out I'm stubborn and difficult and not likely to change. I thought I should get some sex out of it before he realizes he's not going to like me."

His whole body heated up. Oh, nothing was going to happen because he wasn't about to let the gorgeous big-city lady use him for sex, but his hopes had shot way up. "I think you're going to have to risk that."

Her chin came up, a stubborn glint hitting her eyes. "And if I don't want to take the risk?"

"Then we'll try to work well together. How about we run a test? Why don't you kiss me and see if you think it's worth the risk?"

"You want me to kiss you?"

"More than I want my next breath."

"I'm not very . . ." She huffed and seemed to come to a decision. "All right."

She'd been ready to explain to him that she wasn't all that great at the sex stuff. But damn it, she could learn. All of her life she'd had to study. She wasn't as smart as the rest of her siblings. They seemed to breeze through school, but she'd had to buckle down and really study to get the same good grades they took for granted.

She might not be good at sex, but she could change that. She could study and practice.

Was she about to kiss Armie LaVigne? Just the day before she'd kind of wanted to smash his handsome face. Except she really hadn't. Even when the man had given her a ticket, she'd wanted to know how it felt to have those sensual lips on hers. He was right. There was something between them, something she'd never felt before with any man.

Chemistry.

She'd kind of thought that was a myth, something women told other women to explain their utterly illogical attractions. Nope. Here it was, tugging at her every instinct, drugging her good sense.

She moved into his space. He was wearing plaid pajama pants and a plain white T-shirt. He shouldn't look sexy, but he did.

Was she supposed to go up on her toes to kiss him? Or wait for him to make a move? What was she doing? She didn't need this entanglement.

Brave. She'd come to Papillon to change her life, to be a new Lila Daley. The old Lila would never have brazenly kissed a man she barely knew. Of course, the old Lila also wouldn't have called 911 and spent the majority of the evening in a corner being afraid of a dog who was now sleeping in her chair, but she was going with it.

His way-too-gorgeous-for-a-man's lips curled up as she put her hands on his shoulders. The move might have been awkward, but that was where the discomfort ended. His hands found her hips and a flash of heat went through her.

"I'm glad you decided to give it a shot."

Arrogant man. It didn't turn her off, though, because he'd been honest with her moments before. It was his honesty that had done it. She'd been ready to ask him to leave again and mean it this time, but then he'd opened his mouth and said all kinds of things she'd never heard from a man before.

That he wanted her. That he wanted to try.

Maybe she'd heard the first part before, but it was somehow sweeter coming from him. She wasn't fooling herself. This was still about sex and it would only last as long as she managed not to show off her unique brand of crazy. She didn't lie to herself. She was stubborn and controlling and obnoxious at times. She came off snobby and overly intellectual.

But she might have a little time with him. She might find some companionship. And hey, they might become each other's booty call. It didn't have to be all or nothing. That was the beauty of the new Lila. She didn't have to either marry a man or have nothing to do with him. They worked together. Not so closely that it would be weird for them to have a relationship, but she would often have to liaise with his department. They could be friends and a little bit more.

She could make this work. It was a bit disconcerting to realize how much she wanted this to work.

"Did I lose you? I don't mind. I can see you're thinking, and that's a good thing, but I really would like to touch you. Will you let me touch you while you think about it?"

"You are touching me." She could feel his hands on her, his strong chest brushing against her breasts. He was warm and she hadn't realized how chilly it had been before she'd been near him.

His head was close to hers and he seemed to breathe her in. "No, you're touching me. Let me show you what I mean."

He stroked his free hand over her back almost to her neck and then down again. He stopped at her hips but it was like that hand went straight to her core. How long had it been since her body had shivered in anticipation? How long since her head had gone fuzzy with need?

"Lila, baby, I need you to say yes."

She found she couldn't tell the man no. "Yes. You can touch me. I want you to touch me."

He stroked over her back again and she utterly forgot why this had ever seemed like a bad idea.

"Take your time. I'm not in a hurry." He was staring right at her. "That's the funny thing about Papillon. It's like time slows down and we can enjoy things more here. I've lived in the city, and while it has its perks, I like the pace here. Here, I can stop and stare at you for a while. I can study you and tell you how beautiful your eyes are. And your lips. God, I can't stop thinking about your lips." He brought his hand up and brushed his thumb over her bottom lip. "You are an incredibly sexy woman. I couldn't take my eyes off you at the wedding. I was going to ask you to dance with me, but I missed the chance."

It was time for some honesty. "I watched you, too. I knew you were heading my way and I couldn't. I ran away. I spent the rest of the reception in the ladies' room or help-ing clean up."

It wasn't her proudest moment, but then, she'd had a lot of those lately.

He frowned. Even that was sexy. She ran her hand over his cheek, feeling the scruff of a beard coming in. He would have to shave every single day. Or not. He might look hot with a beard.

"You danced with a couple of other men. Why not me?"

"Because I wanted to dance with you and I couldn't let myself. Because you scared me." She took a deep breath, letting the scent of him wash over her senses. He must have taken a shower before he'd gone to bed because he smelled delicious. "But I'm sick and tired of being scared."

Before he could reply, she went up on her toes and kissed him. She closed her eyes and for once simply let a moment happen. She was the woman who plotted and planned every single minute of her day. From childhood, she'd been a list maker, every second written down and crossed off. She couldn't have planned for Armie LaVigne. She'd made the choice before to avoid him, to control herself and the situa-tion, but things were different now.

Now she'd figured out that controlling every aspect of her life wasn't working. It was time to give a little.

She moved her lips over his, thrilled by the way he fol-lowed her lead. His arms had tightened around her as though he was afraid she would pull away. She could have told him she had zero interest in getting away from him.

It had been a terrible day and she wanted this with him, wanted some solace, a few moments where she didn't feel alone.

The kiss was soft at first, and then she couldn't help but run a tongue over his plump bottom lip.

It felt wickedly good to be close to this man. Her inhibitions were rapidly falling off her, a weight being lifted. She should have danced with him that day. She should have sat there and let him ask her, should have given him her assent. It had been more than cowardice. It had been penance, and she wanted to be free of the feeling she didn't deserve anything good.

His lips moved on hers, tongue coming out to play. She let her hands find his hair, sinking into it. His hair was soft and silky. He growled against her lips and then his tongue was invading, one hand fisting in her hair and gently guiding her head so he could have better access.

Her whole body went soft and she could feel herself getting ready for him.

He didn't have to sleep on the couch. He could come to her bed and they could end the night right.

As if he could hear her thoughts, his hands moved again. This time one went around her back and the other under her knees. He lifted her up like she weighed nothing at all. Her heart raced in the best way.

"I think that answers the question," she said, not recognizing the husky sound of her voice. "Risk is totally worth it."

"It will be." He was staring at her like he could eat her up. He cradled her in his arms and started making his way back to the bedroom.

He walked through her bedroom door. She needed to redecorate, make the place her own. For the first time she thought about redoing the house. She'd thought it would only be a place to sleep, but if Armie would be here, she wanted it to be nice. Comfortable. She wanted it to have something of her in it.

Armie started to lay her down on the bed. She would definitely start with high-quality sheets. And she might get some sexy pajamas. She could find those somewhere. She had Internet. Well, sometimes. When it was working. Surely there was a library with Wi-Fi.

She waited to feel the press of his body against hers. He could take control now. She was ready to follow him.

This was what she needed. God, this might be what she'd come here for.

He pulled the covers over her and bent down, lightly pressing a kiss on her forehead. "Good night, Lila."

"What?" She pushed herself up. Was he actually leaving? "I said yes, Armie. It's fine. You don't have to sleep out there."

"Yes, I do, because if I don't we're going to make a hell of a mistake tonight."

She didn't see it that way. "We're consenting adults. It's not a mistake. It's sex."

"Yes, that would be the mistake. It's too soon. It would be sex for you, and I don't particularly want sex. I want something more. I've had plenty of sex."

"Good for you. I haven't had any in a long time." A thought struck her like a slap to the face. She'd felt something. That didn't mean he had, and didn't that hurt way more than she'd imagined it could? "Oh. It didn't really work for you, did it?"

"Hey, you want to take a look at this thing and tell me I don't want you? It's painful and it's taking everything I have not to hop into bed with you, but I don't think you'll feel the same way I do in the morning. I think you'll slap my pretty ass and send me on my way."

Sure enough those PJ pants of his had tented admirably. Frustration welled through her. He wanted her but he wasn't going to take her? He thought she would use him for sex?

She wasn't going to do that. Probably not. She wouldn't have been terribly embarrassed in the morning and kicked him out and not talked to him for days, avoiding him as much as possible.

Damn it. He was right. She wasn't ready.

"Good night, Lila." He stood in the doorway, his big frame in shadows.

She wished she could honestly reach out to him, but she

simply turned over and tried not to think about the fact that once she'd thought she was indestructible.

Life had taught her otherwise. Life had brought her low and showed her how much of a coward she could be.

Still, when she closed her eyes and sleep claimed her, she dreamed of him, and that was worth all the trouble.

chapter six

Armie was rethinking the entire night as he maneuvered the flat-bottom boat toward Petrie Island. That was what the locals called it, but it was really a series of small islands that were high enough that they didn't regularly flood. The Petrie family had lived on those islands for the last century. They made their living as shrimpers, and it made sense to Armie that they would move closer to the marina where their boats docked, but anytime he asked, he was told Petries lived on the island. Always had. Always would.

"You know people are going to talk, right?" Roxie sat at the front of the boat, scanning for anything that might catch on the bottom or the motor.

"Talk about what?" Maybe he should have taken what Lila had offered. Maybe if he had she wouldn't have hustled him out of her house this morning. If he'd been in bed with her, he could have pinned her down and kissed her until she couldn't even think about going to work. He could have woken up to her body cuddled against his. Instead, he might have to ask someone to check him for ticks because Peanut had managed to climb on the couch with him in the middle of the night.

"Talk about the fact that your truck was spotted outside the new girl's house."

Shit. He hadn't thought about that. "Peanut came back last night. He scratched at the back door and scared her. You know how it is when you aren't used to the sounds out here."

Roxie's brow rose. "Peanut? Bill's dog? I thought his son took the dog."

"Yeah, well, Mikey always was a selfish asshole." It shouldn't have surprised him but it did. He'd given Mikey a call this morning and explained the situation. "He gave me some story about how they stopped at a rest stop and the dog ran away. But he also told me to take him to a shelter because he wasn't coming back to get him."

"Asshole," Roxie said with a sigh. "I'll take him in. I've been meaning to get a dog."

"I think you'll have to fight Lila over him. She says she's going to fix him up and then find him a home, but you know how that goes."

"Yeah, in a few days she'll be used to him and she'll think it can't hurt to let him stay a little while longer, and then she's buying him Christmas sweaters and arguing at the town hall for a dog park." Roxie nodded. "She looks like the kind who would dress up her dog, and I think she likes arguing."

Why hadn't he thought of that? He could have gone to bed with her, woken with her, shown back up at her place to fix something—he had his pick since nothing worked—and repeated the whole process. "I think she's too practical to dress up the dog."

"Nah, she only looks that way. Trust me, that dog will have a sweater by the end of the year. Have you thought about how Miranda is going to take your sudden passion for Remy's sister-in-law?"

Miranda Jossart was the local real estate agent. He'd also gone to high school with her. They hadn't been close then despite the fact that there had only been twenty-seven kids in their whole class. When he'd come home, Miranda had been one of the first to show up with a platter of cookies in her hand and a smile on her face, welcoming him back. They'd gone on a few dates, but there had never been a spark between them.

"Why would Miranda care that I'm dating Lila?" He'd missed an opportunity, but she had agreed to go out with him. Even as she'd been shoving him out the door this morning, she'd agreed to go to dinner on Friday.

Roxie stared at him, the same expression on her face she often used on Zep. "You can't possibly be this unaware."

She was underestimating him. "Apparently I can."

"Why do you think Miranda brings cookies to the station house all the time? Do you think it's because she loves law enforcement?"

"I thought it was because she loves to bake and always has too much." She told him constantly that she was watching her figure. He'd never looked at her figure. She was a nice enough woman, but he'd never once thought of her that way.

"It's because she's got the hots for you."

He laughed because that was ridiculous. "She does not have the hots for me. She's just nice."

"Like Annie Dubois is nice? Because when I first came to town she warned me off you. Not like I was ever going to hit that. No. My taste in men is way worse, but Annie showed up at my apartment and explained that you and she were together and I better back off."

"What? I went out with her twice. Years ago." It had been when he'd first come home to Papillon. He'd been divorced and burned out. He'd felt like he'd lost everything. The only reason he'd taken the job had been his old friend Rene basically begging him to do it. Annie had suggested that they have dinner, and he hadn't cared enough to say no.

Then the accident had happened and he'd been forced to care about everything. He'd been forced to focus his entire world on his daughter.

"Well, you made an impression," Roxie replied with a brief smile. "This was a couple of years ago. She might not still be pining. I think there are some women in town who believe that as soon as Noelle graduates you'll look for some companionship. Especially when she goes off to college."

"She's not going off to college." He couldn't stand the thought of her out there in the big bad world. She was fragile, vulnerable. There were other ways for her to get an education. "She's going to do it all online. She doesn't need to be in some dorm where everyone parties. She's not that girl."

Noelle was studious. She took her classes seriously and she was focused.

And what would happen when she graduated from her online school? How the hell was she going to find a job here?

He shook off that worry. It was years away, and lots of people worked remotely these days.

"Well, that's still the prevailing theory around town. You're going to find more and more Mirandas and Annies on your doorstep, and they are not going to be happy about the rumors you started this morning."

"I told you why I was there." But no one would believe him. He hadn't even thought about it. However, he couldn't see how it would do any real harm. "I am dating Lila. Well, almost dating her. We're going to have dinner on Friday."

He thought he might have to avoid her entirely until he showed up on her doorstep. He would do it so she had zero opportunity to back out of the date. She was a polite woman. If he showed up with flowers and dressed nicely, she probably wouldn't be able to send him away.

He turned the boat, giving it a little more gas. Up ahead he saw the turnoff that would take them to Petrie Island. It was marked by a massive bald cypress whose base lay in the murky waters, the branches extending far above into the sky.

He wondered if Lila would like it out here. He liked the quiet. Even when he'd lived in New Orleans, he'd missed this place, missed the calm he found here.

"Are you sure that's a good idea? She doesn't seem like your type."

"I have a type?"

A thoughtful look crossed Roxie's face. "I guess I don't really know. You haven't dated since I took this job."

"I haven't dated since I brought Noelle back here," he admitted. "At first it was too hard. I had to focus everything I had on her. Even after we settled down I couldn't find the time. She'd lost her mom. I didn't love my ex-wife. Not at the end. But I couldn't bring someone in to replace her. Noelle had to know she came first."

"And that is why you're going to have all the Mirandas and Annies chasing after you. You're a good man. I like the new doc. What are we supposed to call her? Nurse Daley? That seems weird. Everyone will end up calling her Doc so she should get used to it. Anyway, I met her the other day out at Guidry's and she seems solid. Practical. I guess that's why I don't see the two of you together."

"Maybe we won't be. I don't know her all that well, but I'm attracted to her." He knew her way better after the night before. He knew there was a soft woman under all her armor. A mystery. He'd told her the truth about that. She was a mystery, and it had been far too long since he'd had one to solve. "She's complex and complicated and makes no apologies for it. I like that she's forthright."

"I liked that about her, too. I don't get all the Southern stuff, to tell you the truth. Like why does every woman in town bless everyone's hearts? It's weird. I've been here for a while and I still don't get it."

He would have to get her a translation guide. "When a Southern woman blesses your heart she means you're an idiot. Southern women are good with the polite passive aggression." He bet Lila would simply call him an idiot. No hiding behind social niceties. He kind of liked that. He hadn't given much thought to how the transition had gone for his deputy. Like him, she'd come from a big city job. Unlike him, she hadn't grown up here. Not even close. "Do you miss New York?"

"Often." She stared out at the water. "And then I remember how crappy it could be. I'm happy I'm here, Armie.

Even if I don't always get the people." She seemed to shake something off. "Speaking of people, I haven't met this Carrie. I thought I'd pretty much met everyone in town. Why does the doc think she's being abused?"

He was going to have to figure out the name thing. Nurse Daley did feel weird. "Lila doesn't know what it's like out here. She also had a friend who was abused by her husband." He hesitated to say anything else. It was her story to tell. "I'm worried she's seeing something that's not there, but I think we should check it out just in case."

"Absolutely," Roxie agreed. "Also, it's not like I have anything better to do. This is the most exciting thing that's happened to me all week. Another reason I like it better here. Working SWAT in New York was not relaxing. I like the fact that the most workout my heart gets is when I do cardio." She sat up. "Is that what we're looking for?"

There was a dock up ahead, another flat-bottom boat moored to the side. The Petrie family relied heavily on boats.

"Yes, it is, and it looks like we won't have to go looking for the house. Hello, Mrs. Petrie."

A stern-looking woman stood on the dock, a shotgun by her side.

It was a testament to how she'd settled in that Roxie didn't put a hand on her gun. It had been a habit he'd had to rid himself of when he'd come home. Out here, shotguns were a necessity of daily life.

"Sheriff. Deputy. What can I do for you?" Mrs. Petrie had steel-gray hair and a look that could freeze the balls off a man at forty paces.

He had to handle this properly. "I wanted to come out and check on your daughter-in-law. I heard she took a pretty hard fall."

He couldn't come out and ask the woman if her son was abusive.

Lorna Petrie frowned. "That girl is always falling or walking into something. She's fine. We sent her to see Doc yesterday. He knows how clumsy she can be."

"Didn't you hear? Doc retired." Roxie stepped out of the boat and tied it off with an expert hand. She'd learned how to handle a boat. It was required training out here. "We have a new person running the clinic."

"Mabel?" Lorna turned on her heels and started back up toward the house. "She's the only one left with any kind of medical training. I might as well send her to Miss Marcelle and see if her hoodoo can fix the problem."

Armie stepped off carefully and followed behind. It was interesting that Carrie hadn't mentioned she'd seen the new nurse practitioner. "No need. We've got a nurse practitioner working under Doc's supervision." A lie, but he would keep it up or they could lose their only clinic. "Her name's Lila Daley. She's from Dallas. She used to work at a big trauma center there. I think she can certainly handle Carrie's mishaps."

Carrie was younger than he was. Considerably. He'd never thought about it, but she was a lot younger than Bobby, too. They'd married before he'd come back to Papillon.

"There's some city girl running the clinic now?" Lorna asked.

"Doc wasn't going to work forever." He wasn't sure what people had thought. Doc had been getting on up there in years. There wasn't anyone else in town even vaguely interested in medicine.

Except his daughter, and that wasn't something she could do online.

"We should have found someone like us. We shouldn't have to go outside the town when we're hiring." She pointedly looked at Roxie.

"We're lucky to have experts who are willing to come here and work with us." It was obvious Lorna Petrie needed to get out more.

"Ms. Daley is very nice," Roxie said, letting the obvious insult slide off her. "I think she's going to be a great addition to the community. And she's got strong ties to here. She's Remy Guidry's sister-in-law."

Lorna turned her nose up at that. "His new wife is from

the city as well. I've heard she's making all kinds of changes at the restaurant. And she's paying less for our hauls. All in all, I don't think the new people are making a positive change."

Good for Lisa. He'd thought that a lot of people had taken advantage of the Guidrys over the years. They were excellent restaurateurs, but none of them had been to business school like Lisa had. Her taking over the business end of Guidry's likely meant it would be healthy and serving the community for years to come.

"Carrie! Get on out here. You have visitors." Lorna strode up the porch steps.

The house had been standing for years, and he had to admit the Petries built houses to last. Despite their isolation, the house looked solid and well kept. Carrie stepped out on the porch, her left arm in a sling. She looked older than she had the last time he'd seen her. Not in a timeworn, normal way. Her youthful cheeriness had been replaced with a weary, haunted look.

When she smiled his way, the expression didn't come close to her eyes. "Hello, Sheriff. Is there something I can do for you?"

Her tone didn't waver. There was no look of surprise in her eyes. When he showed up unexpectedly, it was almost always bad news. One of the worst parts of his job was the look that came over a person's face when they opened the door and saw him. There was none of that in Carrie's expression.

"I heard you broke your arm." He needed to get her away from Lorna. She wouldn't talk honestly around her mother-in-law.

"Yeah, I fell. I was feeding the chickens and tripped," she explained.

"You have chickens out here? Those coops better be up to code." Roxie turned and walked off the steps.

"There's no damn code out here." Lorna took the bait fast, nearly running after Roxie as she started looking for the chicken coops.

He had a couple of minutes. "Are you all right, Carrie?"

She glanced the way her mother-in-law had gone. "I'm fine. The nurse fixed me up. I'll be out of the sling soon."

"Is Bobby treating you right?"

Her eyes flared and then her gaze wouldn't meet his. "I said everything is fine."

Damn it. Lila was right. Something was going on. "If he's hurting you, I can help."

"I'm clumsy. That's all." Her chin came up, and he saw a grim resolve in her eyes. "I should have known that woman would be trouble. Tell that nurse to keep her nose out of my business. I'll find another place to go if I get hurt again. She's got no right to make accusations."

"She's an expert, and she sees a pattern of injuries that don't work with your explanation," he pointed out. "If you're worried no one will believe you, you're wrong."

"Is there a problem, Sheriff?" Lorna was back, her stare going from him to her daughter-in-law as though assessing the situation.

"There's no problem, Mother Petrie." The calm smile was back on her face. "Apparently the new lady at the clinic is very thorough."

"I'm surprised you didn't mention that it wasn't Doc you saw." Lorna managed to make the statement into an accusation.

"I told Bobby about it," Carrie replied. "It wasn't a big deal. Now, Sheriff, please let the nurse know that I'm fine. I'm feeling much better and won't need to come back for a follow-up."

Lorna huffed. "Follow-up? What an idiotic notion. She's fine. She's already working. The girl's tough. She don't need some uppity city nurse to turn her into a whining baby like the rest of them. Now go and get out of here. We have things to do before the men get back. And tell that deputy of yours that we're unincorporated land here. She's got no right to check on anything at all. Only code out here is the Petrie code."

Roxie simply smiled. "The coop's perfectly fine to me.

Not that I know a lot about them, but the chickens seemed happy, too."

Lorna shook her head. "Ridiculous rules."

"Unincorporated land or not, I'm still the law here, and you would do best to remember it." He turned and walked away, knowing Roxie was right behind him. He got on the boat and looked back.

Carrie stood in the doorway, half in and half out, a shadow over her face.

Lila was right and something was happening with that girl, but damn if he knew what to do about it.

"We can't bring the husband in if the wife won't tell us anything's wrong," Roxie pointed out as she pulled the rope in. "Unless you want to start asking around. See if anyone's seen something."

He started up the motor. "No, I would have heard by now. They keep to themselves. I thought it was because they simply liked to live that way. Now I have questions. But they'll have to wait."

He wasn't going to be able to avoid Lila.

He steered the boat away from the pier, his brain working on the problems.

Another day, another list of canceled appointments. It was enough to make a woman wonder if there was something wrong with her deodorant.

At least she had a friend now.

"You know, for a dog who managed to make it all the way home, you don't seem like you want to stay there." She stared down at Peanut, who thumped his tail against the floor and gave her a big doggy grin.

She'd spent her morning cleaning him up. He was in surprisingly good shape for being on his own for months. She'd pulled two ticks off him and his hair was short enough it hadn't matted. He'd needed a bath and food and water, but he was going to be fine. When the time had come for her to go to the clinic, he'd followed her to the door.

When she'd closed him in, he'd whined and cried so loud, she'd gone back to check on him. He'd taken the opportunity to run out to her car and jump around like he knew they were going for an adventure. She hadn't been able to leave him behind.

She should start looking for someone to take him in.

Not today, of course. He'd been through a lot and needed TLC. In a couple of weeks she would start looking around to see if anyone needed a pet.

"Oh, he's attached to you now," Mabel said, leaning over to give Peanut a pet. "That dog went everywhere with Bill. I'm not surprised he found his way back home, and now he's imprinted again."

"I can't keep him." It was what she'd thought about as she'd tried to fall back asleep the night before. She'd thought about the dog and the man who'd been occupying her living room, and how she probably couldn't keep either one of them.

"Why?" Mabel asked.

There were many reasons. She'd wanted a dog while she'd been in Dallas, but it hadn't seemed fair to the dog. It still wasn't. As for Armie, it probably couldn't work for all the same reasons. "I work long hours. I work weird hours. Well, I will if anyone ever actually makes it to an appointment."

Armie worked crazy hours, too. And wasn't his position elected? She couldn't see herself as anything but a liability in a campaign. It might be different if she could tempt the man into some stress-relief sex that didn't have to necessarily end in some kind of happily ever after.

She knew that was something that wouldn't happen for her. She'd lost that chance, or maybe she'd never had it at all.

Mabel shrugged like that was no big deal. "So? Take the dog to work with you. He's perfectly housetrained. We can get a pooper-scooper, and there's a nice patch of grass out back. He's been around town his whole life, and he's a sweetheart."

There was only one problem with that. "You can't have a dog in a clinic."

"Maybe you can't in Dallas, but I don't know if you've noticed, hon, this is not Dallas. Now tell me how Armie LaVigne was in bed. I know I'm married and my Dale is a gentle lover, but I'm not dead."

Lila stopped, hoping she hadn't heard right. "What?"

Mabel shook her head and leaned against the reception desk. "Hon, if you wanted to keep it quiet then Armie shouldn't have parked that big old parish vehicle of his in the front drive. Angie Jones runs the post office. She gets up real early, and she definitely noted that Armie was at your place. She told Dixie, who owns the café Angie eats at every morning. Now, I personally think Angie would do well to avoid Dixie's waffles given those thighs of hers, but that's none of my business. Dixie told her fry cook, who got on the phone with his wife. Now, Frank's wife is Marie, who works with Miss Marcelle at the hair salon. She told Miss Marcelle, who told Delphine Guidry. Delphine told her daughter, Seraphina, who told everyone in her morning yoga group. I know it seems very big-city, but Emma Lorraine got some crazy ideas in her head when she went to L.A. Now a whole group of them meet out in the park and do yoga in the mornings. The pastor of the First Baptist Church has tried to stop them because he calls it devil worship, but they claim it's just a nice way to stretch their lower backs and don't pay him any mind. Kenny overheard the yoga-girls-slash-devil-women, depending on who you talk to, and he told me that you and Armie are having a baby."

She felt her jaw drop. "Oh my god."

"Kenny says that he was there because the park is nice at that time of the morning, but I think he's a pervert and he's watching those women stretch. I should talk to Armie about that. No. Now that you're going to be his baby momma, you should. You tell Armie those women don't need creepy Kenny staring at their butts, though Armie might also tell them that those leggings they wear are damn near obscene."

It was a lot of information to process, but one fallacy stood out. "I'm not sleeping with the sheriff."

"Okay, 'sleeping with' is a phrase we use because we're ladies and don't want to use the other phrases. But it's a euphemism, hon. I know there wasn't a lot of sleeping going on."

"I'm not having sex with Armie LaVigne." Not yet anyway. He turned out to be a very prudish, hot-as-hell alpha male. He didn't want her to use him for sex. It was ridiculous. "Peanut showed up at the door last night and I'm ashamed to say I called 911. The sheriff came out to see if I was okay, and he ended up sleeping on my couch."

"Did he scratch on the door and scare the crap out of you? I can understand that. But why did Armie sleep on your couch?"

Well, she had tried to kick him out. She hadn't been successful. "I told him I was fine, but he thought I would sleep better knowing I wasn't alone in the house. I can't imagine he was comfortable on that couch. It's not very big. But he insisted."

After he'd kissed her and gotten her hot and bothered for the first time in forever. Wicked man. Mean man.

Mabel gave her a knowing look. "He's courting you. I know that's probably not a word you use a lot in the big city."

"I know what courting is." And Armie wasn't doing it because that would be ridiculous, too.

Mabel continued on like she hadn't said a thing at all. "That is when a man does all kinds of silly things to attract a woman he wants to spend time with. It's like in the animal world when a male bird puffs out his chest. Armie is doing the same thing, except he's damaging his spine because I remember Bill's couch and it was from the sixties. It couldn't be comfortable. Didn't he give you a ticket? That was probably his way of showing masculine power. Like a gorilla beating on his chest."

"Well, I didn't find it sexy." She was still thinking about

fighting that damn ticket. "I think that was more about a new coffeemaker than it was about tempting me."

He was so tempting. Something was definitely happening to her. She didn't lust after men. She carefully chose her sexual partners. Well, all two of them. There had been a college boyfriend and then there had been Brock, who'd hit on her sisters because according to him, they were way more spontaneous than she was.

She'd tried to be spontaneous with Armie and that way had led to frustration.

The door opened, bell jingling, and a woman walked in. She looked to be in her mid-thirties, maybe early forties. She had brown hair she wore in a neat bun on the top of her head. She had on a perfectly pressed business suit and carried in a plate of what looked like cookies or brownies or something.

Not a patient, then. It said something about her that she was disappointed that the person walking up to her wasn't covered in blood or didn't have a bone sticking out. She would settle for a nice concussion.

"Oh, lord, it's starting. Batten down the hatches," Mabel said under her breath.

She wasn't sure what was starting, but the woman seemed to zero in on her.

"Well, hello, Ms. Daley. It's such a pleasure to finally meet you. I'm Miranda Jossart. I worked with your younger sister Lisa to get you that jewel of a house. I thought I would stop in and welcome you to Papillon."

Jewel? "Yeah, we should talk about that house. There is nothing jewel-like about it. Well, there's a whole collection of rocks, but the coal sample he has isn't even close to diamond status. Nothing works. I have to kick the washer to get it to start. I won't even go into the hot-water heater. Do you have something going with the inspector?"

Mabel's eyes widened. "I think what Lila is trying to say is that she's had a few troubles with the house. Last night her lights went out."

"Did they, now?" Miranda set her tray down on the counter. "Well, you're used to a high-rise apartment building with all those rich things inside it. You'll have to understand that things work differently here on the bayou."

"Electricity works differently?"

"A lot of things do," Miranda replied as if everything she was saying made sense. Which it didn't. "You're new in our town and it can be hard to fit in, hard to know where the boundaries are."

She got the sense that there was something underneath the woman's words, some subtext she wasn't getting. "Okay. Hopefully someone will let me know. Is there a pamphlet?"

There was a nasty smile on the woman's face. "A lot of fitting in is about good sense. You should take your time. Concentrate on your business. I'm sure a clinic like this operates on the goodwill of the people. You need to ingratiate yourself with influential members of the community. I heard you had a little trouble yesterday."

"Yes, apparently the doctor I bought the clinic from didn't bother to inform the general population that it was happening," she explained.

"She'll settle in," Mabel replied.

Miranda glanced around the clinic as though sizing it up for sale. "I could, of course, help you out. I could let people know that I think you're a good fit here if I thought you were hardworking and willing to be an asset to the community."

"I would appreciate that." She would take all the help she could get.

"I talk to a lot of people and I'll make sure they know it's safe to come here. Doc was a pillar of the community," Miranda continued.

"If a pillar can be held up with Scotch and laziness, then yes he was," Mabel shot back. She quickly looked to Lila. "Not that I didn't love that old man. I'm a very tolerant person."

They had two different definitions of that word, but she was quickly coming to realize that happened a lot here.

And Miranda wasn't offering to help her out of the kindness of her heart. "Why do I get the feeling you're going to want something in return?"

Miranda seemed to consider how to proceed. Or she knew how to draw out a moment for maximum drama. "I'm offering to help you so everything goes smoothly during your transition. I think you should understand that there are certain relationships already in place."

"I would assume so." She was definitely missing something.

"Then there are relationships that are only in one part of the couple's head." Mabel had a hand on her hip, staring down Miranda.

Were those two in some kind of fight?

"Oh, it's real and it's happening, Mabel. You should stay out of this," Miranda replied before turning back to Lila. "Look, it's obvious I'm going to have to be up-front with you. I would like to handle this like ladies. I'm in a relationship with the sheriff and I didn't take kindly to you inviting him to stay at your place last night."

Whoa. Mabel and Miranda weren't in the fight. She was. How had she managed to get into a fight with some woman she'd never met before? "I didn't invite him. I called 911 and he showed up."

The first expression that crossed Miranda's face was one of surprise. Like she'd never thought to do that and what a great idea. The second was a smug grin that came from pure self-satisfaction. "I suspected as much. Armie is very careful about who he's seen with and how he conducts himself. He's got a daughter. I'll let everyone know it was a purely professional visit and they got it all wrong. I'm sorry about that confusion. It's a small town and you would do well to remember that people talk."

She honestly didn't care what people had to say. It was odd but she was remembering more and more shitty things about her childhood, and she wasn't reacting the way she had before. Back in Dallas, she would have thoughtfully gone over what to say and how to smooth over the situation because relationships were important and how the people around her viewed her had been important, too. Now she wondered why she cared. She was smart and worked hard and she wasn't mean. That should be enough. She shouldn't have to spend her whole life being worried about how every single person was going to interpret her actions.

Dallas? It hadn't been Dallas. It had been that night. It had been that night when she'd watched her friend die. It had been the knowledge that Maryanne had done everything she could, everything right, and she'd still died.

"I didn't sleep with the sheriff but I did kiss him, and I'm probably going to do it again. I don't know. He was a great kisser and I'm still considering it this morning, but I think he might be clingy. I might like him being clingy, but am I ready for that? If you're in a relationship with him, you should rethink because he is looking to cheat on you. He asked me out a bunch of times. Wore me down, to tell you the truth. If people are going to talk, they should talk about that."

Miranda gasped, an offended sound. "I never . . ."

"You certainly didn't with Armie," Lila pointed out because it didn't matter. They were already gossiping. They might as well know the facts and gossip properly. "According to him he's hit a dry spell."

Miranda put a hand on her chest like she was looking for pearls to clutch. "I never said I slept with him. We have a platonic relationship, and I know he's merely waiting for his daughter to graduate and then we can be together."

"His daughter is sixteen. She's not a kid who doesn't know her father probably wants to date and do all the other things that go with dating." Remy wouldn't have pointed her in Armie's direction if Armie had a girlfriend. Honestly, she didn't think Armie was the type who would cheat on a girlfriend. He seemed . . . honorable. He certainly didn't seem like the type who would be platonic around a woman he wanted. He would be frustrating. Demanding. But the way he'd touched her the night before had told her the man would likely be very enthusiastic in bed. "I know this is the country, but it's not Victorian England. Adults can sleep together without a bunch of societal consequences."

"Except gossip," Mabel pointed out. "And babies, if they don't protect themselves. Ask Seraphina Guidry about that one."

"Except gossip and babies and potential STIs." She'd come here to live a nice, quiet life, but apparently she was going to have to make a little noise. And she was serious about a community discussion of STIs. They were completely avoidable, and she would be the one who would have to deal with all the nasty things that came with curing them. "If you have a problem with Armie, I suggest you take it up with him. If you think to punish me in some way for being attracted to a man you have no real claim on, then we should talk about that. Well, we shouldn't because I'm not licensed to practice psychology. But I can refer you to a couple of great therapists."

"I came here to be nice," Miranda said.

Mabel shook her head and wagged a finger Miranda's way. "You did not. You think I don't know your tricks? Those are your chocolate chip cookies. They are your second-best cookies. Everyone in town knows when you want to impress someone or be nice to them you bake lemon meltaways. Everyone knows you consider chocolate chip to be for children and people with no taste buds."

"I like chocolate chip." The cookies hadn't offended her. And she was hungry. Since she'd gotten to Papillon, she'd been hungrier than usual, the likely result of having nothing else to do. Usually she was so busy she forgot to eat. Now those cookies looked pretty good. Cookies couldn't be full of malice. Poison, maybe, but she was willing to take the chance.

Miranda grabbed her tray with a shake of her head. "Well, I can see you are not going to be reasonable."

She was. She was being entirely reasonable. She would entirely reasonably ask Armie about it later. If this woman thought she could make her run away and hide or something, Miranda would soon learn that there wasn't a lot of drama she couldn't handle. "Guess not. But remember about the gossip thing. Didn't sleep with him. Yet."

Miranda strode away, banging out of the clinic with a whole lot of fussy sounds.

Mabel turned to her. "Do you have any idea how long I've been waiting for someone to take that queen bee down?"

"If I'd been really smart I could have kept the cookies." It struck her that Mabel knew a lot about the town. "Should I expect other visits from women who think Armie will finally be theirs once his tender innocent daughter is pawned off on a man? Are they waiting for her marriage or just for her to leave home?"

"You trust him that much? You didn't even think twice about it. How do you know he doesn't have a whole bunch of women on his string?"

"My sister likes him and she's a good judge of character. My brother-in-law likes him, too. And I know self-delusion when I see it." She'd seen it in the mirror for years.

The door swooshed open and Noelle wheeled herself in, followed by the man himself. No wonder Miranda had come to protect her turf. That man was fine. He walked beside his daughter, and the man rocked the khakis.

He turned and looked out into the empty parking lot. "Was there something wrong with Miranda?" He glanced back her way. "Hey, did you ask her about what's up with the wiring in that house she sold you? I want to know if she's paying off the inspector."

Even his suspicion was sexy. And great minds and all that. "I did ask her about that and she avoided the question. She did not come here for business purposes. She's angry because I stole her man."

He winced. "Roxie might have mentioned that could happen today. Lila, I've never given her any reason to think we're together."

"You should look out for Annie Dubois, too," Noelle offered with a cheery smile. She didn't seem to mind that Peanut was sniffing all around her. She simply reached a hand out and gave the dog a pet. "Just like Miranda, she's been after Dad since high school, according to the gossip."

"She helped me out in math," Armie said with a shake of his head.

Yep, he was cute when he was confused. It was exactly what she'd thought it was. He was a guy and many, many times men didn't pick up on the subtleties of female desire.

"So I'm not wrecking your future home?" she asked.

The slightest smile curled up his lips. "I am a perfectly single man. I cannot help it if a number of women around town find me attractive. I can assure you I've done nothing to make them desire me. In fact, I gave Miranda a ticket for parking violations a couple of months back." He glanced over at Mabel. "You think she's going to cause trouble? Should I talk to her?"

Mabel shrugged. "She'll try to cause trouble. I don't think Lila is going to be intimidated, though."

She wasn't, though she was still sad about the cookies. She should have known once she blew her tight control on the amount of carbs she allowed herself that her diet would go all to hell. "You should be on the lookout for women around town calling 911 in an attempt to get you to pay attention to them."

After all, it had worked once.

"This is going to be fun." Noelle looked far more enthusiastic than her father.

"It could cause trouble for the clinic," Mabel pointed out.

Lila didn't see how. "No one's coming in anyway. I don't think she can make it worse. Noelle, why don't you come back to the exam room? I want to take another look at that wound."

Noelle nodded up at her. "Sure thing. I need to talk to you about some weird stuff with my period, too."

Gyno. She could handle that. "All right."

Armie shrank back. "I'll wait out here. Lila, I need to talk to you when you're done with Noelle. I made a trip out to visit Carrie Petrie earlier today."

He'd gone to talk to her? He hadn't believed her suspicions, but he'd checked into it? From the grave look on his face he was either worried he was going to piss her off by saying everything was fine or he'd found out it wasn't. Either way, she appreciated him taking her seriously.

"Thank you."

Noelle made her way back, Peanut following and generally proving why dogs shouldn't be allowed in a medical setting.

"I was going to avoid you until Friday, but I thought you should get an update," Armie admitted.

That made her grin because she could guess why. "I was probably going to cancel out of sheer cowardice, but then your real fake girlfriend showed up and pissed me off, so now there's zero chance of me not showing up."

Even though real-real dating Armie was probably going to make the situation with Miranda worse, she wasn't about to back down.

And that felt good. That made her feel better than she had in a long time.

She followed his daughter, and hoped he enjoyed the view.

"You are a perfectly healthy young woman," Lila said twenty minutes later.

"With the exception of the fact that I can't move my legs?"

"Let's just call you healthy." She didn't have any pressure sores or ulcers. Her weight was in a healthy range. It could be hard for wheelchair-bound patients to get enough exercise. Noelle's injury was at L-3, low on her spine. As injuries go, it could have been much worse. And honestly it surprised her that Noelle was completely confined to that chair. "Do you have any feeling in your legs?"

"Some," she admitted. "I can move my toes a little, but I've lost all coordination. It's cool. I'm okay with it. Doc told me about it a long time ago. He said if I was going to walk it would have been in the first few months."

But only with proper PT. Her records showed that she'd gone to a local therapist for a couple of months and then she'd stopped trying to get on her feet. Now her therapy was about keeping her muscles from atrophying and building her upper-body strength. If she had some feeling in her legs and could move her toes even the tiniest bit, then the injury was incomplete. Messages from the brain were still able to get to her legs. She should have more function than she did. "I want you to think about upping your physical therapy. I think you gave up too soon, and I'm not sure these orders the doctor gave you are the best course of action. Given where your injury is, you should be able to stand and perhaps walk with braces."

She shook her head. "Nope. Can't do any of that. I wanted to talk to you about something else."

She was surprised that Noelle wouldn't consider it, but then, she didn't know the case well. She needed to study the records before she pushed harder. "All right. What did you want to talk about?"

The young woman seemed to steel herself. "I want to know how normal you think I can be."

"Pretty normal. Are you having trouble getting around? I've noticed almost every business in town has a ramp of some kind." She'd been surprised at how well equipped the town was.

Noelle pushed her glasses up her nose and shook her head. "I don't mean that. When I came to live with my dad, everyone was great. They tried to make it easy for me. I was talking about being able to do things other women do."

There was something about the way her fair skin had gone slightly rosy that made Lila think she was talking about something beyond braiding her hair or singing karaoke. She'd mentioned her period. "Are you talking about having kids? There's nothing at all in your records that makes me think you would have a problem. Even with a complete spinal cord injury, most women can still have children. Yours is much less severe. It didn't harm your internal organs. Is your period regular?"

She waved that off. "Yeah, it's fine. I didn't want my dad to think he could come back here. He's nosy about the medical stuff. I get some privacy if I mention the girl parts. But honestly, I did want to talk to you about my girl parts. Will they work? Not my ovaries."

"Oh." She hadn't expected that. "Are you talking about your clitoris?"

She nodded. "If I fall in love with a boy, a man, can I have sex?"

Ah, now she understood why Noelle had been desperate to not have her father in here. She was sixteen. Lila was surprised this hadn't come up. "Have you tried?"

"Having sex with a boy? No. My dad pretty much watches me twenty-four-seven, and when he's not someone else is. And it's not like there's a boy I would want to do that with. I don't know yet. I'm asking because I might want to someday, but what if I can't? There's this guy in my physical therapy group. He asked me out. I said no, of course. It's too soon. I'm not looking to have sex with him." She struggled for words.

Lila understood, and she was a woman who planned ahead. "But you want to know if it's possible for the future because you don't want to get into something that can't possibly work."

She nodded. "I know that sounds dumb."

"That is the smartest thing I've heard all day. The short answer is you can absolutely have sex, but depending on what's going on down there, you might have to make some adjustments. How do you feel when you masturbate?"

She went still.

"Sweetie, have you ever masturbated?"

"I've tried." Noelle had gone a bright pink, but she soldiered on. "It's hard for me to touch it. It. I mean my clitoris. I can't arch my hips. I can move side to side, but not up. And my arms are freakishly short. It's hard. I feel warm down there sometimes."

"That's normal when you see something that arouses you. Or you think about it. There's nothing to be embarrassed about, Noelle. This is a normal part of life. Sex and intimacy are a necessary part of the human experience. It's good that you have those feelings, because they're normal."

"But I'm not normal. What if I can feel arousal, but not all the other parts? I don't have a lot of friends here. My best friend doesn't know much more about it than I do. Her dad is the pastor and her mom said she wouldn't talk to her about it until she's ready to get married. I would talk to the other girls my age, but it's embarrassing that I don't know much. I had my period before the accident, and I think Dad thought Mom had covered the sex stuff. She did. I know how it works, but I don't know how I'm supposed to feel. Or what to do because I can't quite touch myself to see if . . . you know."

"If it works." It wasn't surprising that Noelle hadn't wanted to talk to her predecessor about this. It could be difficult to talk to anyone about sexuality, but an older man might be a young woman's worst nightmare. Or her dad. "Okay, we can deal with this."

Luckily, she had some practice with this and she knew exactly what to do.

chapter seven

❧

Armie was well aware that everyone in the diner was look-ing at them. "Maybe we should have gone to Guidry's."

When he'd decided to have this conversation over lunch, he'd thought he could use it to get to know her in a low-key setting. He hadn't realized they would be the center of at-tention.

Damn town.

She shook her head and folded her menu, shoving it back in the holder. She'd ordered a salad and taken off the cheese and eggs and then put them back on. Twice. He still wasn't sure which salad would show up, and he wasn't sure Dixie knew, either.

"I can't take that much time," Lila explained. "I actually have a couple of patients this afternoon. Apparently they called while I was in with Noelle. I'm doing physicals and drug testing for an oil company on a couple of new hires. It's very exciting. Is it wrong that I'm kind of hoping I find some-thing horribly wrong with one of them? Not like cancer. That would be terrible. But something curable would be nice."

She was odd. He wished that made her less attractive to him. And then there was the fact that when Noelle had come out of her checkup, she'd had the biggest grin on her face. He glanced over at her. His daughter was sitting at a table with Beth Burns, her best friend. They were leaning in and giggling while waiting for lunch to be delivered.

She'd been tense lately, as though something was bothering her, and Lila seemed to have set her mind at ease.

He hated that he was about to shake Lila's calm. "It's hard when things are slow. It can be difficult to get used to the pace of life around here. I know it was for me when I came back. It still is sometimes. I often pray for tourists to get lost and fly through town so I can at least say I wrote a ticket that day."

She stared at him. "Yes, you do that a lot."

She was cute when she got mad. Not that he wanted to make her really mad. He got the feeling she could be mean. He should get her to forget the ticket. "So I mentioned I went out to visit Carrie Petrie."

"And?" She said the word with the expectation of someone who wasn't sure she would like what he had to say.

"Something's going on with that family. Carrie's hiding something," he admitted. "I don't know what it is, but she was nervous about me being out there. Normally I would chalk it up to nothing more than not enjoying surprise visitors. People who love being social don't typically isolate themselves on an island."

"Did you know her before she got married?"

"Vaguely, and I know what your next question is going to be. No. She wasn't like this when she lived in town. She's quite a bit younger than me. I know what I know from the few times I met her before she married Bobby. I know him, though. I know I was surprised he married a woman so much younger than him."

"Has he been married before?"

"Yes," he replied. "He married a woman he met when he was working a job in Biloxi. He's got some relatives who run a fishing charter business there. He used to spend his summers helping out before he graduated and he and his brother took over the shrimping business from their father. Susie moved here, but it didn't work out. She divorced him after a few years and moved away."

"Why?"

"The divorce decree merely cited irreconcilable differences. That's all I know. There's nothing else official. When I got back from the visit, Roxie and I looked through old records and couldn't find anything beyond a couple of traffic tickets and some complaints about Bobby's boat waking people up at odd hours of the morning, but that's how the family gets around. I know it might sound weird to be on a boat at three in the morning, but shrimp don't catch themselves."

Lila leaned in. "How did she react to you showing up?"

"Her mother-in-law certainly wasn't happy to see us, but that's not unusual. Lorna comes into town as little as possible. I think she sees herself as the queen of that particular kingdom."

"If she's the queen, is Carrie a princess or her servant? They're the only two women out there? You mentioned a brother."

"Yeah. Bobby's got a brother but he's never been married. Carrie didn't handle it well when I asked her if everything was okay. I'm afraid I might have made things worse since she immediately realized you were the reason I was out there."

"There's nothing else you could do," Lila said. "I *was* the reason you were out there. I wish you could have caught her alone, but I understand. She was angry with me?"

"She said she would find another doctor to help her next time."

"And her mother-in-law was there?"

"No, I had Roxie distract Lorna, but I didn't have long," he explained. "Her words didn't match her initial reactions, in my mind. My gut tells me you're right and something is going on out there."

"But you can't do anything without proof." She sat back with a long sigh. "I know how this game is played, Sheriff, and you're the one in a bad position. Carrie is very likely going to take the brunt of it, but we can't force her to talk to us. It'll be worse now. Maybe I should have kept my mouth shut, but I've seen what happens."

He hated that he couldn't give her more. "I'm sorry if I made things tougher for you."

"I hate the thought of her not getting the medical attention she needs, but honestly, even if she did everything right, she could still end up getting hurt." She glanced out at the street, seemingly lost in thought.

He wanted to get her mind on something better, but he had one more thing to get out of the way. Perhaps if he apologized, they could talk about more than all the ways he'd screwed up. "I'm sorry Miranda confronted you like that. I went out with her on a few dates. Nothing serious."

Her eyes were back on him and there was no question she was curious. "Before the accident?"

"Yes." He didn't want to talk about that time, but she should know since she was dealing with his past. Not that he'd really known his past was a problem.

"I got that feeling. She seems to think that once Noelle is out of the house, you'll resume your previous affair."

"It wasn't an affair." He knew he didn't owe her an explanation and she hadn't seemed angry about the incident. He was discovering that not much got to her. Still, he found himself nearly falling over trying to explain. "It was a couple of dates. Three, maybe. It never got past a single goodnight kiss. I knew there wasn't anything between us. It was . . . boredom, maybe. I was restless when I first got here. I never intended for it to become a relationship."

"But you never had that discussion with her? Because she did not sound like a woman who'd been dumped."

"I was going to talk to her," he explained. "It's sad, but I planned that conversation with far more care than I ever planned a date with her. But then Noelle was in the accident and the problem pretty much faded away."

Lila's eyes widened. "I don't understand. Your daughter was in a horrible accident. Where was Miranda?"

"She backed off." He'd been relieved. The last thing he'd

needed was to have to deal with the situation in the middle of all that chaos. She'd stopped calling and given him some space. It was only in the last couple of weeks she'd started being overly friendly again. Now that he really thought about it, he could see Roxie was right. Miranda had been slowly but surely trying to work her way back into his life. "She knew I needed to concentrate on Noelle."

Lila shook her head. "You lucked out, Armie. You understand that if she cared about you she shouldn't have backed off. On the romance stuff, of course. But you needed help. You needed support."

The passion behind her words warmed him. She seemed ready to do battle with a woman she'd barely met. It was sweet and reinforced some of the things he'd learned about her. She was prickly, but not the kind of woman who folded when times got tough.

"I had support," he said, wanting to reach out and hold her hand. "My dad had passed by then, but my mom rallied in those early days after the accident. So much of it's a blur. I had to deal with the fact that my ex-wife died. She didn't have any family left. I made arrangements for the funeral and handled her house in New Orleans. And there was Noelle. My mom was a rock. I swear she lived to see my baby get better. It's weird to think about it now because those were terrible days."

She was the one who reached out, covering his hand with her own. "And they were precious, too."

Damn. He needed a moment because no one else had understood that. It had been days of mourning and pain, days when he wasn't sure his daughter would live. And yet his momma had been right there. She'd gotten out of her bed, thrown aside her own grief, and supported him. He'd been certain he would lose her shortly after he'd lost his dad, but she'd lived months beyond the doctors' estimates, and he knew it was all because she couldn't leave him alone like that. Only when she was sure her son and grandchild were okay had she rested and joined the love of her life.

He thought his mom would like Lila Daley.

"Why did you come home? Was it your mom?" Lila asked. "You were a detective in New Orleans. It can be hard to leave that kind of adrenaline behind for some people."

He could imagine it was hard for her. The trauma department she'd worked in was legendary for the work it did. "Yes. My parents' health declined to the point that they needed assistance. It just so happened that the man who'd held the office for twenty-seven years was retiring. I'd gotten divorced the year before. I didn't want to be apart from Noelle, but I couldn't leave my parents alone, either. Papillon is only a couple of hours away from New Orleans, so I moved back and took the job."

"I can understand that. Not about the parents, though. I never met my father and my mom and I are just beginning to find our way. She wasn't a good mom. She liked drugs more than she loved any of us. But I would do anything for my siblings. Anything."

"I figured you picked this place because you wanted to be close to Lisa." The sisters were awfully different from one another, but it was easy to see they were close.

She shrugged as her hand played with her coffee mug. "Will and Laurel have each other. They also have a big group of friends. I was on the outside of that. It's my fault I am, but it's still true. I thought maybe Lisa would need me. I was probably wrong about that. She's well on her way to finding her own big group of friends and family. I don't do that well."

But she wanted to belong somewhere. It was there in the bittersweet tone of her voice, in the wistful way she looked at the families who walked in the door. "I think you'll find it easier to fit in here than you think. It just takes a little time. Getting that contract from the oil company is a great start. We have a lot of oil rig families who live here. If you take care of the husbands, the wives and kids will follow."

"Well, it's not like the company has a lot of choices unless they want to bring in their own. It's not a big deal. I'm only doing the checkups for their new hires out here, but they pay well." There was the self-satisfied look of a business owner who knew she'd made the right choice. "That contract alone will help us stay afloat. So how are you going to handle the Mirandas of this town?"

They were back to that? "I can talk to her."

It would be terribly uncomfortable, but he didn't like the idea that Miranda had confronted Lila. He definitely didn't like the idea that she could hurt Lila's business.

"Don't worry about it," Lila proclaimed. "Any way you go you lose. If you're too soft with her, she thinks there's still a chance. If you're too hard, you're an asshole. It's the classic rock and a hard place. Do you want to let her know you're not interested?"

"Yes."

"Are you really interested in me or are you restless again, Armie?" The question came out of her mouth like pure temptation.

Maybe he should play it cool, but there was nothing cool about the way he felt. "I'm madly interested in you."

She moved, her torso coming up over the table and her face leaning toward his. "Then make a statement. I suspect this place is a gossip hub. They heard the rumor that you spent the night last night, but some people won't believe you're interested in the new girl until you show them."

So show them. The challenge was clear in her eyes. Gorgeous eyes and lips he could kiss for days. His daughter was here, and apparently Noelle had been his shield against several women showing their interest. Kissing Lila with Noelle in attendance would make a statement.

It was one he wanted to make. He pushed his body up and leaned over, meeting those lips of hers with his own. The kiss was swift, but his body lit up the minute they touched.

It felt good to be alive sometimes. He'd forgotten that in the last few years. His world had revolved around responsibility and sacrifice. It felt damn good to want something for himself.

"Dad, eww. Get a room."

He glanced over and Noelle was grinning his way.

Lila sat back down. "That should do it. I won't be getting Miranda's cookies anytime soon."

Suddenly the idea that everyone was looking at them wasn't so bad. They were looking at him because he had the prettiest lady in the diner. "That's a shame, actually. She makes delicious lemon meltaways."

Her mouth twisted into the most sweetly cranky expression. "They were chocolate chip."

A little gasp drew his attention and Dixie was standing there. She put his burger and fries in front of him. Dixie seemed to get herself under control as she placed Lila's salad on the table. "Well, chocolate chip cookies are nice. Sorry. I couldn't remember if you wanted the eggs and cheddar or not, so I put them on the side. I can take them away if they're offensive."

Lila huffed, an irritated sound. "I know her chocolate chip cookies are an insult. I don't understand why y'all think food can be used as an insult or be offensive." She took the small bowl of grated egg and cheese and dumped it on top of the salad. "And you forgot the bacon I wasn't sure I wanted until now."

Prickly. She was prickly, and he wished that didn't do something for him.

"Then I will get that for you because I believe in customer service and I am polite." She turned on her sneakers and strode away.

He was going to have to deal with that prickliness or she was going to be in trouble. "Just a tip—politeness goes a long way around here."

Her eyes narrowed as she turned back his way. "You're not always polite."

He wasn't. He could be irritable, especially when he was working. "They expect a certain degree of surliness from me."

"I know Remy can be short with people," she pointed out. "I've heard him argue with local vendors, and no one tells him to smile more."

He hadn't actually told her to smile more, but he let that go. "Again, people are used to Remy."

"And I've met several men who were downright rude," she pointed out.

How did he explain this? "You have to work with the public. It's different."

She nodded and he worried he'd fallen into a trap. "Different for a man."

That wasn't at all what he meant. "If there was a new male professional taking over the clinic, I would say the same thing."

But would he? If a new man had come into town, every woman in the county would stop by to either meet his wife and kids or size the new guy up as a potential partner. Had anyone welcomed Lila?

"Sure you would," she said.

He was on a slippery slope, and he wasn't sure how to stop from falling. "I was only saying Dixie is very popular in town. It wouldn't hurt for you to be a little softer around her."

A sound that was something like a laugh but held no amusement huffed from Lila. "Because she was nice to me? She wasn't. And let me tell you, the women might be polite, but they're not nice. There's a difference. They say one thing and mean another. And how am I not polite? I say *please* and *thank you*. I didn't just then, but she was being passive-aggressive. I've been told that's not a good way to be. I should know because I was that way for years, so I know it when I see it. I have zero fucks to give, Armie. They're all gone. Those fucks I was born with should have lasted a lifetime, but I used them all up and the fuck tank is empty."

Everyone was staring again. Noelle's friend looked like she'd never heard those words before. Of course, Noelle was grinning broadly, like this was the best show she'd ever seen. His daughter had a perverse sense of humor.

A hum was going through the diner, and he knew the gossip mill was at work again.

"Could you keep your voice down? Everyone is listening, and some of them are not used to that language."

She glanced over and her face flushed. Maybe she still had a few fucks to give. "I'm sorry. I'll watch my language."

He leaned over, his voice going low. "I was only trying to point out that you're attempting to fit in."

"I'm not trying to fit in," she replied. "I'm trying to build a life. That doesn't mean I have to make friends. I might be too old for this, Armie. I don't think I can be the good girl you apparently need."

"I didn't say that. And you're not old." Things were starting to spiral out of control. He should have put it better, been more smooth. "You're younger than I am."

"I might not be old in years, but I assure you I feel it. If you need a polite woman who says all the right things and lets her rage simmer under the surface, only coming out in the form of insulting baked goods, go back to the Mirandas of this world. I'm not going to be that woman. I think you're restless again and I'm the new girl in town."

He couldn't help but frown her way because now she was getting under his skin, and not in a good way. "You're making assumptions."

"That's been going on a lot between us," she shot back. "We don't know each other. You saw me. You thought I was new and shiny. I'm not. I'm busted up and battered, and that shine is not coming back. You gave me some advice. I'm going to give you some, too. Don't coddle her. She's smart and capable and she's planning on spending her life here because she doesn't think she can hack it anywhere else. You don't mean to, but you're holding her back."

His blood started to heat up. Had she really just said that? "Are you talking about my daughter? You don't know a damn thing about the situation."

He was a good father. Sometimes it was the only thing he had to hold on to. He'd sacrificed for Noelle, and now some woman he barely knew was criticizing him?

Lila's expression didn't change at all. It was the blank face of a professional stating her opinion. "I know she should be more mobile than she is. I studied her scans. When was the last time she had a physical therapist who got her on her feet?"

He did not have to take this. "That is none of your business."

"I'm her primary care provider. I assure you this *is* my business. It's exactly what you pay me for."

There was an easy solution to that problem. He'd been blinded by her beauty, her drive. She was right. He'd seen her as something different and thought different had to mean good. "Maybe I should pay someone else if you're going to be this nosy."

She sat back and her energy seemed to deflate. "All right, then. I'm going to take this to go, and I don't think Friday is a good idea."

"Maybe it's not." Maybe she was too prickly even for him. "If you can't take good advice, then you won't last long here."

She didn't reply, merely grabbed her purse and pulled out her wallet. "I've lost my appetite. This should take care of my part of the bill. Good afternoon, Sheriff."

She pushed out of the booth and dropped a ten on the table.

How had this gone so wrong? One minute he'd felt close to her and now it was like a damn wall had come up. He wasn't sure he wanted it to come down. But he also wasn't sure he didn't. They'd both said some things they probably shouldn't have said. "Hey, let's take a breath."

She didn't look back as she headed for the door.

She was not going to cry. She wasn't. The tears were right there, pulsing behind her eyes, threatening to rob her of her vision and her dignity. But she wasn't about to shed them. Certainly not in front of this crowd. That's probably exactly what they wanted.

"Hey, are you okay?" Noelle was staring up at her.

Damn it. She shouldn't have said anything. She didn't

think Noelle could have heard the advice she'd given her father. She'd kept her voice low, but honestly, she'd also meant it. Not that she should have an opinion at this point. It hadn't been fair to throw that on him, but she couldn't take it back now. She plastered a smile on her face. The other girl sitting with Noelle stared at her like she expected her to grow horns at any moment.

"Of course," Lila replied. "I have to get back to the clinic. That's all. I hope everything works out for you."

She was going to have to hope since her father likely wouldn't bring her back to the clinic again. Of course, once her father found out she'd helped his daughter with her masturbation techniques, showing her how to order a vibrator over the Internet on her phone, the relationship probably would have gone to hell anyway. Like all her relationships had.

She was too fussy. Too picky. Too intimidating. Too uptight.

Too much.

It wasn't anything she hadn't heard before.

So why did it hurt so damn much coming from him? It was an actual ache in her gut. She should have stuck to her plan. Work. Sleep. Visit with her sister. Repeat.

Except she didn't have much work to do. She didn't sleep well at all. And her sister didn't have a ton of time for her.

When had she become this needy, clingy thing?

"Whatever he said, he didn't mean it," Noelle offered. "He's not good with women. Or people at all, really."

She disagreed. He was excellent with everyone, and he'd meant every word he'd said. "Everything's fine. Like I said, I have to get back to work."

"I guess you changed your mind about lunch." Dixie was staring at her with a frown. "You don't want the bacon anymore? You know we had to make it. We didn't simply have it sitting around in case someone wanted it."

She didn't want any of this. Somehow she'd thought she would come down here and everything would fall into place. It was a sleepy town, and she'd made the mistake of thinking it would be different here. In the city, most of the time people ignored her. No matter how good she was at her job, there was always someone who could take her job. She'd thought she would have a place here. She hadn't expected to make a ton of friends, but she certainly hadn't thought people would actively hate her.

What the hell had she done? She'd given up a great job, awesome salary, pretty apartment, and for what? Everything she had was sunk into a clinic no one wanted to come to and a house that was full of a dead man's junk. Now she apparently had a dog to take care of, and she would have to avoid the hot sheriff at all costs.

Not that she would be here long if the town turned on her.

"I left the cash on the table. I'll brown bag it from now on."

Dixie sighed and put a hand on her hip. "Food's not good enough for you?"

Yeah, she'd gotten a lot of that. "Given the fact that I grew up eating whatever my brother could scrounge from a dumpster half the time, I'm absolutely certain that your food is delicious. You seem to think I'm some almighty, powerful city girl. Yeah, I grew up in a city, but I assure you there were days in my childhood when I would have given anything to have what you have here because most of you had parents who loved you, had someone besides your teenage brother who could provide for you. I had a mom who was in prison more often than not. Your food is fine. What I can't take is the judgement that goes along with it. I'll avoid that from now on."

"Oh, hon," Dixie began, her eyes going oddly soft.

But she was done for the day.

"Lila," a deep voice called out behind her.

She ignored him and the stares of every single person in the dining room who had heard her describe her crappy childhood. That would go a long way to making them embrace her. They would likely think since her mom had been an addict that she was on drugs, too. And she'd outed her sister. God, she had no idea what her sister had said about their childhood. Remy knew, but he had a mom, sister, and brother who Lisa might not have shared her history with.

She strode toward the door and then stopped because there was the horrible sound of tires screeching, and then the ground beneath her shook as a crashing sound hit her ears. The entire café went still, trying to figure out what was going on, but Lila knew.

Car accident. She took off, pushing through the double doors.

"Lila!"

She didn't stop, couldn't stop. This was what she did.

She didn't have far to go. A pickup truck had smacked against the building that housed Dixie's café. It looked like it had struck two cars in the parking lot before it had come to rest against the solidly built brick building. That was fortunate because the other cars had slowed the truck down. What was unfortunate was the man on the ground who had apparently also slowed the truck.

She dropped to her knees because the man's leg was broken and he was losing blood. A lot of blood. It stained the street. She looked down at him and emerald eyes looked up.

"I can't feel it." He was dressed in a dapper-looking suit. His reddish-gold hair had likely been slicked back to perfection once, but now it hung around his face. "I should be able to feel it."

His foot wasn't where it should be. It was at an odd angle. "You have a compound fracture, but what I'm worried about is the blood loss. I need you to stay calm while I find something to use as a tourniquet."

"We can use my belt." Armie was behind her, pulling his leather belt from the loops on his khakis.

No matter what had happened between them in the diner, she was happy he was here. He was calm, his expression showing nothing but stable professionalism.

"Did you call it in?" She took the belt and wished she had her kit. She carried it with her in her car, but they'd walked the block to the café. "And do you have a knife on you?"

"Roxie's on her way and so is the ambulance, but it could be a while. We have one ambulance and it serves the whole parish. They're fifteen minutes out."

Fifteen minutes out. Another thirty to the hospital, potentially. It struck her hard how vulnerable they were. She was the only thing standing between this man and potential death, because he wouldn't last fifteen minutes without care.

"Rene, it's going to be okay." Armie opened the Swiss Army knife he'd pulled from his pocket.

"I'm not even sure what happened." The man named Rene winced as she neatly sliced through his slacks.

"Keep the ambulance coming, but I think we need to call in a chopper." That was definitely a compound fracture, and it was going to require surgery and probably a metal rod. This man was looking at automatic pat-downs whenever he flew from now on. But she was going to ensure he lived so he could endure all the joys of the TSA. If she could stop the bleeding. Unfortunately, she was worried it was his femoral artery. "I need something to stanch the bleeding while I'm putting the tourniquet on."

Armie was on his phone again, arranging for the Life Flight. She might be going into overkill, but they were isolated and moments would matter.

"These are clean." Dixie was pale but she had a stack of towels in her hand. "I can do it. Do I put it over the wound?"

Lila grabbed a couple of the towels. It wasn't gauze but it was all she had. She found the bleeder and eased the towel on. She immediately needed a new one, taking a couple from Dixie and putting them on top. "Come down here and apply pressure. Don't let up. You have to put some strength behind it."

Armie had moved away, going to check on the vehicle. "Lila, it's Janice Herbert, her daughter Hallie, and the baby. The adults are unconscious, but I think something's wrong with the baby."

Shit.

There was a crowd around her, everyone coming out of

the buildings that formed the small square of downtown Papillon. They were watching on, some of the women crying. But she needed help.

It came in the form of her nurse. Mabel was running like a damn track star as she rounded the building, Lila's kit in her hand. She was in her scrubs and Peanut was chasing after her.

"I've got this." Mabel dropped to her knees. "I'll put the tourniquet on. You go deal with the baby."

Out of the corner of her eye, she saw Noelle. Her face was flushed and she appeared out of breath.

Smart girl. She'd gotten Mabel and now they had a chance.

"We're going to need water and maybe more towels. Someone get them." It was often best in an emergency to give people something to do. "And clear a way for the ambulance."

Comfortable that Mabel knew what she was doing, Lila raced to the truck. Her slacks were coated in blood, but she couldn't think about that right now. Armie had the baby in his hands. She was running on pure adrenaline, a drug she knew well. It had fueled her many a crazy night in the ER. Adrenaline made her stronger, faster, more able to focus. It took her to that place where she could do what she needed to do.

The baby was turning blue. There was no blood on the child. "Was she restrained properly?"

"What? Momma?" Hallie was coming to, but Lila didn't have time to update her.

"Yes, I had to get her out of the car seat," Armie replied to her question.

She held her hands out to Armie, glancing into the car. Armie immediately went to Hallie, who was starting to understand that something had gone terribly wrong.

"Gracie!" Hallie was fighting to get out of her seat belt. "Where's my baby?"

She left Armie to deal with Hallie. She needed to figure out why Gracie wasn't breathing. There was a car seat where it should be and a diaper bag beside it. The scent of burnt chemicals filled the air, letting her know without seeing it that the airbags had deployed. Her brain quickly processed the scene, the visuals clicking into place. Baby girl's hands were covered in doughy goo. It smelled like vanilla. Teething biscuit. She'd been gnawing on a teething biscuit and the accident had caused a chunk to lodge in her throat.

The baby's eyes were open, desperation clear in those blue orbs. She couldn't breathe, couldn't cry.

Lila flipped the baby over, cradling the one-year-old head in her hand. She put her foot on the running board and rested her arm along with the baby on her thigh. The baby's delicate jaw was cradled between her thumb and forefinger.

She was ready.

One. Two. Three. Four. Five.

Five firm blows from the heel of her right hand between the baby girl's shoulder blades.

There was a coughing sound as the chunk of cookie hit the back seat. Then the baby wailed.

"Gracie?" Hallie was standing there, holding her arms out.

Lila turned over the baby. "What happened?"

Hallie clutched her daughter. "Momma was driving along and then she went pale and said her arm hurt, and then I swear we were going too fast and she wasn't responding. I tried to take the wheel but I think we hit someone. Oh my god. Is that Rene?"

Lila made it to the driver's side of the car. Hallie's mother was slumped over the airbag, which covered the steering wheel. She was wearing a seat belt and the airbag had deployed properly. Given what Hallie had said, she had to think either cardiac arrest or stroke. No pulse. She had to take the chance and get Mrs. Herbert on the ground, where she could start CPR.

"Armie, help me get her out of here. She's in full arrest. I don't know how long she's been down."

Armie didn't hesitate. He unbuckled the belt and eased Mrs. Herbert to the pavement.

"Get the AED from my kit." She didn't explain to him that she was talking about the automated external defibrillator that would be in the kit Mabel had brought with her. Armie had enough training to back her up and she was so grateful. Lila fell to her knees, found the xiphoid process, interlocked her hands, and started CPR, the rhythm ingrained from years of work. *One. Two. Three. Four. Five.* She kept going until she'd counted to thirty.

Lean over and breathe. Once. Twice. Listen for breath sounds.

Back to compressions.

One. Two. Three. Four. Five . . .

Around her, somewhere in the background, she knew people were crying and the world was moving, but she was caught in this moment. The world slid away and there was only her work. In this place, she was strong. In this place, there was no fear, no hesitation. There was life and death and a battle she knew well.

Armie moved in beside her. "I've turned it on."

Thirty.

She tore open Mrs. Herbert's shirt. Her skin was dry so Lila properly placed the electrodes as the machine began to do its work.

"Everyone stand back." Her patient needed the shock the AED would administer. Lila pressed down on the button.

Mrs. Herbert's body convulsed as her heart started again. Her eyes came open, shock plain in them. She was shaky, but Lila felt her heartbeat pulsing under her fingers.

"Gracie? What happened to the baby? My babies?" She croaked the words out.

"They're fine. Stay down. The ambulance is on the way. I need to check on Rene. Armie, keep her comfortable and find a way to elevate her feet." She stood, positive that Armie would do the job and the AED would keep working if she needed it to.

The deputy had shown up and she was working crowd control.

"Deputy, I need an ETA on that ambulance." She was

going to have to make a decision on who to send in the ambulance and who got the helicopter.

Mabel glanced her way. "Lila, I'm worried he's going to have this tourniquet on his leg for more than an hour if we send Janice in the ambulance and have to wait for it to come back."

"I've got a chopper coming, but I don't know if it can take both of them. I don't know how big it is." He would lose the leg. She was going to have to make a decision.

"Send her," the man Armie had called Rene said. His skin had paled considerably. "I can wait."

She wasn't making that choice. Not when she could make a play to save everyone. "Deputy! We're going to need to get Mrs. Herbert to the clinic."

"The chopper is on its way. ETA is ten minutes," Armie shouted. "There's a landing pad on top of the clinic for just this purpose. The ambulance will be here in five. Who's going where?"

She wasn't about to move Rene more than she had to. And Mrs. Herbert could go into arrest again at any moment. She needed to get to a cath lab as quickly as possible. "I need you to carry Mrs. Herbert to the clinic. Rene is going in the ambulance. The bleeding is controlled for now."

Armie nodded as the sweet sounds of sirens hit her ears.

"I'm fine." Janice Herbert was trying to get up on her own.

Damn stubborn woman. "You had a cardiac arrest. You're still hooked up to a defibrillator and you and I will have a serious problem if you unhook it. You will go to the hospital."

"I want to see the real doc," Janice said.

Hallie had gotten Gracie calm again. The baby clung to her momma. Momma, however, was obviously taking charge. "You will do whatever Ms. Daley tells you to do, Mother. You will let the sheriff carry you to the clinic. You will take whatever drugs they give you, and you will get in that damn helicopter because that woman saved your life.

She saved your granddaughter's life. So shut the hell up and do what she says."

Mrs. Herbert's eyes went wide, but she allowed Armie to pick her up.

The ambulance pulled through and two EMTs got out, quickly taking over for Mabel.

"We got this, Doc," the big man said.

His female partner was already dealing with Rene's injury. "He's stable. He would have bled out if they hadn't gotten to him quickly. I hear you've got a cardiac patient. Do we need to look at her? We can fit him on the bench and her on the stretcher."

She shook her head. "I have a chopper coming for her. She needs a cath lab ASAP."

The EMT gave her a thumbs-up. "You did good work here."

Mabel stood up. They were both covered in blood, but they still had work to do.

She needed to get Mrs. Herbert safely on that chopper and then check out her daughter and granddaughter.

Her day wasn't close to being done.

chapter eight

❧

Hours later, Armie sat in the clinic waiting room, a vision of a blood-soaked Lila Daley single-handedly taking chaos and turning it into survival imprinted on his brain.

They'd been on the knife's edge today. One wrong move and they would have lost Rene or Janice or that precious baby.

She'd been the difference. If she hadn't been there, the day would have turned out very differently.

"What are you doing here?" Lila asked as she walked in. "Of course. You want an update. The good news is Rene came through his surgery with flying colors. He didn't need the rod I thought he might. He was lucky. He'll be in a cast for a few weeks and he'll be weak, but I hear he's already making plans to come home. As for Janice, she had an eighty-eight-percent blockage. They put a stent in and she's resting comfortably now. She's got some lifestyle modifications she'll have to make, though." Lila closed her office door behind her. She'd put on new clothes, taken a shower in the back, and now she looked perfectly clean, but he remembered what she'd looked like when she'd taken control.

She'd looked like a warrior, like a freaking Valkyrie.

He'd been wrong to tell her to fit in.

"I came to drive you home."

There was a weary look in her eyes. "I have a car here."

"Lila, you went through a lot today. Let me drive you home. Or take you to your sister's. I don't think you should be alone tonight."

She seemed to think about that for a moment. "Lisa and Remy are in New Orleans for the weekend. I'm fine. It was a job, and one I've done a hundred times."

It wasn't her job to do that kind of work in the field. He knew how hard it could be. He'd been emotional out there, shocked at how close his friends had come to losing everything. She was certainly feeling the consequences of all the pressure she'd felt today. She'd done a phenomenal job of shoving it aside and doing the job, but she would crash.

"Not when you were the only one responsible, you haven't. When you took over the clinic you took responsibility for this town, and you take that seriously. Even when the town let you down."

"No one let me down. They just don't like me. They don't have to like me."

Her words sounded hollow, and he wondered how much the day had cost her. She'd been there when the helicopter had come to take Janice to the hospital. She'd updated the medics on the patient's condition and the way she'd stabilized Janice. Then she'd rechecked the baby, made sure Hallie was all right, and only then had she done a thing to take care of herself. Only after Hallie's cousin had shown up to drive them to the hospital had she gone to take her shower and calm down.

And he knew she'd needed to calm down because despite her demeanor, she had to be a rolling wave of emotion. Once the adrenaline was gone, the trauma of the day would have been waiting for her. He knew.

Yet from what he understood, while he and Roxie and the new guys had been dealing with the fallout of the accident, she'd spent the rest of the afternoon on her job. She'd done two complete physicals with blood draws and all the paperwork, kept in touch with the hospital, and stitched up a tourist who had cut his hand fishing.

She'd sent Mabel home and finished out the last hour of her shift alone.

She needed someone to take care of her. He damn straight wanted to be the one to do it.

"I think people will have a different view of you after today. I know I do. Lila, I'm sorry about what I said. You be you because we need you. I think *I* might need you."

She sniffled but shook her head. "No. I can't do this right now."

There was a knock on the glass doors. Armie sighed and looked back. Dixie stood outside the clinic, two bags in her hand. He did not need another smackdown between those two, and he wasn't about to let anyone argue with Lila tonight. Tomorrow he would make his position clear to the rest of the town, but he could start here.

He shook his head. "Not now, Dixie. She's going home."

Lila waved her key card over the reader, completely ignoring his words. The doors slid open. "What do you need?"

Dixie strode in and set her bags on the counter. "I didn't know what you would want for dinner. I do know Bill's kitchen is a wretched mess. Miranda never should have sold you that place. Here's the deal. I brought Doc his lunch every day, no charge. It was my pleasure to help out a man who served the community even long after he was good at serving us. *You* are going to be spectacular at serving us, Doc Daley."

Lila shook her head. "I'm not a doctor."

Dixie waved that fact off. "Deal with it. We don't understand the whole nurse practitioning thing. I might have been too sensitive earlier. I apologize." She shook off the emotion he'd seen in her eyes and she was back to professional, practical Dixie. "Like I said, I didn't know what you would want so there's a big salad. I put all the fixin's on the side. There's also some meatloaf, green beans, corn, a big container of red beans and rice, and both bread pudding and chocolate pie."

Lila looked at the big bags and her lips curled up slightly. "Trying to fatten me up?"

Dixie winked her way. "You need it, girl."

"I'm sorry, too," Lila said, holding her hand out to the café owner. "I might not have been sensitive enough."

Dixie shook her hand before she turned and started for the door. "All is forgiven, then. I'll be back tomorrow with a salad and the soup of the day. If you want to change your lunch order, call one of my girls before noon and let us know. Have a nice night, Doc."

Lila frowned, stepping in front of the bags and looking inside. "Do you think she'll come back and take them away? That's what Miranda did. I didn't care that they were her second-best cookies or that she made them to insult me. I liked that they were food I didn't have to cook myself."

Oh, it was bad. The words were coming out of her mouth, but there was absolutely not a hint of emotion behind them.

She stopped and looked around, her eyes flaring. "Where's Peanut?"

He'd already settled Peanut for the night. She didn't need to worry about the dog. She needed all the attention on her. "Noelle has him. Mabel let me take him home when I dropped Noelle and her friend there. They'll take care of him. I gave them instructions on how much food he can have. I know he's got to go slow. Beth is spending the night. He's got two dog-loving teens to lavish him with affection. And Dixie's not going to take your food. I think you made a believer of her. I know you made one of me. Let me take you home, Lila. Let me take care of you. I promise I won't push you. I'll drive you home, make sure you get fed, and I'll sleep on the couch again because you need rest. You had a long, stressful day, and tell me that's not exactly the time when you dream about it. Tell me you won't sleep better in a brand-new place knowing someone is watching your back."

She was still for a moment. "Just for tonight."

Not if he had a say, but they were doing things her way. "Just for tonight."

She started to reach for the bags, but he moved in quickly. "I've got it."

She nodded and went to get her purse. She was quiet as he led her to his SUV, quiet as he drove her past the parking lot where the accident had happened, quiet as he turned onto her street.

She waited as he killed the engine. He was surprised she was still in the car when he got around to her door, but she was staring out the front and he knew she wasn't seeing the yard or the night. She was somewhere else, and it was his job to bring her back to the present with him.

He opened the passenger-side door and held out his hand. "Come on, sweetheart. Let's get you inside. We'll feed you, get you a glass of wine or two, another shower, and put you in bed."

"Okay."

She was an automaton, going through the motions. She let him take her hand but dropped it the minute her feet hit the ground.

"Maybe we should have eaten at the clinic." She glanced back down the road that they'd just driven. "I have a microwave in the back."

"I fixed yours." He hoped what he told her next didn't make her mad. "I might know where Bill kept his spare key and I might have gone into your house after we finished up at the scene and I might have fixed your microwave and the stove and that drip in the bathroom sink. I know I shouldn't have but I had to do something. I couldn't go home. I needed something to do with my hands."

"You fixed my microwave?"

"It needed some rewiring. My dad was an electrician. He worked on the oil rigs. I know a little. It works, though it's ancient. It will definitely warm up those red beans and rice." He got her to the door and used the key he'd taken earlier to open it. "I also stocked your fridge with the important stuff. Wine. Beer. There's a bottle of bourbon in your pantry. That's for me."

She sighed. "I love bourbon. That's mine. You can have the wine. Wait. I think I want the wine, too."

She could have anything she wanted.

"I'm going to get the bags from Dixie's. You go in and sit down. I'll take care of everything." He jogged back to the SUV and grabbed the bags.

He'd hurt her. She'd said some things, too, but he could handle it. He understood her, or at least he thought he did. When she felt hurt, she punched back. He could do that, too. He'd certainly done it before himself. Hell, he'd deserved it. He'd basically told her she needed to fucking smile more.

He locked the car door and ran up the steps. He needed to fix those, too. In the few days she'd been in the house, she'd started to clear out a lot of the clutter. He could move easily through the front hall.

The sound of Billie Holiday's "Fine and Mellow" pulsed through the house. She'd obviously found Bill's old-school stereo. It was really old school since Bill had bought it back in the seventies and had original vinyl from long before then.

It would be good to listen to some old jazz and relax with the bourbon. He would make sure she slept tonight.

"Do you want the salad?" He thought she needed something more, but he wasn't going to argue with her. Not tonight. In the morning he would get up and make her bacon and eggs and gently prod her to eat. "Or I can heat up the meatloaf or the rice and beans."

She stood and turned. "I would rather you kissed me."

He dropped the bags and moved to her because that was definitely something he could do.

She knew she should go to bed. Without him. She knew she was making a mistake, but after the day she'd had she needed hands on her. His hands. One night. That was all she would let herself have.

But why? If it went well why couldn't she continue to have him in her bed? What was the problem?

She shook off her inner questions. This wasn't the time to make decisions. It was the time to fill a need, and he was the only man she'd wanted in years.

The day had been so long.

There had been the thrill of the contract with the oil company. Not that it would be a ton of money, but it meant patients. And then the confrontation with Miranda, the confrontation with Dixie, the one with Armie. So much conflict.

She hadn't thought about it at the time but if she'd been off even a little, someone would have died today. It had all been on her. It would always be on her.

It was only now when the world had finally slowed down that it all hit her. She could cry. She could let out all the tension by screaming until her throat was sore. She could pound on something.

Or she could wrap herself around him, let him fill her up until she screamed for another reason. She could try to finally understand what it meant to need a man.

She'd said it. She'd said she wanted him to kiss her. There was no taking it back because he was already invading her space.

It played through her head that she wasn't this girl. She didn't fall into bed with a man she'd known for so little time. A few days, and they'd spent a good portion of those days fighting.

She didn't want to fight him tonight. She'd made a half-hearted attempt when she'd told him she could drive herself, but she'd caved because she didn't want to be alone. Maybe if her sister had been in town . . .

Her sister didn't make her heart start to thud in her chest, her whole body going electric. He was gorgeous. Armie was a massive wall of muscle who managed to make her feel petite and feminine when she often didn't. He made her think about her body as something more than a tool to use to work.

She'd talked to Noelle about her body today, pretending like she knew what she was saying. She knew all the technical terms, all the functions, but she'd ignored her own needs for so long she'd forgotten how good it felt to want someone.

Or maybe she'd simply never wanted anyone the way she wanted Armie LaVigne.

"I know I should wait, but I can't," he said, getting into her space. His hands came out, cupping her cheeks.

The minute he touched her, the world seemed like a softer place. She could breathe again. "I don't want to wait. I need this tonight."

"I know you need this and I'm going to give you everything I have," he said, hovering over her lips. "But I want you to need me. Only me."

She thought she did, but she couldn't tell him that. After their fight, she still felt vulnerable. "This is only for tonight. I still don't think this can work."

He lowered his lips to hers and held her still for a kiss that sent shock waves through her. When he came up for air, he brushed his nose against hers in the sweetest gesture of affection. "I'm going to prove to you it can. I was wrong today. I was a dumbass guy who was holding you to a different standard than I'd ever want myself held to. This is a small town, and not fitting in can be rough for a woman, but there's no reason for you to not be able to be you. You are amazing. If they can't handle it then they can fuck themselves."

Sweet words, but she couldn't believe them. He was a part of this community, an important part. His job depended on votes, and if the last few days were any kind of an indication, she would cost him. But not tonight. Hell, everyone thought they'd already spent the night together. She'd already done some of the time. It was time to do the crime.

She let her hands drift up to find the silk of his hair as

he took her mouth again, drugging her with pure desire. His lips were soft but oh, the rest of that man was hard. She ran her hands from his hair to the corded muscles of his neck and shoulders. He'd been dependable in the field, never once questioning her.

She'd been able to work because she'd known he would back her up. If only he could do it in real life. He was still in shock. He would wake up in a few days and realize how difficult she was. He would go back to the Mirandas of the world.

But for tonight he was hers, and she was going to revel in the freedom to touch and explore this magnificent man.

His hands went to her hips, dragging her against him. She let her whole body go soft, ceding all control to him. She didn't want to think, didn't want to be in charge. Tonight she wanted him to take the lead so all she had to think about was how her body responded to him.

"I wanted to kiss you the first time I saw you. Lust at first sight," he whispered against her lips.

Maybe that was why she'd really run. She'd seen his interest, his raw sexuality, and hadn't understood it. She hadn't wanted that shot of pure desire that had gone through her. Sex had been something she planned, and yes, she'd enjoyed it, but more for the intimacy than the actual act. Sex had been something she'd thought was normal and natural, and therefore she should schedule it into her life.

Then she'd realized she wasn't in control of anything at all, that control was something that could be stripped from her at any moment, and she hadn't wanted intimacy.

"Don't leave me. I know you get lost in that head of yours, but I want you here with me tonight. Stay with me." His hand fisted in her hair, drawing it out of the loose bun she'd put it in and forcing her to look into his eyes. "Let it all go. There's nothing but the here and now. You and me. Shut everything else out."

The words came from his mouth in a low, sexy rumble. *Let go.* She needed to let go and focus on him. Focus on how warm he was, how vital and alive he could make her feel.

He kissed her again, his tongue surging inside and sliding against hers in a silky dance. This was all that mattered, this moment and this man.

His lips moved across her cheek, making their way along her jawline and down to lave affection on her neck and shoulders. "I can't think of anything but you. Since you drove into this town, you've invaded my every thought, every dream. All I've wanted to do is this—touch you, taste you, feel you."

He pulled her close and she could feel the heat of his body, the thick hard length of his erection pressed against her. She wasn't the only one who wanted this desperately. That erection was a revelation. He wanted her and badly . . . maybe as badly as she wanted him.

When his hands made it to the hem of her shirt, she allowed him to drag it over her head, tossing it away. Cool air hit her skin and she hadn't realized how warm the room had gotten. She let her fingers go to the buttons of his khaki shirt, shaking as she started to undress him. She couldn't quite get them undone.

He reached for her hands, putting them between both of his, and he brought them to his lips. "Let me."

He dropped her hands and reached back, tugging his shirt and the T-shirt under it over his head and tossing them to the side. His chest was everything she'd dreamed of, masculine and warm, muscled, and yet the skin itself was soft. She knew because the minute he'd revealed his chest, she'd put her hands on it, unable to hold back. She wanted to explore him, to memorize every inch of his body.

His hands moved to her back and he proved he did not have the same problem she was having. With a single twist her bra came undone and she let it slip to the floor. Her nipples tightened as he stared down at her, his eyes on her breasts.

"You are so beautiful."

She never felt that way. She was the woman who wanted to turn the lights off, but the look in his eyes told her he wasn't lying. He thought she was lovely, and in that moment, she felt that way, too.

He gently turned her, drawing her back against his chest. His hands eased up to cup her breasts. She could feel how hard he was, but the man seemed determined to take his time.

"We should go to bed," she suggested.

"Not yet. Not until you understand how much I want you, how much I want to give you. I want to play with you, explore you. Maybe when I've kissed every inch of this body I'll take you to bed."

He was going to kill her. "I'm ready right now, Armie."

"But I'm not." He nipped her earlobe, sending a shock of lust straight through her.

She wiggled against him, against that part of him that seemed perfectly ready. "I think you are."

He was priming her in a way she'd never felt before. Her whole body had gone warm and soft and ready for him.

And he was being frustrating. His big hands held her still as he ran his tongue along her ear. A damn ear shouldn't be an erogenous zone, but she shivered at every caress. His hands molded her breasts as he kissed her neck and shoulders again.

"Let go, Lila. Let me take care of you."

Why was it hard to let him take control? He obviously knew more about this than she did, but it was right on the tip of her tongue to argue with him.

What would it feel like to give over to another person? To trust someone so much she could let her mind flow, knowing he would ground her, not let her get too far from herself? "I want to."

His hand started to trail down to the waistband of her scrubs. "Then do it. Stop thinking. Let go. Tomorrow you can go back to work and you'll kick the day's ass, but tonight, you're all mine."

All his. His to protect and take care of. His to pleasure and lavish with affection.

She relaxed, her decision made.

His hand slid inside the waistband of her scrubs, inching closer and closer, but she wasn't going to hurry him along. He wanted to indulge in her, and she wasn't about to stop him. She would be patient with him and it would pay off in the end.

"Trust me." Every word out of his mouth was a silky seduction.

She did. At least in this she did. She could trust him with her body. Her heart? She wasn't sure about that, but she abandoned the thought for the evening. This was what she'd needed all day.

"How long has it been for you?" He whispered the question as the song changed. The sultry sounds of jazz formed a soundtrack of pure seduction.

"A long time. Over a year."

He chuckled and she was surprised how intimate the moment was. Not because his fingers were teasing under her panties, but that she could feel him laugh, the sound rumbling over her sensitized skin. "I've got you beat. It's been two years for me. Two years and a few days, so I'm going to make you come for me a couple of times before I get my turn. I'm not sure how long I'll last. I want you so much and I'm out of practice."

She didn't understand. Yes, his daughter had needed him, but he could have found a lover. He was beautiful and it wouldn't have been hard to find a partner, even one who would accept nothing more than quick sex from him. "Why? The women of this town obviously adore you."

"I didn't want them. I'm too old for meaningless sex. I need more. I don't want a woman who follows me. I want a woman who kicks my ass when I need it, one who can be a partner in every sense of the word. I want her to stand by me, but I want to stand by her, too."

"I can't tonight." She couldn't think about the future. She definitely didn't want to think about the past.

"No pressure. Well, maybe a little pressure." His finger found her clitoris and pressed down, sending sparks through her. "I know what you're thinking. You think we can go back to where we were in the morning. Go back to our corners, but I'm done fighting. You win. I won't even stop you the next time you speed like a race car driver."

"I wouldn't have been speeding if it hadn't been for that alligator. It's not . . ." She'd been ready to point out that it wasn't normal for an alligator to sit in the middle of the road, but his finger made a circle around her clit and she suddenly couldn't breathe.

"I'll let you fly around this town, and everyone will know how sweet I am on you. They'll be afraid of you because the sheriff won't do a damn thing to stop his lady from doing anything she likes. *Tu tiens mon coeur entre tes mains.*"

She could barely stay on her feet. And those words sounded entirely sexy, and she didn't understand them at all. She could speak a little Spanish, but she was pretty sure she knew what language he was whispering in. "You speak French?"

The words came out on a gasp because her whole body was melting under his clever hands. She could feel the orgasm building and they weren't even naked yet.

"My mom-mom didn't speak a lick of English. She was pure Cajun. She used to live out on the islands. Disappointed her family when she moved to the big city, and yes, they meant Papillon. If I wanted to talk to that old woman, I had to learn her language." He'd found a perfect rhythm. *"J'ai besoin d'apprendre ton langue."*

She leaned back against him, letting him control her body and her balance. "Armand . . . Armie . . ."

"That's right," he cajoled. "Let it go. Let me take you away."

He pressed down and she went flying over the edge. The world fell away and there was only him, the feel of him, his masculine scent. He filled her senses, surrounded her entirely.

For the first time she could remember, she utterly surrendered.

chapter nine

Armie held her up, still rubbing that sweet button of hers. His dick was dying, but he wasn't going to give in. He wanted her to understand that there was no going back in the morning. He'd meant what he said.

She held his heart in her hand. Maybe it was far too soon to think that way, but he didn't care. Today had proven to him that she was it. Full stop. No moving on from this one. She was the one he'd waited for all his life, the woman who could handle him. Lila wouldn't wither when times got tough. She wouldn't beg him to find a safer job. He might have to beg *her* to play it safe from time to time.

And he meant the other thing he'd said to her in French. He would learn her language. It was different for a woman like her. He couldn't win her over with presents or taking her out. She would need something more to teach her how serious he was. She would need patience. She would need to be able to poke and prod at him without losing him. She'd been hurt and she would need time to trust him.

Tonight, he intended to make a start. If she could trust him physically, at least they were on their way.

He adored how she'd gone soft against him, her whole body dependent on his strength. He picked her up, her slight weight no problem for him at all. He could carry her around all day, not letting her feet hit the ground until her unique skills were needed.

Her eyes fluttered open and she looked softer than she normally did. This was a look only he'd seen. He knew it instinctively. This was a side of Lila she wouldn't share with anyone but a lover.

"Are you taking me to bed now?" And her voice was soft, too.

He loved how no-nonsense she could be, but damn that dreamy voice hit him square in the gut because he'd been the one to get her here. He'd been the one to chase that haunted look from her eyes and replace it with the satisfaction he saw there now.

"Oh, yes, *chère.*" Even he could hear how deep his natural accent had gotten. "But don't think you're going to get everything you want. Not yet. Not until I've had my fill."

"You're an obnoxious man." But the words were said with a sigh that let him know she didn't mind his obnoxiousness.

She might tomorrow when she realized he wasn't going to be put back in the neat and tidy box she'd placed him in. But that was a problem for another day. The good news was he would sleep in her bed tonight. He would wake up next to her and if all went right, she would find herself in his bed tomorrow night.

He would greatly prefer his house since he could easily carry her through his hallways.

"Sorry," she said as he tried to get around a stack of plastic containers. "I think those are his collectible action figures. They're toys still in their boxes."

"You need to have the world's largest garage sale," he muttered. They were definitely going back to his place tomorrow night.

The good news was the bedroom was neat and tidy. She'd replaced the LSU blankets and pillows with pretty, feminine bedding. Like the woman herself, the décor in the bedroom was lovely and restrained.

He laid her out on the bed and eased off her sneakers and socks. He was going to take his time, lavish every inch of her with his appreciation. He brought her foot to his lips and gently kissed the arch. He should be in a frenzy to have her, but he couldn't give in to that side of his nature. Tonight she needed to be worshipped for the goddess she was, to understand that she was worthy and should expect his every tender care.

"You're going to drive me crazy." She looked up at him but made no move to push him along.

"I'm planning on making you so crazy you sleep like a baby tonight." And crazy enough to stay with him, but he couldn't say that yet.

"I don't feel tired anymore."

He gave her other foot the same treatment, taking it between his hands and rubbing strongly before kissing every toe. He kneaded the arch of her foot and was rewarded with a long groan.

Billie Holiday floated through the ramshackle house, lending an air of dreamy seduction. Time seemed to slow down, cocooning the two of them. He didn't think about anything but this woman. She was his to please, and that was all that mattered.

He pulled at her scrub pants, dragging them down her body and tossing them away. She was left in nothing but a pair of white cotton underwear that was already damp from the orgasm he'd given her. They could go, too. He pulled the underwear from her and she was naked and laid out for his delectation.

The sweet scent of her arousal filled the air. He breathed her in, dropping to his knees in front of her. He took her ankles in his hands and rubbed upward, easing the tension from her calves. He let his hands and his mouth work her flesh, strong caresses and gentle kisses. He took his time, moving slowly and making certain he didn't miss an inch of her sweet skin. He was an explorer and he would map her, noting every curve and freckle, memorizing how she shuddered when he licked the backs of her knees, how she squirmed and sighed when he gave her a nip. She was incredibly responsive, and she was true to what she'd promised him. Her hands had fisted in the comforter as though she needed to hold on to something, but she hadn't moved, hadn't tried to take control.

The trust she was placing in him made him determined to pay her back.

He dragged her down the bed, putting her in the perfect position for what he'd wanted to do all night. All night? Damn, he'd wanted to get his mouth on this woman from the second he'd seen her. Even as she'd been running away from him, he'd thought about how much he wanted to get to know the woman with big intelligent eyes.

"Ne t'éloigne pas de notre amour." He knew she didn't want to hear that in English. He would simply tell her how he felt in French. No more running. He had her in his world now and he would make it so nice she wouldn't ever want to leave. Of course, that would take some work, but he was willing to do all the heavy lifting.

And this . . . oh, this was no work at all. He stared at her gorgeously splayed out for him. She was a buttoned-up, somewhat tense professional, but right now she was a sultry, wanton woman waiting for her man to give her what she needed.

Luckily for him, what she needed was exactly what he'd been dreaming of for months.

"Armie, please." The words were breathless.

He lowered his mouth down, kissing his way up her thigh to the juncture of her legs. He put his mouth on her, unable to hold back a single second more. It was everything he'd dreamed of, the connection flowing between them, and it didn't take long before her whole body went taut and she called out his name. She went still beneath him and his heart pounded in his chest.

It was his time and he didn't have to wait a second longer. He got to his feet, fishing the condom out of his pocket and shoving his pants and boxers down. He was so hard he could barely breathe, but that wasn't going to stop him.

He managed to get the condom on, managed to shift her up so he could cover her body with his. He wanted to be close to her, wanted to feel her moving against him. Her arms locked around his back, her legs clinging to his hips. She opened herself for him, holding nothing back. When he looked into her eyes, the dreamy quality was gone and replaced with pure need.

"I want you." She arched her back as though offering even more of herself—all of herself.

He would take it. "Then let me give you what you need."

He thrust inside her, groaning at the exquisite feel. Heat and silk surrounded him, drawing him in. She was tight and it was a delicious fight to work his way inside. Her nails dug lightly into the flesh of his back and he welcomed it, welcomed every twist and turn of her body as she moved with him.

Their bodies found a rhythm, moving to the music and the beat of their desire. Over and over, he meshed his body with hers until he couldn't remember where he ended and she began. He didn't want to remember. He wanted to stay in this place where he was more than himself, where he wasn't lonely anymore. Damn, but he hadn't realized how alone he'd been until he'd met her.

He had to find a way to stay with her, to make himself meaningful to her life, because he was fairly certain he'd never felt this way about a woman before and never would again.

She called out his name and her body clamped down around his, throwing him over the edge. He lost control, thrusting in hard again and again, giving her everything he had.

He dropped down, not holding his weight off her, but she didn't complain, merely held him closer.

"Stay with me," she whispered. "Spend the night with me."

Hearing her ask was everything he'd wanted. "Yes."

He held her, the world warmer than it had been before.

Blood coated her hands, her knees, her legs. Anywhere her body met the cold of the ER floor. She'd been around blood. Blood didn't bother her. Patients bled. It was part of the process, part of how medical professionals saved a person.

But not this time. This time the blood was merely wasted, like the life of the woman on the ground in front of her.

"It's okay." Maryanne slurred the words, blood dribbling from the corners of her mouth. She sounded like she was drunk, but it wasn't from alcohol. It wasn't sweet wine or hard vodka that made her friend's eyes seem opaque. It was death. "Doesn't hurt."

"Doesn't hurt?" A massive figure looked over Maryanne's body, the same devil who'd shot at Lila when she'd tried to handle the bullet wounds on her friend's body. "I hurt every day and you were the reason. Why couldn't you love me?"

Her friend was nothing but a prize to be won. Maryanne had been this man's property and when she'd tried to break away from his abuse, he'd killed her. He hadn't cared how strong and brave she'd been, didn't care about Maryanne's intelligence or how much she cared about every patient that came into the hospital. She was nothing but property to this man, and he wouldn't allow anyone to take what he claimed as his.

He fired again, the sound jarring through her as Maryanne's body jerked one last time.

The light in her eyes died.

Lila looked up and into the barrel of the gun and knew her life was over.

And that it had all been meaningless.

She gasped as she came out of the dream, her whole body shaking. It took a moment to remember where she was. Not in Dallas. She wasn't in Dallas, and it had been a long time since she'd faced down Maryanne's husband, since she'd looked up and known he would pull that trigger and that no one would miss her. That wasn't true. Her brother and sisters would mourn her. Her mom might think about her from time to time, but they would all move on and she would be nothing more than a memory. She hadn't been essential to anyone.

She'd never truly loved someone, and in that moment, she'd understood that loving someone was more important than anything else. Not having someone love her. It was different. She wanted to look into that gun and pray for one more minute with the man she loved, but all she'd felt was impatience to get it over with, regret that she didn't care more.

She took a deep breath and tried to calm down.

"Come here."

Oh god, she wasn't alone. Not that she could forget that Armie LaVigne was in her bed since he was taking up almost all the space. She should get up and let him sleep. When she dreamed about that day, she never got back to sleep. It was only four in the morning. Armie didn't have to be back at the station house until nine. He needed rest.

"Go back to sleep. I'm okay." She hated this, hated that she would think about it for the rest of the night, hated that it was going to ruin what had been almost perfect.

Almost? He'd been beyond perfect. He'd shown her how good sex could be, and now that seemed to be erased.

She wanted to go back to that moment when he'd been her whole world. For a brief time, everything else had fallen away and Armie had been all that mattered. Armie had played her body like a master, drawing her out of herself and giving her pleasure and more importantly, peace.

His hand came out, reaching for hers and drawing her toward him. "Tell me about it. You had a bad dream, right?"

He was so damn sexy lying there taking up two thirds of her bed. Moonlight streamed in through the filmy curtains and illuminated his sleepy eyes. Her comforter was down around his waist, showing off that cut chest with its dusting of dark hair.

But she couldn't go there with him. Not now. This was a one-night thing.

Why? Because he said something that pissed you off? I don't know if you've noticed but you get pissed off pretty easily. You said some stuff you shouldn't have said, either, and he's still here. How about you chill and see where things go? You do not always have to know where a relationship is heading to enjoy one.

He tugged on her hand and she decided to indulge him. She slid under the covers and let him pull her close. She sighed as his arm went around her and her head found his chest.

"It was only a dream," she said, settling in. She would wait until he fell back asleep and then she would sneak out of bed. Or she could lie here and hold him and try to think about something other than the demons that hadn't stayed in Dallas, where they'd belonged.

"Dreams can kick your ass," he murmured with a sleepy sigh.

"You have nightmares?"

"Yeah," he replied. "I have some recurring dreams that aren't so pleasant. A couple of them come from when I was on the force in New Orleans. I got pinned down in a nasty neighborhood once. My partner and I were chasing a suspect and ended up in a part of the city where we weren't welcome. We wound up in an alley with nowhere to go. He took a bullet to the chest. I had to drag him behind a dumpster and keep him alive until backup came."

It was easy to forget his job hadn't always been as sheriff of a sleepy town, where most of his job was enforcing the speed limit and making sure the tourists didn't irritate the locals. "Was your partner okay?"

"Yeah, but it was a close thing. I couldn't sleep without dreaming about it for months afterward. And I swear I still dream about the accident Noelle was in and I wasn't even there. My mind fills in the blanks. Sometimes I feel guilty that I wasn't in the car, that I wasn't the one who got stuck in that wheelchair. Hell, sometimes I wish I was the one who died. I worry Noelle would have been better off with her mom."

"That's not true." Her body wasn't in line with her head. Her body had relaxed the second he'd put his arms around her, going soft and sleepy again.

Because she was safe.

"I don't know about that," he said with a long sigh. "I'm not good with the whole teenage-girl stuff."

She could imagine he was made distinctly uncomfortable by certain parts of raising a daughter. "Somehow I think she'll find her way. She seems to have a lot of friends and she's good at utilizing her resources."

"I'm hoping you'll be a good resource for her. I know she was excited to have a doctor she wasn't going to be embarrassed talking to. It's good to have someone to talk to."

"I dream about what happened." She hadn't meant to say the words, but they came out as though she couldn't keep them in anymore, as though they didn't have a place to hide in the sweet, happy world she'd found in this bed and this man.

"Of course you do, *chère*." His hand moved over her flesh, stroking her with easy affection. "You go through what you went through and it sticks to you the rest of your life. But you don't have to go through it alone."

She was quiet for a moment, the silence oddly comfortable. It should be awkward. They were new to the lovers thing, but it felt . . . right. Normal. Like they'd been here a hundred times and it was her right to take comfort from him. "Sometimes in the dream I look down and I'm the one dying on the floor. He wouldn't let me help her. He shot at me when I tried to stop the bleeding."

His arms tightened around her. "I can't imagine how hard that was on you."

It had been the hardest moment she'd ever faced. That one moment was beginning to define her life. If she wasn't careful, she might be attempting to atone for a moment she couldn't control for the rest of her life. Sometimes she closed her eyes and couldn't see anything but Maryanne.

"I could have saved her. I was in a trauma room. We would go in there when we needed a couple of minutes of peace. We would get to take a breather and we would talk. Even a couple of minutes helped. I was the one who talked her into leaving her husband. I know that was the right thing to do. I know it in my head, but there's a part of me that thinks she would be alive if I'd left things alone."

"He was physically abusive?"

"Oh, yes. He was good at hiding it, or rather Maryanne was, but he beat her on a regular basis. It was more than physical abuse. He tried to isolate her. He bullied her constantly. We were friends for seven years and I watched her go from a scared mouse to a woman who valued herself. It was a long road. She got out and he still killed her. Should I have left her alone? Would she be alive if I had?"

"Probably not."

It was soothing that he didn't make a big deal out of this conversation even though it *was* a big deal. He didn't turn on the light or force her to sit up and look him in the eyes. He held her and let her wrap herself around him like he was the best teddy bear ever.

"That's what I tell myself. He wouldn't have stopped. I wanted to get her out of the situation before they had kids," she explained.

His hand moved up and down her back. "Lila, you have to know you did everything you could. And that it's normal to feel guilty. You survived. Your friend didn't. You wouldn't be human if you didn't feel it."

No "You're crazy. It wasn't your fault." No "How can you possibly think that way?" Just a steady "Of course you do."

He understood her.

"I know it's stupid, but I feel like I should have been able to fight through the man with the gun to save her. I didn't think I would sit there, afraid for my own life."

He kissed her forehead. "Because you are not the type

of woman who ever puts herself first, and that's something we're going to deal with. *Tu es mon raison d'être, chérie.*"

"I get the feeling you are saying things you think I'm not ready to hear yet."

"Tu es la plus intelligente femme que je connaisse." He kissed the top of her head and sighed, a contented sound. "I want to forget the things we said at the café. Can we erase that part of the day? I was wrong. Please forgive me."

She could forgive him. That part was simple. "Of course, and I'm sorry, too. But, Armie, I'm still not going to fit in the way you need me to."

"I don't need you to fit with anyone but me."

It was a lovely thought. "You're an elected official. I don't think it's going to help you to be associated with me."

He chuckled, his whole body moving. "I'd love to see them bring someone else in to run against me. No one wants my job. No one wants to deal with the crazies, I assure you."

"They're not so crazy." It felt good to be here with him, too good. "I never thought I would be here. I actually was very against my sister marrying Remy and moving here."

Armie chuckled. "As you should have been. Have you met his family? Sera is okay, but Zep keeps an overnight bag at the station house because he's in jail so much, and I swear Delphine Dellacourt Guidry is a con artist of the highest order. She's worked some kooky schemes with Miss Marcelle. Makes us all crazy."

"It wasn't about that. I didn't think he was good enough for her."

"He's definitely not."

"I'm being serious."

"No, you're piling on and you're trying to put up walls I have to climb over to get to you because you're afraid you've done bad shit in the past, which means you don't deserve to have a man as sexy, smart, and unbelievable as me."

She snorted, a completely unsexy sound, but she couldn't help it. "Think a lot of yourself, huh?" But he wasn't necessarily wrong. He was all the things he'd said he was and she was definitely scared of falling in deep with him. "I was just pointing out that there are reasons I don't fit in here."

"Give it time. You'll fit in nicely once people get used to the idea of you. Folks around here don't like change because change is almost always a bad thing for them. You're a good thing. It'll all be okay."

She wasn't sure about that. Today had been out of the norm. "Even as I was stabilizing Janice today she told me she wouldn't come back. She actually said to me she wouldn't go to a female doctor. She told me she remembered how she'd been when she used to have periods and she wasn't about to risk it."

He chuckled again, the deep sound soothing. "Janice is a character. And I think she'll come around because you definitely made a believer of Hallie."

"It was one day. They'll forget. Something else will happen and they'll forget about it and I'll be the new girl again." She was afraid she could live here for twenty years and she'd always be the new girl. Her sister was far better at fitting in than she was.

His big body moved and suddenly he was rolling on top of her. His eyes gleamed in the moonlight as he reached out and pinned her arms over her head. His body weighed her down deliciously, making her sink into the bed. "That's where you're wrong. That's where you don't understand this town. Nothing else will happen. Not for a long time, and people here have good memories. They don't go from one crisis to the next because there are almost no crises to be had. What happened today will be talked about for years. Likely as long as you live. You'll be the woman who saved four people."

"Only three."

"Oh, I think Hallie would disagree. I think she would say you saved her life today, too."

It hit her all at once. She was used to being in an ER, being in a trauma situation, but she wasn't used to being alone. She'd been in the field before, but she'd always been support. She hadn't been one hundred percent in charge. She could have lost that baby or her grandma. One wrong call and she could have lost a man who was in the prime of his life.

It had all been on her. Every second of the fallout from that accident had been on her.

"It's all right, *chère*. Cry. You need it. You deserve it. You got through it all and you performed magnificently. Now let the pressure go. Let it out. You're safe now."

It welled up, a volcano she'd thought was dormant. The day flashed through her, the sights and sounds, the knowledge of the edge she played on. One wrong move. Only one wrong word from her mouth and the day would have ended differently. Lives would have been changed.

The tears flowed freely. "I could have killed them. It's every nurse's fear. Every medical professional's. That we'll make the wrong call and have to live with it forever. When you're in an ER, it's easier to distance, but I won't be able to do that here."

He shook his head and his eyes shone in the dimly lit room. "No, you won't. You'll eventually know these people and you'll feel every death. It won't matter if someone dies from old age or in an accident. You'll feel it, Lila, and it will be the single best thing that ever happened to you because it will mean you cared, you loved. The pain is going to be worth it because they will love you, too, if you're patient enough."

She'd held herself apart for so long. Her life had been safe. She'd closed herself off, sinking into intellectualism and professionalism, but it had left her behind walls. Those walls had crumbled and it was time to decide if she was going to rebuild them or find a new life.

She held on to Armie and cried out the stress of the day.

He shifted and drew her close, resting her head on his chest as he let her cry.

She fell asleep to the sound of his heart beating. Safe, this time, didn't mean alone.

chapter ten

‿

The knock on the door damn near shook the house. It made him shoot out of bed, but Lila merely turned over and yawned before her breathing became easy again. The woman needed sleep and according to the clock on the nightstand, she should have at least another forty-five minutes before she had to get up.

The knocking began again and he hustled to drag on his slacks. The shirt would have to wait because he was about to have a conversation with whoever was knocking on the door at damn 7:14 in the morning.

He worked his way around the plastic containers and nearly tripped on a surprising amount of buttons, but he managed to get to the door before a third set of thunder shook the place. "What? Did you know it is illegal to knock on the door before eight a.m.?"

He asked the question as he flung the door open and then had to sigh because he couldn't tell the two people standing there to go away. Remy and Lisa Guidry were on Lila's doorstep. Her sister looked like she hadn't slept and Remy had a fierce frown on his face.

"You started making up new laws now?" Remy asked.

It had been worth a try. Sometimes he could intimidate people into doing the right thing. Remy wasn't one of those people. "It would have been a misdemeanor. I take it you heard about what happened yesterday? Come on in, but she's asleep and she needs it. I'm not waking her up until I have to."

Not even for her sister. Lisa could wait forty-five minutes more to assure herself that Lila was okay.

Lisa stepped inside, followed by her husband. "I was so worried when she didn't answer her phone. She always has her phone on her. I didn't hear about what happened until late last night. I tried to call but it went to voice mail."

"We had a couple of business meetings and then we went out to dinner," Remy explained. "When we got back to the hotel, I called Seraphina to see how things had gone at the marina. She told us what happened."

"I wanted to come home, but Remy wouldn't drive me until this morning." Lisa entered the living room and turned to look at him, her arms folding over her chest. "Is there a reason you're in my sister's house? And do you own a shirt?"

She glanced down at the couch and he could see her make note of the fact that no one had slept on it.

"I'm in your sister's house because I slept here last night. I don't have a shirt on because I was trying to ensure that your sister got all the sleep she could after a very rough day. I ran to get the door before you woke her up." He moved into the kitchen. Lila would need coffee and breakfast before she went to work. "I drove her home last night."

"And decided to stay?" There was a well of judgement in Lisa's tone.

"*Chère*, tread carefully," Remy warned his wife. "You didn't like your sister getting into your business."

"And yet she did," Lisa replied tartly. "So she shouldn't be surprised that turnabout is fair play. She's new in town and I don't want some Romeo law enforcement officer coming in here and showing off his abs and taking advantage of her."

He pulled out the coffee filters and found the can of coffee. He was going to have to suck it up and drink it. He preferred chicory because the normal stuff was bland comparatively. "I'm not the one taking advantage. I've made my intentions plain. Your sister is the one who wants to use me for sex. My abs were my only way in."

Remy laughed and shook his head. "I told you Lila can handle herself."

"Not with men she can't. But first off, how is everyone? I heard Rene almost died," Lisa said, moving into the kitchen beside him, pulling a can from the cabinet. "I cut those bland beans of hers with about a quarter of this. I bought it when I stocked up her kitchen. I planned to come over for coffee and start making the switch. Lila has to be eased into change. She struggles with it."

"Yes, and she's had a lot of change lately, so maybe she should have the coffee she likes." He wasn't going to force anything on her.

Lisa finally gave him a half smile that didn't hold a hint of judgement. "I lived with her most of my life. Trust me. She'll love it if you can get her to try it. It's a leftover from our childhood. We never had a ton of food and she had to eat stuff she didn't like. Now she almost always ends up ordering the same thing because in the back of her head she's afraid she won't like it and she'll go hungry. She'll eat steak and salad and chicken breasts and nothing else if you let her. I managed to talk her into jambalaya the other day. It was the blandest jambalaya ever, and I had to promise our chef that he could start having a chef's special once a month to get him to actually make it. She's now had it three times, and I've been gently pumping up the spice."

"She did mention that the last batch she had was the best," Remy admitted.

He couldn't stand the thought that she'd been a hungry child. She was so put together as an adult it was hard to believe her childhood had been rough. Of course, sometimes the roughest places turned out to be the most beautiful. It took time and pressure to create a diamond.

Well, if she hated it, he could always make another pot.

He couldn't blame Lisa for easing her into the coffee. Wasn't he trying to ease her into a relationship?

Lisa took over. "Why don't you see if she's got some bread for toast and I'll make breakfast. That way you've got total deniability. Now give me an update."

Lila's sister was a force of nature. He backed off. He wouldn't mind a little deniability, and he would like it if he didn't have to make two pots of coffee every morning because they couldn't stand to drink the same one. If he could get her to half and half, he would compromise. "Rene is coming home today. Janice will be in the hospital a couple of days. The baby is fine. None of them would have survived if your sister hadn't been there."

"Is she okay?" Lisa asked.

There was no question who she was talking about. "She had a rough day, but she's all right."

"She bottles things up. She won't even acknowledge that anything is bothering her," Lisa explained. "You have to push her to get her to talk about it, and even then, she might not tell you anything."

"She's all right, Lisa. She had a good long cry and she managed to get some sleep." She'd also wrapped herself around him. She'd held on to him while she'd cried, and he wasn't sure he'd ever felt as good as he had when she'd needed him.

Remy and Lisa both stopped, staring at him.

"Lila cried?" Remy asked.

"Lila rarely cries. Never in front of anyone but her family." Lisa glanced back at the bedroom. "Well, there was the once, but that was more like a total breakdown, and she had her reasons for it."

"Well, she had a good cry last night, and I think she's feeling better now." He wasn't going to tell Lisa that her sister had a nightmare. He probably shouldn't have told her anything, but she seemed so worried. "Are the rumors already flying? What exactly is being said?"

He knew the way the gossip mill worked in town. A big

event like this would be talked about for years, and it would take that long for some people to get the facts right. Oh, it would start out with eyewitness accounts, but it would roll downhill from there.

Remy chuckled as he sat down at the small bistro table. "Well, the way Sera told it, Janice had a heart attack while she was driving and Rene was in the way. The baby choked on a teething biscuit and Lila saved the day. My momma heard it a bit differently."

Delphine Dellacourt Guidry was one of the town's eccentrics. "Good lord. Tell me."

Lisa looked far more cheerful now that she knew her sister was all right. She pressed the button to start the coffeemaker. "Janice tried to run Rene down because he wouldn't marry Hallie all those years ago. Hallie was forced to marry an outsider because Rene spurned her. Janice saw him on the street walking by and her rage flashed through her and she was out of control. In that particular scenario, Lila and Rene made an obvious connection and that's why she saved him first. There also might have been mention of some hoodoo Rene worked to make himself attractive to all women. I think he should have used the hoodoo to make his bones a little stronger."

"She saved him first because she got to him first. Tell me they're not matching Lila up with Rene." That wasn't happening. It didn't matter that Rene was a better match, damn it. He didn't care that Rene was incredibly wealthy and could give her a life of ease. Or that Rene was arguably handsomer. And younger. And without a kid who would need help for the rest of her life. Lila was his. He'd seen her first and he'd gotten his hands on her first, and Rene could deal with it.

Not that Rene wanted Lila. Or Lila wanted Rene. Damn rumors.

"She's having his baby soon," Remy said with a grin. "Hey, it got them to stop talking about how your vehicle was seen here in the early-morning hours, though they'll probably start talking about how you're trying to break them up since your vehicle is right back out there this morning. And might I mention I called this one? Lisa wanted Lila to fake date Rene, but I knew she'd be real dating you in no time at all."

At least someone believed in him. "I'll put those rumors to rest."

"I only thought she should fake date Rene because he fit more with the kind of guy she liked in Dallas." Lisa shrugged as she found a carton of eggs in the fridge. "Except for the part where Rene is a nice guy."

"She didn't like nice guys?" It occurred to him that he could learn a little more about her from her sister.

Lisa frowned at the stove. "Well, she thought they were nice. They were good at pretending to be nice, but they were often assholes. I'm afraid to turn this thing on."

"I fixed it." He grabbed the bread. The toaster looked like it was new, so Lila had probably brought it with her. "It works, and so do all the lights. I'll check out the plumbing next. Now tell me why she dated assholes."

"Because every man Lila has dated since college has been the *right* kind of man. At least in her head. She dated a couple of doctors, and then there was Brock. He was the CEO of a fairly successful company back in Dallas. I think in her head she believed he could give her the life she thought she was working for. He was incredibly supportive of her career, wouldn't ever tell her what to do. In fact, he pretty much did what she wanted him to do. She was almost one hundred percent in control of that relationship."

"And the percentage she wasn't in control of?"

"That was the part where he hit on anything with boobs, including her sisters."

"Lila only thinks she wants to be in charge," Remy pointed out. "Don't get me wrong. She's a strong-willed woman and she's smart as a whip, but I think she picked men who didn't challenge her so she didn't have to get close to them. She's got serious intimacy issues, but she's better now."

"Well, nearly dying will do that to you," Lisa said, her

voice somber. "I think she had to face a whole lot of reality that day." She took a deep breath and nodded, obviously choosing to be positive. "It was a good thing for her to get out of her comfort zone and come down here."

"The question is what happens when she's healed," Remy said, concern in his eyes.

"What do you mean?" Armie asked.

Lisa waved him off as she started cracking eggs in a bowl. "It's nothing."

"It's not nothing," Remy replied. "What happens to this town when she's feeling better and realizes she needs more than this place can give her? Lila likes nice things more than you do. She likes the theater and fancy restaurants."

"New Orleans isn't that far away." He'd lived in the city for years, but when he'd needed to, he'd settled back in. Lila could do the same. She hadn't grown up wealthy. Of course, didn't that mean she would want all the things she'd worked so hard to have? Wouldn't she want educated conversation? Not that there weren't educated people in town. There were plenty. And they had plays. Twice a year, Alma Hannaford and her Papillon Players put on a show at the rec center, and the local high school had a band concert he was forced to survive.

She might get bored.

A knock on the door sounded through the house and then there was a deep bark.

He rushed to the door because that could only mean one thing.

Noelle was on the porch, having used the ramp Bill had put in when his wife had gotten so sick. Noelle grinned his way and pointed to a big box emblazoned with the local donut store logo. "Morning, Dad. Beth had to help her mom with the church's pancake breakfast so Roxie came over and gave me a ride."

His deputy gave him a nod as she opened the driver's side door of her SUV. "Morning, boss." She shook her head.

"How could you come between two new lovers? Rene is going to be so sad."

Armie groaned. "You know she met Rene when she was putting a damn tourniquet on his leg. Don't let that rumor get out there."

Roxie shrugged. "I don't think that's my job, boss. Good luck."

Noelle grinned as Peanut lumbered in around Armie. "I heard Lila is my new mommy."

He grimaced for more than one reason. He was never going to be able to get Noelle's chair through the hallway because they hadn't moved all the storage boxes out. "The chair's going to have to stay on the porch."

"I'll trade you donuts for a Dad taxi ride," she offered.

He leaned over and picked her up. It was something he'd done a million times in the months since the accident, and it always reminded him how small and fragile she was. His heart ached at his daughter's slight weight in his arms.

He knew Lila had been lashing out at him, but he couldn't help but think about the words they'd had the day before.

I know she should be more mobile than she is.

He shook it off as he carried his daughter to the living room. He'd learned long ago to accept the things he couldn't change, and this was one of those things.

"Morning, Noelle." Lisa smiled at his daughter. "Are those donuts? If they are glazed and coated in sprinkles, you're my favorite."

"A donut is not a donut without sprinkles." Noelle settled down on Lila's couch. "I will trade you a pink sprinkled for a cup of coffee. I'm all about negotiating today."

Noelle offered up her box of treats and Armie noticed she also had a couple of envelopes in her hands.

He passed the box to Lisa. "Did the mailman come early?"

"Is there a reason you've invaded my home, sis?" Lila yawned as she entered the kitchen. She wore pajama bottoms and a tank top, a brightly colored robe around her shoulders. She looked gorgeous and rumpled and perfect. "Should I leave a sock on the door or something?"

Lisa flew over to her sister, throwing her arms around her. "I'm so glad you're okay. We didn't hear about it until last night and then it was late and we'd had some hurricanes, but we should have come home."

"Three hurricanes," Remy pointed out. "And they were not light on the pours."

Lisa ignored him. "And you wouldn't answer your phone."

Lila hugged her sister, but her eyes found Armie's and she smiled. "I was busy."

"She was busy with my dad," Noelle said with a grin.

Lila's eyes flared as she seemed to realize her sister and brother-in-law weren't the only interlopers. "Hey. I . . . uhm . . ." She shook her head and obviously gave up. "Yep. I was. No way around that one."

It was good to know she wasn't going to try to hide the relationship from his daughter. He had no plans to.

Lisa frowned and took a step back. "I was worried about you."

"I wasn't the one with a compound fracture that managed to nick the femoral artery," Lila pointed out. "Nor was I the one who had the heart attack. I'm fine. All in all, everything went our way and everyone is healthy and happy."

"But it must have been traumatic," Lisa insisted.

Lila simply nodded. "That is why they call it trauma. I'm feeling good today. The coffee smells great."

"And you are looking good, too," Remy said with a grin. "Especially given your blessed state. You are glowing, girl."

Noelle clapped her hands. "I heard that one, too. Beth and I spent most of the night calling around and finding out all the crazy rumors about the accident. Did you know that Mabel actually set up the whole thing so that Doc would come back and save the town because she's been secretly in love with him for years?"

Lila frowned. "She's married. I know that because she regularly overshares about her sex life. She's quite flexible for her age. And why would I glow?"

"She's not pregnant." Armie sent Remy a dark stare.

Lila turned the sweetest shade of pink. "What? Why would you think I'm pregnant? I just slept with him and he used a condom and everything. I'm on the pill, by the way, but I'm going to need a test on you. Sexually transmitted infections can lie in wait for years. I'll do one on me, too. We can exchange them over dinner."

"That's very modern of you," Noelle said, watching the conversation like it was the best tennis match ever.

Lila's skin went from pink to red. "Damn it. I should not have said that. I've been around Mabel for too long. I'm starting to put everything out there."

"Well, I think it's refreshing," Lisa said, moving back to the stove. "I like this side of you. And according to all the rumors, Armie shouldn't have any trouble passing that particular test."

"He hasn't had sex in years and years," Noelle confirmed. "It's been a long drought for him, and it makes him cranky. I would have asked you for some kind of sex toy for him that I could slip into his nightstand, but I don't know if they have those for men."

He turned to his very precocious teen. "You asked Lila about sex toys?"

It was Noelle's turn to go pink. "Just joking. Maybe. It's doctor-patient privilege."

He put his hands on his hips. "Not until you're eighteen."

He turned to Lila, ready to find out exactly how much she was already influencing his daughter.

How could her morning have already gone so wrong? She'd woken up only moments before. She shouldn't be dealing with this kind of drama. The night before had been a revelation, but she was confronted with all the reasons they might not be able to work this morning. All it had taken was the addition of a few people and she was right back to worrying they didn't really fit together.

"I think this is a conversation we should have in private." She loved her sister and she should have called her apparently. Back in Dallas, it would have been no big deal. Lisa likely wouldn't have even heard about the incident. Here, she was discovering, everything was a big deal.

Maybe he would see reason and she could put off the conversation until they could have it in a professional setting. Like the clinic, where she would be properly dressed and in the right place to deal with the fact that she'd had a conversation with his daughter he might be angry about.

"Hey, the eggs are ready." Lisa stepped in and gave her another hug. "I'm glad you're okay, and I will see you the day after tomorrow? Remember? We've got a day of beauty scheduled at Miss Marcelle's."

"I might need to work." She didn't need a day of beauty. She needed patients. She needed to not step on the land mines that seemed to be buried everywhere in this town.

"You don't." Lisa took her husband's hand. "I already had Mabel clear your calendar."

That probably hadn't taken much. But yesterday had proven that even though the people in town might not like her, they sometimes needed her. "Emergencies. I need to be available for emergencies."

Lisa shrugged. "It's okay. The beauty parlor is a block away from the clinic, and Mabel can call. She has your full schedule for the rest of the week and she's ready to take care of everything. I'll be by to pick you up for lunch." Her voice went low. "And don't think we won't talk about this. Because we will. All of it."

There might not be much to talk about given how grim Armie looked.

Remy frowned the sheriff's way. "You think before you say anything you can't take back, because you do not want to have a talk with me. Remember who she is."

"Why would you forget who I am?" She watched as Lisa and Remy headed out.

Armie sighed. "He didn't mean it that way. He meant if I hurt you, he'll kick my ass."

"Why would he do that?"

"Because you're his sister-in-law, and that's how we do things down here. I'll be honest, though—I'm more worried about Lisa. Now tell me what's going on."

"Dad, it's private." Noelle shifted, her frustration at not being able to move evident.

But she moved more than Lila had seen her move before. Her hips actually shifted a bit. With some serious PT, Noelle might be able to have more freedom. She needed to do some research. Armie hadn't liked her talking about this yesterday, but maybe if she came to him with hard facts and a plan, she could convince him. Of course, he might not talk to her at all after this morning. "Noelle and I had a talk. She had a few questions and I answered them."

"What were the questions?" Armie asked, looking from her to his daughter.

Damn, that man could be intimidating. She'd worked with law enforcement a lot over her years, but she'd rarely met one who could make her think about backing down. "She wanted to know what the normal flow for a period is. She's worried hers is quite heavy."

Noelle had asked about that. And she'd told Lila it was the way to shut Armie down. Technically HIPAA didn't protect children under the age of eighteen from their parents asking for medical information, but Noelle should have someone she could talk to.

Armie winced but soldiered on. "No. I don't think that's what she meant. She talked about sex, Lila. I want to know what's happening with my daughter. She's sixteen years old. She's not an adult and I have the right to know what's happening."

She squared off with him. "And she has the right to some privacy when it comes to her own body."

The moment lengthened, silence between them.

"Don't be mad at Lila," Noelle said. "I asked her to do it, to order it for me."

Armie's jaw tightened. "Is this about that boy? Caleb Granger?"

"Not exactly." Noelle had gone bright red. "Caleb is just a friend. It was about something else. I . . . I wanted to know if it worked. My female parts. I want to know if I can have sex."

Armie's eyes went wide. "No. No, you can't have sex. You are sixteen and you are far too young and it's not happening. Not on my watch. I swear I'm going to talk to that little shit. Sniffing around my daughter. He can spend some time in jail and then we'll see if he tries to take advantage of my daughter again."

"Dad!"

Lila had to step in front of him. "Stop right now. Cool down, Sheriff. She is a responsible young woman. She didn't ask me for condoms, although you should know that if she had, I would have given them to her. She isn't trying to have sex with some kid. She's trying to experiment, and she has every right to do that. Just because she's in a wheelchair doesn't mean she can't eventually enjoy sex, and that includes masturbation. And don't you dare give me some moral lecture on the evils of masturbation. I bet you can't tell me you didn't do it when you were her age."

He stopped, his whole body going still. "You talked to her about . . . that? You talked to her about how to do that? She's not pregnant?"

"Dad, eww, no. I haven't done anything that could get me pregnant. Why would your brain even go there? Why?" Noelle shuddered.

"Likely because he was doing far more than self-pleasure at your age." She couldn't imagine teenage Armie hadn't been the local player.

"When she said you ordered something, I thought it might be a pregnancy test," Armie said.

"I bought her a wand," Lila admitted. "It's for clitoral stimulation. I think she should start there."

"I want to die." Noelle picked up a pillow and muffled her scream into it.

Armie's shoulders dropped. "So you talked to my daughter about sex and bought her something to help her feel more normal?"

Lila nodded.

Armie sighed, a deeply relieved sound, and then he was wrapping her up in his arms. He lifted her off the ground and held her against his body. "Thank you for being so kind to my daughter."

"You're not mad at me?" She let her arms drift up around his shoulders. "Because I meant what I said, Armie. I think she has the right to have a private life."

"She does," he agreed. "I'm sorry I reacted the way I did, but you're right about what I was doing at her age. And she's my baby. I worry about her."

She could understand that. "You can't arrest every boy who wants to date her."

"On this we are going to have to disagree." Armie set her on her feet and kissed her forehead. "So I will happily give you permission to talk to my daughter about all the female stuff, and I will not ask about it again."

He'd ceded that fight quickly.

"Can I die now?" Noelle asked.

Armie ignored her, his eyes on Lila. "I want you to take your coffee and sit on the back porch and enjoy the morning. I'll get everything else ready and we'll have a nice breakfast."

"Or I could help you. Actually, I don't normally eat breakfast," she admitted.

Noelle's head came out of the pillow. She managed to go from embarrassed to disappointed in a heartbeat. "But I brought you donuts. They're my favorites from this place in town. I would have brought beignets, but they don't travel well. The donuts were a way to say thank you."

It wouldn't hurt to have one donut, though she didn't see the need to sit on the porch.

Still, she found herself being hustled outside, a mug of coffee and a donut in her hands.

She sank down in the surprisingly comfortable rocker. There were two of them, side by side. She could imagine the couple who'd owned the house sitting here, watching the sunset.

It was quiet in the early morning hours, the world seeming softer. Maybe it was simply that she'd gotten sleep the night before. Maybe it was that she'd never taken the time to sit in Dallas, never gone on the balcony of her condo and watched the city come to life around her as she sipped coffee and ate donuts.

It wasn't terrible.

She took a deep breath and let her mind float, let the sights and sounds of the world around her sink in.

She sipped the coffee, feeling more peaceful than she had in years. She could hear Armie in the kitchen and Noelle telling her dad how he was doing everything wrong. It was nice to not be alone all the time.

And maybe she should get her nails done. It might be fun.

She sat back and sipped her coffee.

That was damn fine coffee.

chapter eleven

Two days later, Lila looked over at Remy's sister and wondered if she'd ever been that young and enthusiastic.

"I think we should go with something a little bigger. You've got such amazing hair. It shouldn't be in a bun all the time." Seraphina Guidry was all of twenty-five years old and was brimming with enthusiasm for her new job.

"I was only looking for a trim," Lila explained.

Seraphina had long blond hair. At least four hundred pounds of it, and it was teased into something that would make a showgirl jealous as hell. It was gorgeous on the lithe young woman but would look utterly ridiculous on her. There were people who could pull off teased hair. She was not one of them.

Sera frowned at her in the mirror. "You don't need a trim. You need to let it grow out. It barely brushes your shoulders. I think you need to let it get about halfway down your back and then we can do the most gorgeous updos. I was first in my class in updos."

"She recently did a wedding for a bride two towns over and all anyone could talk about was the bride's hair." Lisa gave her a thumbs-up.

She was not getting married, and big hair had no place in a medical clinic.

"I need a no-nonsense cut. I don't spend a lot of time on my hair." Most mornings she washed it, dried it, shoved it in a scrunchie. "I won't need much. I color the grays once every six weeks or so. I promise I'll be very low maintenance."

"There's no such thing," Sera declared. "Not here. Beauty takes work, and you're a beautiful woman. We need to find your style."

"What if my style is scrubs and scrunchies?"

"It kind of is, most of the time," Lisa interjected. "But when she goes out, I like to call her style modern stick up the ass."

Lila rolled her eyes. "It's understated elegance."

"I like my version better," Lisa quipped.

Sera giggled. "Don't be silly. Let me grab the biggest barrel curling iron I can find and we'll have so much fun. How do you feel about a total makeover?"

Terrified. Completely terrified.

"Non, non, ma fille." Marcelle Martine was a stately looking woman. At least five foot ten, she towered over Seraphina, but the differences didn't stop there. Miss Marcelle, as they called her, despite her marital status, was one of those women who didn't look her age. Oh, she'd read the woman's file and knew she was sixty-two, but Marcelle could have been in her forties for that barely lined face. Her hair was up in a turban and she wore a brilliantly colored caftan that contrasted her dark skin. "You work on Lisa's hair. I will deal with the town heroine myself. Girl, everyone is talking about you."

If only they would come into her clinic. It was a little better than it had been before the accident. She'd had a follow-up with Hallie Rayburn, who'd promised to bring her baby back for a full well check soon. A local teenager had decided making videos of himself doing skateboarding tricks was a good idea. He'd discovered the joys of getting a cast.

Lisa was sitting in the chair beside her and gave Marcelle a smile that came nowhere near her eyes. Not even close. "Really? Because I was thinking it would be a fun way for Sera to get to know my sister."

Ah. She knew all her sister's tricks. "I think I have to go with Miss Marcelle. Everyone says she's the finest hairdresser in town, and obviously Sera would know exactly how you like your hair done since you're so close."

Sera practically vibrated with enthusiasm. "Oh, I've actually been dying to get my hands on your hair, Lis. It's so thick. I can make it go a mile high. You're going to love it."

Sera clapped her hands and ran toward the back of the salon.

Marcelle shook her head Lisa's way. "You should be ashamed, trying to sic that puppy on your poor sister. You know she's going to try to talk you into highlights. Unless you want to leave this salon looking like a broke-down disco ball, you will hold that line."

"You hired her," Lisa said, the words coming out in a whisper as she made sure Sera wasn't around.

Marcelle shrugged. "She'll be good one day. It's not like I have a lot of options since Francine took off for Florida to live out her dream of working at a retirement home. I've never known a woman so focused on the elderly. I miss her. Sera finally finished cosmetology school and she's willing to do ten perms a day on some of the oldest, orneriest clients you've ever met, and I include your mother-in-law in that group."

"You are my mother-in-law's best friend," Lisa pointed out. "And her partner in crime."

Marcelle waved that off. "I don't consider it a crime. I put the hex on the tourist. Delphine takes it off."

"For forty bucks," Lisa explained.

Marcelle put her hands in Lila's hair, getting a feel for the texture. "And the tourist gets an authentic bayou experience. We all win. And the fact that Delphine and I have been through all sorts of ups and downs over the years is another reason why I had to hire Sera. Like I said, she'll be good in a year or two. Until then there's going to be some awfully big hair for you white girls in the parish. You're welcome. I'll be right back, Miss Lila. You remember this when my next checkup comes 'round. I'm the reason you won't walk out of here looking like a pageant reject."

She sashayed away.

Lila turned on her sister. "Traitor. After everything I've done for you, this is what I get."

Lisa had the good sense to wince. "Sorry. There are only the two of them working today, and Marcelle is the best. Sera . . . Sera is very enthusiastic. I let her do my nails a couple of weeks back and I had claws. Actual claws. I couldn't work my phone or drive until I managed to get those fake nails off. I'm trying to support her because she's really gotten her shit together in the last year. Being a single mom in a small town is rough."

She could only imagine. "I think being a parent anywhere is rough." It had been three days since the accident and that first night with Armie in her bed, but it already felt like the world had changed. "I'm worried about Noelle."

Lisa turned her chair toward her. "What's going on? I thought she liked you. You seemed to get along fine the other day."

"It's not about that. I like her a lot." She'd spent the night before at Armie's. He'd shown up when the clinic closed and convinced her that coming back to his place for dinner was a brilliant idea. She'd followed him, promising herself that it was only dinner and it might convince people that she wasn't after the richest man in Papillon. The gossip game was strong in this town and there were still rumors about her and Rene. She'd spent a pleasant evening watching Armie cook and then sitting around the kitchen table and listening to Noelle talk about her day. They'd watched a movie and she'd fallen asleep, leaning against him. He'd carried her to bed and made love to her, and she hadn't had the dream. But she did have concerns, and she wasn't sure how to go about addressing them. "After you left the other morning, Armie, Noelle, and I had breakfast. While I was cleaning up, I found a large envelope I didn't recognize. It was halfway in the trash. I opened it."

"Of course you did. I would, too. What was in it? Was it crazy police stuff?"

Her sister sometimes treated the town like it was all a TV show meant to entertain her. "No. It was a report from Noelle's college counselor."

Lisa sat back, crossing one leg over the other. "I thought she was homeschooled."

"She is, but it's through a school in California," she explained. "They offer her a lot of things a physical school does, from what I understand. I know I should have tossed it out. That's obviously what she was trying to do, but I couldn't. It was a letter asking her if she'd considered applying to any of the colleges that are interested in her. Apparently her PSAT scores made some colleges take notice. The counselor thinks she could be accepted into an Ivy League school."

"That's amazing. I don't see what the problem is. I knew that girl was smart the first time I met her."

"She's insisting on taking online courses instead of leaving Papillon." She'd gently questioned Noelle the night before during dinner. She hadn't told her she'd found the counselor's package. Armie had seemed perfectly happy to go along with whatever Noelle wanted. "I asked about her plans and she shrugged and said she would work part time at the station house and maybe take some online courses. That kid needs to go to college."

"You can get a lot done online these days," Lisa pointed out.

It wasn't the same. "She needs to see more of the world. I get that this is her home, but I know that going to college and having the experience of being independent was incredibly important for all of us."

They'd been a chain, each sibling leaning back to support the others. Will had worked his ass off to send Lila to college, and Lila had done the same for her younger sisters. They'd slowly climbed their way out of the poverty of their childhood. Noelle wasn't poor, but she had so much potential. There wasn't anything wrong with staying in her hometown if that's what she wanted, but Lila suspected there were other reasons Noelle was staying in Papillon.

"How do I talk to Armie about this?" It had been bugging her for days.

Lisa thought for a moment. "You're really starting to care about him, aren't you?"

"I am. I know it's weird and that we don't seem like we would fit together. He's not my usual guy, but I feel different around him, like I don't have to put on a front with him." One of the things she'd figured out was that her usual guy had kind of sucked. Her usual guy had basically been a prop, an accessory she selected to go with the life she thought she'd wanted. Armie was real. A relationship with him would be difficult, and he could truly break her heart if he wanted to. And she was still going to try.

Lisa reached out and put a hand on her arm. "I'm glad to hear that. I'm so proud of how you're opening up."

It was odd because she'd always been the older sister, but in this Lisa was the leader. "So help me figure out how to deal with this, because Noelle is becoming important to me, too."

Lisa nodded and settled back in her chair. "Armie is pretty protective of Noelle. I think he feels guilty. Divorce is always rough, but then he had to leave New Orleans and he saw less of Noelle."

"Are we talking about how Armie coddles that girl?" Marcelle was back, Seraphina behind her. "Because he does. I worry about her. She needs a momma. Daddies are too soft on their daughters, and she needs some tough love or she's going to end up living in her daddy's house for the rest of her life."

"There's nothing wrong with living with your parents," Sera said with a frown. "Just until you can save enough money for a place of your own." She sighed. "Except it's got to be close to my momma or I won't have a babysitter for Luc. I'm a little worried about that, though. I think Momma might be planning on training Luc to help her with short cons."

Marcelle waved that off. "Boy's gotta have a profession.

And it's not the same. You'll eventually find a nice man and settle down. You have a job and you get out in the world. Noelle isolates herself. I don't think she's been out of this town since the accident except for doctor's visits. Armie tried to take her to Disney World for her sweet sixteen and she wouldn't go."

"I've offered to pay her to babysit Luc for me, but she told me she couldn't because she's in a wheelchair," Sera said. "I don't see why she can't. At the time he didn't do much more than sleep and poop, and she could always have called someone if she needed help."

"She won't try," Marcelle pointed out. "She's scared of everything, and I understand that, but her daddy needs to push her."

"You know why he won't." Sera started combing through Lisa's hair. "I heard him talking to my cousin one night at the bar. He had a fight with his ex-wife the day of the accident and he told her she had to bring Noelle to him for his time with her or he would take her back to court. She was on the road that night because Armie insisted on it."

Insisted on seeing his daughter? Of course he had. "It wasn't his fault."

"It can be hard to see that." Lisa stared at her pointedly. "Sometimes a person does everything she can to help someone out and it doesn't work. It's not her fault."

Yeah, she'd been told that a hundred times and she did understand that. But logic and that terrible feeling in her gut were two different things. Armie had the same trouble. The only problem was she agreed with Marcelle. Noelle needed a push.

And she'd just thought of the way to do it. It was something she'd been planning to do anyway. After she'd studied Noelle's charts, she'd decided they needed to try something new.

Maybe she needed to try something new, too. "How do you think I would look with bangs?"

"I think that would be amazing and Lisa needs some highlights," Sera said, her joy obvious.

Before Lisa could bark out what had to be a denial, the door flew open and Mabel was standing there.

Lila stood up and turned to her nurse.

"You've got a patient. She needs you," Mabel said.

Lila grabbed her purse and didn't look back.

She pulled the last stitch on Carrie Petrie's cheek through and started the process to tie it off. The woman hadn't even winced when she'd given her the local. She'd been sitting on the exam table like a zombie, no expression at all. She did everything Lila asked her to, but she'd said very little.

"How did you get here?" She was fairly certain Carrie didn't have access to a car.

"I took the boat," she said in a monotone. "Bobby and his brother are working. Mother Petrie visits a couple of other families who live out on the islands every week. Today's the day. Normally I would go with her, but I couldn't hide this. When she left, I took the old boat out and came here."

She went silent again.

Lila finished her work and studied Carrie's face. "I think I've got the stitches tight enough that it shouldn't scar, but you have to understand how close this was. If he'd hit you an inch higher, he could have seriously compromised your eyesight."

"It was an accident." The words were hollow. Carrie had been almost silent since Lila had entered the room. All she would say was she'd had another accident.

Her stomach twisted and what had happened with Maryanne was right there, bumping up against the surface, threatening to break through. But what the hell was she supposed to do? She had legal obligations. "It wasn't, and I'm going to have to tell the sheriff."

Carrie's jaw went stubborn. "You don't know that it wasn't an accident."

"I know someone's fist met your face." There were some injuries that couldn't be explained away, and Lila had made damn sure she'd detailed every single element of this one. She had X-rays and pictures. The fact that Carrie had allowed her to document her injuries made her think she was on the edge of admitting what was happening. "This wasn't a door or you falling down. You were in a fight and you lost."

Carrie was silent for a moment, staring down at her hands. "You told Sheriff LaVigne about the other day and Bobby was so mad."

At least she'd admitted it. She needed to get Carrie talking. "I have a legal obligation to talk to the sheriff if I think you're in danger, and I definitely think you're going to keep getting hurt if you stay where you are."

Carrie's stare was on the floor. "He said he won't do it again. He brought me flowers this morning."

"But he didn't bring you to see me."

"He put a bandage on my face. He tried to take care of me when he realized what he'd done."

"Then why did you come in here? You risked a lot to come to this clinic." And that's why she had some hope that she could get through to the younger woman. She wouldn't be able to cover up the fact that she'd gotten medical attention. "He's going to know you came here. You couldn't do those stitches yourself."

"It wasn't closing up right." She brought her hand up to touch her cheek.

"I think you know you have to get out. I think you know he's going to take it too far one of these days, and then no amount of sweet words or apologies is going to bring you back from the dead."

Carrie sniffled and used the tissue Lila had given her when she'd started crying during the exam. "I thought he loved me."

That was the horrible thing about it all. She was sure Bobby told her regularly that he did love her. Bobby likely thought he loved her. "His love is twisted. It's a nasty, selfish thing. It doesn't have to be this way. There are good men out there."

Men like Armie LaVigne, who had all the strength in the world and chose to use it to protect the people around him. He had the scars to prove it.

"None of them were ever interested in me," Carrie said forlornly. "No one ever noticed me until Bobby. I thought I would spend my whole life alone, but then he asked me on a date and it was good. I know he was older than me, but he was handsome and he said he needed me."

She'd heard that story before. "When did the abuse start?"

"The first time he hit me was a few days after our wedding. He never did anything to me before that. He was nice. Quiet but nice. He was good to my mom, and she was sick at the time. But then we came into Papillon for supplies and I met up with some friends from school. He didn't like that. I wasn't doing anything. I wasn't flirting."

"It wasn't your fault." She needed to make this very clear. "Carrie, even if you had been flirting, he didn't have the right to hit you. If he walked in and you were making love to another man, he doesn't have the right to lay a hand on you."

Tears slipped from her eyes. "Mother Petrie told me it was my fault and I had to learn how to submit to my husband."

"Mother Petrie is a righteous bitch."

Carrie's eyes widened and then she laughed. "She is. She really is." She sobered. "She told me she went through the same thing with her husband and I should suck it up and be a woman. She told me she would kill me herself if I turned in her son. She doesn't care about anything but her sons."

She might need to have a conversation with Mother Petrie, but first she had to get Carrie to understand what needed to happen. "You can't go back there."

"But then where would I go?" The question came out in a dead tone, like she'd gone over this a thousand times and believed there wasn't an answer. "My mom died a few years back. I have a cousin I grew up with, but she's got three kids. I can't put them in danger. I don't have anywhere to go. Would they keep Bobby in jail?"

The court system worked slowly. It was what had happened to Maryanne. She'd gotten away, gotten her husband arrested. He hadn't had a record so he hadn't served any actual time. He'd been put on probation and told to stay away from his wife. The restraining order hadn't stopped him from walking in and killing her. He'd done it three days before his trial was to begin. She'd never even gotten her day in court. She'd gotten a funeral.

She had to be honest with Carrie. "Probably not. The sheriff can arrest him but if he can make bail, they'll let him go. We can get a restraining order, but it can't work if he refuses to honor it. It's possible if the sheriff thinks it's serious enough that you could be put into protective custody, but they don't typically do that for domestic abuse cases."

"Bobby will come after me. I don't know what I was thinking." Her shoulders slumped. "I looked at myself in the mirror and realized if I didn't get someone to stitch me up, I would look at that face for the rest of my life. It was like I needed to hide it, even from myself. He finally did something I can't hide. What will he do when he realizes I came here? I don't know how to explain this to him."

"You don't have to explain anything." She couldn't let this young woman walk back into hell. There were other ways. "If I found a women's shelter for you, would you consider going to it?"

"A shelter. Is that like a homeless shelter? Because that's what I'll be."

There wasn't a shelter here in Papillon, but there was a well-run one in New Orleans. When she'd bought the clinic one of the first things she'd done was study up on all the resources she would need. Her clinic was about more than medicine. In a rural setting, she was the first line of defense when it came to a lot of her patients' problems. "It's not a homeless shelter, though many of the women who go through them are homeless. You would get a room and food, and more than that you'll get counseling to help you set up a new life for yourself."

"It's just a house?" Carrie asked.

"It's a house, but they have lots of security and no one would know where you are. I'll take you there myself. I assure you I won't tell anyone where you are. But it's important that you file charges against him."

"I don't know." There was a wealth of uncertainty in Carrie's tone.

"You talked about how you ended up with Bobby because he was the first man to show you some attention. Was your father not in the picture?" She had to keep Carrie talking. If she backed off, she would lose her and then she might have to deal with signing her first death certificate.

Carrie's eyes came up. "My dad was the best man in the world. I loved my dad, but he died long before my mom. I was seven when he passed."

She took the chance. She reached out and put her hand over Carrie's. "Do you think your father would want you to go back to Bobby, or would he want you to fight for your life? I know you think that having someone to love you is the most important thing in the world, but that has to start with loving yourself. It's not selfish to want to live, to want a good life, but it has to start with respecting yourself and understanding that you are worth more than this."

There was a knock on the door and Mabel stepped in.

"Lila, I have a test result you should look at." There was a grim set to Mabel's expression. She held out a printout.

Unlike the first time she'd seen Carrie, this time she'd run all the tests she could. Including a urinalysis.

She glanced down and saw the one thing she hadn't wanted to see. Damn it. "Carrie, you're pregnant."

It would very likely send her straight back into that nest of snakes. If she was afraid to be on her own, how would she feel about raising a child without any help?

Carrie sat there for a moment. "I'm pregnant? Are you sure?"

"Tests these days are very accurate." She would run it again, but the result would be the same.

"I'm having a baby." Carrie put a hand on her belly.

"You are and you need to think about that." If she could get Carrie to see the counselors at the women's shelter she might have a shot at convincing her to leave the toxic situation she found herself in. If she didn't, then she wasn't sure what she would do. She only knew she wouldn't be able to sleep knowing what was happening on that island. "You're going to need prenatal care. You can get that at the shelter."

A long silence stretched out and it took everything Lila had not to push. She had to be patient. She couldn't overwhelm Carrie or she might lose. This had to be her choice.

Her head came up, her eyes lit with will for the first time since Lila had met her. "My husband hit me. He was angry that you talked to the sheriff. Apparently Armie has been asking questions around town, and he even got in touch with Bobby's ex-wife. Bobby started drinking last night and that's when he punched me. And two years ago he kicked me in the stomach and I lost our first baby. My baby. It was my baby, and this one is my baby, too, and I cannot lose it."

Then again, some women found an iron will of strength when they realized they were going to be mothers.

"I always wondered about that," Mabel said quietly. "I remember your first miscarriage. Doc didn't ask, and I thought we should. He told me we had to keep our noses out of other people's business. He was old school, but I think in this case he was wrong."

He'd had a duty and he'd failed. She was not going to. It didn't matter that it might not work, that she was putting herself in a position she'd been in before. There was right and there was wrong, and her own fear had no place here. "Let me get you to that shelter."

Tears dripping from her eyes, Carrie nodded.

chapter twelve

"He's already lawyered up," Roxie said, her voice coming over his cell phone. "His brother found a lawyer from New Orleans who's willing to work with them since Quaid turned them down."

Armie sighed, but Roxie's news hadn't been unexpected. "He can't post bail tonight. We've got at least until tomorrow morning."

He stared down from the balcony. Bourbon Street was well warmed up for the night. He knew he should have picked a quieter hotel, but Lila had never been to New Orleans and he wanted to show it off to her.

They'd left Carrie at the nondescript house at the edge of the city that served as the women's shelter for this part of Orleans Parish. It was a large home in a nice neighborhood. If a person wasn't aware of what the home served as, he or she might think it was simply an upper-middle-class home where they took security seriously. It was peaceful, and damn he hoped it stayed that way.

He'd managed to talk Lila into staying in town for dinner. They'd checked into one of the nicer hotels in the Quarter, had dinner, and walked the streets, her hand in his. Still, he was worried about her.

"I will give it to the man. He's good," Roxie said. "He

didn't break character even once. Major and I were waiting for him when the fishing boats came in. Arrested him right there on the dock and all he did was ask about how Carrie was. He gave some song and dance about how weird she'd been acting lately. I think he's setting it up to look like she's crazy."

"The medical records will disagree with him." Lila had explained it all as he'd driven them from Papillon up here to New Orleans. She'd described how Carrie couldn't have possibly given herself the injuries documented in her records. In this, the Petrie family's desire to be isolated worked against them. There was no one else to blame the abuse on since Carrie rarely left the island. Or had been allowed to leave the island.

Why the hell hadn't he seen it?

"Well, he's locked up nice and tight for the time being," Roxie assured him. "I'm going to stay overnight and Major's here until midnight. Vince comes on for the night shift, so we've got this covered. Judge won't be in until eleven tomorrow. I've been told he goes fishing every morning and no one is to disturb him."

Ah, the joys of small-town living. "I'll be back before then, but it's late. We checked into a hotel for the night. Noelle is going to stay at Beth's, and Mabel said she would take Peanut home with her. I think Lila needs a night away."

"She probably saved Carrie's life, but you have to know this fight isn't over yet. Bobby, for all his calm, isn't going to go down easy. He'll try to get Carrie back."

"But you didn't have trouble bringing him in?"

"Not a lick," Roxie replied. "Like I said, it was almost like he knew this would happen one day. He's smooth, and that makes him more dangerous in my mind. There's something dark in that one. He did ask about Lila."

A chill went through Armie. "What exactly did he say?"

He turned and looked back into the room he'd found for them. He still had connections here in the city, and he'd managed to get them a table at Arnaud's. She'd seemed to relax after two Sazeracs. He was fairly certain a lot of memories were playing through her head, and none of them good. If he'd taken her home, she likely would have insisted on going back to the clinic and updating files. She would have found an excuse, but he'd put her in a corner, telling her he was too tired to drive.

She needed someone to take her out of her head for a while, and that was his new favorite occupation.

He also needed to let her know that this wasn't just sex for him. He wanted to take care of her.

"He asked if his wife was with Lila," Roxie explained. "You have to know that neither I nor Major would ever have told him a thing."

"He's not an idiot. I went out there right after Carrie saw Lila the first time. This has apparently been going on for years. Carrie comes in, tells Doc it was an accident, and nothing happened. She sees Lila once and we were on his doorstep. Did he threaten her in any way?"

"No. He asked if Lila had taken care of her. He's a careful little shit," Roxie said with her usual candor. "If he'd said anything even indirectly, I would have called you immediately because he's got a brother and I wouldn't put it past them to work together."

"According to Carrie the brother never touched her." He'd had a long discussion with Carrie while Lila had been on the phone to the shelter. He'd documented years of abuse, and the guilt sat in his gut. "The mother never physically abused her and I can't put people in jail for being assholes." God, he wished he could. "Call me if anything else happens. And treat Bobby Petrie like gold. I'm not joking. I don't want anything sketchy about this arrest."

"Got it. And, boss, this isn't on you."

"I've been the sheriff here for years."

"And she was good at hiding it," Roxie replied. "Doc was good at pretending it didn't exist. He should have told you. You have a big jurisdiction. You can't patrol every inch of it every day. Believe me, I know. You did good today, and tell your girlfriend that she rocks. I'll hold the fort down here. You relax."

He glanced at the bathroom door. It was slightly open and steam poured out. "I'll try to do that. I'll be back tomorrow before his arraignment. Be careful and keep your eyes open."

"Will do."

He hung up and stepped back into the room. They'd stopped at a convenience store and grabbed a few things they would need, but he hadn't thought about the fact that she didn't have clothes for tomorrow. Not that she would need them tonight.

She was inside the gorgeous stone-and-glass shower. His eyes caught on her graceful body, but there was a weariness to the way she held herself that kicked him in the gut. She was feeling every minute of the day.

He tugged his shirt over his head and ditched the rest of his clothes. He kept thinking about how much she needed him, but it was all a cover. He needed her. He thought about her all the time, his life utterly revolving around her moods and desires. If she smiled at him, he was happy. If she was sad, he had to try to fix it. There was no fixing what was bothering her now, but he could help her forget for a while.

He stepped into the shower. "You know you did good today."

Her eyes came open and she glanced his way. "I hope so. I don't know. The truth is she could be right back in his home in a couple of weeks. I've seen it before. I've seen it all, the same women coming through time and time again and having the very men who put them in the ER pick them up. It was different in the ER. I didn't get to know anyone. I wasn't completely responsible, if you know what I mean."

He stepped in behind her and picked up the soap, building up a rich lather in his hands. "I know exactly what you mean. I used to be responsible for any number of cases. But it was easy to distance in the city. I know every one of these people. Maybe not as well as I should, as today proved, but I know them. They're not names on a file I can't quite recall. They're the people I grew up around. Carrie's mom was friends with mine. They used to bring by a tray of

Christmas cookies every year. She was younger than I was, but I can remember her standing next to her momma and delivering treats. How did I not see she was hurting?"

He put his hands on her shoulders and started to wash her skin. She sighed and let her head drop forward. "That's not your job. It's mine. You can't do a thing if she won't talk to you. You can't force her to tell you the truth. From what I can tell they purposefully isolated her."

"Well, I'm going to check on the people who live on those islands more often," he promised. "I'll try to make it so it's a friendly thing, but I need to make sure nothing's going on out there."

"When you do, can you tell them Doc retired? I'm so tired of explaining I'm not his new nurse." Her muscles started to relax. "I kind of hate that man. He was lazy. That feels so good."

He pulled her back against him and loved the way she relaxed as though she trusted him not to let her fall. He moved his hands up to her breasts, cupping them and feeling the way her nipples pebbled against his hand. "I have you right where I want you now, *chérie*. Away from all the stress of work. I think every time you get too caught up in all the drama that town can make, we'll come up here and eat and drink and I'll take you back to some elegant hotel room and I'll do this. I'll get my hands on you and I won't take them off until you've screamed my name three or four times."

"I would never," she said with a husky chuckle. "I'm a lady, Sheriff."

"You're my lady." Desire thrummed through his system and he realized what he'd forgotten. Damn it. "Lila, baby, I'm going to need to run back downstairs."

Or he could call downstairs and have someone bring up condoms. Surely they had condoms.

She turned and her head tilted up. Her hands went to his pecs and she ran them up to his shoulders. "Armie, I was joking about the STI tests. I know you had a full physical three months ago. It included a blood panel and testing for just about everything. By the way, we're going to talk about your cholesterol soon. Have you had any unprotected sex since then?"

"The only person I've been with in years is you. My player days were over long ago." Was she saying what he thought she was saying?

"Like I told you, I'm on the pill and I haven't had sex with anyone but you for over a year. So don't make some poor bellman run out and get you condoms. Make love to me, Armie."

He didn't need to be asked twice. He covered her mouth with his and let himself go.

Lila knew she should have gone back to the clinic, but when he offered to take her to dinner, she'd wanted her time with him. She'd wanted to be alone with him.

How was she in so deep with this man in so little time? He wasn't at all the partner she'd envisioned for herself. She'd thought she needed someone successful, highly educated, motivated.

Turned out, kind and sexy and focused on her trumped all the other stuff. Armie LaVigne was a man who knew how to love, and whoever he ended up with would be one lucky woman.

Why shouldn't that woman be her?

He kissed her like he needed her. His hands slid down her spine to cup her backside.

He was having an effect on her she hadn't expected. She'd thought maybe she could enjoy a physical relationship with him, but it was going deeper. So much deeper. She liked him, liked his daughter, loved feeling in some small way like they were starting to become a family. It was dangerous, but she couldn't stop herself. She couldn't make smart decisions about this man.

He was addictive. She softened and let his tongue invade her mouth, sliding against hers and causing a fresh rush of arousal to make her head spin. She ran her hands over the strong muscles of his back and enjoyed the sensation of being caught between his warm male form and the heat of the shower. Sometimes the world seemed so cold, but she was safe here.

Maybe that's what she was truly getting addicted to—feeling safe. Oh, she knew the world wasn't safe. That damn accident and what had happened with Carrie reinforced what she already knew, but there was a place that was safe. This place she'd found with Armie.

"Tu me rends fou, mon ange." The words were whispered over her skin as he kissed his way down her throat.

"I want you to teach me. I want to learn how to speak French." It might help with some of her patients. Some of them spoke a combination of French and English and pure Cajun that she couldn't completely understand.

His head came up and his lips split in the sexiest grin. "I can teach you. Repeat after me. *Armie est le meilleur amant du monde.*"

She knew a trap when she heard one. "Am I saying something about you being the sexiest man?"

He shook his head. "The best lover."

She could learn those words because they were true. She went on her toes and lightly kissed his lips. *"Armie est le mellar amour da mande."*

He grinned. "I have no idea what you said, but I love the way you say it." One hand came back up to find the nape of her neck. "Let's go slow. Repeat this. *Armand est mon homme.*"

"Armand est mon homme."

"I'm your man, *chérie*. It's all I want to be."

"You're my man." They weren't words she'd thought she would ever say. They were words meant for romance novels, not ones she would claim for her own. Now she realized it was because she'd viewed them in the wrong way. Armie wasn't saying he owned her or she owned him. Those words were a declaration of intent, the intent to try, to be together, to support each other. He was telling her she could count on him. "I'm your woman."

"Tu es ma femme," he agreed and took her mouth again.

Then there was no more talking. There were his hands and his mouth and his body against hers. There was communication, communion through kisses and caresses and the way his big body shuddered when she touched him.

She explored him. Somehow it always felt like discovery when she touched Armie. He let her explore. Her hands skimmed over his torso and down to his strong legs. He'd been so giving with her in bed, but they'd forgotten a few things. She'd been so wrapped up in his dominance in bed that she'd forgotten how much fun it could be to give back.

She dropped to her knees, the warmth of the shower at her back.

"Tu vas me tuer, mon amour," he said, his eyes hotter than the shower.

She didn't need any translation for that one. She'd rarely done this. Sex hadn't been an indulgence. It had been a bodily function, a thing to enjoy and forget and get back to work or sleep after. Now she wanted to revel in it. She wanted to try all the things that had seemed unimportant before. She reached out and stroked him, loving the feel of him in her hand. The skin was soft but he was hard, wanting.

"That's what I need, *chérie*. I need you to touch me everywhere." His head was down, watching her as she played with him. His hands came down to toy with her hair and she knew it wouldn't be long before he'd fisted them there and he took control.

She was all right with that. He'd never led her the wrong way, but she was going to enjoy these few moments where she was in charge. She leaned over and licked the head of his cock. It tried to leap in her hand, but she held him firmly. She stroked him again and gave him another teasing kiss.

"You're going to pay me back, aren't you?"

She simply smiled up at him. The man could spend hours playing with her. She'd never had any lover lavish his affection on her the way Armie did. She needed to give the same back to him, to let him know exactly how much she enjoyed him.

And she did. Every moan and hiss that came from his mouth let her know how much she was affecting him. Those hands in her hair tightened, the way she knew they would, and she chuckled.

"I love the way you laugh. I love it even more when I can feel it on my cock," Armie said, his voice deepening along with his accent. When he was deeply aroused, his Cajun came out more strongly than it did in his everyday life, as though when he was with her in the most primal, intimate sense, he became more of himself. Like she got a part of Armie no one else did.

He was the only man who regularly made her laugh. If she was getting some secret part of Armie, he was getting a piece of her she hadn't known existed. With him, she was discovering that she wasn't so afraid anymore. She could relax. The man and this place were definitely having an effect on her.

"Take more," he demanded gruffly, his hands gently clutching her hair.

She even liked the slight sting of him tugging against her scalp. It sent mini shock waves through her.

She softened her jaw and sucked him, whirling her tongue around and around. Humming around him, she stroked him with one hand as she moved up and down.

He tugged on her hair, pulling her off. "I can't. I need to get inside you. I missed you all day."

His hand came out and she took it, allowing him to help her to her feet. Her whole body pulsed with desire, as though she could feel her blood pounding through her system. He pulled her in close and suddenly her back was against the stone of the shower wall.

"J'ai besoin de toi," he said, lifting her up. "Put your legs around me. I need to be with you."

She needed it, too. She needed to feel that connection to him. It was visceral and real and undeniable when he was making love to her. She locked her legs around his waist as he stroked into her. The orgasm struck and she called out his name. She clung to him, giving up all control and riding the magnificent wave.

His body stiffened as he came, bucking into her.

She held on to him, sweet languor invading her veins, and wished the moment never had to end.

Hours later, Armie laid back and took a contented breath. Lila shifted and put her head on his chest. The second go around had been every bit as good as the first. His body was sated, his soul content. This was how he'd ended the last few nights, and he wasn't sure he could go back to sleeping alone. Still, he didn't want to push her.

"Did you talk to Roxie?" The question was asked in a quiet voice, but it managed to shake his peace.

He didn't want to talk about this, but he knew she would worry. "Bobby's in jail. He won't have a chance to get out until tomorrow when the judge is in court again. But you have to know he's going to post bail."

"I know. I've seen it happen before. I know how a man like that can work the system."

"Are you all right?" He looked down at her, taking in the curve of her cheek and soft fall of her hair. "It had to be hard for you to do that today. You had to be thinking about your friend."

She was thoughtful for a moment. "I'm in a position I can't get out of. As long as I work in the medical field, I'm always going to be here. I'm always going to have to make the call whether I involve you in a patient's life, and the minute I involve you one of two things is going to happen. I guess three, really."

He knew exactly what those things were. "She gets away. He gets her. Or she goes back to him and he still gets her. He might not kill her, but her life won't be what it could have been. She won't have the opportunities she should have. She'll live in fear. You will always have to make that decision, but I want you to know that I will always back you up. I have to follow the law, but I'll do everything I can to help you."

Her arm wound around his waist. "Thank you. That makes it easier. Cops in the city, they care, but they don't have the time to follow up more than once. There are too many people they have to deal with. You and I could make a difference if we tried. If I can get people to trust me."

He smoothed a hand down her back. "They will. It takes time, but you can make a huge difference here. I know that things change fast in the outside world, but we're isolated, and it's worse in the outlying areas of the parish. Seeing a woman running that clinic might teach our girls there's something more out there than marriage."

She sat up, not bothering with pulling the sheet with her. Her breasts were bare, her hair around her shoulders. She looked like a woman who'd been well loved. She also looked like a woman who wasn't sure what to say next. Lila bit her bottom lip and stared down at him.

"Whatever you're going to say, say it." Was this when she told him she'd figured out she needed the city?

"Did you know Noelle scored crazy high on her PSATs?"

He relaxed back. "Hell, yeah. She had great scores. I have no idea where she got her smarts. Let me tell you, her mother and I weren't that great in school. Noelle was definitely the best thing we ever did."

It didn't hurt so much to think about Monica now. She was a fond memory tempered by wistful regret that she wasn't still here. The accident hadn't been her fault. She'd been a good mom to Noelle. She simply hadn't enjoyed being a cop's wife, and she definitely hadn't wanted to live in Papillon.

"You know how incredible that is? She's got a lot of options, Armie."

But she didn't, and already the conversation was making him uncomfortable. He hated the fact that his daughter wouldn't have the same opportunities other kids would have, but he'd dealt with it a long time ago. He made the best of things. "Yes, online schools can do amazing things these days. Did she talk to you about her tests?"

"Not exactly." She took a deep breath before proceeding. "She threw away a letter from her counselor. I found an envelope half in and half out of my trash can. I didn't remember putting it there. I opened it to make sure it wasn't something I needed to keep. The counselor is encouraging her to apply to several well-known and respected colleges. Not online schools. UT Austin sent her information on how to apply."

His daughter in Austin? No way. Still, he was surprised Noelle hadn't mentioned the counselor's letter. Or maybe he wasn't. How must it feel to know she would be accepted and not be able to go? "Noelle knows what she's doing."

"See, I don't think she does. She's sixteen. And I'll be honest, I don't think the PT the doctor prescribed for her is enough. He's basically got her going in so her muscles don't atrophy. I think he should have done everything he could to see how mobile she can be. He didn't do a lot of testing."

"He knew how mobile she could be." Which was not much at all. He'd been sick when he'd realized there was nothing he could do to help his daughter.

"I don't think so."

He sat up because it looked like their sweet time together was over. "Why don't you think so?"

"Because of where her injury is," Lila explained. "It's very low on her spine and it's incomplete. She has some feeling. I've even seen her move her hips a bit. I think with time and patience, she could potentially walk with braces."

"That's not what the doctor said."

"It is what the specialist said."

He'd been over this a thousand times. "The specialist we saw said it was very unlikely."

"He said without proper PT she wouldn't be able to do it," she argued.

He shook his head. "He told us it would be difficult and painful and likely wouldn't help."

"And what did your second opinion doctor say? Armie, I know this makes you uncomfortable, but it's important. I looked into the specialist Dr. Hamet sent you to. He was an old friend. *Old* being the operative word, and he worked in a small hospital."

"Are you saying we don't have good doctors?" He should have known she would come up with that argument.

"I'm saying there's a reason for the old phrase 'Hire an old lawyer and a young doctor.' Younger doctors keep up with new research. I'm not saying older doctors can't be great, but if this specialist was anything like Dr. Hamet, he thought the old ways were best. I'm shocked at some of the meds Hamet still has people on. There are better medications out there now with less side effects. He has no protocols for talking about nutrition and how it can affect diabetics. He simply gave them meds and told them to deal with it. I think that's what happened with Noelle. He took the lazy way out."

The old guilt was rising inside him, and he definitely didn't like the word *lazy*. "I did everything they told me to do. Noelle didn't like physical therapy. It hurt and it wasn't going to work anyway. Do you know what it's like to watch your child in pain? It's not like she's skipping therapy. She works out. She has good upper-body strength."

"And that's great, but I think I'm going to prescribe some new therapies for her. There's a lot more we can do to help her now."

He sighed, wanting to end this conversation. She was the expert here. If she thought she could help, he wasn't going to stop her. "All right. I think we're willing to try, but I don't want to give her false hope."

"If you were in her place, wouldn't you rather try and fail than not try at all?"

She looked so earnest it made his heart break a little. He leaned over and kissed her. "All right. I'll talk to her and you figure out what you think is best. I'll make sure she goes to all her appointments."

"Thank you. It's been worrying me." She laid back down.

He followed, happy that was over. It might be good for Noelle to get out more. He would talk to her about the colleges. She obviously couldn't actually attend a college since she couldn't live on her own, but he could talk to her about community college. There was one an hour away. It would be hard, but he might be able to find a way to get her to and from school.

"Have you thought about having other kids?" Lila asked.

The hits kept on coming. "Not really. I'm forty."

"That's not old. A lot of people are starting families at forty these days."

"A lot of people don't have a disabled kid to deal with."

"She's not a kid, though, is she?" Lila mused. "She's a young woman, and she won't always be at home."

He supposed Noelle might find a husband. Probably would since she was lovely. God, he couldn't think of a single teen in town he would trust with his daughter. He rolled onto his side. "Why are you asking?"

Her eyes were on him, soft and luminous in the low light from the lamp on the nightstand. "I don't know. I'm curious, I guess."

This was getting serious. He knew it, but he wasn't sure he was ready for this conversation. "I hadn't thought about it at all. Monica had a rough time when she was pregnant with Noelle. She didn't want to try again. I suppose I got used to the idea of having one kid. Then we got divorced and the accident happened and I haven't thought about remarrying or even dating at all until I met you. I kind of thought you wouldn't want kids."

That seemed to startle her. "Why?"

This was a conversation filled with land mines. "You're very focused on your career."

"The funny thing is if I was a man, you wouldn't even consider that being a barrier to me wanting a family. The other funny thing is a couple of years ago I would have said you were right. I would have said the last thing in the world I wanted was to be a mom. I didn't have one. I mean I did, and she's all right now, but when we were growing up . . . Kids need stability. I did not have that."

"Because your mom was an addict?"

"Oh, yes. She was addicted to a lot of things. Mostly I think she was addicted to not dealing with things. She always wanted to be out of her head. It started with liquor and men."

"When did she start going to jail?"

"The first time I was six," Lila explained. "My aunt came and stayed with us while my mother was incarcerated, but she wasn't terribly interested in four kids under the age of ten. She was there but she wasn't. She spent most of the time teaching us how to take care of ourselves. It felt harsh, but I was grateful for the lessons later."

He didn't like to think about her childhood. "She should have taken care of you."

Lila shrugged. "We weren't hers. She never wanted kids and she wasn't going to spend her life cleaning up her sister's mess. We found that if we didn't ask much of her, she was willing to help us with CPS. That was our whole life, trying to convince CPS not to split us up. No one wants to foster four kids together. We learned how to take care of each other, how to push each other to excel because it was the only way we were ever getting out of that trailer park."

"You grew up fast."

"I didn't have much of a childhood, but I've been thinking a lot lately about how I might be able to offer a kid a good one. Childhood, that is. For a long time I thought I shouldn't have kids because my own childhood was rough, but I know what not to do. That's something."

What would it be like to start over? Did he have any right to when he had Noelle to take care of?

"Hey," she said, reaching out and touching his hair, a soft look on her face. "I'm just talking, Armie. I'm not demanding sperm. I promise I'm really on the pill."

"I wasn't thinking you lied to me." He trusted her.

"But you are wondering how we could work long-term if I want kids and you don't," she pointed out.

"I haven't thought about it. Honestly, I haven't thought

much about the future at all since the accident," he admitted. "I've gotten through the days. I've sat up nights praying my daughter will be okay. She was depressed after the accident."

"Of course she was."

He hated even thinking about those first few months. "I would go into her room at night to make sure she was still alive. Like when she was a baby and I had to get up in the middle of the night to assure myself she was still breathing."

"You've done an amazing job with her. Don't think that my wanting to try something new with her therapy says anything about what a great dad you are." She moved to him, cuddling up. "We don't have to talk about this now. I don't know why it's on my mind. We should just have fun."

"This isn't fun, Lila." He was serious about her, and that meant getting real. "I'm not playing around. I'm not having some fling. Can I think about this for a while? I don't know what I want when it comes to more kids, but I know I want you in my life. I want this."

He kissed her and felt her relax against him.

The buzzing of his cell phone interrupted the moment. He wanted to ignore it, but he had to pick it up because Noelle might need him.

There was a smile on Lila's face. "Go on, Sheriff. I'm not ever going to give you hell for needing to answer your phone. I'm on call most of the time, too."

There were distinct advantages to dating a woman who was also a first responder. He kissed her forehead and rolled over, grabbing his phone.

And his skin went cold because it wasn't Noelle, who might call him because her tablet froze and she didn't remember how to fix it. It was Roxie, who would never disturb him unless it was serious.

"What's happening?"

"You need to come home, boss," Roxie said. "There's been an incident. A house burned down. The fire department is trying to save what they can right now, but I don't like their chances."

"Whose house?"

He knew the answer before she said the words. "It's Lila's place."

He stood up because their night out was over.

chapter thirteen

"I don't know what you want me to say, Sheriff." Bobby Petrie stood in the small cell, his hands on his hips. "Obviously, I couldn't have burned down anything. I was here."

"I'd like to know where your brother was last night."

He suspected Donny Petrie had been busy the night before. Lila's small home had been completely gutted. They'd made it back to Papillon in the middle of the night, but the morning had brought with it the sight of her destroyed house. She'd held his hand tight as she'd stared at the house she'd briefly called home and then she'd gone to work.

And so had he.

Bobby looked like he'd slept perfectly fine. He was bright-eyed this morning as he looked at Armie through the bars on his cell. "You would have to ask him, but I suspect he was busy trying to find me a lawyer since the only one in town turned us down. He probably spent the whole night on the phone trying to work something out. I assure you my brother wouldn't have burned down some random woman's house."

He could feel Roxie moving to stand beside him. Likely she was going to try to make sure he didn't murder their prisoner. "She wasn't a random woman and you know it. You're lucky Dr. Daley wasn't in the house at the time."

Bobby shrugged. "Why would I want to hurt Lila Daley? All she's ever done is try to help my wife out. She doesn't understand how sick Carrie is. I blame myself. I should have talked to her. I should have let her know that Carrie can be delusional at times and she loves to get my attention. That's all this is. You should talk to Doc Hamet. He knows all about my wife's problems."

"You can't fool Dr. Daley the way you did Hamet." He wasn't about to let Bobby muddy the waters by bringing the doc into this.

"Not trying to fool anyone. I'm worried about my wife." He managed to sound like he gave a shit. "Look, I understand that she told you a bunch of stories about how I hurt her and I have, but not physically. I've been having an affair with another woman. This is how she's trying to get back at me. We'll go over all of it in court, I suspect. If I could talk to her, explain to her that I'm sorry about cheating on her, I'm sure we could handle this on our own. You know how women can be."

"I don't," Roxie interjected. "Why don't you tell me how women can be."

"Vindictive," Bobby replied, his eyes sharpening. "Sometimes nothing you do is enough for a woman." He seemed to shake off the darkness that had briefly clouded his eyes. Or he'd managed to get his mask back on. "Marriage is hard. It's definitely more complex when the wife has a mental illness."

It was easy to see Bobby knew how he was going to play this. The problem was Armie could see some people buying into what Bobby was saying. Lila would be the one who had to explain to the judge and any jury how those injuries couldn't have been self-inflicted or accidental.

Lila could be the one who tipped the scales of justice in this case, and there was zero question that she would do it. Lila wouldn't back down.

"Sheriff, can I talk to you in your office?" Roxie turned away from the cell.

She was obviously trying to get him to back off, and she

was right to do it because if he didn't put some distance between them, he might reach in and throttle the asshole. Lila was going to be in this man's way, and he'd already proven he was capable of hurting a woman.

He'd listened to Carrie on the long drive to New Orleans and he believed her. Even if Carrie hadn't told him her story, he would have believed Lila's logic.

Losing his cool here and now wouldn't help Carrie or Lila down the line. He took a long breath and faced Bobby. "You settle in. I heard the judge is moving slow these days. I'll let you know if your lawyer shows up. And don't think that getting out on bond means I won't be watching you. I see you even breathe around Lila Daley and we'll be right back here."

He turned and strode away before Bobby could get another word in. He nodded as Major walked in, ready for his shift. Roxie had spent the night at the station house, but she looked none the worse for it.

Ah, youth. He was getting old, and late nights showed on his face. He wanted to be just waking up, warm and happy with Lila cuddled up beside him. He would have kissed her and made love to her again, and then they would have gotten dressed and walked to Café Du Monde hand in hand. He would have driven her back, talking to her the whole time.

Damn, but he was falling in love with that woman, and that could be dangerous because she might want more than he was willing to give.

"We have to bring in an arson investigator from New Orleans. He'll be here tomorrow afternoon, but right now the fire department boys are saying they think it was faulty wiring," Roxie said as soon as she closed the door. "They think it started in the laundry room, and the place went up fast. Something about old newspapers."

Lila had been planning to recycle the massive stack of papers Bill had collected but hadn't gotten around to it. And there was no doubt the place had bad wiring. He'd seen it himself. Still, it was awfully coincidental. "I want to know where Donny Petrie was, and while we're on it, I want to make sure Momma Petrie was out on her island last night. I wouldn't put it past her."

"I'll get right on it. You don't buy what the fire chief is saying?"

"I don't know. He's a good man, but he's not an arson inspector. I'll wait until we get that report in. Until then, I want us to keep an eye on Lila." She'd lost everything. She didn't have clothes. He was certain her sister was already working on that problem. Lisa had shown up at the site a few minutes after they'd gotten there, throwing her arms around her sister and crying freely.

Lila wouldn't cry. Not in public. She would wait until they were alone, and even then he would have to make love to her. When he'd stripped down all her walls, she would give in and let the tension out.

Was she planning on moving out to Guidry's? There was an apartment over the bar. Or she could stay at Lisa and Remy's home close to town.

He didn't want that. Was he being a bastard by thinking about using the situation to get her to move in with him? If she did move in, would she get comfortable, maybe so comfortable she forgot the problems they had? Could he convince her to forgo the possibility of having children of her own?

Did he want to do that? The idea of Lila with a baby in her arms was a pleasant one.

The idea of loving that child, of worrying about that child, of potentially losing that child was the thing that made him hesitate.

There was a knock on the door and the very object of his worry opened it.

"Dad, is Lila okay?" Noelle moved into the room, her backpack on her lap. It would include her lunchbox, a couple of books, and her laptop so she could catch up on schoolwork when she wasn't answering the phone.

Would she be stuck here, working dispatch in a tiny station house for the rest of her life? She'd always been fascinated with chemistry. When she'd been a kid, she'd wanted a chemistry set when other girls her age had asked for Barbie Dolls for Christmas. The fact that she couldn't walk didn't disqualify her from working in a lab. But she would need the education to get there.

How would she do that? She couldn't live in a dorm. His house was equipped to handle her wheelchair and all the problems that came with her lack of mobility. He couldn't send her out into a world where no one would care.

But wasn't that the worry every parent had to face?

"She's fine," Roxie said. "Lila wasn't in the house at the time. She was in New Orleans with your father."

"I didn't mean physically," Noelle replied. "She lost her home. I would be devastated."

"Daley's a tough one." Roxie eased around the wheelchair to get to the door. "She's already back at work. I like her. I would have her watch my back. Boss, I'm going home. I'll be back for the night shift. Call me if you need anything."

Noelle turned to him as the door closed. "Seriously, is she okay?"

"As okay as she can be," he replied. "I need to talk to you about that. She doesn't have a home. She could go to her sister's."

"Or she could stay with us," his daughter replied quickly.

"You understand that there might be a reason her house burned down." He wanted to be careful about this. He didn't want to scare her. "It might be faulty wiring."

"Or it might be that jerk in the jail cell." She pointed toward the station house main floor. "Maybe he didn't do it personally, but he had it done. He wanted to hurt Lila because she helped Carrie get away from him. I've heard all sorts of terrible things happened to her out on the islands. Did you know some people think the Petries run drugs?"

He groaned. "Don't listen to gossip." Although it might be helpful now. "They're not blaming Lila for sticking her nose in other people's business?"

"I was in the café last night and someone called Lila an

outsider and Dixie nearly took his head off," Noelle explained. "I swear she told everyone if they had a problem with the new doc helping women leave their abusive husbands, then they should understand they weren't welcome in her café. There were a whole bunch of old guys who shut their mouths real fast."

Since Dixie's was one of the only places in town to get a good breakfast, he could bet they had. It was good to know they had at least one person on their side. It didn't solve the problem, though. "I don't have any proof that the Petries had anything to do with the fire, and it could be a while before I do. That means Lila could be in danger. If she comes to stay with us, that means you might be in danger, too."

"I'll be fine, and I think they'll think twice before coming after her in the sheriff's home. She should stay with us."

That was what he'd hoped she would say. And the truth of the matter was the Petries would be stupid to push it any further. He had a security system, and his house wasn't vulnerable the way hers had been. "I'll talk to her. Now tell me why you threw away the counselor's letter."

Her eyes widened and a fine flush made her skin pink. "How do you know about that?"

"Lila found it. She didn't know what it was."

Noelle frowned. "I wish she'd given it back to me instead of reading it."

"Why, sweetheart? That was nothing to be ashamed of."

"And it was also nothing to get excited about. It doesn't mean anything. I'm going to find an online school and I'm going to get a business degree. I might look into accounting. There's always work for accountants."

Somehow he couldn't see her as an accountant. "I thought you wanted to be a chemist."

"I can't get an advanced degree in chemistry online, not one that would get me a good job, and there's not a lot of call for chemists in Papillon. I'm realistic, Dad. The counselor can talk all she wants, but she's not the one who would have to figure out a way to get around campus. It's fine here."

"Lila thinks you might have more mobility if she changes your physical therapy." He didn't want to give her false hope, but he also didn't want her to not try.

A long sigh came from his daughter's mouth. "She wants to fix me."

That might be the case. "I think for Lila this is a way to show she cares about you. You have to go, so why not try? After all, she's helped you out before. After that purchase she helped you make, I'm fairly certain our electricity bill is going to double."

The quizzical look on her face was quickly replaced with one of complete horror as she realized what he was talking about. "Dad!"

She turned her chair and stormed out.

Armie smiled as he watched her go, and he thought about how to get the two women he loved under the same roof. Maybe he could show her how good a family they could be.

She had nothing. Absolutely nothing. She was in her mid-thirties and she had absolutely nothing to her name. She didn't even have a shitty trailer to call her own. How the hell had she ended up here?

She used to have nice things. Oh, she'd worn scrubs to work, but on her days off she'd worn designer clothes and one of her precious two pairs of Louboutins. She'd carried a Chanel bag she'd scrimped and saved for. The apartment she'd shared with Brock had been beautifully furnished. She'd left most of that behind when she'd left him, but she'd thought somewhere down the line she might fix up her dumpy bayou home.

And it hadn't been so dumpy. In the beginning it had seemed like a trash heap, but slowly she'd found small treasures—books she'd wanted to read, records to listen to, a book of recipes to try. All gone.

A thumping tail told her she wasn't completely alone. Peanut was sitting beside her, his head up, big doggy eyes staring at her like she knew what the hell she was doing. She had to buy dog food. And a bowl. And a bed. And everything. Did she even have the money for that?

"Lila? Are you all right? That was our last appointment of the day." Mabel stood in the doorway, her purse on her shoulder. "Is Lisa coming to pick you up? Hon, you can come home with me. I might even have something that fits you."

Only if Mabel used to be about four inches taller. She hadn't even thought about what she'd do for clothes. She had two sets of scrubs here at the clinic. They would have to do until she could go shopping. Where would she go shopping? At least she still had a car. Not that she'd used it much lately.

"Thanks, but I think I'm going to stay here and make a couple of lists of things I'll need." She knew Lisa would come get her, and she would likely be more than willing to go and shop, but she couldn't face her sister right now.

She wondered if she could stay here. There was a perfectly nice on-call room. It wasn't normally used because the clinic wasn't open twenty-four-seven, but there was a cot and a bathroom with a shower. There was a fridge and a microwave in the break room.

The bell that let them know someone was at the entrance chimed through the clinic.

It might be her sister. She'd told Lisa she would call when she needed help, but Lisa wasn't all that great at listening. She moved toward reception, Mabel and Peanut trailing after her.

A familiar young woman stood on the other side of the glass doors, bags in her hands and a stroller at her side. Hallie Rayburn smiled and Lila opened the doors.

"Hey, Hallie. Is everything okay with your mom?" Neither Hallie nor the baby had an appointment. She'd heard Janice was doing well now that she was home from the hospital, though she wasn't happy about not being able to pour butter over all her vegetables. She'd gotten an earful about fried chicken not being on the list of acceptable foods Lila had given her.

"She's okay, though I will admit she was easier to deal with when I could tell her I was hungry to get her off my back for a while. Now that she's on the heart-healthy diet, she's all about getting in my business. But I'm here for another reason. Me and Seraphina went around and got you some things we thought you might need. Dixie told us you were back in the clinic after last night, and we figured you wouldn't have time to go shopping. It's nothing much but it should cover the basics."

There were a couple of big bags sitting by the stroller. "You didn't have to do that."

"Oh, it was a ton of fun, and once people heard we were going, they pitched in with some cash. The insurance might take a while, so we all know you'll need a few things. It can be hard to get adjusters out here quickly. Besides, we got to drive into Houma to go to the new superstore there. I know it's not anything special, but they have the basics. We got you jeans and undies and bras. I know it sounds weird but I'm excellent at discerning bra size. My husband says I was a perverted man in my last life. You're a thirty-four B."

She was. Lila nodded, still trying to figure out what was going on.

Hallie grinned, obviously pleased with herself. "There's shampoo, conditioner, and Miss Marcelle threw in some anti-frizz gel. We got you some makeup, too. You're definitely a fall. That was the color palette I got you. I also bought you socks. Socks are important. I hate it when my feet are cold."

They'd bought her makeup? She didn't know these women very well, but they'd gone out of their way to ensure she had little comforts? "This is very nice of you."

"Well, you saved my baby. You also saved my momma's life. It happened recently enough that I'm still grateful, so bask in the attention, Doc. And there's also the fact that you're here. I know I wasn't easy on you that first day, but I feel better about Gracie's future knowing that you're here and you're going to do everything you can to make sure she stays healthy. If you hadn't taken over the clinic, we would have to drive an hour to get any kind of care. Thank you."

The world went watery. No one outside of her siblings had ever done something like this for her. She looked down into the bags. There were jeans and T-shirts, a package of plain white cotton undies and two bras. And there were socks. Fluffy, pink-and-purple unicorn socks.

Nothing designer or flashy. Nothing that said *I'm successful.*

A whole lot that said *someone cares about me.*

"We went by the pet section, too. We figure Peanut's stuff didn't survive, either," Hallie explained.

They'd bought food for her dog.

"Hey, the waterworks are starting early," a deep voice said. Armie. Armie was here and he looked so big and safe.

She threw herself into his arms and wrapped herself around him. "They bought me socks."

"Does she not like socks, Sheriff?" Hallie asked.

Armie held her close. "I think she likes socks a lot. I bet it's been a long time since anyone but her siblings tried to take care of her."

That was wrong. She brought her head up so she could look him in the eyes. "You take care of me."

The softest look came over his face. "Yes, I do, *chérie.* It's all I want to do."

She pulled away and turned to Hallie, wiping her tears. "Thank you. And please thank everyone who helped. I can't tell you what it means to me."

Hallie hugged her. Lila didn't hug patients. She didn't do the get-close-to-people thing because people often let her down.

This wasn't a high-powered ER where the patients would come and go and she would barely remember their names. She would know these people, come to care about these people, and that was so scary to her.

She'd come to this town to hide away, but it was going to

force her to change. She'd gone into medicine because it had seemed like the best way out of the poverty of her childhood. It had made her feel smart and strong and powerful. It had been something to conquer.

She would have to be more here. She would have to continue for different reasons. She would be a primary care provider because these people were her neighbors, her community.

Her family.

She hugged Hallie and somehow despite everything that had happened, she felt larger than she'd been before.

Hallie and Mabel left a few minutes later, seeming to understand she needed some time to settle down. She was left alone with the man she was falling in love with. She hadn't thought this would ever happen to her. She'd thought she wasn't capable of feeling so much for anyone outside her family.

What would it feel like to make a child with this man? Another thing she'd never wanted before she'd met him. With Armie by her side, she might be able to do all the things she'd been too afraid to do.

He stared down at her. "I was coming over to take you out to dinner and try to convince you to come home with me."

"You want me to spend the night?"

"I want you to move in." He set his hat down on the counter and looked ready to plead his case. "I know it hasn't been very long. I get that we're probably moving faster than we should, but I also believe that things happen for a reason."

"My house burned down so we could move in together?"

"No." He was incredibly cute when he was flustered. "That didn't come out right. I guess what I am trying to say is sometimes things happen and we have to react to them. And my first reaction was to hold you as close as I could and take you back home with me. Well, not my first reaction. My first reaction was to go and find Bobby Petrie and that brother of his, throttle both of them, and leave them for the gators. But I didn't do that because I'm trying to be less violent. So I'm going with my second reaction."

"Which is to haul me back to your lair." God, she was crazy about him.

She seemed to stump him. "Not like that. It's your choice . . . You're screwing with me, aren't you?"

She nodded.

"You're coming home with me."

Again, all she had to do was nod.

He moved into her space. "I want you home with me and so does Noelle. I want you in my life and my bed every single day."

"Yes." She was taking the leap. It didn't matter that they hadn't worked everything out. All that mattered was being with him.

His face split in the most beautiful smile. "Yes?"

"Yes."

He crowded her and she found her back up against the reception desk, his hands on her hips. "I like it when you say yes to me."

She let her hands move up to his broad shoulders. She was going to live with him. It made losing her house easier to take. She might have lost a house and gained a family. "I intend to say yes a lot."

He lowered his head to hers and his lips were about to close in, when there was that chime again. And someone pounding on the glass doors.

"Doc! Doc! Stop kissing the sheriff and let me in." Zep Guidry stood outside, his sister standing with him holding a small cooler.

"Lila, Zep is an idiot who thought he could trim the branches better than the local landscape guy," Sera yelled through the door.

"I was trying to save Momma some money," Zep argued.

"You were trying to charge her yourself, you ass." Sera shook her head and held up the cooler. "He's not so good at trimming branches, but he successfully trimmed off his pinkie finger. I've got it in here."

Lila rushed toward the door because that was going to be a challenge. "Come on in. How clean was the cut?"

"Oh, he did a great job on it," Sera said with a sigh, passing over the cooler. "It's perfectly clean. Be careful, though. Momma freaked out and I think she and Miss Marcelle might show up to perform a ritual or something. You might have to work around that."

"I can handle it." She started to lead Zep back.

Armie sighed and sat down. "I'll be waiting here."

It was good to have someone waiting, and even better to know he would be waiting to take her home.

chapter fourteen

Armie came awake to the smell of coffee and the sense that all was right with his world. Damn, but he loved waking up and knowing Lila was somewhere in the house. She almost always woke up before him. He was going to have to set an alarm because he was missing precious time with her.

In the two weeks since she'd moved in, she'd had a definite impact on his household.

The best thing she'd done was get Noelle out more often. She'd gently pushed and prodded his daughter into going to church with her. Of course that had meant *he'd* had to go to church. That wasn't a ton of fun, but Noelle had spent time with the youth group and had even gone out to the movies with some friends she'd made.

Lila had held his hand as he'd watched them drive off with his daughter. She'd been the one to convince him she had to go out on her own again, and he had to trust her enough to have some kind of a life.

Lila had also been the one who'd sat up with him waiting for her to come home, watching the little signal on his phone that showed him where she was.

"Hey, sleepy head. It's almost time for me to head out. You on night shift again?"

He rolled over and got his first look of the day. He liked starting the day alone with her and finishing it off the same way. Even when she was asleep when he came in. He'd snuck into bed at four a.m. and she'd turned as though even in her sleep she'd known he was there. She hadn't opened her eyes but had let him wrap her up in his arms as he'd gone to sleep. "I am. How did last night go?"

"Good. Noelle worked on her history project and then we watched a movie." She was dressed in scrubs, her hair up in a neat bun that made him want to sink his hands in and mess her up a little. She looked gorgeous right after sex, when she was completely open to him. He'd come to understand that was a side of Lila Daley that was saved for him, a gift to him.

"I'm glad to hear it. My night was all about the damn golf carts. I swear those damn things are a menace. Arnold Butler kitted his out with twinkle lights and oversized tires. He was going fifteen miles an hour and holding up traffic." And that old man knew a whole lot of rude hand gestures, all of which he'd used on Armie when he threatened him with a ticket.

"We were fine, so you can probably pull Major off sentry duty so you can stop working like a crazy man," she said pointedly. "You can go back to day shift and let Major deal with the crazies."

He wasn't sure about that. He'd had Major or Roxie doing regular drive-bys when he wasn't at home. So far everything had been quiet. According to the reports he'd gotten, Bobby and Donny Petrie had been getting on their boat every morning to head out into the bay to shrimp and going back to the island at night. "He doesn't mind. Neither does Rox."

She sat down on the bed beside him. "I know they don't, but it isn't necessary. The arson inspector said his results were inconclusive. Unfortunately, Bill stored gasoline in the garage, and that was right next to the laundry room. I hadn't even started to explore that garage. I was intimidated by it."

Because Bill had been a hoarder and his garage hadn't been filled with cars. He should have checked out the house more thoroughly. "I know. I read the report ten times. I'm thinking about asking for a second opinion. There was an accelerant used, but it could easily have been the gas because while Bill was apparently prepping for the apocalypse or something, he didn't use safety storage procedures. I'm going to sue that home inspector. I think I'll sue Miranda, too."

Lila's eyes went wide. "Don't you dare. She sent over the lemon cookies and they were incredible."

"Those were 'I hope you don't sue me because I screwed you over' cookies."

"Regret and fear never tasted so good," Lila replied with a shrug. "It's fine. The insurance money should come in soon. I don't think it was the Petries. I think maybe Carrie moving out proved to him that she was too much trouble. Maybe he realized how close he came to doing something that would have ruined his life. He apparently hasn't even tried to contact her. I spoke to her yesterday and she's good. She's in therapy and talking about finding a job. She's thinking of moving to Dallas."

He could imagine that a change of scenery would do her good. "I'm glad for her, but I hope she plans on testifying against him. I would hate for him to get away with it."

"I think she will. Scoot over. I have ten minutes before I have to leave." Lila laid down next to him and put her head on his chest. "I think Bobby gets that he's in trouble and he'll start looking for another punching bag. You can let up. I know where the shotgun is, and I know how to use it. I've also taken self-defense."

"I'll think about it." He hated the idea of someone out there waiting for his chance to get to her, but then, he was likely paranoid. The arson investigator had told him her house had been a bomb waiting to explode. Maybe she'd been damn lucky.

"Noelle's first PT didn't go well," she said, her voice turning careful.

He looked down at her. "She said it was fine. She said the new massage therapist was nice."

"The physical therapist didn't think she was trying."

"The therapist is wrong. She works hard." She always had.

"I'll go down today and check it out," Lila promised. "Noelle told me the same thing. She said it was fine but nothing happened. She seemed very disappointed. Patience is the key here. This could be a long process."

"That could yield absolutely nothing. You need to be patient with her, too. She's settled her mind around being strong with what she has. Neither one of us knows what it's like to be where Noelle is."

She was silent for a moment. "She was happy when she came home the other night. I think it was good for her to go out with her friends. But I know they asked her again this weekend and she said no. I overheard her on the phone. She said you told her she couldn't go."

"I never said that, but I did tell her she could throw me under the bus if she didn't want to do something." It made him worry that maybe that night hadn't gone as well as he'd thought it had. "I'll talk to her."

This was their only point of tension. The weeks since Lila had moved in had been some of the happiest he could remember, but he could tell it was starting to bother Noelle when Lila pushed her about the future. He'd saved a couple of dinners by turning the conversation away from where Noelle would go to college, what Noelle wanted to do with her life.

It was worse when Lila started talking about all the new therapies and research being done.

He knew she was only trying to help, but it was his responsibility to make sure Noelle was comfortable. It was his job to let Noelle know that she was enough.

"Okay. I'll drive her out to the therapist's today," Lila said. "I don't have anything after two, when I get to recheck Zep's finger. Luckily it was something I could handle. It was just the tip. Don't. You have no idea how many jokes he made about that."

He was sure that dealing with Zep Guidry as a care provider was almost as bad as dealing with him as a law enforcement officer. "I can imagine."

"What are you doing today?"

He was not looking forward to his day. "I get to attend a planning meeting. The town fair is next week. I have to make sure there's some form of security. We've got a couple of volunteers. I get to teach a class on our crowd control protocols."

"We have crowd control protocols? We have crowds?"

He was looking forward to taking his honey to her first big town party. "Oh, you haven't seen what can happen at one of these things. Especially at some of the food stands. They brought in fried butter last year and nearly started a stampede."

Lila groaned. "I am going to make pamphlets warning of the dangers of both fried foods and butter. And fair food. Are we sure the vendors all have health department clearance?"

"I thought you were trying to make people like you."

She shrugged. "They'll like me when I save their arteries."

"They won't," he insisted. "They don't even know what their arteries do. Besides, your sister would be leading the revolution if you got fried food banned."

"That's true." She kissed his chest. "Gotta go, babe. There's coffee when you're ready and yes, I finally figured out you've been putting chicory in my blend. It's delicious."

"Hey, you love all things Cajun."

She wrinkled her nose and stalked off.

He forced himself to get up. She was right about working crazy hours. He wasn't going to be able to do it much longer. He was starting to get irritated due to worry and lack of sleep. Just yesterday, he'd actually given out three tickets for dog doo violations when he would usually issue a warning. The owner of a Labradoodle with an obviously healthy colon had accused him of being the po-po who was too concerned with poo-poo.

He couldn't deal with these people on no sleep. Coffee and a hot shower would only keep him going for so long. He'd managed to keep his irritable mood from Lila and Noelle, but the rest of the town was definitely starting to notice. He was a bear.

Noelle sat with her laptop at the breakfast table, a big bowl in front of her. She glanced up. "There's oatmeal. Lila made it in the slow cooker last night. It's pretty good."

Her eyes went back down to the screen.

He grabbed a cup of coffee. He was too tired for this, but he didn't like the fact that there seemed to be some tension to his daughter he didn't understand. "I heard you decided to not go out this weekend. I thought you had fun."

She didn't look up from her computer screen. "I did. The movies were good, but I've got a lot of work to do."

"I get the reports on your pacing. You're ahead, sweetheart."

"I don't want to go."

"Did those girls say or do something they shouldn't have?"

"No. I just don't want to go. And I think you should talk to your girlfriend about the fact that she's not my mom." Noelle's lips firmed. "Look, I like Lila. I like her a lot, but I'm starting to think that maybe she doesn't like me."

"Why would you say that?"

"She's always talking to me about how smart I am and how much I could do."

"That doesn't seem like a bad thing."

"It is when you really can't do any of those things. I can't go to college, Dad."

"I've been thinking about that. Maybe we can work something out. I mean, I'll be honest, I don't see you going to UT Austin and living completely on your own, but maybe we could start looking around for a community college we could get you to. And maybe we should think about getting a car you could drive."

Her skin paled in the morning light. "I'm not driving. I'm not."

"Sweetie, you have to learn at some point." Had she honestly believed she wouldn't drive at all?

Now her eyes met his and there was disappointment in them. "She got to you."

"Got to me how?"

She shook her head. "Nothing. Like I said, I like Lila."

Frustration welled inside him. "Tell me. I can't solve the problem if you don't tell me what the problem is."

"I've started to wonder if maybe she doesn't want to be burdened with a stepdaughter in a wheelchair. She keeps pushing me to try things I can't do. Maybe she wants to send me away so you can start a new family and not have to deal with me."

Oh, they were going to have to have a meeting. A family meeting. "That's not what she wants. She's thinking about you and what's best for your future."

"I don't have a future," Noelle shot back with a savage anger he hadn't heard from her before. "Not one that includes going to college and living in a dorm. I can barely manage to get in my chair from bed, much less getting myself around a campus. I'll go and do the PT because it seems like that's something she needs me to do in order to be okay with me, but I don't want to listen to her complain about how lazy I am."

"Nobody is saying that. Lila certainly isn't. Is she saying things when I'm not around?"

"No. Not like that," Noelle replied. "She's always positive about it, but I have to wonder. I know I'm a burden."

"You're not a burden. You're my daughter and you still come first in my life." She had to. He was pretty sure he wanted to marry Lila, but Noelle still had to come first. "I'll talk to Lila. Maybe we should all sit down and talk."

There were tears in his daughter's eyes. "I don't want her to hate me. I want things to stay the same. Can't she like me the way I am?"

"She does like you." His heart ached for her, but she was wrong about Lila. She had to be. "Are you okay with her taking you to therapy? I can pick you up, but I have a meet-ing that will likely run long."

Could he get out of it? He would send Roxie, but she was even less tolerant than he was and might end up arresting the board members.

Noelle sniffled. "Yes, I can go with her. We're fine most of the time. We had a nice night last night, although she tried to teach me how to make the oatmeal. I can't cook. She keeps trying to teach me things."

She was trying too hard. "Lila is the type of woman who throws herself into everything she does. She's a type A. She has to be to do her job the way she does. She's trying to solve problems and be a good role model to you. Be patient with her. She means well."

"I hope so." Noelle looked back to her computer.

He got himself a cup of coffee and thought about how to navigate this new land mine.

Frustration sparked through Lila, and she was about ready to pull out her own hair. "I know that didn't go the way you hoped, but it's early and you need to try it again."

"I don't want to try it again," Noelle complained, staring up at the parallel bars like they were a snake about to bite her.

Unfortunately that snake was the only way to get to where they needed to go. After the physical therapist, a young woman named Tanya, had told her Noelle had been very stubborn about the new regimen, she'd decided to come in and take it over herself. Noelle hadn't been happy when she'd walked into the facility with her. She definitely hadn't been happy when Lila took over the session. She hadn't seen another way. At first, she'd meant to simply watch. She'd come in and stayed in the background. Noelle ignored everything her therapist said, and the minute Tanya turned her back, Noelle chose to flirt with the teenage boy who was rehabbing a broken ankle. It was typical teenage girl stuff, but she had to do something about it.

Noelle had been okay through the warm-up and the TENS unit treatment. It was when they got to the exercise portion of the afternoon that Noelle had turned stubborn. Lila had watched her carefully, and all evidence pointed to the fact that Noelle simply didn't appreciate her normal routine of denial and flirtation being interrupted. In some ways it was reassuring. Noelle always seemed so perfect. This proved she could be a rebellious teen like all the rest. It meant there was some fire under her placid surface. They were going to need that.

She'd responded well to the warm-up. All her charts showed she was past ready for this. But the real struggle had been getting her on her feet.

"I think you should go another ten minutes." They had actually made the tiniest bit of progress. She was sure Noelle couldn't see it, but that was exactly why she had a therapist.

"Definitely." Tanya nodded with obvious satisfaction. "I've been trying to get her to do this for months. I don't know why but she thinks she can't do it."

There was only so much a therapist could do, but Lila was something more. At least she was to Noelle. She could take this further.

"It hurts." Noelle stared up at them with a sullen frown on her face.

Of course it hurt, but sitting in that chair for the rest of her life and never giving herself a chance to try would hurt more. The trouble was sixteen-year-old girls thought they knew everything. She should know. She'd been one. "Pain is feeling, and feeling is good in this case."

"I've been telling you this for months. It will hurt, but it will also get easier every time you do it," Tanya explained. "You've got this. You can do this."

Noelle said nothing, her eyes not meeting either of them. Lila glanced around. They were the only ones left on the floor. Maybe privacy would be a better idea. Maybe then Noelle would actually tell her why she wasn't trying. "Tanya, I think I can handle the rest of the session."

Tanya nodded as though she understood and then sighed as she looked down at Noelle. "You should listen to her, sweetie. I've been trying to get Doc Hamet to change up your PT for months. I would trust this woman with my own daughter. I'll see you next week."

Lila waited until she was gone and they were alone before turning back to her very stubborn patient.

"Noelle, I need you to trust me. I know it doesn't feel like it, but this has been a very encouraging day. Let's do ten more minutes and then we'll get you back to massage."

She would take little victories with Noelle. If she were anyone else, Lila knew she likely would have given her the tough-love speech and walked away until the patient was willing to do the work. She knew damn well that unless the patient wanted it, no amount of pleading or bargaining would work.

But this was *her* patient. Her kid. She knew she shouldn't think of her that way, but she'd come to love Noelle. She wasn't willing to let this lie, and she knew after today that she was going to have a big discussion with Armie about this. It might break her if he wouldn't listen. She wasn't sure she could live with herself if she didn't convince them to try.

Noelle stared at her, a stubborn set to her jaw. "I can't walk, Lila. I've told you that a hundred times today."

If only she would put as much will into actually trying as she did arguing, she might already be walking. "Do you think I didn't see your hips move? It wasn't the wind that moved them."

A startled look came into her eyes. "You saw wrong. I didn't move them. I can't move them. I can't move anything from the waist down."

She was so frustrating and they were so damn close. "You did. You move them more than you think. And you have feeling below your waist. We both know that. I've explained to you that given where your spine was injured, there's a good possibility that you can get some mobility back. But you have to put in the work. Noelle, you only have so long before you won't be able to come back from this. I know what the doctor told you, but he was wrong."

"And you're right?"

Dr. Hamet would eventually show up since he was supposed to be "overseeing" her practice. He was going to get a massive earful and a hearty definition of the word *incompetence*. "I am. So let's get up and do ten more minutes and then you can rest."

Noelle's deep brown ponytail shook. "Ten more minutes of hell isn't going to fix anything."

This was it. She'd seen it before in other patients, heard about it from her friends who'd specialized in physical therapy. There was often one chance to convince a patient they could do it. Especially with the hard cases. If she'd been working in Papillon right after Noelle's accident, they might not be here. Noelle would likely already be up in her braces, and these sessions would be all about pushing her limits and making her strong. Instead, Noelle and Armie had been fed crappy information and they'd accepted it because they'd both been too traumatized to think to go for a second opinion. She had to get over those hurdles or this wouldn't work. "No, it's going to be a long road and it's going to hurt, and you'll be walking at the end of it. You might not ever be able to walk without a brace, but you'll be mobile."

"Then why don't I stay in the chair?" Noelle asked, her exasperation evident. "I know you're doing this because you think if I can move myself around I'll go to college and study something important, but what about when I actually get there? It'll still be hard to get around. I still won't be normal. Do you want to be the freak who everyone stares at?"

She wasn't even going to deal with that. It was ridiculous. It was time to start some of that tough love. Begging wasn't working. Softness would let Noelle know she could keep fighting and eventually get her way. "Noelle, get up and finish this out. We're not moving from this spot until you finish. We can stay here all night. Your father will come looking for us and then you can explain to him why we can't go home."

"I'm tired."

"I don't want to listen to excuses. You can come up with a million and one and none of them are valid. People will always find a reason to point and stare. You think the braces are worse than a wheelchair? God, is that the reason you don't want to try? Because if you try you won't have an excuse to not leave town? Are you afraid of the big bad world, baby girl?"

Finally there was some real fire in her eyes. "Screw you, Lila. You think I don't know why you're doing this?"

Sometimes a knock-down, drag-out fight was exactly what was needed. "I'm doing it because you'll thank me in the end. In here I'm not your friend. In here I'm your primary care provider, and what I say goes. I won't coddle you."

Noelle got enough of that at home. It had become very clear to her as she'd watched Noelle deflect every time the therapist tried to get her out of the chair that something was driving Noelle, and it wasn't pain. It was fear. There was only one way to break through it, but they were running out of time. They'd already wasted a bunch of it. She wasn't going to be the one who simply let this brilliant young woman throw away a chance at more normalcy.

"You're not my friend at all. You're trying to get at my dad."

It was obvious this would get nasty. Luckily she didn't back down from a fight. "I already have your dad. Believe it or not, I'm doing this as much for him as I am for you. One day he's going to figure out he handled this wrong, and that guilt will eat him up forever. Now give me your hands and we'll get you on the bars."

"You want to get rid of me."

She couldn't help but roll her eyes. "Sure. I want to get rid of you. I want your dad all to myself. You're wasting my time."

Tears shone in Noelle's eyes. "Why are you so mean?"

The shift was obvious. Again, it was something she'd

absolutely seen a hundred times. The patient started out aggressive, and when that didn't work, tried to play on her sympathy. She couldn't afford sympathy. Sympathy would leave Noelle in that chair. "I'm mean because you're too stubborn to see that you're allowing your fear to keep you in that chair. Is that what you want? Do you want to sit there the rest of your life? Do you want the rest of the world to wait on you hand and foot? That sounds awfully easy."

The words were mean and utterly untrue, but Lila was trying to shove Noelle into a corner where she'd fight for herself. Fighting for herself might lead her to break out of the cycle she was in. If Lila had to be the bad guy for a while, she was willing to do that. Sometimes the patient needed someone to fight, some villain to overcome and prove something to.

"It is damn fucking hard."

Unfortunately, that hadn't come out of Noelle's mouth. She looked over and Armie was standing there, his eyes cold as ice. He wasn't in uniform today. He wore slacks and a dress shirt and loafers. He looked like he'd just come out of a business meeting, which according to what he'd told her this morning, he likely had. And he looked angry.

She had a lot of explaining to do. She knew she would have to eventually, but she hadn't expected he would walk in at the worst possible time. They needed to show a united front or Noelle would use it as another way to stay in the box she'd put herself in. "Let's talk in the office. Noelle, this isn't finished."

Noelle started crying in earnest, her big eyes shimmering and her face going red. "Daddy, I want to go home."

"Noelle, I need to talk to Lila alone for a moment. Why don't you go and get your things and wait for me in the lobby," Armie said in a tone that brooked no disobedience. The sheriff was in the house.

Noelle looked up at her, but there was no triumph in her eyes. She was crying. "I'm sorry I wasn't what you needed me to be."

Lila groaned and started to lean over.

Armie stepped between them. "Don't you say another word to her."

Noelle made her way to the hall.

"What is that supposed to mean?" It was very obvious he'd misunderstood what was going on. This was sometimes how therapy went, and it was absolutely how parental figures and teens went at times.

"It means I can't believe you talked to her that way."

"I know I was harsh, but we're on a deadline, Armie, and gentle prodding isn't working," she explained. "There's something going on with her and she won't talk about it. Something is holding her back, and I need to get her to acknowledge it so we can get her on her feet before she loses this window."

"That window closed the day she lost use of her legs," he insisted. "I am not going to have you make things harder on her."

Why wasn't he listening? He could be so logical but about this he was a freaking rock she battered her head against. "That's what I am trying to tell you. I don't think she has to lose it all, but she's afraid."

His hands found his hips and he loomed over her. "Yes, she's afraid of you. She thinks you're trying to get rid of her, and after hearing the way you talked to her, I have to question every damn thing I know about you."

How to explain this to him? "Physical therapy can be a difficult process. Have you ever known someone who went through it? You said your partner got shot once. Did you ever go to one of his therapy sessions?"

He shook his head. "It's different. He was a cop. He could handle it."

"Noelle can handle it, too. Do you know what I would have done to anyone but a family member who refused to do the work? I would have told them they could find me when they got serious about healing and I would have walked away."

"Well, I wish like hell you would have done that here because the one thing she doesn't need is more negativity."

"No, she needs to believe she can do this, and you are not helping her. You are holding her back by coddling her." The minute the words were out of her mouth she knew they were a mistake. "Armie, I know you're trying . . ."

He cut her off. "No, please tell me what you think. I'm not a good enough father? How the hell would you know? You never had a father. You can't possibly know how to raise a child because you never had a parent."

Wow. She took a deep breath because the cruelty of those words had kicked her in the gut. She'd talked about her childhood because she loved him and wanted him to know everything about her. Not so he could throw it back in her face, weaponizing the words to win a battle she hadn't even thought to fight.

She had to keep it together or she would end up crying, and she wasn't going to do that. She was going to keep this professional. "My lack of parental love has nothing to do with my medical knowledge. All of the studies show if I don't get her on her feet soon, she'll never walk. I do not understand why you want to keep her in that chair except that you're afraid and you feel guilty and you're indulging her. You got to do that when she was young because you were the dad. I bet your wife was the disciplinarian. Well, she's gone and sometimes you have to be tough. Noelle is smart and strong, but she's also sheltered."

"How can you say she's sheltered? Do you know what she's been through?"

"I know she's willing to sit in that chair instead of trying to walk. I know she's willing to give up all her dreams because it seems easier than doing the work. Honestly, even if she was going to spend the rest of her life in that chair, she can go to college. People do it all the time. She can have a life. She can be strong and independent."

Armie's eyes widened. "You do want to get rid of her."

"Are you kidding me? Because I want to help her have a life I'm some villain plotting to exile my rival? What world are you living in?"

"Obviously not the same one you're in," he shot back.

"Here we don't harass people we love. We don't break them."

"She's already broken, Armie. We're all broken. Every single one of us. How we put ourselves back together and move on is the measure of our souls. Don't take this fight from her. This is her life. Do you think I haven't seen this? My mother said she would get clean. She said she would start tomorrow and tomorrow never came, and that's how she spent most of her life, letting it waste away."

He shook his head. "Do not compare my daughter to your drug-addicted mother."

"Why not? She's addicted to that chair. Do you know how many people who have no choice would kill to be in her place? To be able to do the work, to feel the pain so they might have a chance to walk again? Tell her. Tell her to be brave. Tell her to try. Tell her to make you proud by being the warrior you raised her to be. Don't let one moment define the rest of her life."

Well, she'd definitely left doctor mode behind, but she wasn't going to cry. She could feel the tears right there, but she couldn't make this fight about her. It was about Noelle.

"It already did, and I'm not going to put her through this." Armie stepped back. "I'm taking my daughter home now. I hope she's welcome back in this facility because I do understand she needs maintenance therapy, but I don't want you in charge of her sessions anymore. She needs to go back to Tanya."

He wasn't going to listen to her? Maybe she needed to step back and come at this from another angle. They were both emotional at this point. They needed to calm down, get a glass of wine, and logically discuss this. "Of course she's welcome."

He stared at her for a moment. "She's my daughter, Lila."

"I know that. Why do you think I'm fighting so hard?" She reached for him. This was their first real fight and it had been a doozy.

He closed his eyes as her hands found his arms. "I have to do what's right for her."

"I know that, too." They would talk and he would see that was all she was trying to do.

His eyes opened and she realized this wasn't going to go the way she thought it would.

"I think you should go to your sister's. I think we need some time apart. I should concentrate on Noelle."

She took a step back, his words not making sense to her. It was a fight. They weren't supposed to break up over an argument. "You're kicking me out because Noelle and I had a disagreement?"

"You were saying terrible things to her. I can't allow you to do that."

She could barely breathe. "Did you think we would always get along?"

"Noelle gets along with everyone."

"Yes, and that's a problem. Can't you see that? Can't you see it's not normal for her to never fight with anyone? She's afraid to fight even for herself."

He held a hand up. "I'm not going to listen to this crap. She's a nice young lady. And she doesn't have to fight for herself because I'm here to fight for her."

"But you're not." Anger started to thrum through her. He'd been an illusion. If he wilted because they'd had one damn fight, they would never have worked. She was difficult. She knew that, but she'd thought he was the one man in the world who might stand beside her. "You're not fighting for her at all. You're sheltering her, and you'll do it until she can't have a life, and the crazy thing is, you won't, either."

A single brow rose over his eyes. "Oh, because I won't let her put up with your abuse, I can't have a life?"

"You're stuck in that moment, too. You can't forgive yourself for not being in that car with her." She knew he wouldn't listen to her, but she couldn't stop talking. She loved him. She probably wouldn't love anyone else the way she loved him, but she also knew when a man was done with her. "It wasn't your fault, but this part is. You are her father. You have to protect her. Even from herself. I'll send someone by to get my stuff. Not that there's much of it."

"You could apologize." He took a deep breath and seemed to come to some resolution. "You could apologize to Noelle and then maybe we could work something out."

And the next time she made a wrong move? Would she spend the rest of her life apologizing? "The trouble is I don't think I was wrong and I never will. Not about this. Good-bye, Armie."

She walked out, turning to the hallway that led to the parking lot. She could barely see for the tears in her eyes. She'd held them off until now.

Noelle was sitting there. She was a mess, her mascara dripping across her cheeks. "Lila, I'm . . . I'm sorry. I didn't mean to do that to you and Dad."

This really wasn't her fault. She sank down to the bench beside Noelle's wheelchair because she didn't want to loom over her. What she had to say needed to be said eye-to-eye. "I know, sweetie. I want you to think about this. You are enough. You are enough to get up and fight through and walk. You are the only one making yourself small. If you need me, you know where to find me."

Armie stood in the doorway.

She got to her feet and walked away, feeling his eyes on her the whole way.

When she got to her car, she forced the tears back and drove toward the only place she had left to go.

chapter fifteen

"Hey, I brought you some tea." Lisa stepped into the small apartment over Guidry's that would serve as her temporary home.

"Thank you." She'd held it together for hours, something she'd learned after years of working in trauma. Her own trauma could wait. Although when she thought about it, maybe she'd learned it in childhood.

Peanut looked up from his place beside her. The dog seemed to know something terrible had happened and he'd stayed close to her.

Lisa sat at the end of the bed, a worried look on her face. "I wish you would come to the house and stay there. I want to take care of you."

Being taken care of was what had gotten her here in the first place. She'd fallen into the softest, sweetest of all traps, the one that seemed like heaven. But this afternoon that trap had sprung, and she'd been broken by it. She'd managed to crawl away, but she feared she'd left a big old chunk of herself back in that house where she'd briefly been happy. "I'm fine. It didn't work out. We moved way too fast."

That was what she was telling everyone who asked. It had been a mistake to move in together.

What would Armie say? Would he put it around town that she'd abused his daughter? Would he trash her reputation to get her to leave? She would have said no, but then, she hadn't realized how far he would go to protect Noelle and himself. He'd found a place after trauma where he was comfortable and life seemed okay, and she was threatening that.

"No, you didn't. What happened?" Lisa's shrewd eyes pinned her. "I won't go away until you tell me. You know how tenacious I can be. It's all you'll hear for the next few weeks. 'What's wrong, Lila? How can I help, Lila?'" She touched her chest and gave her a shocked expression. "'Oh my, did I do something wrong, Lila?' Now that is a manipulation because I know damn well I didn't do anything wrong, but it's going to annoy you so I'll go there."

This was what sisters did. They poked and prodded and didn't care about personal boundaries when they meant well. This was what she'd tried to do with Noelle because she knew it was what any of her siblings would have done for her.

Armie was wrong. She might not have had two loving parents, but she'd had Will and Laurel and Lisa. They'd loved and supported each other. They'd taught each other what it meant to be a family.

"We had a fight. He broke up with me." She petted Peanut, taking comfort from his closeness.

Lisa gasped. "What did you do?"

"Why do you think I did anything at all?"

"Because I've known you my whole life. You can be a bitch."

She could, but this time she'd been a bitch for all the right reasons. "I pushed Noelle at PT. I tried to get her up and walking and I said some nasty things about it being easy to stay in that chair. I think I was close to getting her mad enough that she would have done it just to throw it back in my face."

Lisa sighed. "Like you did when I was flunking physics. I remember that well. You and Will thoroughly pissed me off enough that nothing was going to stop me from passing that class and showing you two up. You know Laurel did the same thing and you simply helped her. She got a C and you were happy with that. I got an A-minus and all you did was pat me on the back and tell me you knew I could do it."

She'd been only a few years older than her younger siblings, but she'd been the one to make sure they did their homework and ate dinner. "Laurel was never good at math and science. It didn't come naturally to her. She had other talents. You were being lazy and floating by on your innate intelligence. If you had flunked that class, the school would have wanted a parent-teacher conference. We didn't have a parent to send."

Those years had been so rough, always walking a tightrope. She couldn't do it again. She couldn't simply apologize for something she wasn't sorry for and go back to him. It was inevitable that she and Noelle would clash from time to time and she would go through this all over again. She would walk a tightrope, the same one she had in childhood— be perfect or she would lose it all.

"Huh, I never thought of it that way. As a teen it just felt unfair," Lisa said.

"Yeah, well, I'm sure Noelle would agree with you. Armie certainly does. He asked me to leave because if I stayed he wouldn't be putting Noelle first. The funny thing is, I'm trying to do the same thing." She'd known they would fight about it and she'd done it anyway.

"He doesn't want her to do the physical therapy?"

"He believes what the old doctor told him. He doesn't want a second opinion because he doesn't want to give Noelle false hope. I personally think it's better than no hope at all. At least if she thought there might be a chance, she would try to figure out how to be more independent. Armie's rigged the whole house so she doesn't have to struggle. That's great, but the world won't be like that. It isn't like that for anyone. He's done a great job of making her comfortable, but he won't teach her life skills. I've been trying to teach her how to help around the house. She tells me she can't do it. Do they honestly believe people in wheelchairs can't cook or do laundry? Because that's ridiculous. Even if she never gets out of that chair, she can be independent. She can go to college and study whatever she wants. She can have a full life where she does amazing things, but she can't if she won't believe in herself."

"You need to talk to him," Lisa urged.

"I tried that. He said the only way he'll consider talking to me is if I make an apology to Noelle. I assume he'll also want me to stop pushing on getting her to walk." There were other things she feared. "Maybe it's for the best. Not for Noelle, but for me. I don't think we would have worked out in the long run because I don't think he'll ever take the chance on having another child, and I don't know that I can live without trying to have one."

Lisa's eyes went wide. "He doesn't want more kids? I mean, I do get it that he's been through it once, but he told you flat out he won't have kids?"

"He said he needed to think about it. Maybe if I'd met him at another time. It's not wrong or bad for him to be done with having kids. It certainly doesn't make him a bad person, just a wrong match." Or perhaps they were simply far too different to ever have worked. She was so tired. "I think he enjoyed the idea of having a woman in his life, but the reality turned out to be not so great. I was convenient for a while and then I wasn't, and I was out."

"I don't think that was it. I saw you two together. He was happier than I've ever seen him."

"Well, I wasn't worth fighting for," she said wistfully. "Do you think he'll tell everyone I tried to hurt Noelle?"

"What? Why would he do that?"

"Because if the clinic fails, I'll leave town," she explained. "I'll have to. I have to have a job. The clinic doesn't make much money. Not much at all, really, but I have to have a way to pay Mabel and keep the lights on. I'm starting to get a good flow of regular patients, but Armie could stop that with a couple of words. I'm the outsider."

Lisa's eyes went steely. "If he bad-mouths my sister, he'll have to deal with me."

She didn't want to get her sister in trouble. Lisa fit in here. She loved it here. Lila was starting to feel at home in Papillon, but she couldn't fight if Armie decided he didn't want her here. It could harm her sister's business. "I don't know. Maybe I should try to find someone to take my place. The last thing I need is Guidry's to lose business because I'm your sister. If I leave, they might forget."

The door came open and Remy stalked in. "You're not going anywhere, Lila. You belong right here, and I assure you nothing Armie says can hurt this business. Dixie and I are the only games in town, and she doesn't have a bar. I assure you, when it comes down to pleasing the sheriff or pleasing me, they'll think about the fact that I won't serve any person who tries to drive one of my family members out of town."

Lila stood up and Peanut jumped to the floor, taking his place beside her. "You were listening in?"

Remy had the good grace to flush slightly. "Well, Zep was already doing it, and I didn't think he should know more than I did."

Zep's head popped around the corner. "Sorry. I saw that Doc there was upset and I wanted to know if I should punch someone."

She sighed. "First off, I'm an NP. Secondly, no. If you punch someone and you injure that finger again, I'm not sewing it back on twice. If you like your pinkie finger, stay out of fights for the next eight weeks or so."

Zep shook his handsome head. "No one's going to call you Nurse Practitioner Daley. It's too long. And I will find another way to defend you, then. I can come up with all sorts of ways to annoy the shit out of the sheriff. You can't leave. We need you. I recently realized that having a member of the medical community in the family is important. If I get a bad hangover, I can pop into the clinic and you'll rehydrate me. Also, I can get you to write me a note about passing my STI tests. It cuts out a whole bunch of steps."

At least there was still someone who could make her smile, even if it was because he was such a dumbass. "I'll write you that note. You should laminate it. But I have to consider that it might be hard to practice in this town. Remy, please don't say anything. I don't want to make this into some kind of feud. In a day or two, I'll talk to him. I'll promise to stay out of his way and be professional when we do cross paths."

Remy frowned. "In a few days, he's going to realize he's been an idiot and he'll come around. Are you ready for that?"

She wasn't ready to think about anything beyond getting into bed and going to sleep. If she could get to sleep. "I don't think so. Even if he did, it would only be a matter of time before I did something to annoy him again."

Looking back, she could see that it had only been the accident that saved them the first time. She'd embarrassed him in the diner that day, and only the town coming to see her as heroic had changed his mind. If it hadn't happened, they wouldn't have gone on. It might have been better because it wouldn't be so hard to work with him now.

"I'll go get your things," Lisa promised.

"No, I'll do it." Zep nodded Lisa's way. "If I let you do it, you'll probably end up in jail because you can be mean when you want to. Remy would definitely end up in jail. He promised Armie an ass kicking if he hurt you, and my brother always follows through. Turns out I'm the reasonable one here. Who would have thought?"

Certainly none of the three of them. "I'll text and let him know you're coming. Thank you. It's a single bag and Peanut's stuff. Not much at all."

She didn't have much, and it looked like that wasn't changing anytime soon.

"I think what the two of you need is a bottle of wine and some of the best tater tots you'll ever have. At least that's what my cook claims." Remy gave her a half smile. "You want it up here or you want to go out on the patio? It's nearly empty and the water is pretty this time of day. I think Otis is hanging out."

Wine and gators. "Sure. The patio sounds lovely. Give me a minute and I'll come down. Thank you for letting me stay here. I could stay at the clinic, but this is nicer."

"That's not saying much, *ma soeur*," Remy replied. "But you're always welcome. And I hope you'll seriously consider staying in town even though the sheriff is an ass. Sometimes men are dumb creatures and we need time to sort things out."

Remy walked out and Zep followed, giving her a salute with his bandaged hand.

The door closed and she was left alone again with her sister and her dog.

Lisa was quiet for a moment. "It's okay. It's going to be okay."

She nodded. "I know."

But inside, the pain . . . god, the pain. He was gone. He probably hated her. He thought she'd intended to hurt his daughter. That was the worst part. He wasn't out there worrying about her. He was out there hating her, and she missed him. She already missed him.

Lisa walked up and put her arms around Lila. "Don't make old mistakes. Let it out. Let me be here for you. Don't hold this in and pretend like it's okay. Let me call Laurel and put her on video chat, and let us take care of you for once. You loved him. It's not wrong to admit it. Please don't hold this in. If you honestly are this calm, that's fine. It's good. But if you need to cry, don't hide it. No one is going to come and take us away. Do you think I don't know how hard it was for you and Will? I know. Let me be strong for you for once. Please let me pay this back. And yes, I'm making this all about me because I am afraid you won't ever let anything just be about you."

Her sister's kindness worked where Armie's coldness hadn't. It was true. She held things in, a remnant of childhood, but one she didn't need anymore. She was never going to be the woman who cried at everything, but some things were worth tears.

Her love was worth a few.

"I loved him. I never . . ." The words wouldn't come.

Lisa held her tight. "You never met anyone like him. I know. It's okay."

Lila let go, let her sister comfort her. The tears she'd held in all day finally flowed.

He was gone and so was a large piece of her heart.

Armie felt like he was a zombie. He was moving, saying all the things he should say, but he couldn't quite feel anything. He'd gotten Noelle in the car, driven home, stayed calm, but he felt like he was still stuck in that moment when he'd realized he was going to have to leave Lila.

He already missed her.

He had to focus on his daughter. She was the one who needed him.

"Do you want something to eat? I can call in pizza." He knew he should make something healthy, but if he opened the refrigerator, he would see what Lila had planned to cook for them. It would be sitting there, prepped and ready to go because his girlfriend was incredibly organized.

Not his girlfriend, and that was the stupidest word. She wasn't a girl, and she was so much more than a friend. His lover. His companion. His every waking thought and comfort.

How had it gone so fucking wrong? He'd thought Noelle was safe with Lila. It had been the biggest relief that someone had been there to support him, to partner with him. He could work the night shift without worrying every second. He could trust her when Noelle needed a ride somewhere.

Do you want the rest of the world to wait on you hand and foot? That sounds awfully easy.

Nothing about the last year had been easy on either of them. Noelle needed someone who would support her, not yell at her.

Like your dad yelled at you when you spent too much time chasing girls in high school and none on your homework? He'd been hard as hell on you and you thanked that

old man for making you go to college. You would be work-
ing at a fast food place if it hadn't been for him kicking
your ass.

His father. He'd been the tough-love king. But Noelle
didn't need that. She didn't.

"I'm not hungry." She sat at the table as quiet as she'd
been during the car ride home. She'd cried, but silently, and
it made him all the angrier.

How could he not have seen it? "Has she always been
that mean to you?"

She turned her head, looking up at him, her eyes red
from crying. "No. Not at all. Dad, we were arguing. She
was pushing me, and I didn't want to do it."

"She had no right to talk to you that way."

"She was being a bitch, but I was, too."

It didn't matter what Noelle had done. "She's the adult
and I doubt very much you were being a . . . I don't want
you to use that language."

Noelle's hands fisted, her body going taut. "I'm sixteen.
I'm almost seventeen, Dad. I assure you, I use that language
a lot. Can't we talk to her? Maybe if we talk to her she'll be
okay with the fact that I'm going to be in this chair for
the rest of my life. I know she's trying to help."

Was she? He'd thought she was. But if that was how she
helped, then she had no place in his home. He had to take
care of Noelle, and that meant being supportive.

Can't you see it's not normal for her to never fight with
anyone? She's afraid to fight even for herself.

Was Noelle's passiveness normal? She'd always been a
quiet, studious girl, but after the divorce she'd never fought
with him. Not once. He'd always thought he was lucky, but
what if it wasn't that she thought he was always right? What
if her willingness to go along with what he wanted was
because she was afraid of what might happen if she caused
waves?

"You're happy here, right, sweetheart?"

The tension left her body with a long sigh, like a cord
had been cut. "Of course."

"It must have been weird to have to move here after your mom passed."

"Dad, I like it here."

Lila was wrong. Lila didn't understand what it meant to have a child with disabilities. She didn't know what it meant to worry about a kid, to have everything he did affect his daughter's life.

There was a knock on the door and he glanced at the bag he'd packed. When Remy had called, he'd forced himself to gather Lila's things and place them in a paper shopping bag. Her things. God, there were so few of them. He'd kicked her out with so little. She had a couple of changes of clothes, some flip-flops, a sad amount of feminine things. He hadn't had time to take her shopping, and she hadn't once complained. She'd merely borrowed from Noelle and joked about how when the insurance money came in, she and Noelle would tear through some stores.

Had it all been a lie?

He was not looking forward to this confrontation. Remy didn't have kids, either. Not yet. Remy would only care about the fact that Lila had been hurt. There was no question in his mind that he'd hurt her. It had been there in the startled look on her face, but she hadn't cried. No. She would bottle that up and there wouldn't be anyone there for her to wrap herself around and share that secret soft part of herself with.

He opened the door and practically breathed a sigh of relief.

Zep stood in the doorway, that perpetually amused look on his face. "Hey, I'm here to grab Lila's stuff." He walked in when Armie stepped aside. "Hey, Noelle. How's it going?"

Noelle moved from the table, wheeling into the living room. "How is she?"

"How's who? Oh, Lila." Zep shrugged. "You know me. I'm not good at reading women. If I was, I would get tossed in jail way less than I do because I would remember not to sleep with deputies."

"Zep!" Armie was fairly certain Roxie wouldn't want that one-night transgression to get out around town.

Noelle rolled her eyes. "Everyone knows, Dad. And everyone knows Roxie's still got a thing for him and hates herself because of it. I want to know about Lila. Does she hate me?"

He needed to make something very plain to his daughter. "This was not your fault. None of this is your fault. Why don't you go and pick out a movie and I'll order pizza."

For a second he saw something flash in Noelle's eyes. Then she shut down, her gaze going tired. "I have a project to work on. I'll be in my room."

Damn it. He had to give her time. He needed time, too. Lila had come in like a storm and she'd left like one, leaving a mess in her wake.

She didn't leave. You kicked her out. She could be here right now, discussing the situation, if you had taken the time to cool off before giving her ultimatums.

He wasn't listening to his inner voice right now. His subconscious was looking for any excuse to forgive her and bring her back. It was selfish. He wanted her for himself. It had been all right when she'd been what was best for Noelle, too, but today had proven that instinct wrong.

He walked to the counter where he'd put her bag of personal items and the other brown paper bag he'd used to gather the dog's things, and guilt sliced through him. He wasn't even sure what he was feeling guilty about—asking Lila to leave or the fact that he'd brought her into their home in the first place.

"She'll be fine," Zep said, glancing around. "Don't worry about Lila. She's strong."

"Yes, she is." She had a forceful personality. It had sometimes rubbed the wrong way, but oh, when they were in sync he'd never felt better about life.

"She's got her job. She's very invested in that clinic of hers. I personally am happy to have her there."

Armie nodded and wished that Zep would get out so he could sit and brood and try to put his life back together.

Zep's brows rose. "She does still have a job, right?"

"What is that supposed to mean?"

"It means I'm real bad at eavesdropping and by bad, I really mean good. I overheard Lila asking Lisa if she thought you would try to run her out of town."

She thought that? "Why would I . . . I wouldn't deprive the town of a medical professional so I didn't have to deal with my ex-girlfriend."

"Good, because I think she's worried you'll do that."

"I've never given her reason to think I would be cruel to her."

Zep nodded. "Yeah, well, sometimes things aren't the way they seem to be. Not that I know much, but there was this perception thing I remember from high school. I was just thinking about that for some reason. I guess she has the wrong perception of you."

"She definitely does if she thinks I'm going to run her out of town." That was ridiculous. He'd never done a single thing that should make her think he was that kind of man. Sure, he could be short, and when he was working he used a different tone of voice. He had to. "I'm the sheriff. I have to be intimidating on some level, but I've never tried to intimidate her."

"You can be intimidating even when you're not trying," Zep replied. "I should know."

Zep turned and Armie meant to let him go. He meant to let him walk out that door and not say another word.

"Is she really all right?" He had to know.

Zep held both bags in one hand. "She's sad. I think she thought you were the one. I don't get that, either. I don't think there's some mystical 'one' out there, but it's obvious she thought you were special. I've never seen that woman cry. Still haven't, but I heard her."

"She cried?" Armie hated the thought that she'd cried. She kept her emotions so private, controlling them always except when she was alone with him.

"I think Lisa convinced her it was okay to. She needed it." Zep gave him a friendly slap on the arm. "So, there you go, Sheriff. You don't have to feel bad. She's cried, and when I left she and Lisa were going out to the patio to have some wine and probably talk about what an asshole you are. She's already well on her way to moving on. You're lucky. Lila isn't the kind to try to cling to a man. She won't come running to you, begging you to take her back. You caught a break with that one. Got away clean."

"I wasn't trying to get away from her."

A brow rose over Zep's eye. "So you're the one who's going to be clingy?"

"No. I told you. It didn't work out. I was only trying to explain that I didn't wake up this morning planning on breaking up with her."

"Oh, I thought maybe you realized you didn't like living with her," Zep commented. "I know you're, like, an old guy and stuff, and old guys like to settle down. I thought you figured out she wasn't good at the whole keeping a house thing."

"I wasn't interested in her keeping my house." Though she'd done it far better than he did. He could keep the place clean, but Lila had come in and organized things, kept them to a good schedule so he wasn't rushing out of the house every morning. She'd started trying to teach Noelle how to cook. Although Noelle had said she couldn't do it.

It was dangerous. His stove was gas and it wasn't built for a young woman in a wheelchair. So was she never going to cook? That would be hard. The world wouldn't change to accommodate her. She would have to adapt. Adaptation was necessary to a good life. He'd had to adapt. Everyone had to adapt.

"Sorry," Zep said, sounding anything but apologetic. "Didn't mean to offend. Like I said, I don't understand this whole romance thing. Sex, I understand, but from the way that woman was crying, I suspect this was about more than sex."

"Not that this is your business, but we had a disagreement about how to deal with my daughter."

"Oh, god, if I don't understand the romance thing, I

definitely don't get the kids thing. I will get these back to Lila." He stopped at the door. "I shouldn't ask this, but I am confused. So you wanted her to have a relationship with Noelle? Or you didn't?"

"Of course I wanted her to have a relationship with Noelle. I can't be with a woman who doesn't have a relationship with my daughter. I guess I thought Lila would want to be a mother figure to her. I was wrong." Because mothers weren't tough on their kids.

His had been. His had been a righteous warrior woman, raining hell down on him when he'd needed it.

But she wouldn't have said those things to him if he'd been in a wheelchair. If he'd had everything taken from him, his mother would have been loving and kind.

Zep leaned against the door. "Oh. So she ignored Noelle? That doesn't seem nice."

"She didn't ignore her. She was mean to her."

"That also doesn't sound like Lila," Zep mused. "She's sarcastic and a little cold, but she's not even mean to me. Oh, she'll offer up an ass kicking, but she's only watching out for me. Doctors can be that way. I have found that the entire medical profession can be way too honest with a man. Not always easy to hear, but necessary. But what do I know, man? Hey, I'm going to a friend's bachelor party next Friday. Could you stock up on Dr Pepper? I need one in the morning, and we both know I'll end up in jail. Night, Sheriff."

Zep closed the door behind him and Armie was left knowing exactly how alone he was.

chapter sixteen

"I got a call and the sheriff is bringing in someone," Mabel said four days later. "Apparently there was an incident on the highway and he needs a blood draw. The driver won't take a breath test. He did, however, fail the field sobriety test by falling into the bayou and twisting his ankle."

Her gut clenched, but she'd known this would happen. She'd known eventually she would have to confront Armie. They were both first responders in a tiny town. It was inevitable they would work together at some point.

What was shocking was what she hadn't been forced to face. She'd expected a flurry of gossip to surround them. Everyone in town knew she'd moved in with Armie and Noelle. A couple of people had already started gently prodding her about when the wedding was. Of course, those people were the town florist and Dixie, who was already planning to cater the reception.

No one had said a thing to her. It was like they didn't know she was no longer the potential future Mrs. LaVigne.

"What's the ETA?"

Mabel was already prepping paperwork. "He said he was five minutes out. It's not an emergency. Armie doesn't think he broke the ankle, but he wanted to be careful. He didn't want to throw the kid in lockup until you have a look at him. I'll go prep room one."

She was gone before Lila could call her back to let her greet the sheriff.

She was not this woman. She was not the woman who lost her cool when an ex walked in the room. Hell, she was friendly with some of her exes. Not the one who'd hit on her sisters, but a couple of the men she'd dated in college were people she would stop and say hi to and ask after their families.

Of course she hadn't cried over those men. She hadn't woken up in the middle of the night, reaching out for them and praying it had all been a terrible dream. Those break-ups had been logical. She'd moved on without this horrible ache in her gut that something was missing and couldn't be replaced.

The doors swooshed open and there he was—big and manly and gorgeous. The fact that he was an asshole who couldn't see past his own fears didn't change the way her body responded to him. She wanted to do nothing more than walk into his arms.

Except his arms were full of whining drunk boy.

"Didn't do anything wrong. It was the gator. That gator made me swerve." Every word came out slurred.

Mabel rushed in, pushing a wheelchair. "Put him down here, Sheriff. I'll take him back and get started on his vitals and the initial exam."

"I'll come back with you." It would be a good excuse to not be alone with Armie. "He looks like he'll be a lot to handle."

The kid was in his early twenties, but he grinned up at Mabel like she was the hottest thing he'd ever seen. "Hey, pretty lady."

Mabel frowned and looked back at the sheriff. "I'll definitely run a blood test. I can handle this puppy. Lila, you stay here and find out what happened. I'll call you back when he's ready for the exam. Hush now, you infant. And don't you try to flirt with me. I like my men elderly and somewhat infirm. Don't you knock it 'til you've tried it."

"Sorry I didn't give you more warning." Armie stood in her waiting room.

She picked up her notepad. Professional. That was how she got through this. It was the first time and it would almost certainly be the hardest. It would be easier in a couple of weeks. She would be able to smile at him and not feel sick inside. In a month or two, she wouldn't feel sick. She would be wistful. In a year, maybe she would question what she ever saw in him. All she had to do was wait and time would work wonders. It always did. "How did he come to be injured, Sheriff?"

He hesitated as though he'd expected something different, but he quickly regained his footing. "I pulled him over on the highway. He was swerving, and it wasn't all about Otis. He ran his car into a ditch. I think he was trying to get away from me. Didn't do a good job."

"So he was in a car accident?" Was it wrong that she was hoping for something complex? Maybe he had internal injuries. That would take her mind off things.

"Not exactly. He was going about twenty miles an hour. I'm pretty sure he thought he was in a high-speed chase. There might be more than alcohol in that kid's system. He went off the road and slid into the mud. It's been raining, so that land off the highway is incredibly soft. Herve is going to have to haul that car out."

She knew the place. She avoided it. If Otis was on the road at that point in the highway, she waited him out. It was precisely why she'd loaded up her phone with audiobooks. It wasn't because she'd read a couple of old-school bodice rippers she'd found in her now torched house and gotten addicted. "So how did he injure his ankle?"

It was the romances. She could blame them for all the heartfelt icky love stuff. She'd read too many romance books in the last couple of weeks, and they'd affected her brain.

"I tried to give him a field sobriety test," Armie admitted. "I know. It's obvious he's plastered, but I have to follow protocol. He tripped and landed wrong. I knew I needed to bring him in here before I take him to lockup. I don't think he's dangerous or I promise I would have brought in Roxie or Major to stay in the room with him."

"It's okay." It wasn't anything she couldn't handle. "I've dealt with plenty worse. The hospital I worked at in Dallas served the county jail system, so it won't be the first time I've treated a prisoner. Is there anything else? I'll go take a look at him and then we'll get an X-ray."

"Are you all right?" Armie asked, his tone going low.

She gave him a smile she hoped didn't look as fake as it was. "I'm fine. Thank you."

There was an awkward pause where they stared at each other. She tried to come up with something witty to say, but that had never been her strong point. Perhaps she should turn and go.

"It's going okay? The clinic, I mean." His deep voice betrayed his awkwardness.

Only days ago, he'd been comfortable around her. He'd sat in those chairs waiting for her to be done with work so he could drive them both home. "It's picking up. I'm happy with it. I've done a lot of well-baby checkups thanks to Hallie and Seraphina talking to their friends. I'm in good with the young moms club. And I got Gene to do some blood work."

"Really? How did you manage that?"

It hadn't been easy. "I talked podcasts with him and I took him on a tour of how the lab destroys samples so they can't be taken and left at crime scenes so innocent people can be implicated in murders. I then signed a document stating that I would never frame him for a crime he didn't commit. I then listened to three hours of how the police screwed up a murder in Lafayette. I'm going to admit, it was a lot, but I don't have to do it again for a whole year."

His face split in the most heart-stopping grin. "Oh, I wish I'd seen that. I'm glad it's going well. I told you this town would settle down and accept you." He sobered and the light left his eyes. "I've missed you."

Damn him. She wasn't going there. Wasn't. "I miss you, too."

Why had she said that? She knew better, but he was standing right in front of her.

"What should we do about that?" His face had softened, and it was almost possible to forget how cold he'd been to her that day.

Almost. "I don't know that we do anything about it."

His jaw tightened and she could see the stubborn will in his gaze. "Maybe we should sit down and talk. Maybe I heard things wrong. It has been pointed out to me that perception and point of view are important things and can be misconstrued. Did I not understand?"

"I said exactly what you heard, Armie. I didn't mean that I thought Noelle's life was easy. That was a manipulation to try to stir up some fire in her. I wanted her to want to prove me wrong." She wasn't sure why they were going over this again, but hope sparked through her. If he was willing to listen, maybe they could try again. They would go slower this time. It had been a mistake to move in. They should spend more time together, all three of them.

"But you meant well?"

She hated the fact that he felt like he had to ask her that. "I meant to get her to try something she didn't want to try, something that could end up being incredibly good for her. Sometimes in therapy you have to be tough, but it's all about the patient's best interest."

He thought about that for a moment. "Okay. I'm sorry I spoke to you the way I did. I was upset. I think we both were and we let things get out of control."

Was it really this easy? "I'm sorry we fought and I'm sorry I didn't figure out something nicer to say to Noelle. I've been doing this for a long time and I can seem cold even when I'm not. I hope we can sit down and talk this out because I meant what I said. I do miss you."

"I miss you like crazy." He reached for her hand. "I want

to see you again. Maybe I can come by and we can have dinner and talk."

She would like that more than anything. They had a lot to talk about. "That might be nice. I just need you to promise me that you won't toss me out the next time Noelle and I clash, because it's normal and natural to do that. When it happens, we should all sit down and work it out. Or we could find a therapist. Actually, I think regular therapy sessions would help all of us. Especially Noelle."

She couldn't walk on eggshells.

He dropped her hand. "I wasn't going to bring Noelle into it. I think that's where we made the mistake the first time."

"Not bring Noelle into it? Not bring her into what?"

"Our relationship. I think we should keep the two things separate. It's obvious you have a problem with the way I'm raising my daughter. I've thought a lot about it, and the solution is to keep the two parts separate."

A numbness started to creep over her. She needed to be numb or she would crack open again. "So I don't ever come over to your place? You show up at mine and we fuck and then you leave and go back to your real family?"

His jaw tightened. "That's not the way I was looking at it."

If he didn't want her around Noelle, he didn't really want her at all. His life revolved around his daughter. He was asking her to accept an ancillary role. She wouldn't even be his girlfriend. She would be his booty call. She didn't miss the irony. In the beginning that was exactly what she'd wanted. When they'd met, she'd wanted to put him in a box and keep him there. It was brutal karma that he wanted that type of relationship now. Because she'd found so much more, come to want more. It was like she'd been the Grinch and her heart had done that growth thing, but the Whos suddenly didn't want to sing. "I happen to love Noelle."

"You did a damn fine job proving to her that you don't." The ice was back in his tone.

"If she truly believes that then I'm sorry because I do

love her, but love isn't always cuddly and sweet. Sometimes it's hard. Cuddly and sweet can be very fragile. Love shouldn't be fragile, but yours certainly was, Armie."

"I'm sorry you feel that way. It didn't feel fragile. I still feel more for you than any woman I've ever known, but she's my daughter and I have to put her first."

"I'm not trying to take her away from you, but you won't listen to sound medical advice."

His hands fisted at his sides. "I don't want to push her."

"Sometimes we need a push," she insisted. "You are treating her like she's made of glass, and she's not. She's strong, and she'll be even stronger if she can push her way through this."

He took a step back. "I can't believe I thought this would work. I don't understand why this is an argument. Do you always have to be right?"

"I am right about this. I don't understand why you're not in there coaching her. She's got a shot at walking again. I know you feel guilty about the accident, but . . ."

His whole body went rigid. "Stop. I took a shot that you would want to at least salvage some of the relationship, but I can see this isn't going to work."

A bit of anger started to thrum through her system. "Salvage the part of the relationship where you get sex and I'm not any part at all of your real life? Thanks a lot. That's a hard pass from me, but go find the Mirandas of the world. I'm sure they'll play the part you want."

"Part?"

Anger felt so much better than desolation. "Yes, the part where your significant other is sweet and agrees with you and makes your life comfortable and you never have to fight and life never changes."

He squared his shoulders, standing right in front of her like a boxer facing his opponent. "Is that how it is? I've got to wonder why you stayed. If I took everything and gave nothing back, why were you with me?"

A million tart, nasty responses shot to the tip of her tongue. *Because you give great orgasms. Because I'm ob-*

viously a masochist. She dropped all of them because anger hadn't worked, either. A deep sense of sadness flowed over her. "Because when you loved me, really loved me, I was a better person for it. Because I could open up to you and finally figure out who I am. I don't know. Maybe it's not only you. Maybe it was what happened in that ER. If you'd met me before that day I would have taken what you offered and not thought much more about it. I certainly wouldn't have lost the best relationship of my life over a sixteen-year-old girl, but this is Waterloo. This is where I stand and plant my flag, and you don't understand it, but I do it because I love you and I love her and I can't watch the two of you let one moment wreck the rest of your lives. Because I want more now. You made me want more. In the end, I'm going to walk away because I love me now in a way I didn't before, in a way you taught me I could. I can't accept a half life and you shouldn't, either."

He stood there, staring at her. "I don't know what to say to that."

"Because you're not ready. Maybe if we'd met at another time things would be different. I wish you luck." She felt the tears on her cheeks. Stupid tears, but they were there for a reason. They were there because she'd loved him. They were there because she loved herself, too. That was the crazy thing. She'd discovered she couldn't love anyone until she was okay with herself. "I'm going to work now."

"I won't say anything," he said as she started to walk away. His words made her stop and turn. "About us breaking up. If anyone asks, I'll tell them it's none of their business."

"I'll do the same."

"And I wouldn't ever say anything bad about you. I know you're good at your job. I'm grateful you're here. I'm sorry it didn't work out. Damn, Lila, I don't want to do this."

But he had to because he wasn't ready to move on. That was the saddest part of all. He'd helped her. She was ready to step out of that terrible moment and move on with her life and he wasn't. She hadn't done the same for him. In the end, she wasn't the woman who could bring him out of himself.

Her sister's words came back. She'd loved him. He hadn't loved her the same way. That wasn't his fault. "It's going to be okay. If we try, we'll get through this and we'll be able to look at each other and not feel bad."

"I'll always regret losing you."

She turned because there was nothing left to say.

"Hey, Armie. You going to play or sit there and look at your cards?"

Armie came out of his misery long enough to stare down at the cards in his hand. King, queen, suited. He glanced at the three cards on the table. A queen and an ace and a two of clubs. Nice hand, but the ace made him nervous.

It didn't fucking matter. He mucked his cards and sat back. "I'm out."

It had been four days since he'd spoken to Lila. He saw her regularly. She'd taken to walking Peanut around the town square during her lunch break. He found reasons to be outside the station house during the noon hour so he could nod as she passed by. Her walks were getting longer and longer as people around town stopped and asked her questions. He was certain that was what they were doing because they inevitably pointed to some body part and then Lila would get that look on her face that let him know she was being patient.

When would he stop thinking about her every second of the day?

Rene stared at him across the table. It had come down to the two of them in the hand. Major and Remy had already dropped out. "Either you are getting very good at reading me or your head is not in this game."

Rene flipped over his hand and showed him the ace and queen that would have cost him three dollars.

They never played for much. This monthly poker game was more about friendship and having a night out than making money. He'd played once a month since he'd come home and Rene had decided they all needed a boys' night out. Of course, it wasn't a night out for Rene, since they almost always played at his place, but the Darois mansion had ten bedrooms, a large room devoted entirely to wine, a movie theater, two different kitchens, and a wing for servants' quarters. Armie supposed that getting to the pool house could be considered a vacation for Rene.

They sat around the custom-made poker table, but Armie's head was miles away.

Remy sat back, shaking his head. "Damn, I'm glad I got out of the way."

He'd expected some anger from Remy. The fact that Lila's brother-in-law would be sitting at the table had made him think twice about coming. He'd called Rene and tried to beg off, but Rene had insisted, playing the guilt card since he'd been stuck in the house alone after he'd been released from the hospital. He'd needed his friends.

Remy had simply shaken his hand when he'd walked in, and things were oddly normal.

Major stood up and stretched. "I'm getting a beer."

Quaid Havery nodded his way. "Get me one, too, if you don't mind."

Rene simply picked up the crystal decanter in front of him and poured a couple of fingers into his glass. "I'm sticking with this absolutely perfect Scotch."

Armie frowned Rene's way because Rene's leg was currently in a cast, propped up on a stool. "Aren't you on painkillers?"

He was certain Lila wouldn't like the fact that her patient was drinking and taking narcotics.

Rene waved him off. "I got off those things days ago. I'm probably going to wish I hadn't when I get through my first therapy session, but for now I'm feeling pretty good."

Quaid leaned in. "You'll feel better when we sue."

Rene groaned. "I'm not suing Janice Herbert. It's bad

enough that she's got her Bible study group coming here once a day to pray for me. I can't imagine what those women would do if I sued her." Rene raked the pot and took a sip of his Scotch. "Where's Noelle tonight?"

"She's got Beth spending the night with her." He rarely left Noelle alone. Had Noelle been by herself for more than a few minutes since the accident? She used to crave that time. Even as a child she'd been the kid who would sit in her room for hours reading books. Now he was terrified something would go wrong and she wouldn't be able to take care of herself.

"I heard Beth is rebelling." Major chuckled as he passed Quaid his beer.

Quaid slapped at the table with a wide smile. "Her daddy asked me if he can legally block her from leaving the state. I told him that he would have to make a deal with his boss because the court is going to rule against him incarcerating his daughter in their home so she can't go to college."

"Why wouldn't he want her to go to college?" Armie asked.

"Ah, it's not college Marge and Hank have a problem with. It's the fact that Beth got a scholarship to UCLA that has them up in arms," Quaid explained. "He's absolutely certain that the minute Beth steps foot in California she'll either be murdered or join a cult."

"Good for Beth," Remy said with a nod. "It's important to get out and see the world. Where's Noelle thinking of going for college?"

Why did everyone ask him that damn question? "She's looking at some schools. I think she's going to study business."

"Really? I thought she liked science," Rene mused. "I seem to remember you always talking about how crazy she was about chemistry. Wasn't she in AP Chemistry before the accident? Was she able to finish that up?"

"She decided to go another way." He'd been surprised

because her school offered it as a course. He'd figured she had enough to deal with and he hadn't fought her on it.

"All that work and she didn't finish?" Remy asked.

"She was going through a lot at the time." And he'd been dealing with it, too. Was it time to stop merely trying to get through a day and start worrying about the future? "I'm surprised Beth would even think about going to California. She's so close to her family."

Quaid shrugged. "She wants to see the world."

"Has she ever been on a plane?" Beth was as sheltered as Noelle.

"She's got to start somewhere. I think I might need to set up a scholarship fund." Rene glanced over at Quaid. "Hey, when Hank sues me for paying his daughter's travel expenses, you can defend me. Now, why don't you and Major go and grab that tray of sandwiches the housekeeper left for us? I think she left some sweets, too. She told me boys need fuel when they're playing. Her sarcasm is sharpening with age."

Armie started to push his chair back. "I'll go."

Rene held up a hand. "No, I'm sending them off because I'd like to have a chat with you and Remy."

Major sent him a sympathetic look as he stood, but Quaid couldn't seem to get out fast enough.

"Come on, friend. I happen to know where Rene stashes the cigars," Quaid offered.

Rene shook his head. "I never should have shown him the humidor."

"What do you need?" Remy asked once they had left. "Is the leg bothering you?"

"The leg aches every day and I loathe and despise not being on my feet, but that's not what I want to talk about. I need to know if the two of you are okay with each other. I don't know what happened, and I don't need to know, but it's obvious Armie is no longer dating Lila Daley. I know Remy likes to protect the female members of his family in some barbaric ways."

"I don't call them barbaric. Maybe my justice is biblical, but it's also effective." Remy turned to Armie. "Armie and I are fine. Lila explained that it wasn't a good fit, and as long as he treats her with respect, we won't have any trouble. Hey, not every relationship works."

But theirs had. It seemed to work beautifully, except that one problem. "I'm not going to do anything to hurt her. We didn't break up because we didn't care about one another. If she ever needs anything, I'll be there."

Rene nodded. "Excellent. I wanted to let you both know that I intend to ask Ms. Daley out. The accident taught me something. I'm not getting any younger and that woman is a damn rock. I'd like very much to see if we're compatible."

"No." The word came out of his mouth before he was smart enough to stop it. He didn't have any right to tell Rene he couldn't go after Lila. He'd always known Rene was a better match. Rene was younger than he was, didn't have children. Wanted children.

Except he'd dreamed the night before of what it would be like to have it all again, with the right woman this time. He'd married his ex-wife because she'd been pregnant. Having children with Lila would be a deliberate act of will.

An act of hope.

What would it be like to raise a couple of kids he got to see every single day? To raise them with a woman he truly loved? He adored his daughter, but he'd missed so much by being her weekend father.

It was pure bad timing that the minute he lost Lila was also the minute he knew he wanted that family.

"I'm sorry, what does that mean?" Rene was staring at him.

"I'd like to understand that myself." Remy frowned his way. "I wasn't happy with how you treated Lila, but I understand that she can be a handful. She also told me I wasn't allowed to punch you, so tread carefully because I'll ignore that if you annoy me."

He didn't have the right to tell Rene no, but he did have some questions. "I don't like the idea of you deciding it's time for you to settle down and picking Lila because she's standing in front of you. She deserves more than that."

Rene watched him with shrewd eyes. "She was standing in front of me saving my life. It wasn't like she was a random pretty lady I decided to choose because I was bored. She was a damn warrior. Even as I was bleeding out on that street I was thinking about how amazing she was. As I sat in that hospital I came up with all the ways I was going to seduce her. Imagine my surprise when I got home and all the talk was about how the sheriff had made his move."

He didn't like how passionate Rene sounded about Lila. But then, who wouldn't be? She was complex and difficult and worth every bit of trouble.

"Armie, it's obvious you miss her," Remy said quietly. "I know it's hard to apologize when you're wrong, but trust me, it works. Groveling is something we all do."

It wasn't that simple. "She doesn't get along with my daughter."

"Lila loves Noelle," Remy said gravely. "I'm struggling to understand this. She's crying every night. You're obviously upset."

"What went wrong?" Rene asked. "There's no gossip, and that tells me you're both playing this close to the vest, but I want to know because I think I could care about her. I know I care about you. Give me a good reason why I shouldn't go after her."

"I can't," he replied. "If you're smart, you'll chase after that woman and raise a family with her because I think one day she'll be an amazing mom. Maybe she just has to go through it for herself."

"Lila's been through it. Lila was raising kids when she was a kid," Remy pointed out. "That's why she and Lisa have a somewhat contentious relationship. You know Lila was in charge of that household when she was ten years old, right? Her brother did a lot, but he left her in charge of Laurel and Lisa."

They didn't understand. "I have to think about Noelle. I'm stuck in a bad place. The reason for the disagreement is that Noelle thinks Lila is pushing her too hard on the rehab training."

"What do you think?" Remy asked.

"I don't know what to think. In the moment I was upset that she was talking to Noelle like an angry football coach. Now I worry I've missed something and I need to get a second opinion on Noelle's condition. But if I do that, I worry that I would be giving Noelle false hope. I hate this. I hate that I don't know what I'm doing. I hate that I'm alone in this."

"It doesn't sound like you are," Rene pointed out. "At least you weren't. It sounds like Lila was taking charge in a place where she knows more than you do."

He shook his head. "You weren't there. You didn't have to watch your girlfriend make your daughter cry. I have to put Noelle above everything else."

"It sounds like Lila was doing that, too." Remy had his arms crossed over his chest. "Do you think she didn't understand this could go sideways? She knew how touchy you are about Noelle."

"I'm not touchy. Okay, if I'm touchy it's because she's fragile. She lost everything in that accident." He wasn't sure why he was defending himself. "I don't know what her future holds. I only know that I have to make life as comfortable for her as possible, and Lila disagrees with me. She seems to think that I should drop my daughter off in Austin and not look back."

Remy chuckled. "Somehow I don't see that. Lila wants Noelle to have as much of a life as she possibly can. No one ever got anything done because they were comfortable. Comfort is something you earn later in life."

"She earned it by surviving," Armie insisted.

Rene shook his head, leaning back. "Wow, it's interesting how different our reactions can be. I was laying there bleeding out on that concrete and all I could think about was getting another couple of moments, another few days. I've been comfortable and it's held me back. Time is a funny thing. It seems long and never-ending in the beginning, and then you realize it's gone by in a flash and you can't ever get it back. I worry Noelle is too young to understand that. Can I ask you a question?"

"You've asked me plenty. What's one more?" He was sure whatever it was would make him look like an idiot. The last few days of his life had been one long session of self-doubt. This was what he truly resented about what Lila had done. His life had seemed calmer. It had normalized. Then she'd walked in and shaken it all up, and he didn't like where he'd landed.

"Will you be satisfied with the job you've done as a parent if Noelle gives up her dreams?" Rene leaned forward. "I outfitted this town to make her life easier. I didn't do it so she would never leave and you wouldn't ever have to worry about her again."

Would he be satisfied if Noelle never tried? What was his job? Since the accident it seemed like it had been about protecting her from everything and anyone who might possibly hurt her. Was he protecting her from a future, too?

"You seem to think Lila was pushing her out," Remy said, his voice softer than before. "But what if she was merely trying to push you all forward? You've been looking for someone who would get along with your daughter, someone who would make your life easier."

That wasn't what he'd been looking for at all. "I just wanted someone I could care about."

"You need to want more, brother," Remy replied. "You need to want to love a woman, and that is neither comfortable nor easy. When it's real love, it's hard and you're going to fight, and if you're in love with a woman like Lila Daley, she's going to push. You should want a woman who loves you and your family enough to put it all on the line, and that's what she did. I've known my sister-in-law for a while. I knew her before she was nearly killed in that ER. Trauma like that can make or break a person. Lila chose to move forward. She chose to change, but in ways that made her stronger. I'm proud to be her brother-in-law. And what she's trying to do for Noelle isn't selfish. It's the opposite. If you can't see that, then you're the one with the problem, and that's my tough love for you. We've been friends for years, Armie. I knew the minute Lila decided to take over the clinic here that you and she would spark off each other. I knew you would either hate each other, or you might find something special. You both went through something terrible, but she's ready and you're not."

"What does that mean?"

"It means you're still stuck in that moment when you realized you could lose your daughter, and now you've wrapped a cocoon around her and she's going along with it, but that cocoon is either going to stifle her or hold her back. Sometimes you have to be tough with the ones you love so they can reach their full potential. That's what Lila was trying to do. She wasn't being a bitch, man. She was being a mother."

Armie's heart seized up at the thought. Was he holding Noelle back? Was his guilt costing them the one woman who might make both their lives complete?

"I'll talk to her. I'm miserable without her, but I don't know that she'll want me again." It was his fear.

"You should understand that if this doesn't work out, I'm taking my shot with her," Rene vowed. "I'll give you a couple of weeks, but when I'm walking again, if you're not with her, I'm going to try."

He was on a clock. He had to figure it out or he could lose it all.

"All right, then." Rene glanced around. "Where are those sandwiches? Let's play some poker, boys."

Armie sat back. The game didn't matter, but he would have to make the biggest gamble of his life.

On her. On them.

chapter seventeen

⌐◦⌐

Lila watched as Noelle stared at the parallel bars. She'd stood in the background, hopeful that the last session had taught Noelle something, but it was apparent that all it had taught her was she could get away with not trying.

Awesome.

Noelle looked up at Tanya and shook her head. She'd been completely willing to do all the upper-body exercises, all the stretching that was part of her therapy. She'd chatted happily while attached to the TENS unit. Then they'd gotten to the bars and Noelle had completely shut down.

Lila was left with the distinctly crappy choice between walking away or getting into more trouble. She'd avoided Noelle's father for three days. It had been fairly easy. He was on night shift for two of the days and she'd taken off the other, choosing to be on call. She wasn't sure what was up with Armie but suddenly he wanted to talk, and that hadn't worked for them before.

The truth was she'd done a hell of a lot of soul-searching and she couldn't do this again. He wanted to talk because he missed her. She missed him, too, but she couldn't trust him. The next time they clashed—and they would—she would get her heart ripped out again.

That clash was coming sooner than any of them suspected. It was coming right now.

If Noelle didn't choose to try soon, there would be no reason for her to try. Armie wasn't thinking. He was reacting to something terrible that had happened, but Noelle didn't have time for things to normalize. Her time was running out.

If she did this, she might be risking her job.

But if she didn't do this, she wouldn't be *doing* her job.

She stepped out and nodded Tanya's way. "I'll take it from here."

Noelle's eyes widened, but she didn't see fear or anger in there. "Lila. I'm glad to see you. I thought about calling you a hundred times. I'm so sorry about what happened."

"I'm sorry, too." She wished it had ended on a better note. Well, she wished it hadn't ended at all. She still couldn't sleep without dreaming about Armie. And beyond Armie, she missed Noelle, but there were some things worth fighting for, some things worth losing it all over. "Now let's get you up on the bars."

Noelle sighed, a frustrated sound. "That wasn't what I meant."

She braced herself for the fight. "I know, but it's what you're going to do. I didn't come here today to try to talk you into asking your father for a second chance. I came here because I believe in you. Just because your father gave up on me doesn't mean I'm giving up on you. Do you understand me? I'm going to be here for every session until he gets a restraining order. I'm not going away until I'm forced to, and you are going to get on those bars and do what I tell you to do."

Her face had flushed and she gripped the arms of her chair. "Why? Why is it so important to you that I walk? Why can't you like me as I am?"

She had to wonder how often this tactic had worked for Noelle. "That's not going to work on me. I love you and that's why I'm not giving up. Sometimes when you love someone you risk everything for them—even your relationship. I will not let a soft heart cost you years of your life. Tell me why you don't want to walk."

"Are you fucking with me?"

It was the realest thing that had come out of that child's mouth in weeks. "No. I am not fucking with you. You won't try so I assume you don't want to walk."

It was obvious anger was starting to bubble up in Noelle. "Of course I want to walk."

Anger could be an excellent motivator. "Good. Then let me help you up."

"Fuck you."

This was what Noelle needed. A foe to defeat. "Yes. Fuck me. Now we're going to get up. Tell me what you're afraid of. Because if it's falling, don't be afraid of that. It will happen, and guess what? We'll try it again and I will be right there with you. I will be there for you to fall on."

Her whole face had gone a brilliant scarlet. "I hate you."

"I'm okay with that. You can hate me all day as long as your ass is up on those bars."

"This is all that matters to you, isn't it?"

"Yes." She'd lost Armie. She couldn't lose this fight, too. When she thought about it, she'd kind of been prepping her whole life for this. It was time to let Noelle understand exactly what was at stake for her. "Do you know I've never really helped anyone I truly loved? I got into nursing because I was good at it and it was a profession that would lift me out of the poverty I grew up in. I was surrounded by all these vibrant women who treated it like a calling. They talked about how they wanted to help all these people. I did get that, but I'm going to admit that I'm far more intellectual than emotional. Except about the people I love. I thought all those years ago I went into nursing to lift myself up, and when I found myself with a gun pointed to my head and my life on the line, all I could think about was that nothing I had done to that point mattered."

"You're talking about what happened in Dallas?" The anger seemed to have fled, but tears shone in Noelle's eyes.

"Yes, I'm talking about that moment, that one excruciatingly long moment that seemed to mean more than all the others that came before it. The one that taught me I was helpless. But I was listening to the wrong message. Sometimes we don't see things clearly until we're on the other side of it. I would never have had what happened to my friend happen, but I can't change that. All I can do is look for meaning, and here you are, Noelle."

Her eyes widened. "What do you mean?"

In all the misery she'd gone through agonizing over Armie, she'd found this one truth. "I mean if that day doesn't happen, I don't come here. If I don't have that gun aimed at me, watching my friend die in front of me, I don't question everything I've ever known about myself. I don't make the illogical move to come to a crazy town where the brightest young lady I've met in a long time isn't getting the treatment she needs. If I hadn't grown up poor, I probably don't become a nurse and I don't end up here and I don't meet your father. And you don't walk. This is my calling, Noelle. You. Right here and right now. So don't think you can sway me. Don't think you can push me off. You will try. I will give you everything I have and even if you never walk, I will help you become independent so you can have the life you deserve."

"Noelle, you will do everything she tells you to do," a deep voice said. She turned and Armie was standing there. Armie, her big, strong sheriff, was standing with his hat in his hand and tears in his eyes. He seemed to suck those up as he looked at his daughter. "Go on, now."

Noelle's jaw firmed. "You're taking her side?"

"No. I just realized that she was always taking your side and I was siding with my own guilt. Get on the bars," he said, striding over to them. He looked to Lila. "How can I help her?"

Finally he got the point. It broke her heart that it was far too late for them, but it wasn't for Noelle. Noelle could still get everything she needed, and that included a couple of people who cared about her enough to not give up. "She's got great upper-body strength. We're going to get her on the bars and see what happens. Armie, this isn't going to be pretty."

"No, this is going to be painful and rough," he replied, his voice hoarse. "It's going to take incredibly hard work, and it might not pay off."

"It will. Whether she walks or not, she's going to know that she tried. She's going to be stronger even if she fails. We learn everything important in life from failing and trying again." God, she hoped so, because some days those lessons were all she had. That and a prayer that everything she'd been through would be worth it.

This would be worth it—even the pain of losing Armie—if Noelle had a good life.

"I don't want to." Noelle sniffled, tears in her eyes.

"I don't care what you want." Armie stood firm. "You have two years before you can get out from under my roof, and during that time I will expect certain things from you. One of those things is going to be PT and doing everything Lila asks of you. I'm indulgent but I can't be moved on this, sweetheart. This is your future."

"You don't want me here. You want me to leave," Noelle choked out.

"No, but I damn straight want you to be able to leave if that's your choice. Now get on those bars and get started," he commanded.

Lila waited, her heart in her throat because this was such an important moment between father and daughter. Armie might not understand it, but he was choosing to walk again, too. He was choosing to try to move forward and find another path.

Noelle sat there for a moment and Lila worried she was going to refuse. The truth was they could push all they liked, but in the end, Noelle was the one who had to do the work. She was the one who had to take the pain and try.

She shook her head, but there was a spark in her eyes. "You two want to watch me fall? You want to see me fail? Fine. Fucking fine."

"Noelle," her father admonished.

Lila put a hand up to stop him. "No, she's making an adult choice. Here in this place she gets to use any language she needs to in order to get through a session."

Armie nodded. "You're right." He turned back to his daughter. "So do it, Noelle. Get up there and try."

She seemed to understand she was in a corner and there was only one way out. "Fine. You'll see. You'll be the one who's disappointed because your only child is broken and damaged. This is for you. Maybe I won't be a burden if you can get me to walk."

Armie paled.

"Don't give in to that." Lila had seen it all. "That's not Noelle. That's her fear trying to find a way out, and fear doesn't play fair. So don't play at all. Get on the bars, Noelle."

Noelle huffed, but shifted forward in her seat.

Her father was right there, lifting her up. "Do I settle her on here?"

"The bars have been adjusted to the proper height, and I know she's scared of falling but the floor is padded." It would still hurt, but she'd made the place as safe as she could.

"I'm not worried about falling. Who cares about me falling?" Noelle asked. "What's one more injury as long as I can prove to you that I'm a fucking invalid? Maybe you two can move me into a nursing home after this and you can have some perfect, non-flawed kids you can actually love."

Armie looked like he wanted to throw up, but he didn't falter. "We'll talk about that in a while, Noelle. Not now. Now you work. LaVignes work."

"I'm not much of a LaVigne, am I?" Noelle said even as she gripped the bars.

She was going to fight until the end. Lila ignored it. "I need you to balance on the bars. Your feet are flat on the mat. That's good. Today we don't have to do anything more than get used to being on the bars. Find your balance."

"I don't have any fucking balance." Noelle seemed intent on using her new freedom of language.

She said she didn't have balance and yet she was standing with both feet planted and her hips only slightly off. The therapists had done an excellent job keeping her muscles strong. And her slender arms held a wealth of strength. Still, her face contorted as she held herself up.

"It's okay. We'll go slow. I'd like to try fifteen seconds at a time. We'll try it three times today and work our way up," Lila explained. "The injury you have has a good chance at healing if we do this right."

"Fifteen seconds at a time? No. I'm trying this once and then I'm done." Noelle shifted her arms and that was when it happened. Her right leg moved from the hip but in an odd, coltish fashion. Her foot slipped and Noelle headed for the ground.

Her father was the slightest bit too slow to catch her. She hit the ground with a dull thud.

The room went silent. Lila knew it was a good thing, but sometimes the patient didn't understand. She knew Armie was going to break soon. He wouldn't be able to watch his baby in pain.

He dropped to his knees beside his daughter. "Sweetie, are you okay?"

"It hurts," Noelle said, her shoulders shaking.

"I'm so sorry." Armie's whole being was focused on his daughter.

"Daddy, it hurts." Noelle's head came up, and sure enough there were tears streaking down her face, but a smile was there as well. "My leg hurts."

Pain. It could be sweet. The world went watery, the two people in front of her crystalizing in a picture she would never be able to get out of her head.

It was enough.

It had to be.

She looked at Armie and Noelle, holding on to each other, and she wanted to be with them. It was an actual ache in her body, but she took a step back. She wasn't a part of that family and it was time to let them be, to let them bond over this new beginning. She would be there for the next session. She would watch as Noelle healed and took back her future.

And maybe someday Armie would be ready for a relationship. It probably wouldn't be with her, but she would be happy for him because she loved him. Her heart hurt as she forced herself to walk away. This was love, the real thing. It wasn't selfish. It wasn't the mad passion of her youth. It was a quiet belief in another person, a prayer that her love could protect him whether or not he could return the feeling.

"Could you finish up the session for me?" she asked Tanya. She knew she should stay there to make sure Noelle got back in her chair and to talk to her about some exercises she could do at home, but she couldn't face them right now. They would likely reach out for her but it would be out of gratitude. Next time she would be more emotionally prepared to deal with it, but for now she needed to go to the clinic, grab her stuff, and head out to Guidry's, where she would cry on her sister's shoulder for a while.

Tanya nodded, her eyes bright with tears, too. "Of course. Lila, you did something great today."

Lila thanked her and moved from the cool air of the building to the heat of the Louisiana summer. Night had descended and Mabel would have already closed up the clinic. She hurried down the street because lately she got stopped by anyone walking along the block that connected the clinic to the therapy gym. They asked her about whatever ailed them or gave her the latest gossip. Seraphina would talk about her son, Luc, or Dixie would pop her head out of the café's doors to ask how she'd liked the soup of the day.

Papillon was home.

Funny how that had happened.

She used her key card to open the clinic doors, a bit surprised it hadn't been manually locked.

"Mabel? Are you still here?" She wanted to clear out before Armie showed up. He would absolutely walk in at some point and want to have a long talk. He would say all the right things but, again, they would be about gratitude.

They needed a good long time to figure out what they wanted free of the turbulence of breaking out of the places they'd been stuck in.

The smell of gasoline hit her nose. Where was that coming from? The gas station was over a block away. She'd never smelled it here.

"What the hell are we supposed to do now?" a deep voice said.

They didn't have any patients. Not any with appointments, but there could have been an emergency. She wondered why Mabel hadn't paged her. She strode through the waiting area toward the exam rooms. The smell got worse. Hopefully they hadn't had some kind of accident with gasoline.

Except it smelled like it was coming from reception.

The computer was wet.

"How was I supposed to know the bitch would still be here?"

Her whole body went cold because she was in trouble again.

Armie could barely see his daughter through the tears that clouded his eyes. She'd moved her legs. It hadn't been much of a movement and it had sent her straight to the ground, but hope was an amazing thing.

Lila had given that to them. She'd been a fountain of strength, unwavering in her belief. He'd walked in and seen her, and his first instinct had been to drop to his knees and beg her forgiveness. He hadn't been shocked by the fact that Lila had shown up for Noelle's session. She'd ignored his calls and texts for days, but she hadn't given up on his daughter.

"Sweetie, I'm so proud of you."

Noelle's face was flushed with emotion as she pushed up

to a sitting position. "I'm sorry I wouldn't try. I didn't want to fail."

"The only way to fail is by not trying." He understood that. He always had, but the lesson he'd learned when he was a child had gotten lost in his pain and worry for her. "Was that the only reason? Sweetie, you need to talk to me. We've both been holding back. You haven't wanted to learn any of the things Lila's been trying to teach you. Why are you afraid of being more independent?"

"I know how hard it was for you to change your whole life after Mom died and I got stuck in that chair. But it also brought us closer together. I didn't want things to change. This is going to be hard, and you hated to watch me struggle. It upset you so much. I didn't want to hurt you more."

Oh, they'd needed to have this talk for such a very long time. "It was not hard. I hate what happened to you and your mother, but getting to spend every day with you was the best thing that ever happened to me. Being your dad has been the joy of my life, Noelle. But I've done you a disservice because I was happy. I wanted things to stay the same so I didn't have to worry about you again. If you were home, you were safe. Life isn't about safety, baby girl. Life is about taking risks and pushing yourself to be the best Noelle you can be. I forgot that."

"I love you, Dad. I'm sorry I was so stubborn."

She hadn't been the only one. "I'm sorry, too. Know that I'm going to push you from now on. I was afraid, too. I put you in that car."

She shook her head. "You wanted to see me. I wanted to see you, too. It had been too long. I could have waited until morning, but I didn't want to waste the time we did have together. I fought with Mom that night."

It wasn't anyone's fault. They'd all meant well. It had been an accident and one it was long past time to forgive themselves for. "We're going to move past this. We're going to do it as a family. I promise the next time I'm feeling guilty, I'll talk about it. And the next time you think you're a burden, tell me and I'll remind you of all the ways you're loved."

He got to his knees and looked around for Lila. She should be here with them. She was the reason they were here. God, he needed to hold her, to tell her he was sorry for not understanding what she'd been trying to do.

He needed to tell her how much he loved her.

"I think she left," Noelle said, allowing him to help her up.

Tanya was there, holding the wheelchair steady as he got to his feet and picked his daughter up. "She went back to the clinic. I think she was trying to give you two some space. Oh, Noelle, I'm so happy for you."

His daughter was light in his arms, but he'd mistaken her size for fragility. Noelle was strong, and she could fight her way through this. He would be by her side. He needed to make sure Lila was with them. They weren't complete without her.

Noelle settled in and nodded up at the therapist. "I want to try again. Lila said I should try at least three times."

"I can make that happen, but we're going slow. Lila will chew me out if I let you hurt yourself." Tanya smiled Armie's way. "It's okay, Sheriff. I can handle the rest of the session if you want to go to the clinic and talk to her."

"Can I have a minute with my daughter?" He needed to make something clear. There was no way to move forward without the most important part of his personal future.

"I'll go grab us some water," Tanya said with a wink. "Be right back."

He turned to his daughter. "I'm going to marry Lila. I love her and I love you. I will always love you, but . . ."

Noelle held up a hand to stop him. "But I won't be here forever, Dad. I'm going to go to college. I'm going to be a chemist and I'm going to have my own family. I love Lila, too. I can't think of anyone I would want as a stepmom more than her. And, Dad, I know you're scared of having more kids, but I think you should. I think I would be a great big sister."

Something had happened to her in those moments when she'd taken her first faltering steps. Something mature and confident had come over his daughter. She'd been a scared little girl, but a woman sat in that chair now, one who would fight for herself.

He leaned over and kissed her forehead. "I agree. I think any kids who get you as a sister will have a hell of a role model. I'll bring her back. I promise."

He nodded to Tanya as he strode out of the building.

It was time to bring his wife home.

chapter eighteen

"I think you boys should get on out of here." Mabel's voice was clear, but there was a shaky quality to it.

Lila started to back away. She didn't recognize the voices, but she was worried she might know who they were. If she was right, they were absolutely not here for medical care. The computer had been coated with gasoline, and so had the filing cabinets from the looks of it. Someone wanted to get rid of all her patient records, and there was only one person she could think of who might want to do that.

Bobby Petrie's trial was going to come up in the next few months, and the DA would want those records soon. They would want to depose her and get all the medical information she had. If she didn't have the X-rays and notes, the tests that had been run, all she could offer was her testimony, and it might not be enough.

"Yeah, because you'll pretend like this never happened, right?"

There was a hitch to Mabel's voice. "I don't have to tell anyone."

Her sweet friend was so scared. It was right there in that tremor she heard.

Armie. She needed to get to the therapy gym and get

Armie. She wasn't sure how many people were in the back. She would bet both of the Petrie brothers were there, but she was sure they had cousins somewhere. Everyone who lived in the bayou seemed to have labyrinthine family trees, and they backed each other up.

She started to turn, but she was too late. Mabel stumbled through the hallway, her lip bloody and a gun at her back. It was held by Bobby Petrie. Bobby's brother was with him, and he immediately pointed his pistol at her.

"Don't you fucking move."

For a moment she was back in that room, the door barricaded and blood on the floor. She could smell the coppery scent, taste the blood in her mouth because she'd bitten her lip to stop from screaming, could hear the choked sound of her friend trying to breathe despite the fact that her lungs didn't work anymore.

She was here again, but this time she had so much more to lose. She wouldn't see Armie or Noelle again if she died. This time she wouldn't simply die. She would lose the life she longed for. Why had she walked away? Why hadn't she told Armie that he wasn't ever allowed to leave her again, that they could fight but they couldn't be apart because they were supposed to be together? Come what may.

God, it was worse when she had so much to lose.

The danger was real, but she wasn't in the same place. She had to remember that. She was in Papillon, and she had to deal with this because she wasn't going to lose Mabel.

"Lila, I thought you were gone." Mabel held her hands up as Bobby moved in behind her, wrapping his arm around her throat. The gun was against her temple.

There would be no coming back from that shot. There wouldn't be time to fix Mabel if he pulled the trigger.

"We thought you were both gone," Bobby said. "The clinic is supposed to be closed this time of night. You close at six today. It's seven thirty. You should both be at home."

"I stayed to do the inventory on the exam rooms so you didn't have to do it in the morning," Mabel explained. "But I turned out the lights. They thought we were closed.

I didn't hear them until I came out to pack up and go home."

"It's going to be okay. Bobby, I need you to stay calm. You can still get out of this." Each word was a struggle, the desire to scream profound, but it wouldn't help her. Rage wasn't her friend at this point. That could come later. For now she had to stay calm. "You haven't hurt anyone yet."

She was so happy she'd left Peanut with Remy today. Peanut would have barked and tried to protect Mabel, but Remy had convinced her to let the dog go fishing with him and his friends.

Donnie Petrie was dressed in all black despite the heat of the evening. She would bet he'd come in the back way. It was secured, but a desperate man could find a way around most locks. "Get on your knees. If you even think about moving, I'll fire. I can set this whole thing up to look like a burglary."

She had to stay calm. "You need to think this through. You kill the two of us and there's no going back from that. Like I said, you haven't hurt anyone yet."

That gun didn't move and she held her hands up, but she wasn't getting on her knees until she absolutely had to.

"No, but you two have," Bobby said. His words came out slurred, and now she noticed his eyes were red. "You two have managed to ruin my life. I want to know where Carrie is. I let that first bitch go, but I'm not doing it again. I'm not going to be the laughingstock of this town."

"Shut up, Bobby." Donny's stare remained firmly locked on her.

"I don't think anyone is laughing at you." She looked at Mabel, who was tense but calm.

"I am certainly not laughing, young man. I don't think anything about this is funny, and if you hold me here much longer, I'm going to miss dinner and tonight is taco night. I love taco night." Mabel's voice trembled slightly, but it was obvious she wasn't about to break.

He shook his head and everything about his manner seemed sloppy. She would bet he'd been drinking most of the day. "You know what I'm talking about. Everyone thinks I abuse my wife, and it's all because of the two of you."

"No, I think it's because you hurt her," Lila said slowly. "I've got records of all her injuries. You only got away with it for this long because Doc Hamet didn't want to be bothered."

He sneered her way. "Doc knew when to keep to his own business."

"Mabel was Doc's nurse, too. She didn't have anything to do with the sheriff arresting you. It was my call to go to him. Why don't you let her go and we can talk about this?" If Mabel was safe, her options would open up. If she was the one he was holding, she might have some moves to get herself out. It would be risky, but anything was better than watching another friend die.

Bobby obviously didn't want to listen. "There's nothing to talk about. I want to know where my wife is. You take me to her and I'll let you live. I don't have anything to lose and if I'm going down, I would love to take the two of you with me."

This was the real Bobby Petrie. The other one was nothing but a mask. What had set him off? He'd seemed so calm these weeks. Since he'd been arrested that first time he'd laid low, staying out on his island and showing up for his court dates.

"You have a lot to lose," she pointed out. "Think about your family."

Donny huffed. "This is all about family. Carrie sent paperwork today filing for divorce. We're not stupid. Momma made her sign some papers so she wouldn't be able to take part of our boat and the business like the other one did, but that uppity lawyer she got in New Orleans thinks she can get around it."

"Carrie's lawyer is going to try to break the prenup because of the abuse she suffered?" It seemed like therapy had empowered Carrie in ways Lila hadn't imagined.

"Yes. We're going to have to fight her. We lost the first time and had to pay. How was I supposed to know my first wife would get a lawyer?" Bobby complained.

"How about you stick to hookers from now on, asshole," Donny shot back. "Momma won't deal with this again. You know what she's going to do if we don't handle this properly."

"Then I think you should talk to your momma," Mabel replied.

Bobby's arm tightened again. "It's Carrie's greed that needs to be dealt with. She needs to understand that she's not getting anything more out of me. I did her a favor when I married her. She was nothing. No man was going to look at that skinny bitch. No one wanted her until I did. She doesn't get to take everything away from me."

"You couldn't expect her to stay with you." She needed to talk him down. He might sober up a bit and realize what he was doing. He'd been careful before. He'd obviously not wanted to get into more trouble. Maybe if he realized how bad this could get, he would calm down. There was still time. "You hurt her."

His face contorted. "I didn't mean to. She wouldn't listen. I'm no worse than my daddy was. And I never hurt her when she didn't need it. It wasn't my fault. She was a bad wife and now I hear she's going to file the paperwork soon and she's going to testify against me. She's determined to ruin my whole family."

"We're not going to let that happen," Donny vowed. "She doesn't get to hurt my family that way."

"I think they want to get rid of the records," Mabel managed to say.

Yes, she got that.

"You're the one who burned down my house?" She needed to keep him talking because she had zero doubt that Armie would show up after the session was over.

"I thought maybe it would convince you that you didn't belong here." Donny started to stalk toward her. "We don't need some uppity city girl coming in here and telling us how to do things. And it wasn't that hard. That house went up real easy. It was a beautiful sight."

And he'd gotten away with it. The trouble was he wouldn't get away with this one. They weren't thinking straight, and she had to wonder if she pointed out all the fallacies in their plan if they wouldn't kill her just because she got them angry.

Donny came into her space, his dark eyes roaming across her body in a way that made her stomach turn. "Not that you aren't a pretty lady. Too bad you feel the need to come in and judge everyone else."

Yes, she totally judged assholes who beat their wives. She forced herself to stand still because while Bobby was a pathetic piece of crap, Donny was a predator. He was the truly dangerous one and he was close, that pistol at the ready.

"What do you think you're getting out of this?" Mabel seemed to be trying to go for reason. "Bobby, you have to know that the sheriff is in love with Lila. You kill her and he won't stop looking for you. For what it's worth, neither will my husband. Oh, Dale will come after you in a scooter, but he's surprisingly mean."

Armie would be here soon. How long would it take to finish up the session? How much would Noelle want to do? A spark of terror ran through her.

God, would Armie show up with Noelle? Panic threatened. She couldn't put Noelle in the line of fire.

"I'll take you to Carrie. You should talk to her. Maybe you can work this out." She wouldn't, but she would do anything to draw this man away from a place where he could potentially hurt Noelle. If it had simply been Armie she was worried about, she would have settled in and let him do his job, but if Noelle was with him . . .

Mabel's eyes went wide. "But, Lila . . ."

Bobby's arm relaxed slightly and his face had softened. "You know where Carrie is? She didn't just run? I knew you probably gave her some money and helped her out, but I didn't know you took her somewhere."

He was the weak link. He still wanted to find his wife. Bobby likely thought he was in love with her. His love would be the death of her if he had his way, but she would manipulate those feelings if it meant getting them out of here before putting Noelle on the line.

"I know exactly where she is." She had him. If she played her cards right, she might be able to get them all out of this building. "I dropped her off. I can talk to her, get her to meet with you. This doesn't have to end badly."

When she got him to the car, she would try to figure a way out. The last thing she would do was take him to New Orleans. Armie would see her car was still here. He would see that the back door of the clinic had been jimmied and investigate. He would find the gasoline and make the right connections. God, she hoped the car they were in had GPS he could track.

He would find her. He wouldn't stop until he found her because that man loved her. She was back in the place where she was fighting for her life, but this time she knew the man who loved her would be by her side. Not physically, of course, but his heart would be with her.

He would be out there and all she needed to do was survive long enough for him to find her.

"I would like to see her," Bobby said gravely. "I need to apologize to her for that last night. She made me mad."

"I'm sure she wants to apologize to you, too." She was close to convincing him.

"Lila, what are you doing?" Mabel asked.

She shook her head vigorously. "We can't fight them. Maybe we made a mistake. I can take him to her. I know she wants to see him."

Her heart was racing because they could be here at any moment. Armie would never be able to handle something else happening to Noelle.

"Come on," she said. "She's in a safe house. It won't take

us long to get there, but we should go now. The sheriff is on his way."

Donny frowned his brother's way. "Tell me you're not this stupid."

"It's not stupid to want my wife back," Bobby argued.

Donny shook his head. "It's stupid to think this woman is telling you the truth." He stood in front of her. "I didn't want to do this, but we've got no choice now. We'll leave them here and let the fire do its work. Don't worry. We've got an excellent alibi, and I'm sure you've pissed off plenty of people. Time to go night-night."

She started to back away, but he was too quick. He caught her arm and then brought the pistol down on her head. She heard Mabel shouting as the world went dark.

She prayed for one more moment with Armie. Just one where she could tell him she loved him.

Armie jogged down the block, needing so badly to see her. He hoped she hadn't run. Not that it would matter. He would find her tonight and make things right between them. There was no way he was letting Rene get his rich, pretty hands on her. Lila was his and he would make sure she understood that tonight.

When he thought about it, his best bet might be getting on his knees and groveling. No man in the world would ever love her the way he would. He was all in, and as far as he was concerned, they could throw away the condoms and she didn't need to take another pill. They weren't getting any younger and he wanted to see her with a baby in her arms. Their baby. Their dumbass boy or super-smart girl with her momma's smile.

He wanted that life with her but he knew he was going to have to convince her. She would think he was grateful for what she'd done for Noelle. It was probably running through that brilliant brain of hers right this second. He was about to cross the street when the door to Dixie's café opened and Dixie walked out, frowning.

"Hey, Sheriff. Are you going into the clinic?" Dixie asked. "Mabel closed it up over an hour ago. She mentioned she had a little cleaning up to do, but she was supposed to pick up her to-go order twenty minutes ago. It's not like Mabel to be late taking Dale his supper. He called looking for her because she's not answering her cell. I called the clinic line and it went to voice mail."

It was supposed to go to either Lila's cell or Mabel's, unless neither of them was picking up. He glanced over and the lights were all off. "I'll go check. Lila only left the therapy gym about fifteen minutes ago. She might be trying to avoid me, so I'm hoping she didn't hop in her car and drive off."

"I haven't seen her car. She parks around back, but she drives by to get out to Guidry's. I could have missed her, but I don't think so. It's been slow." Dixie started to walk across the street. "Something's wrong. I can feel it."

He didn't like the fact that no one was answering the clinic line. He jogged ahead of Dixie and looked through the glass doors.

And immediately took a step back because a fine cloud of smoke was rising from behind the reception desk. He tried to get the door to slide open, but it was locked down and he didn't have a key card. The glass was thick, far too thick for him to break without some serious equipment. It would take too long to get through that door. Panic started to bubble up inside him. The front reception area was dark with the exception of a glow coming from behind the desk, faint at first and then the whole thing caught fire.

"Call the fire department, Dixie." He was already starting around the back. It was a simpler lock and he should be able to get through it. "Then call the station house and watch for my daughter. If you can, call Tanya and get her to hold Noelle there. Tell her to lock everything down."

Because he had no idea who was in there or who would come out.

God, now he prayed Lila had gotten straight into her car and ran as fast as she could from him. He would do just about anything if she wasn't in that clinic. He hadn't seen her, but he couldn't see much from his vantage beyond the reception desk. Though it was getting easier to see in the dark clinic because the fire was growing, glowing with ghostly light.

Dixie nodded. "I'll get Roxie here as soon as I can. Be careful."

The station house was just around the block. Roxie and Major were both on duty. They wouldn't bother with a car. They would come running, but he couldn't wait.

Dixie raced back to the café and Armie pulled his side-arm. The reception desk hadn't set itself on fire, and Lila wouldn't have done it. Now he knew the arson inspector was wrong. Her house had been purposefully set on fire. There was no question about it.

"I don't see why we had to do that." The words were in a harsh whisper, but Armie could hear it plainly because the night was quiet around them.

Fucking Bobby Petrie. He should have found a way to keep him in jail. He should have protected her better.

If she was dead, he wasn't sure what he would do. He might lie beside her and let the fire take him. God, she couldn't be dead.

He forced the terror down and clung to the side of the building, stepping as lightly as he could. Every bit of training locked in, holding the fear at bay and allowing him to go cold.

"Listen here, little brother. I did what I had to do for the sake of our family." That had to be Donny Petrie.

"But she was going to take me to Carrie," Bobby insisted with a nasally whine.

"She was lying. Carrie isn't coming back, and you need to man up or we're going to lose half our damn boat. Now we need to get out of here. Those two bitches will die from smoke inhalation and we'll have an alibi. No one's seen us since we went out on the boat this morning. We get back to the boat and bring her in and head into Guidry's. I want her own brother-in-law to have to testify we were out on the water all day long."

That was not going to happen.

He couldn't wait for Roxie or Major. Lila was inside and it sounded like she'd been alive when they'd started that fire. He couldn't waste a single second. He came out from behind the wall and rounded on the Petrie brothers, getting them both in his sights in an instant.

"Put your hands up. Now."

The world seemed to slow down, everything stopping in an instant. This was when he had to make the decision. He took in both men. Bobby's eyes went wide, his shock obvious. But Donny didn't hesitate. He pointed his gun and fired.

Fire licked across Armie's shoulder, but he stayed on his feet and took a shot of his own. He was a professional. He didn't miss. Donny's body jumped as the bullet entered his chest. He let go of his pistol and slipped toward the concrete, his eyes going dead before he ever hit the ground.

Bobby stared down at his brother's body, his face going pale.

"Drop your weapon." His shoulder was on fire, but he couldn't care about that now. He needed to get Bobby Petrie under control so he could get Lila out of that damn building.

"You killed my brother." Bobby's eyes came up. "You killed him."

Bobby turned and ran back into the clinic.

The instant Bobby moved, Armie shot again, but he was already inside.

He cursed inwardly. "Come on out, Petrie. There's no getting away at this point."

His left shoulder screamed in pain, but he kept his weapon up as he followed Bobby. The back of the clinic wasn't bad. Smoke was just starting to billow through, but up ahead he could see the plumes of black and gray starting to rush around. How long had the fire been going? How much smoke had she already inhaled?

He reached over and flipped on the lights. At least they were working. Bobby was nowhere to be seen. He searched his memory, trying to count the number of rooms the clinic contained. He was in the back where they stored supplies. Up ahead there was a break room to the left, Lila's office ahead of it. To the right were two exam rooms. He wanted nothing more than to rush past all of them to get to the reception area.

Please let her be alive. He couldn't have lost his chance with her. He would give up his own life if only she got out of this. His daughter would be safe with Lila. She wouldn't let Noelle down.

"Sheriff." Roxie stepped up next to him. She had her sidearm in place and took her cues from him. "How many are we dealing with?"

That was his deputy. Cool under pressure. "I think it's just Bobby Petrie. He slipped in here before I could take him out."

"You can't say the same for his brother. Where's Mabel and the doc?"

"I don't know, but they must have disabled the sprinklers. This fire is going to move and fast. We need to get Bobby and find Lila and Mabel. I have no idea how much smoke they've already inhaled."

They moved cautiously, clearing the room before moving to the hall.

The smoke was getting thicker and thicker the closer they came to the front of the clinic.

"Major is working the problem from the front, and Joe and the boys should be here in ten," Roxie said, her voice low.

From here he could hear the crackling of the fire, feel the heat. How much time did they have? The fire department would be here soon, but they might have only minutes before the fire got to Lila. Where was she?

He had to take the chance. "I'm going to the front. From what I overheard, Donny knocked them out and left them. I think they'll be close to the fire."

"I'll watch your back, but be careful. He could be anywhere in here."

This wasn't how he should do it, but he couldn't care. He had a damn bullet in his shoulder, but he wasn't about to stop. She was somewhere in here and she needed him. He couldn't let her down. Not again.

In the distance he heard the sound of sirens. They would be here soon.

He strode down the hall, being as careful as he could, but more worried about Lila and Mabel than getting shot again. It would be far easier to get shot than to know she was gone.

He stepped out of the hall and into the reception area. He could barely breathe.

Something banged against the walls, the sound louder than the crackling of the flames that had completely overtaken the reception desk.

Major was trying to get the doors open. Armie could find the fire extinguisher, but it was too out of control.

"Sheriff." Roxie was behind him. "There are oxygen tanks in the back. We need to move fast."

He hadn't even thought about that. Where was she?

He waved a hand in front of his face and finally saw a body. He rushed to get to the still form on the floor. She wore scrubs but she was smaller and lighter than his love. Mabel. He checked her wrist and sure enough, she was alive.

If those tanks blew, the whole block might go up. "Roxie, get Mabel out of here and then come back for those tanks if it's safe."

"I can't leave you," she argued.

"You have to. Start getting those tanks out or we're going to have more than this building to worry about."

"He's in here somewhere," Roxie insisted.

He couldn't worry about that now. "I gave you an order, Deputy. I have to find Lila. Get out and have Major help set up a perimeter."

He moved on as Roxie holstered her weapon and picked up Mabel, getting her over her shoulder in a fireman's hold.

He glanced back and saw her running toward the door. She wouldn't stay away for long. His orders wouldn't keep her from putting herself on the line to try to save him.

Some of the smoke cleared and he saw her. Lila was lying on the ground facedown, her arm reaching toward him as if she'd known he was coming.

Unfortunately, she wasn't alone. Bobby stood over her, the flames illuminating his body and the way he pointed his gun at Lila's head.

"If I can't be happy, why should you?" Bobby asked.

Armie lifted his weapon but he knew he would be far too late.

A flame from the couch licked up and struck like a snake. Bobby's shirt caught fire and he jerked as he pulled the trigger, launching the bullet away from Lila, but toward another target. Armie felt the bullet hit his gut and the pain flashed through him. Bobby screamed as the fire engulfed him.

The sounds would haunt him, but he couldn't give in to the horror. Lila was too close to that fire, and Bobby could still take her out if he fell on her. He thrashed and tried to drop to the floor, but it was too late.

Armie gripped Lila's hand and dragged her back. The pain was starting to get to him, but he couldn't falter. He forced his body to work, holstering his weapon. If another bullet was coming his way, there would be nothing to do but take it. He leaned down and lifted her up even as Bobby's screams shook the building.

He had to get her out, get her breathing. Was she breathing?

Every step was agony, but he made it to the hall. The fire chased him and he knew there wouldn't be a way to get those tanks out in time. Roxie met him halfway.

"Joe's coming in," she shouted.

He shook his head. "Tell everyone to get back. Those tanks are going to blow."

She turned and shouted to the men starting to come into the building.

He ran, knowing their time was almost done. Lila hadn't moved at all. She was dead weight in his arms, but he would stay with her. He would get her out or go with her.

He hit the back door running.

Then the world exploded. He held her close and prayed he could stay with her forever.

chapter nineteen

The world was a foggy mess as Armie came to some semblance of consciousness. His whole body felt heavy. Voices pierced the veil of his haze.

"The doctor said it could be a few weeks before he's on his feet again."

"I doubt that, hon. That father of yours will be up and irritable as a bear in no time at all," a familiar voice said. "I'm more worried about how he's going to handle what happened to Lila."

Lila. It all came rushing back. They'd been in a fire. They'd nearly died. He'd had her in his arms when the oxygen tanks had exploded.

What had happened to Lila?

"It's such a shame." That was Dixie's voice. She'd been there.

"I know." His daughter was here, too. "Dad's going to be so upset."

He was going to be sick. The fog was all around him and he had to fight his way out of it. Lila. What had happened to her?

He couldn't have lost her. They'd been so close. They'd come so close to making it out and having the future he'd dreamed about.

"Lila." The word was mumbled.

"Dad?"

He felt someone touch his hand. Noelle. He opened his eyes and her face came into focus. "Where's Lila?"

"Dad, are you okay? Dixie?"

"I'll be back." She rushed out of the room.

Noelle squeezed his hand. "Dad, you've been in surgery. You had a bullet in your shoulder and another one in your gut. You need to stay still."

He couldn't. Not until he'd found Lila. She should be here. She should be with them. It was where she belonged, and he'd screwed everything up. He hadn't even told her he loved her. He started to try to push himself up.

"Oh, you are a stubborn man. Lie back down, Sheriff." Lila's pretty face loomed over him. "If you pull your stitches and have to go back to the OR, I'll be very upset."

Her voice was husky but that seemed to be the only side effect. She looked gorgeous, like the best present the universe could have given him.

She took his wrist in her hand and felt for his pulse. "You're in the hospital. You took two bullets, one to your left shoulder. It didn't hit your scapula, so you'll heal fairly quickly from that. The bullet to your abdomen was worse. The doctor managed to save your spleen, but it was a close thing. You need to rest for a couple of days."

"Love you." He wasn't going to waste another moment.

She stilled over him and finally looked down. "I love you, too. But, Armie . . ."

He knew what she would say. She would give him all the reasons they didn't work. He'd done that to her because the truth of the matter was they worked beautifully together. "Love you. Want to marry you."

"Noelle, could I have a minute?"

Noelle looked up at Lila. "Okay, but don't forget what I told you."

Lila nodded and Noelle wheeled herself out. She turned back to him. "Armie, you've been through something traumatic."

She was going that way, was she? His faculties were coming back to him and it was easier to focus. He turned his hand over, catching hers. "Yes, and the whole time all I cared about was getting you back in my arms. I was wrong. I was scared of things changing. You are the best thing to happen to me and Noelle."

"I want to believe you, but when things got rough . . ."

"I faltered and I won't do it again. I will never let you down again. I know who you are now, Lila Daley, and you are a woman I want to spend the rest of my life with. You're the woman I've been waiting all my life for."

There was still uncertainty on her face. "You think you know me so well?"

"I do. I know that you never back down from a fight. I know that even after everything you just went through the next time a woman walks into your clinic and she needs help, you'll give it to her. You'll do it every single time. You won't ever stop. And that's why we need to build a women's shelter, one you can oversee. I don't want us to have to drive two hours to protect our vulnerable citizens."

Tears made her eyes shimmer. "Armie, that could be dangerous."

"Life is dangerous. I'll go you one better. Noelle is going to want to help you and I will not stop her. I want her to be every bit as brave as her stepmom."

Her hand squeezed his. "Please be sure. I don't know if I'd be able to stand it if you changed your mind."

"I never changed my mind," he promised. "I never stopped loving you. I made a bad call as a father. I didn't see what Noelle needed, but I know now. She needs what I need. She needs you."

"The clinic is gone," she said.

That was what Dixie and Noelle had been talking about. "Then we'll rebuild it."

"I don't have any money left. I don't know what insurance is going to do. This wasn't an accident."

"I'll find the money. Otis and I will produce a speed trap unlike anything this town has ever seen. I'll let Roxie arrest

Zep as often as she likes. Those two things alone will bring in more than enough revenue." He had to make her understand that this was her home, and he would do anything to make it right for her.

"You can't build my clinic with traffic tickets." But she was smiling.

"Watch me."

"Be sure," she said, her fingers tangling around his. "Be sure you want me."

"I've never wanted anything more. Stay with me. Be with me. Build a family with me."

"But you . . ."

"Am being brave like my wife."

She stood up and leaned over, pressing her lips to his. "I love you, Armie. I would be so proud to be your wife."

"Oh, thank god," a feminine voice said from just outside the door of his room.

"Noelle," he admonished.

"Well, the waiting was killing me." She pushed the door open slightly. "And you won't have any problem rebuilding the clinic. Rene already pledged to do it. I think he'll pay for the women's shelter, too, if you play your cards right."

"She's not playing any cards with Rene at all." Even through the pain, he could find a way to be jealous. He might always have this problem because his wife was stunning and sexy, and there would always be men attracted to her intelligence and complexity.

But he would also remember that she'd chosen him.

She wrinkled her nose his way. "He's just doing it because I saved his life."

Noelle shook her head. "Nope. According to everyone in town, he's mad crazy in love with you and wants to marry you."

He was going to kill Major. Or Quaid. One of the two had been talking. Hell, maybe it had been Remy. He wouldn't put it past Lila's brother-in-law to try to shake him to his senses. He didn't need it, though. "Rene is going to have to find his own city-slicker bride."

"Is that right?" Lila asked, her lips curled up.

"Damn straight." His body was in pain, but his soul had finally found some peace. "But, *chérie*, you're going to have to take care of our honeymoon. I'm an injured man."

"Eww," Noelle said, and she turned and started out of the room. "Too much information."

"Payback can be hell, baby girl," he managed to shout.

The door closed and he was alone with Lila. With his love, his almost wife.

She leaned over to kiss him and it was more than enough.

One month later

Lila looked at the clinic with its shining countertops and all that glorious brand-new medical equipment sitting in boxes. Turned out there was plenty of money for her brand-spanking-new, top-of-the-line clinic. Doc Hamet hadn't seen the point in applying for state or national funds. Lila didn't mind. She'd had plenty of time while the clinic was being rebuilt to fill out a whole lot of paperwork. Between two large grants, Rene's donation, and the shocking number of tickets Armie could write, the Papillon Parish Clinic would be open for business soon.

"It's looking pretty good, huh?" She glanced down at her constant companion. Peanut liked coming up to the clinic. He'd kind of become their mascot.

The big dog thumped his tail and gave her one of those doggy smiles that always made her lips curl up. Even when she was in the worst of moods, that dog could make her smile. Not that she had many bad moods.

Well, except when she'd had to go out to the island and pronounce the last of the Petrie family dead. Lorna Petrie had been found dead in her small home, a week after her sons had been killed. The cause of death had been an opioid overdose. Lila had no idea where she'd gotten the pills.

There was no record of her ever coming into the clinic. Doc Hamet certainly hadn't written a prescription, but that was a mystery for another day. She wanted to settle into her new clinic and enjoy her life for a change.

"The phone lines work and I've got the schedule for our first week," a chipper feminine voice said.

Lila looked up at the newest member of her staff. Carrie was standing behind the reception desk. Even though they weren't open for business yet, she'd embraced scrubs as workwear. "How's it looking?"

There was something confident in the younger woman, something peaceful that hadn't existed before she'd made the decision to fight for herself. Lila rather thought being welcomed back in her hometown with open arms and apologies had done wonders for Carrie, too. She'd been surprised when Carrie had shown up on her doorstep asking for a job, but Carrie had told her this was her home and where she wanted to raise her baby.

"We're going to have a full week," Carrie replied. "Also I scheduled some extra time because Gene is due for a colonoscopy and you're going to have to explain that."

Lord. She would need a good argument for why the government didn't need to probe his colon for information. "I'm going to give it some thought."

"Or we could just sneak up on that old man, give him a nice dose of sleepytime drugs, and haul him in." Mabel joined Carrie at the desk. The pair had become a formidable twosome. Mabel had taken the younger woman under her wing. Carrie's baby wouldn't lack for a grandmother. "When you think about it, it plays into all of Gene's crazy conspiracy theories. It's a gift to him."

Gene wouldn't see it that way. She would likely spend some time in that jail cell. Of course, then the sheriff would have to perform a search to make sure she didn't have any weapons, and that might go really well for her.

"Hey, pretty lady."

She hadn't heard the doors open, but oh she knew that voice. For a big man, Armie moved so quietly. He could sneak up on her, but he was always a good surprise. She sighed and leaned back against her man, breathing him in. Armie wrapped her up and kissed her cheek. "Hey, babe," she greeted him. "I'm ready to go. You said you wanted to take me somewhere."

She hoped this was it. Since that day in the hospital he hadn't breathed another word about getting married. He'd had her move back in with him and they'd found a wonderful rhythm. Both he and Noelle went to PT, and Lila and Mabel had set up a temporary clinic at the gym. She would watch her two favorite people in the world as they worked their way back.

Noelle had found her strength. She was a warrior in that gym, and she was starting to find her balance. It would always be a struggle, but she was far more independent than she'd been. Although Lila wished she'd never mentioned that Noelle should learn to cook. There were some acts that could never be taken back, and Noelle's meatloaf was one of them.

But Armie hadn't mentioned marriage again. She hadn't pushed because he'd been getting back on his feet.

She also had to wonder if he'd changed his mind. He'd been through something harrowing. She was perfectly happy she'd been unconscious for the last part of that particular adventure. She'd woken up in the hospital with her sister holding her hand. Lisa had been the one to tell her that Armie was in surgery and that her clinic had gone up in smoke. Luckily the fire department had managed to keep the fire contained.

"If you're ready, then we should head out." Armie was back at work but looking for a new station house manager since his daughter was now devoted to her PT and taking dual credit classes at a community college an hour away.

"You two can handle it, right?" she asked, smiling at her employees.

Mabel had returned to work after taking some time off. She claimed a week at a casino was all she needed to get back on her feet, but Lila had insisted they both talk to a counselor. They had a standing date with a lovely young woman who was guiding them all through the aftermath. Even Armie was going in for sessions.

"We've got it. We'll be ready when we open up tomorrow." Mabel winked her way. "You two go and have some fun. You've been working like a dog for weeks."

She took Armie's hand and he led her out toward his SUV, Peanut following behind. "Where are we going?"

"Somewhere I've been wanting to take you for a while." He opened the door and helped her up. The dog hopped into the back and took his normal seat. There was nothing Peanut liked more than hanging his head out the window and watching the world go by. "But the time is right now."

"The time is right?" She rolled her window down, too. She kind of liked the fresh air as well.

He kissed the palm of her hand. "Yes, I'm working on my timing and now it's right, though you should know my life became right the day you walked into it."

"I drove into it and you pulled me over."

"You're a speed demon, my love. Now hush and enjoy the ride."

He was being awfully mysterious, but she'd learned to trust him. He'd said he was all in, and she'd seen nothing from him that made her doubt it. He'd supported her in everything she wanted to do even when it meant cutting his red meat intake after she'd gotten his cholesterol numbers back. They'd settled into something amazing.

And he'd been more than supportive when she'd announced plans for the Maryanne George Women's Shelter, serving all of Papillon Parish. She was using the land she'd bought and building something new and safe for any woman who needed it.

He was right. She wouldn't give up on them.

And she wouldn't ever give up on her town. She was quiet as Armie started to drive them through the town toward the bayou. How odd that she'd spent all those years of her childhood dreaming of some high-rise, thinking wealth would make her happy, and only finding the meaning of that word here. Her happiness wasn't found in money or things. It had been found in this place, in serving her neighbors and discovering what it meant to be a mother and a wife. Finding her place in this tiny town had given her a freedom she'd never thought to have.

Armie parked in front of the remains of her old house. He opened the door and Peanut bounded out.

"Are we taking a tour ahead of the wreckers coming out?" In a few days they would clear out the entire lot and get it ready to rebuild it as a modern, secure home. She liked that she wouldn't be too far from it.

He shook his head. "No. We're going to one of my favorite places in the world. It's a little out of the way, though. I guilted Major into coming out here and fixing up your dock. It still needs work, but it's safe and I parked a boat there for us."

She would go anywhere with him. "Let's go."

She let him lead her down to the dock, looking wistfully at her first house on the bayou. She loved Armie's home, her home, but this one had been a nice introduction to her new life.

He helped her onto the flat-bottom boat and she enjoyed the beauty of the world around her. Peanut didn't mind the boat at all. He simply laid his head in her lap and settled in for the ride. She'd never done this before, never simply let the loveliness of a place wash over her knowing she belonged amidst the trees and water, the sky and land. She didn't even question where they were going, simply let Armie navigate the boat out and into the mighty forest that rose up from the water. It was a magical place.

"Do you know why they call this Butterfly Bayou?" Armie slowed the boat down, and up ahead she saw a small island and another couple of boats tied to the tiny dock there.

"I know Papillon means butterfly. Lisa said they migrate

through here." Was someone waiting for them? She thought she recognized one of the boats.

"Yes, they do, and they're here now. They love this island in particular." He tied the boat off and helped her onto the spongy earth. Peanut immediately started chasing bugs.

That was when she saw what had been hidden by the bushes.

Her family. They stood in a semicircle, her brother, Will, and his wife. Laurel and Mitch. Remy and Lisa. Noelle was in her chair next to Lisa. They were joined by what had to be thousands of butterflies. They clung to the trees and the plants, landed on her clothes. Their wings fluttered and her breath caught.

"I thought this was the proper place to do what I need to do. They come here on their way to Mexico. Butterflies transform and you transformed me."

"And me," Noelle said with a grin.

She could feel the tears start to roll, but they were sweet this time. He hadn't changed his mind. He'd had a plan. "Tell me you didn't ask my brother for my hand."

Sometimes folks around here could be a bit on the old-fashioned side.

"I would never do that. No one can give you away, *chérie*. You are a force of nature. And I'm not asking you to give yourself to me. I'm asking you to bond with me, to take what was singular and turn it into something more. Turn it into a family. Turn us into a family." He dropped to one knee and pulled out a ring. "It's not much, but it has history. My father gave this to my mother. He spent every dime he had on this ring and told her they would live on hope if they had to. They lived on it for fifty years, and I want all that and more with you."

The ring was beautiful, the sentiment behind it even more so. She got to her knees with him because they were always equals. "Yes."

"I love you." He slipped the ring on her finger as her small crowd cheered.

"Excellent. I brought the champagne," Lisa said.

"Good, because I think we should stay out here for a long time." Will was smiling.

His wife shook her head. "He says that because the baby's teething and we left all the kiddos at Guidry's."

Remy frowned. "Where my brother and sister are supposed to be watching them. I hope they're still whole when we get back."

Her family started arguing about the pros and cons of life on the bayou, but she was far too busy kissing her almost husband.

He pressed his lips to hers as the butterflies flittered around them.

Life was good on the bayou.

acknowledgments

Special thanks to my agent, Kevan Lyon. I love working with you and look forward to many more books. Thanks to my editor, Kate Seaver, for seeing how much fun we could have on the bayou. A shout-out to the Berkley publicity team, Fareeda Bullert and Jessica Brock. Much love to my publicist, Jenn Watson, and the whole Social Butterfly team, as well as my social media guru, Jillian Stein. I would like to acknowledge the great work my beta readers do. Stormy Pate and Riane Holt always keep it real for me. Liz Berry manages to ensure I don't go crazy. Kori Smith and Sara Buell—if I got anything right with the medical aspects of this book, it's because of you! As always, thanks to my personal team: Kim Guidroz, Maria Monroy, Margarita Coale, and my husband, Richard.

Look for Lexi Blake's next Butterfly Bayou book

Bayou Baby

Coming soon from Berkley!

Ready to find
your next great read?

Let us help.

Visit prh.com/nextread